# Forever the Road

Anthony St. Clair

**rucksack**
*universe*

Rucksack Press
Eugene, Oregon

*To that spring morning in 2003,
cycling on the bike path
by the Willamette River in Eugene
just as the sun was coming up.*

*I pulled off quickly, sat on a tree stump,
not caring if I was late to work.
I had to write down the first thoughts
that one day, over 10 years later,
would grow up to be this story.*

# CONTENTS

"Agamuskara shares its name with the river that runs through India's holiest city, which is also its unholiest. While no records survive to tell us when Agamuskara was founded, local lore maintains the area was settled by the first people to come to the Indian subcontinent. History also does not explain why the city and the river should be named what, in the Hindi, translates as 'smiling fire.' This mystery, the delights of daily life and Indian culture, and the unrivaled drinks at the Everest Base Camp Pub and Hostel continue to attract travelers from all over the world."

— Guru Deep, *India Through the Third Eye*

# I

"IT COULD BE a mirror eclipse," Rucksack said to Jade. Her hand jerked. The pint glass banged against the tap, sending the black Galway Pradesh Stout foaming and sloshing. She set it down so the beer could settle before resuming the seven-minute pour that made for a perfect pint of GPS.

"But there hasn't been a mirror eclipse since The Blast," she replied. "And that was nearly two hundred years ago."

Rucksack looked up from the newspaper and ran his gloved left hand over his bald brown head. A dark sadness flickered over his eyes, as brown and black as earth and trees. "Well, in two month's time, there may be." His accent, an ambiguous combination of Irish and everywhere, refused as usual to acknowledge the sound "th," so "there" sounded more like "t'ere." His gaze flicked from Jade's face to the bottles at the back of the bar, then slowly came back to her.

"Mirror's not for certain, though," he said. "They won't know till closer to the time. Just says the atmospheric conditions may be right." He harrumphed. "Bloody irresponsible, saying that. All it'll do is scare people. And mentioning the damn Blast on top o' it..."

Jade poured, then set down the brimming pint so it could finish settling, black beer under snow-white foam. "Let me guess," she said. "There's no cause for alarm."

"O' course," Rucksack said. "It's all coincidence." His thin, tight smile said the rest.

Even the steaming-hot India day outside couldn't alleviate the chill in Jade's gut. She remembered talking of The Blast as a schoolgirl, scared hushed whispers after history lessons about the strange double-sided eclipse that had burned before Night's Day, then a world changed and scarred. As an adult and a Jade, many times she had tried to ask The Management what role The Blast was supposed to play, but they never spoke of it. Then again, there were many things they never spoke of.

Jade handed Rucksack his pint. The heat didn't matter. At her touch, the glass and beer became the perfect temperature for the stout, as if the Irish pub were in Ireland itself, instead of the middle of one of India's hottest cities.

"I'll be outside," Rucksack said. "Suddenly I feel a chill."

*You're not the only one,* Jade thought as her first

customer of the day opened the double mahogany doors. Flat yellow sunshine spilled heat into the pub, but she still felt cold.

Once the doors closed, Jade eyed the liquor, where not so much as a speck of dust dulled the bottles or the glass shelves. The bar's lights glinted off the bottles, which sat on shelves against the mirror that ran from the ceiling to Jade's waist, as wide as the length of the bar. It was well stocked for now, though later she knew there'd be a run on the cheaper stuff: Ram Rum, Liquid Courage, Manager's Reserve, Jimmy Runner, Potato Juice, Blue Label Special, Nirvanic, Captain's Special Box.

The knock-off Indian booze might all taste like sugary antifreeze, but it had the best names. Jade chuckled and wondered who had thought of them all. In the mirror, the light caught her smile and her blue-and-gold eyes, framed by her almond face, olive skin, and the kinky brown-and-black hair that hung just past her shoulders.

Then she reached down, just there on the paneling, just below the bottom shelf of the mirrored bar, just below the phone that never rang. Jade tapped the spot and the cabinet opened. Unseen and unseeable by anyone but her—though lately she wondered about Rucksack—the cabinet held her true duty.

A soft, silvery light shimmered from no distinct source. The cabinet could have opened to the sky; the small space inside seemed to have no back, no bottom, no sides, no top. *All these years,* Jade thought, *and sometimes I still don't know.* She reached inside, wondering if she would just keep reaching and reaching, but as always her knuckles rapped on the wood at the back of the cabinet, the same deep mahogany of the bar and the doors.

The bottles seemed to float on the light: Green #2, Red #4, Brown #5, Yellow #6, Blue #7, Orange #9, Silver #10. Almost an ordinary day, except that there was extra Blue #7 and Red #4. No Gold #1, Gray #3, Purple #8, or Black #11, but those came only with special circumstances. Two or even three could be combined. All eleven were never supposed to be mixed together, except under personal guidance from The Management. For a moment Jade wondered why The Management had never been able to figure out a twelfth elixir. It was said that they nearly had, just before The Blast, but after the catastrophe they had stopped trying. The twelfth elixir remained a myth that could not be made real.

Jade glanced at the clock. Early the hour and empty the pub, but hot was the day, and people would be thirsty. The news spoke of The Blast and another mirror eclipse. People would be scared, indecisive, unsure. The people would need those extra elixirs, and Jade would be ready to steer them.

She closed the cabinet, rose, and turned to face the doors. Her eyes blazed, but her insides still felt cold. For a moment, her mind faded back to long ago, to another life that seemed further away than The Blast.

"Why are you posting me here?" she had asked The Management.

"Because of who you are," the three hooded, floating figures had replied. The voices of The Management always seemed at once like three voices in perfect unison and like one voice that they passed to each other like a ball.

"But I'm just me," she had said.

If they knew her thoughts, they gave no indication. Jade couldn't figure out if they read minds or not. All you could ever see were the hoods—never a face or limb or any indication of what The Management were behind their cloaks. In a way that still haunted her every move and decision, they had replied, "You are here because you are the best of us, Jade Agamuskara Bluegold."

She hoped she still was. Lately, she didn't feel so certain. No matter how perfect the drink, no matter how she steered the drinker down the path that life needed him or her to take, she no longer fully trusted her decisions or her own path. Whoever she helped, her own choices rang in her mind all the time. *Who am I now?* she thought. *Why did I choose this, instead of saying yes in Hong Kong when he asked?*

But that was another life ago.

When the pub door opened again, her thoughts returned to where she was: behind the bar of the best pub and hostel in Agamuskara, India. A man entered and sat at a table. His straight black hair hung ragged, as if he'd given himself a haircut after drinking a few beers—a common look with many of the budget backpackers she'd seen pass through the hostel. His clothes suggested a young American, and in his brown eyes hung doubts of his place in the world, how he was trying to find it but had a hard time knowing where to look. He stuck his nose in his guidebooks, a dry thirst in his throat and a yearning in his heart.

Jade ignored him.

A few minutes later, a woman came in, sat at a

different table, and quickly buried her nose in her guidebooks. The pub lights gleamed off her short blonde hair. A ferocity burned in her, one that Jade knew well: a brittle wall, hard voice, and driving velocity that concealed intense fear and doubt.

Jade ignored her too. *The less you do,* she thought, *the more they do what they were supposed to do anyway.* So Jade stood behind the bar, her back to the tables. After a few more minutes, first the man and then the woman approached the bar. Jade kept her back to them, waiting.

"Excuse me," the man said.

"Oy!" the woman said.

Jade turned around. "Oh, hello! What can I do for you both?"

"I've been here for—" they both began in unison.

"Oh, oh, so sorry!" Jade replied. "What can I get the two of you?"

"We're not together," the woman said, looking at the man for the first time.

"No, um," the man said, looking back at the woman, "I'm, um, over there."

"I'm surprised," Jade said. "I would've thought you were traveling together."

The woman's eyes widened. "Why do you say that?"

Jade pointed at the book each was carrying. "You each have *Deep's Enlightened Guide to Spiritual Travel* and *India Through the Third Eye.* Seemed like a for-sure." Jade shrugged. "Even a bartender can't be right all the time."

"Oh," the woman said, not just looking at the man but also paying attention to him for the first time. He looked at her, then at the worn, identical book in her hand. "Are you heading to Godhpur?"

"Um, yeah," said the man. "I was, I mean, it's—"

"It's amazing!" the woman said. "I've been wanting to find myself there for years!"

"Me too!" the man said. "Well, I mean, find myself, not yourself. I, um, you know…"

*Gotta be Californian*, Jade thought as she smiled at him. "You want a Deep's Special Lager," she said, then nodded to the woman. *Australian, no doubt.* "And you want a chardonnay."

Both nodded.

"I'll bring your drinks right over. Why don't you sit and swap travel plans."

They both wandered over to the woman's table and resumed talking.

*Now for the hard part.*

While they pointed to the same highlighted sections in their guidebooks, Jade looked at the paths of their lives—how they connected, intertwined, ran together for so long.

How they broke apart.

*Falling in love*, Jade thought. *It's easier than falling down the stairs.*

But he would never show his confidence, and she would never let down her guard. In time, their bright eyes would turn cold, their words sharp. Eventually, there would come a day when they would turn away from each other, preferring the coldness of the world to the frigidity of each other's company.

*That's the future*, Jade thought. It was all there in the paths that only Jakes and Jades could watch—and influence. She grinned as the tapped the cabinet.

*Unless I do my job.*

Neither the man nor the woman saw Jade pour the beer and the wine. Nor did they see her smile as she pulled out Red #4 and Blue #7. "Best to you both," Jade whispered, tipping drops into each glass. The drinks brightened for a moment, as if revealing some inner divinity, then faded back to their usual merely golden selves.

*They should be lifelong,* Jade thought. *But they will let themselves get in the way, instead of trusting each other enough to be their true selves with each other.* Jade set the drinks on the table.

*The challenge isn't falling in love,* she thought. *The challenge is landing safely and staying in love.*

An hour later and well past their first round, the man no longer stammered, and the hard edge of the woman's voice was gone. The woman looked deep into his eyes, one hand near his, almost but not quite touching. Not yet. Though too far away to hear, Jade needed only to watch to know what was happening. They sat closer now, knees touching, hands occasionally tapping a shoulder, arm, or thigh. From serendipitous wonder had come laughter. Now the talk was serious with "you do? me too!" moments.

Then it happened.

Mid-sentence, the talk ended. The man and the woman looked deeply into each other's eyes. He leaned toward her, his hand on her hand. She leaned toward him. They connected in the smallest, most passionate, tender, relieved-to-have-found-you-in-such-a-random-heartless-world first kiss.

The couple left soon thereafter, toward their shared lifetime ahead. Jade smiled, but only for a moment. *I can help anyone fall in love,* she thought, *but myself.* Like the smile, this thought lasted only a moment. *I am a Jade,* she thought, *and I am the best. Love has no place in decision and destiny.*

She went back to work.

THE NO-SHOCKS, NO-WORRIES TRUCK clunked in and out of another pothole. For the millionth time since hopping in the back of the truck at Mt. Everest Base Camp in Tibet, Jay bounced up and slammed back down into the truck bed. His bruised body seared under the blazing Indian day. He hardly winced anymore. The effort wasn't worth it.

When Jay was crammed into the corner where the truck bed met the cab, the jarring and jostling affected him less. He tried sitting on his backpack again. Instead of merely pounding his arse, each bump nearly tossed him onto the cracked road.

Jay sat back down on the hot metal of the truck bed and patted his backpack. Faded, black, waterproofed by dust, nearly as wide as Jay, and as tall as his tenderized torso, the backpack dozed next to him like a dog beside its master. A round lump stretched the fabric at the top of the pack.

It had come back.

Again.

A triple shot of fear, awe, and revulsion washed through him. Jay had lost track of the number of times he'd dropped the *thing* off cliffs, flushed it down toilet holes, and lobbed it into rivers. Each time, he'd hardly zipped up his pack when the lump would appear again. Jay looked away. Instead of thinking about the... thing, Jay tried to think about Agamuskara. Guru

Deep's *India Through the Third Eye* called it "India's holiest and unholiest city," though the guidebook never explained why.

Jay couldn't explain to himself why he felt so compelled to go there. It was said that people went to Varanasi to die holy, but they went to Agamuskara to live fully. Jay figured he really must want to live, even if his manner of getting to the city suggested otherwise.

After three days of the truck's tires barely not going over the edges of cliffside roads in Tibet, nearly crashing to a halt from axle-bending potholes in Nepal, and using endless horn blasts to navigate the oncoming trucks and standstill cows of northern India's river plains, Agamuskara couldn't be much farther now. Before setting out this morning, the driver had told Jay they would not be going to the city center, but that was fine. He'd make his own way to the middle of town, even if he had to walk. With his skin clogged with grit and his throat caked in dust, all Jay wanted right now was a hot shower and a cold beer. India was India, though. He suspected he would get the opposite. But he would rest and clean up. Then he'd find his way through the city and figure out what he had to see, what drew him so.

The rattling truck moved so fast that the world passed in a blur, but Jay marveled at all he saw. Countless people wore brilliant colors and smiled from weathered, driven faces. They defied the washed-out landscape and the humid mat of the air. Every village had been here before time was time, it seemed. Each village also brought a glimpse of temples and shrines, elephant-headed gods, bulls, monkeys, multilimbed deities rendered in brick, stone, concrete, and reverence.

Approaching Agamuskara, Jay now understood that India was four things: heat, humans, history, and gods. They shaped India not so much into a country or a culture but a world. India was all of the world, all of time in every passing moment, and every emotion, every depravity and transcendence, every hope realized and every futility suffered, of all the human race.

And, gods, was India heat. Humid, blazing, sopping heat. India felt as if wet blankets had been baked for an hour in a pot of water, then, steaming and boiling, wrapped around the country. Even Jay's sweat glands felt sluggish. The humidity jellied the will. It softened the wood of the few meager trees. Even the concrete blocks of houses and shacks seemed to sag, drip, and simmer in the midday, clear-sky blaze of sunlight.

The truck turned onto a highway, renown throughout northeastern India for being maintained. The road reminded Jay of the interstate highways of his left-long-ago home, except that as far as the traffic was concerned, the four lanes were simultaneously one lane, three lanes, twenty lanes, and no lanes. Still, the truck's consistent speed and motion brought a soothing breeze to Jay's skin, and the smooth road took him from a blazing sear to a nearly gentle simmer.

For once, Jay's tenderized rump stayed in one merciful, bounceless spot. After a few kilometers, he relaxed like a roast chicken resting after coming out of the oven.

The view from the highway wasn't as interesting.

The heat haze dulled the flatlands, and it seemed as if a wink and some rupees had made the scenery vanish. Jay almost pined for the cliffs that, just a couple days ago, had dropped off from the side of the truck. Every rock bouncing down into nothing had terrified him, but the trees, cows, and occasional village had been fascinating.

"Namaste la vista, baby," Jay said, mimicking the formerly white t-shirt he was wearing. He lifted the shirt to gain access to the treasures below. Wrapped around his waist and tucked into the front of his tan, dusty cargo pants, the thin fabric of his money belt was already soaked through. But no matter. The treasures would be dry and safe. Jay took out a wad of plastic, then unrolled, unfolded, flipped, and eventually unwrapped his most prized possession: the small, dark-blue booklet of his US passport.

The formalese of government speak greeted him: "...requests all whom it may concern to permit the citizen/national named herein to pass without delay or hindrance and in case of need to give all lawful aid and protection..."

Jay wondered how much he still looked like the photo. The green-and-gold eyes were the same, as was the light-brown hair. But the skin of that face? Dust, heat, sun, cold, ice, rain, beer, hot breakfasts, cold breakfasts, no breakfasts had all leathered his face, hardened his eyes, softened his smile. But it was still Jay. Jay, once from Idaho, now of the world.

He flipped through the pages—past the backgrounds of cacti and mountains, past the important information that addressed everything from about your passport to loss of citizenship. Then he opened the last five years. Visas, stamps, signatures—most of them official and some, to put it mildly, questionable. Jay thought about the so-called visas that had been added not at an official immigration checkpoint, but by hands unsteadied after a bit of backroom blather, boozing, and baksheesh. He flipped through the countries: South Africa, Tanzania, Kenya, Gambia, Morocco, Ireland, England, Scotland, Belgium, France, Spain, Italy, Austria, Croatia, Germany, Sweden, Russia, Kazakhstan, Mongolia, China, Tibet.

There should have been a visa for Nepal, but instead there was only a blank page. Before arriving at the border checkpoint between Tibet and Nepal, the men in the truck had hidden Jay under a blanket. Jay didn't ask why. They'd hardly slowed down since.

And now—officially—Jay was in India.

Adventures taken, people met, sights seen—all condensed to stamps on pages. Jay re-wrapped his passport in the plastic and stuck it back in his money belt, behind the photo where the man and woman always smiled at him.

"I hope you're still having a good time," Jay said to the couple in the photo. For a moment, his anywhere voice lost all the twangs and lilts of his globetrotting, and he was just a regular guy from Idaho again. He started to take out the picture, but the truck's grinding, slowing gears stopped him. The driver stopped blaring on the horn just long enough to slap the door twice. Jay rustled his money belt and clothes back into place.

*End of one road,* he thought. *Now for another.*

The truck stopped. Jay grinned. He grabbed the

pack, ready to lose himself in all the adventures that came from putting one foot in front of the other on an unknown road—a road that could be the one that would finally go on and on forever, as long as he just kept traveling.

At the edge of the city, Jay jumped out, thanked the two men, and handed them some worn notes. The drivers nodded and laughed at the crazy traveler who thought he'd just stroll into the center of the city. As the truck rumbled off, the indistinct faces of the two men slipped out of Jay's memory. He couldn't understand why it was so hard to remember what these men looked like, especially after spending so many days traveling together. *Must be fatigue,* he thought.

Jay swung on his backpack, set its buckles, and adjusted its straps. Despite the ringing in his head, the tiredness, the bruises, and the extra weight, the touch of the pack to his back brightened his eyes and straightened up his stooping body. It'd be a good walk. A long walk. A tough, hellish walk, sure, but then again, travel wasn't supposed to be easy. The pack did feel heavier, though, now that the little... thing spun in there again.

If anything weighed him down, it wasn't the road-weary fatigue, the not-quite-remembered moonlit night at Mt. Everest, or the Chinese police and all those Dalai Lama portraits. It was the quiet, slow, incessant *shr-shr-shr* as the thing turned, rubbing the fabric of his faithful backpack.

"One foot in front of the other will put it out of your head," Jay said, the Idaho gone from his voice and replaced by the patchwork of places stamped in his passport.

The city center couldn't be that far. *Once there,* he thought, *I'll beeline to a pint, a shower, and a bed—in whatever order works best. For once, I even know where I want to go.*

Backpack-laden, his skin and clothes were so soaked he wondered if sweat glands could get sore. With every step, Jay tried to understand how the Indians did it. Children ran, laughed, smiled, circled him, joked, and asked for a pen or a piece of candy. Women, wrapped head to toe in yards and yards of sari fabric, walked everywhere carrying baskets. Men in pants and long-sleeve shirts held hands with each other and talked like they were all brothers. Their animated voices and gestures defied the dulling, steaming humidity.

Jay had no idea what the men said. The women didn't look in his direction. The kids tired of him and returned to their games.

With every step, the age of the country seemed to whisper alongside the *shr-shr-shr.* All around him, in every pebble and blade of grass, in every buffalo-dung patty drying as fuel on the sides of shacks, Jay saw and felt the gods whose presence and personality had shaped all people, all moments, all things.

The acrid scent of burning tires stung the air. A cow rooted through plastic and garbage. Jay wondered why the gods couldn't have made things smell better.

As he pressed on, the heat melted his resolve. He was now wearing a boulder, not a backpack. Sweat poured and feet dragged, but Jay kept going. Some old saying about single steps and thousand-mile journeys flitted through his mind. It had to be close, though, had to be. The miles pounded the bottoms of his worn boots, and the scene around Jay changed. At least the ground was flat. Other than a tall hill off to the west, the land here was even, with hardly a rise at all.

Covered in drying dung-fuel patties, the shacks gradually gave way to one- and two-story buildings. Shops. Homes. Offices. Sometimes distinct, often all jumbled.

The humid floating dust changed character too. The scent of fields, cow dung, and fires still clung to his pores and his soul, but a new layer of sound and soot settled on him: car and rickshaw exhaust, cooking food, open sewers. Jay had always heard of India as a land of diversity. Walking it now, he understood they meant the smell.

Stopping a moment to rest, Jay had hardly stood still when an open-sided, three-wheeled black-and-yellow rickshaw taxi pulled up next to him like a buzzing, rattling bumblebee.

"You need a ride?" the driver said. "Get in. I will take you to my friend's hotel."

"No, I'm fine," Jay replied, but the driver was already running over to him.

"So tired," the driver said, reaching for Jay's backpack. "Let me put that in for you."

Jay's eyes widened and he stepped back.

"I'm fine," he repeated, his voice flat and final. "No taxi."

"Cheap ride."

"No taxi."

"Special price, my friend," the driver said.

Jay flung out his hands, shook his head, and started

walking away.

The driver shrugged. "You tourists."

"I'm not a tourist," Jay replied. "I'm a traveler."

The driver smiled. "You tourists. Always walking around with houses strapped to your backs! But it is okay, my friend. Sooner or later, you always need a ride, and when you need a ride, I will take you."

Jay left the taxi behind, but the taxi didn't leave him. As he trudged onward, the taxi would flit beside him or buzz behind him or singe Jay's nose with a whiff of putrid blue-black exhaust.

A few kilometers later, Jay stepped wrong and tripped. Banging his knee on the rough asphalt, he winced and his eyes watered.

When he looked up, the rickshaw had stopped in front of him.

"My friend," the driver said. Something about the man's indistinct face seemed familiar.

Jay sighed. He looked past the driver to the skyline of the city proper.

"The heat makes things seem closer," the driver said, "but it is still far."

"How far?" Jay asked.

"Farther than your feet."

The rickshaw's back seat looked soft. There weren't any springs poking out, and the roof would keep the sun off him. Jay's knee throbbed. His feet threatened mutiny and blisters. Jay sighed and surrendered.

"Everest Base Camp," he said, limping into the rickshaw and setting his pack at his grateful feet.

* * * * *

"OY! JADE!"

The laughter-laced shout blasted through the pub door and nearly made her drop the glass she was polishing.

*Ah,* Jade thought. *Rucksack must be ready for his next pint.* She brought a fresh glass to the tap. As she did, The Management's strange warning rang in her head, the way it did every time Rucksack was around: "This man is dangerous."

She thought back over the last few months to when the three hooded figures had appeared in the pub. It was just minutes after the letter had arrived and she'd read it. Later that day Rucksack had come in for the first time—but The Management had visited first.

The surprise had made her drop the letter. The Management hardly ever came to the Jakes and Jades in person. Or in being. Or whatever they were. "Why is he dangerous?" she had asked, picking up the sheet of paper. "Who is he?"

"Some say he's a broken hero," said the figure in blue and green.

"Some say he's the world's only Himalayan-Irish sage," said the figure in brown and black.

"Some say he's just a freeloading drunk," said the figure in silver and gold.

"None of these things has ever been proven," they all said together. "All we know is that he is an unknown quantity."

"An unknown quantity?" Jade had said. "What does that even mean?"

"It means he has no destiny. He is as a ghost to us. He is outside of us all."

"How is that even possible?" Jade had looked at

each of the three figures. If they could look sheepish, this was the closest they had ever seemed to it. "What do you want me to do?"

"Your duty has many guises, Jade Agamuskara Bluegold, and some are more dangerous than others. We know little about Faddah Rucksack and far less about his path. Be wary of him but watch him. Learn from him but keep your distance. Stay close but do not get involved. A man without a destiny is a man who might do anything."

The Management faded away into nothing, as they always did. Jade stood alone, still holding the letter.

She came back to the finished pour. *Who are you, indeed?* Jade thought. Blinking at the glaring midday sun, she carried the brimming glass out into the bright world.

The white walls of Agamuskara collected light, stored it, packed it tightly, and shot it back into the world like munitions. People, bicycles, vehicles, and animals trudged and flowed—a river of thousands moving past one-story, two-story, and three-story buildings.

The brown-and-black sari was a shadow amongst the white glare and the thousands of colors. The woman caught Jade's eye for a moment. Then the woman was gone, downstream in the river of flesh and steel.

Scooters, rickshaws, taxis, trucks, cows, dogs, children, men, and women teemed through the streets. Many things tried to occupy the same place at the same time. Not even a square of dirt or pavement showed beneath the slow incessant press of tires, feet, and paws. From the people rushing and meandering to the buildings that seemed to shimmer and wobble in the light, all the world moved.

Except for him.

Faddah Rucksack sat at the black iron table, the pub's single table outside, to the right of the door and near the corner of the building, where two wide streets met at an acute angle. His back to the pub and dressed all in black, he sat like the city's shadow—the only shadow amidst the white walls and brilliant colors of the people and trucks. Clad in a black leather glove, his left hand rested on the table next to an empty pint glass. His bare right hand seemed simultaneously earth-brown and cloud-pale.

He read a sheet of paper covered in a scrawl whose language Jade couldn't determine. As she approached, he turned it over and set it down. Rucksack looked toward the roving people. Jade couldn't see his eyes, but everything in how he stared said that the man sitting right here was also hundreds of years and thousands of miles away. He set his left hand on top of his right.

Jade blinked. Coming from the low lights of the pub, it was hard adjusting to the sunlight. She looked at his hands again. Maybe it was the glove, but his left hand seemed smaller than the right.

"Rucksack?" she said. "Are you okay?"

He turned his head and noticed her for the first time. It took but a moment for the faraway man to return. Rucksack's face was everyone and no one, everywhere and nowhere; he could've been from Ireland, Tibet, Kenya. For all Jade could tell, he could've dropped out of the clouds. His tight face let loose a wide smile, bright as the city walls. "There's never a fear, as long as there's beer, there's only smiles and glee," Rucksack sang. "Now that you're here, let's drink in good cheer. Hey, barkeep! How about a couple for free?"

Jade laughed. "Have you ever paid for a beer?"

"It's like a dog, only more loyal and useful," Rucksack said. "I cannot help the extensive credit that insists on following me wherever I go."

*And that comes ahead of you too,* Jade thought. The letter had arrived an hour before he had first walked into the pub all those months ago. The Deep, Inc. stationery was familiar enough, having appeared on many an invoice and letter accompanying kegs of Deep's Special Lager ("Thank you for making *Every Night Special!*" and Galway Pradesh Stout ("The World's #1 Beer!"):

> One Faddah Rucksack, a traveler of worlds and doer of deeds, does come to Agamuskara for an indeterminate length of time. Mr. Rucksack's purchases are free of charge and will be reimbursed to you. Thanking you in advance for your understanding.

The scrawled signature had been as indecipherable as the strange language on the paper Rucksack had been reading, but the money had come every week. *Good thing too,* she thought. *It's so bloody hot here, I hardly ever carried GPS until he arrived. I swear the man could put a straw in a keg and drain it.*

Jade set the pint on the table. The beer's white head wobbled just above the rim. "I'll never understand how you drink stout in this heat."

"A pint at a time, my lass," Rucksack replied. With a tilt of his head, he raised his glass to her. "Besides, o' all the barkeeps from Ireland to India, not a one pours a GPS as fine as you do, Jade. And believe you me, I would know."

Jade couldn't help but grin. All these months and they had hardly spoken, except to exchange pint orders, natter about the weather, or discuss the day's headlines. "Such a compliment," Jade replied. "You're not... drunk... are you?"

Rucksack dimmed his smile, a seeming seriousness in his eyes. Then he winked. "There are two things I never do," he said. "I never stop drinking. And I never get drunk."

"It's just that when I came out here, something about you seemed off."

Rucksack looked at her in a new way. His gaze moved from Jade to the paper, then back to her. "Have you ever lost someone, Jade?" he said. "Someone close to you? Someone who mattered more than all the world?"

For a moment, she was there again: painted concrete, his outstretched hand, the shape of his mouth, the glint of the ring in his fingers—and then all the world had gone still. "Yes," she said. "Long ago. In a different life."

"In a different life." He nodded, clenching and unclenching his left hand. "Yes, that's a good way to put it. I have too," he said. "Lost someone. Long ago."

"I'm sorry."

"And I thank you, as I am for you too." Rucksack traced a bare finger over the sheet of paper. "I got a letter recently, saying that the someone I lost, I only thought I lost. And that if I came to Agamuskara, I'd find her."

*A lover? A wife?* she thought. *A sister?* Jade took a step toward the table. "Who was she?"

Rucksack opened his mouth to reply, but the words froze. All the world seemed to hold its breath.

Both Jade and Rucksack doubled over, as if they'd each been punched in the stomach. On the two streets, everyone and everything stopped moving. No one spoke. Thousands of eyes only looked around, wondering what was so suddenly different about the world.

The glaring walls of the city grew brighter yet softer. From the Agamuskara River, a breeze blew whispers and wet earth, caresses and cool summer nights. A million dawns rose from every soul in the city. Every dream shimmered like gardens in the first morning light, dewy green leaves scintillating. Though it was midday, the world seemed like the slimmest golden glimmer of sunrise, like the birth of a child, like the first time you see the person you fall in love with.

Jade fell onto one knee, her right hand grabbing the other chair at the table. All that had happened, all the doubts, all the wonderings and questions, all washed away. She was only Jade, no longer a Jade or the Jade. Just Jade. Just herself. Not her decisions and her destiny, only her possibilities. *I can do anything,* she thought. *I can be anyone. I can choose anything and nothing and everything.*

The world shimmered. Double helixes of silver-and-gold light rained down.

Shaking, Jade staggered back to her feet. Helixes. Ever since her training, The Management had said to think of decision and destiny as a double helix, the DNA of existence that flowed forever, intertwining without touching, influencing the other without crossing paths.

Of course, no one else noticed that part. She glanced.

Except Rucksack.

As quickly as the world had held its breath, it exhaled. Life began moving again.

Jade looked at Rucksack and caught him staring at her. The world teemed by again. Rivers of endless people, animals, and objects flowed and flowed as if nothing else had happened but moving forward.

"No one else saw it," he said. "But you did, didn't you?"

She said nothing.

Rucksack smiled. "I figured you were one o' them. You're not the first I've ever seen or known, Jade Agamuskara Bluegold. I've seen as many o' you as pubs I've lightened kegs in over the years—dozens o' you the world over. I still don't know quite what you do with that special wee cabinet that no one else is supposed to see, but near as I can tell you don't do anyone evil by it, and I'm okay with that. So, let's not lie to each other here."

Confusion flooded her. *How did he know my full name?* she thought, looking away from Rucksack to the people. *How could he have seen the helixes? Only Jakes and Jades can see them, and I'm the only one in Agamuskara.*

The Management's cryptic warning whispered through her: "Learn from him but keep your distance."

But Rucksack wasn't shying away from what they'd seen. *If I were to get close,* she thought, *if I wanted to understand him, then he would have to understand some of me too.*

The Management hovered in her mind, and their warning coursed through her again: "A man without a destiny is a man who might do anything."

*Okay,* she thought, *so what is he going to do?*

Jade smiled. "Seeing destinies," she said. "We've got that in common. Usually it's obscured, tucked just beneath the skin of all things. What we just saw, it's like suddenly seeing the air we breathe."

Rucksack sighed and drained his pint. "There was a time I would've been able to read every one o' those lives wandering by, helixes to heads. I would have known them all." His fingers touched the paper in front of him. All the bluster, the bombast, the big smile, and the bigger words all vanished. He looked away from her. "I can't do that anymore."

The rest of him seemed as withered as his hand. Jade's confusion turned to pity. She pulled out the chair and sat down. "Maybe. Maybe not," she said, getting her mind out of the way and letting her instincts, her training, take over. "But I know what you can do."

"What?"

"You can help me figure out what that was."

Rucksack shrugged. "Things happen that don't necessarily mean anything."

"Tell that to anyone in western Ireland just before The Blast," Jade replied. "That meant a lot."

"What does The Blast have to do with any o' this?" The letter crumpled beneath his fingers.

*It happened so long ago,* Jade thought. *Why does it bother him so much?* Instead she leaned forward, locked her gaze onto him, and said, "From every person and animal and object, the helixes trailed away like paths. They should flow like bright water."

Rucksack stared at the wrinkled sheet of paper and nodded.

"Then tell me, Faddah Rucksack, why did so many of them wither into black and ash and nothing?"

He turned to look at her, his left hand closed tight. "We don't know," he said.

"We don't," Jade said kindly. "But I think we owe it to these people to find out. It just might save their lives."

For a while, Rucksack said nothing. The city wandered. The sun blazed. A meandering cow walked by and left behind a steaming pile of dung.

*Forget it,* Jade thought. She started to go back into the pub, when at last he spoke.

"Whatever changed just now," he said, "we'll figure it out."

Jade turned around. "Where should we start?"

Something in Rucksack relaxed, as if he were relieved. When his gaze held hers, earth turned to stone and a fire blazed up inside his brown-and-black eyes. "I'm going to start right here, have a think and a pint. There's tales o' this city I need to remember. That... and I need to wait for something."

Jade nodded. "Okay," she said. "It's a start. What should I do?"

"Make sure you have a bed available," Rucksack said. "And bring me another pint o' GPS. I need to see clearly."

"I thought you were staying a few blocks away?"

"I am," he replied. "It's not for me. We'll find out who it's for soon enough."

"Then I'm going to get back inside and see what else the day brings."

She walked to the door, thinking of helixes. Then it hit her—the last thing she'd seen before the helixes had faded from sight. They had trailed from every person, every object, every animal. So many of them flashed like bright chains, only to blacken, char, and disappear.

Except him.

Rucksack had sat there, staring out at the still crowd, at the shimmering helixes. But no helix had come from Rucksack. No chain of destiny, no flowing paths of decisions and possibilities. The Management was right. Rucksack was like a ghost yet alive. Wandering but without a path.

His voice stopped her at the door. "Who were you before?"

Jade looked down at the cracked, somewhat-white pavement. Years and lifetimes coursed through her like blood. She opened the door and said, "Who were you?"

Neither answered.


A POTHOLE sent Jay lurching to the right, and he nearly tumbled from the rickshaw. A chunk of asphalt bounced the three-wheeled putt-putting bumblebee into the air and flung Jay back into his seat. Through the open sides of the rickshaw, the blazing blue sky for a moment took on a silvery glow. The world seemed to pause, as if holding its breath, but Jay realized that it was just him not exhaling yet.

The wheel smacked back down onto the pavement. Like a punch in the stomach, Jay doubled over as the impact knocked the air out of him.

He gasped and coughed, seeking air amidst bumblebee exhaust and the scent of cow manure. The driver smiled over his shoulder. "Welcome to Agamuskara, my good friend!" he said. "We are now in the city proper!"

"How can you tell?" Jay asked, coughing again.

"You are not truly in Agamuskara," the driver said, "until you see the river." He pointed west, to their right.

For a moment Jay thought back to his time traveling through England, the only place in the world where people drove on the left. Madness, he'd figured at the time. It was absurd, but you couldn't give the Brits too much flack. *Given how the entire island was nearly wiped out by The Blast,* Jay thought, *the Brits can drive on whatever side of the road they want.* But here in India, Jay was glad the traffic went on the right. Otherwise, he wouldn't have been able to see the river.

After the truck had passed through the Nepal-India border and resumed its bouncing, jostling ride toward Agamuskara, Jay had passed some kilometers looking through his guidebook, Guru Deep's *India Through the Third Eye*:

```
Agamuskara shares its name with the
river that runs through India's
holiest city, which is also its
unholiest. While no records survive to
```

tell us when Agamuskara was founded,
local lore maintains the area was
settled by the first people to come to
the Indian subcontinent. History also
does not explain why the city and the
river should be named what, in the
Hindi, translates as "smiling fire."

As Jay stared at the wide river, he understood how it could be mistaken for a smiling fire. The ruddy water glowed harsh and golden in the sun, and it burned Jay's eyes to look at it too long. Even the ancient river flowed sluggishly in the heat, but the driver was right. The Agamuskara's bends and straightaways, every curve and line, held a majesty that belied the brown water. As they drove, the river coursed along with them.

The map in the guidebook had shown that the river flowed from the north, out of the Himalayas. At Agamuskara the river's course turned sharply west, then curved south and east, creating a nestle of land where, it was thought, the original riverside village had been founded. As the city had grown, it had built up on the north side of the river. Then the city crossed south and continued growing. Today, the Agamuskara bisected the city then emptied into the Ganges farther east.

"It is beautiful," the driver said, looking more at the river than the road in front of them.

Jay turned to agree. Then he saw the cow standing still in front of them and instead he screamed.

The driver hardly turned his head, but he pounded

on the horn. The cow blinked but did not move. Not bothering to look, the driver swerved right. Jay looked over. Beside them, chains flapped from the yellow bed of a large truck. Red wheel wells blurred as they turned. Jay grabbed the supports of the rickshaw.

*I'm going to die,* he thought. *And I only just got here.*

As the horn blared, a hole opened between the truck and another vehicle. The rickshaw swung into place with inches to spare on either end.

As they passed the cow, Jay was certain it winked at him.

The driver spat at it. "Bloody cows."

"Aren't they holy?" Jay replied.

"Cows give us many gifts," the driver said. "Milk and butter to nourish us, dung for our fires. We do not eat them and we do not hurt them, but it doesn't mean we like them."

"Since they think they own the road?"

The driver laughed. "Yes, my good friend. I like how you say that." One foot on the gas and one hand on the bleating horn, the driver swerved, zipped, and putted. The rickshaw swerved in and slipped out of every scant space not possibly big enough for it, yet somehow there was always just enough room.

Jay stared at the river as they traveled farther into the city. Had this water come down from the Himalayas at the same time that he had? As the rickshaw zipped in and out of meandering livestock, bell-ringing bicycles, grumbling trucks, and horn-tooting taxis, a breeze passed over Jay. It wasn't particularly cool, but it felt good on his skin. If his clothes couldn't dry out in the soggy hot air, at least they didn't feel as sticky. And the drive was certainly not boring. Jay let go of the rickshaw supports and sat back in his seat.

The river disappeared behind some buildings. Jay's backpack sat quietly on the floorboards between his knees, and he rested his hand on top of it. As they passed the white walls of the city center, the close buildings reflected the light and trapped the heat. The weight of gods and ages pressed on Jay, compressing humanity and humidity in a slow boil.

Out of the corner of Jay's eye, in front of a copy-machine-and-long-distance-calls shop, a blue humanlike figure sat proud and smiling on a cow. Dressed in gold, the figure was maybe male, maybe female, but it definitely had four arms and held some sort of staff. It winked.

Jay's head snapped to the right to look more closely, but only the cow remained.

He'd barely seen it, but since of course there was no way it could have been there to begin with, he hadn't seen it anyway.

*I'm so tired and dehydrated,* Jay thought. *I'm starting to hallucinate. That's all.* Jay swallowed dust. *I need a beer. Even a Deep's Special Lager would be good enough for right now, though I wouldn't really call that beer. I've drunk more flavorful water and passed tastier piss.*

The rickshaw squealed to a stop. Jay folded forward. Five years of traveling clamped his hand to the top of the pack so it didn't tumble out of the rickshaw. The driver stomped the brakes and cut the engine. Jay tried to ignore the *shr-shr-shr,* but the outline of the thing pressed into his hand.

Hundreds of people banged instruments, sang songs, and paraded down the cross street in front of them. Jay couldn't understand the words, but he understood the feeling—a hope for tomorrow, a wish for the next life, a joy in spite of today. The singing cooled him like water, like a spring night back home. He sighed. For a moment, his addled weariness faded. The *shr-shr-shr* seemed louder.

Another flash of blue turned his head. So did flashes of gold, brown, white, and red.

Cows flanked the rickshaw. Taxis, bicycles, and large trucks all stopped at the edge of the procession. When Jay looked directly at any of the motionless cattle, he saw only cows. When looking from the far edge of his peripheral vision, though, Jay thought he saw more figures, multi-armed and gold-adorned, aiming inscrutable smiles at the parade. But whenever he turned to look directly, he saw only cows.

Jay tapped the driver's shoulder. "What is the parade for?"

"For the gods, my good friend."

"Which one?"

The driver shrugged. "All sing to all, and all listen, and all praise."

Jay wished he didn't suck so badly at languages. Other than a rough French *bonjour*, the only other language Jay knew was the "I'm not dangerous" smile, the "where's the nearest toilet?" anguished leg scrunch with side-to-side wiggle, and the cupped fingers raised to the mouth that could serve for "hungry" or "oh great keg in the sky do I need a beer." But this? This was all Hindi to Jay.

Hundreds upon hundreds of paraders passed. All of their disparate songs should have been disjointed caterwauling, but they weren't. The upbeat danced around the slow. Low, mournful notes fell low in Jay's ear, but songs of celebration leaped over them. Jay picked out harmonies and tunes; they blended, played side by side, built on each other's pitch and cadence. His hand pressed harder on top of his backpack as he leaned out of the rickshaw to better see the procession.

Out of the corners of Jay's eyes, all the multi-armed, multi-colored blurs turned to look at him. Before he could cry out, the tune and the lyrics skipped his ears, stunning him silent as the paraders' songs sang directly into his mind.

"Let the love of ages be the love of my heart..."

"A hot meal and a warm thigh, a hard kiss and a soft sigh..."

"May my sons be as the sun and my daughters as the earth..."

"Return the life to the flame and to the Smiling Fire, be the cinders and the burn of the life of the world..."

Jay sat up, banging his head on the rickshaw's roof. His hand flung from the pack to the top of his aching head. The song vanished. Out of the corners of his tearing-up eyes, he saw nothing but stalled traffic and shuffling cows.

The driver turned around at the noise. "Are you okay?"

"I think so."

The driver smiled, looking at Jay's head and the slightly dented roof. "Not the way one usually sings, my friend, but then, you tourists have strange ways."

"I'm not a tourist," Jay said. "I'm a traveler."

The driver bobbed his head side to side. Jay didn't

need to speak Hindi to know that this meant, "Maybe yes, maybe no, maybe maybe. All the same to me."

The parade ended, its fading songs mere whispers to the words sung and singed into Jay's mind. The pain faded only once the street had cleared and they could continue again.

The driver soon stopped at a nondescript hotel. "Here we are," he said, getting out and reaching for Jay's backpack.

Jay batted away his hand. "This isn't Everest Base Camp."

"No, no, much better, you will like it, my good friend. Much better."

Head still throbbing, feet still hurting, and throat a cup of desert sand, Jay felt how tempting it was. He was here. He was so tired. It was so hot.

But there were no signs of a pub. He recalled what he'd been told: when in Agamuskara, the only place for a traveler to stay was at the Everest Base Camp. Some said it was the best pub and hostel in town. Some said it was the best in India. Everything else was for tourists and tossers—which was he?

Jay pulled up all the will he had left, along with some money in his pocket. He set the bills on the seat, grabbed his pack, and got out.

The driver cried out, but Jay ignored him. Then, from behind, an impact made him stagger. Jay couldn't ignore that he was almost falling.

One hand on the pavement to keep from smacking the road, Jay looked up. His backpack grew smaller as it bounced down the street, seeming to struggle in the arms of a teenage boy but already far away.

Jay's feet protested with pain and fatigue, but his backpack was everything. He began to run.

THE HEAVY PACK made Jigme's arms throb, but he ran faster. The reason for the running had changed, but the running itself had started just as it had for days now. Because of her. Always her.

"Mum?" Jigme asked.

Her blank eyes stared.

He switched back to Hindi. "Amma?" No answer. No response but a raspy breath.

She lay on the hard pallet in the small, dim, dusty room, her skinny body blazing hotter than the day. If her thin blankets were ever wet now, it was with Jigme's tears. She didn't sweat anymore, didn't cry, didn't even drool. He missed that now. At least when she'd drool he'd known there was moisture in her, or reaction, or feeling. When she had sweat, she held his hand and said her love was now his strength. When she had cried, she touched his cheek and told him that he must find courage—a man's courage, beyond his sixteen years.

Now she said nothing. He brought her water but she did not drink. He brought her food but she did not eat. Her arms lay limp at her sides. When he tried to hold her hand she didn't even look at him.

Gradually, she faded into what he guessed was sleep. After the sleepless night, he felt relieved. Once her eyes were closed and her breathing was ragged but even, Jigme squeezed her hand and kissed her brow. He wished he could sleep too, but his body refused any notion of rest. So he left.

There was no food in the room and no money in the little drawer by the bed. So out into the bright day Jigme went, his belly and pockets empty. He closed and locked the faded red door behind him. He usually left the little room earlier to try to find work for the day. Today he'd left too late. *We'll get by,* Jigme thought, *but tomorrow I must find work.*

The white walls and brown dirt strip of the narrow alley glared with sun and shadows. The bright sun did not shine as fully here in the slum's alley, but the contrast was stark enough to make it hard for Jigme's eyes to adjust. Whenever he first went outside he always felt blind.

But the sight was not nearly as overwhelming as the sounds. Inside the dim room, there was only his and Amma's breathing. Outside, other children played and squealed. Men worked on projects and women cooked and cleaned. Everywhere was talk and songs, the sounds of dough being smacked and shaped, the smells of spices and frying. People spoke of the strange hot wind that had blustered up the alley earlier; Jigme had wondered what had rattled the door while he'd sat with his amma.

Younger children and children his age went to school and came home from school, but Jigme couldn't look them in the eye. Once Amma had fallen ill, he had left school to learn from the streets and the endless people who lived in Agamuskara and who came through here from all over the world. Leaving school allowed Jigme to make money to buy food and medicine for him and his mother. Not that Jigme had been able to look the other kids in the eye much anyway. The children of the alley didn't want to be friends with Jigme, the child of Asha, the woman with no husband.

The moment Jigme's eyes adjusted, he ran. As long as he ran, as long as his feet smacked the pavement of the streets and the dirt of the alleys, as long as his legs throbbed, his breath rushed, his skin tingled with the sharp sun, and his heart pounded like a bomb, he felt alive. Lately, as soon as he went back to the little room, he felt as if he had died.

He only ran toward the mouth of the alley. He never ran the other way. No one ever walked any farther than their door, though the alley's white walls seemed to go on forever. Past their door, the strip of dirt continued down a shaded part of the block to a bend and then, as far as Jigme understood, onward to the very heart and center of the city.

Back when she still talked with him, Jigme had asked Amma what was at the other end of the alley, but she had no answer.

"No one knows," she had said, "which can only mean that what is there is not for us to know. It must be a place of the gods and only for the gods."

Then she had smiled, patted his hand, and asked him what he had seen in the city that day. He had told her of the tomato cart, the monkey taking the camera out of the tourist's backpack, the tourist chasing the monkey then slipping on crushed tomatoes and falling into a pile of cow dung. He and Amma had laughed so hard. Just when he thought he couldn't laugh harder, she had said, "I hope the monkey took a picture of such a soft landing!"

But Amma did not laugh anymore. She no longer shared her funny way of seeing the world. The absence of her laughter was like the absence of breath.

Jigme ran faster toward the city, where he could lose himself in the endless people and boundless sounds. Past the small statue at the corner, from the mouth of the alley, the world opened up.

People filled the side street. Jigme smiled, remembering what someone once told him: "You could run from one end of Agamuskara to the other in an hour," the woman had said, "but because of the crowds it would take a hundred years."

It had taken Jigme a day. At least then, Amma was still well enough to be worried when he came back late. Now he wondered if she would notice at all. His eyes stung, but crying was the one thing that he could not allow when he was feeling alive. To cry was to stumble and to stumble was to fall and to fall was to stop. He would not stop.

From the alley, he turned right, toward the main street, where all the world's inhabitants seemed to live. He ran past the skinny men on the stoop in their doorway, begging bowls out to support their seemingly never-ending fast. As far as Jigme could tell, they were always perched there. Even sitting, their bare bellies hardly bulged over the dirty *lungis* that covered their loins and thighs. They alternated between chanting and waving people over to talk and put money in their bowls. They nodded at Jigme, but he didn't stop. They never asked about his mother.

He never understood why the fasting men held their vigil so close to The Mystery Chickpea. He didn't understand the ancient wheeled cart either, for that matter. Every day it was there from daybreak till sunset, steam rising from the two large, dented, shiny, bubbling pots beneath a sign suspended from two posts at either end of the cart. No one ever seemed to eat there, yet there was always a crowd. And there was always the silent old man, his face partially shrouded by the endless clouds of steam.

"He says nothing," Jigme had once heard someone say, "yet I know no one else who I would rather talk to."

Jigme smiled as he blurred past the cart. He had the feeling that the silent old man always asked him how Amma was doing.

Then he left the side street, came onto the main road, and was in the city.

Jigme's heart beat faster and he started to smile. Tourists would be wandering, their absurdly large packs like cows on their backs. People would be buying snacks and vegetables, jewelry and cloth. The smells from the *bhel puri* vendors already tugged him by the nose and the stomach. The clean smell of hot puffed rice washed away his worry. The raw red onion cracked its pungent knuckles at him, and the tang of tamarind sauce scrubbed him like a bath.

Jigme's belly groaned, but he ignored it. *Maybe I should consider it a fast*, he thought. *I won't eat till Amma is well enough for both of us to eat together again.*

*Nice idea, but we'd starve to death first.*

He ran faster.

Jigme focused on the crowd, on the movements of what was both a mass of individuals and a single being of person, animal, street, machine, and city. Only a few people looked wide-eyed and panicked toward the crazy skinny boy, his ragged white shirt flying, his brown arms pumping. He knew their thoughts. He was heading straight for them, and in the press of people they had no escape. He'd crash into them. There would be falling and pain as they hit the ground, but all breath would be gone. When collisions happened, you could hardly breathe, much less shout.

But none of that would happen. Jigme understood now. *You just have to find the cracks in the crowds*, he thought as he barreled toward the throng, looking left and right for the tiniest opening where he could dash in and keep going.

*Once you find the cracks, you can go anywhere.*

The mass of people shuffled, going only as fast as the person lingering longest over the stalls that lined the street as solid as walls. Not even Agamuskara's stray dogs wandered in and out of people's legs here; too many of them had been kicked and trampled.

In the back of Jigme's mind, a flame of doubt flickered behind a shadow fear. *No room*, he thought. Too fast to stop, too fast to change direction. The woman and man in front of him would fall, and what if they shouted for the police? Jigme tried to swerve and dodge, but there was nowhere to dash in, nowhere to slip out.

And then there was.

The woman in front had kept going, her red and blue sari brilliant in the light, but the man behind her had stopped to look at something and tap his large mustache. The gap between them widened to at least a foot. Jigme adjusted his course slightly. The man's eyes widened as he saw Jigme sprinting toward him. "No, no!" the man began to say, waving his arms, but Jigme slipped past his frantic arms, through the next layer of meandering people and into the relieving heat and press of the city's throngs.

Jigme slowed to his usual crowd-jogging speed. A heartbeat before his feet got there, a space opened for him. He did not think. He did not analyze. He moved.

Whether it was his instincts or the gods, capricious luck or the sometimes-gentle hand of the harsh city, Jigme didn't care. He ran through the crowd again, dodging surprised gasps, feet in mid-step, pointing fingers, and overflowing baskets. Some people saw him and had no reaction; they recognized the running boy of the alley. Some people jumped back in fright, nearly knocking over the people behind them. That always made Jigme grin.

Through the crowds, down the street, and through other streets he ran. The heat of the day and the mass of the people pressed at Jigme like a flame approaching a dung patty. Sometimes he wondered if you could catch fire from being in the crowd too long.

*As long as I move, I'll be okay,* he thought. *As long as I run, I can see the city.*

Jigme thought about searching for food. Then he could seek out the man who yesterday had sold him strange medicines in strange bottles, all the while looking around and around. He only looked at Jigme once the gleam of coins was in the boy's hand. But that didn't matter. Jigme had the medicine.

*As long as I run,* Jigme thought, *Amma is asleep and not dying.*

"This I only have just gotten for the first time," the man had said. "It will help her immediately. She will seem as if she were twenty years younger. Her sickness will be but as the memory of a bad storm."

Such relief also cost every coin and note they had left, plus a few trinkets Jigme had put in his pocket while Asha slept. He hoped she would be so relieved at her new good health that she would forgive him—or even better, not notice the absence of the objects. Jigme doubted he would be so lucky.

The incense pot, she had once said, had been a gift from his father. Other than Jigme, it was all she had left of him, wherever he was now.

The medicine man took everything and gave only a crooked smile and a small bottle of pills in return.

That night, Jigme had given Asha the two pills as the man had instructed. All night she had thrashed, saying nothing, making no sounds except those of her limbs flailing over her small pallet. All Jigme could do was stay awake and keep her from throwing herself onto the dirt floor. The next morning, Asha's glassy eyes burned like the embers of a dying fire. Jigme had been too afraid to give her another dose.

The memory nearly tripped him, and an elbow knocked into his ribs. Jigme stumbled. A shin caught his foot. A swinging hand bashed his nose, followed quickly by a thin trickle of blood out of his left nostril. The people continued on their way. A boot's heavy weight crushed into Jigme's ankle.

Jigme cried out but no one spared any room for the skinny boy with tears in his eyes. A body bashed him sideways. Jigme's balance wavered.

*I'm going to fall.*

Through his blurred vision, something seemed different about the space between the people in front of him.

Stumbling and doubling over, he lunged forward.

He landed outside of the throng, on the quieter, wider main street that led in and out of Agamuskara. No crowd jostled. A small boy stared at him as Jigme stood bent over, his hands on his knees, trying to get his breath back as burning drops of sweat, tears, and blood fell onto the dusty street.

Jigme looked up and glared. The boy ran away.

*Sometimes,* Jigme thought, *I hate this city, this world, everything. I hate that it made my mother sick. I hate that it took my father from me. I hate that it just tried to kill me.*

Hunger growled but worry for Asha sliced through his heart. They had no money; they would not eat today. The pills were more poison than medicine, Jigme had decided. They would not help Amma. Nothing would.

*Unless...*

A few meters away, a yellow-and-black rickshaw pulled up to the curb. Jigme did not hear the words exchanged between the driver and the dusty-skinned foreign tourist in the back seat. The tourist was angry as he got out of the rickshaw, Jigme saw. Angry meant distracted.

The man pulled out a massive backpack. *Those backpacks must contain such wonders,* Jigme thought as he stared harder.

The men spoke loudly and angrily to one another, not seeing Jigme move forward. He no longer noticed the sore parts of his body where the crowd had nearly smashed him to the ground. His breath came back. His heartbeat was calm, slow, and even. *Rich tourists,* he thought. *What does it matter? He must have so much money he can get everything back in a heartbeat. Maybe there even is some money...*

While the men argued, Jigme clenched the backpack's endless straps. By the time the driver saw him and shouted, Jigme was already out of reach and gaining speed.

The pack was heavy, but Jigme's heart was light. *We will eat today after all,* he thought. *I will find real medicine for Amma. I will not deal with the medicine man anymore. Things will be different. Amma will get better, and she will be as she was before.*

Around the corner and away from the main throng, Jigme ran faster. *I just have to lose the tourist,* he thought. *Then everything will be all right.*

THE UNEVEN STREETS AND SIDEWALKS buckled, wavered, and corrugated in the exact sequence needed to constantly trip him. Jay panted, continuing to chase the backpack with heavy-booted, tired steps, despite his wish to collapse. He rounded another corner and again nearly knocked against a wall of people. He tottered back a moment, regained his balance, tried a different way.

The crowd was thinnest against the buildings. When you can't go through, he thought, go around. Jay stuck close to the white walls and ran forward again, dodging people and dogs, stalls and tables. Ahead, the backpack bobbed, its dusty blackness a fleeing shadow among a rainbow of women's saris.

The crowd always seemed to part for the boy, only to wall off as Jay tried to pass. His rushing body knocked bags out of hands and made people stumble. Jay kept his balance, but his pace slowed. His ragged breathing stabbed his side. And no matter how he dodged, no matter what last few drops of adrenaline he squeezed into his body, the backpack always seemed smaller and smaller.

He turned one more corner. *I have to catch him,* Jay thought. *I have to get my pack back. The thing came to me. I have to get it back.*

Reality caught up.

*There's no way I can catch him.*

Jay tripped.

*My pack, everything inside it, it'll be lost. Even the thing...*

He got up, kept chasing, but his pace faltered. A heat, a flush, hit his face.

*It's all gone.*

The boy kept running, now approaching the next corner, almost beneath a large sign with the outline of a mountain on it.

*I can catch him,* Jay thought.

His legs buckled.


WAS IT THE BOUNCING of the running or the awkward weight that made the backpack seem like it was fighting him? Jigme shifted his arms again, trying to keep the pack still. If he could lose the tourist, he could stop and put the pack on properly, even though it was nearly as tall as he was.

Jigme chanced a quick look over his shoulder. The pack saw the distraction and thrashed back and forth, left and right. But Jigme held on tighter, running toward his hope: Amma sitting up in bed, a smile on her face as the sickness fled her eyes.

Looking ahead again, Jigme smiled. *I'll lose the tourist for sure now.*

Ahead, the two widest, most populous streets in the city connected. *I'll duck left, cross, and be gone before the tourist can make out which way to go,* Jigme thought. *Then Amma will get better.*

He swerved to dodge around a man in black sitting at a table.

Jigme's knees smacked the hard concrete as he fell.

The backpack crumpled his folding body, knocking out his breath, and making a sound like, "There!"

Jigme pressed his hand into a round bulge at the top of the pack. For a moment a light shone brighter than the sun, but it did not blind him. It shined into his eyes, his soul, his lives now and then and to come. He felt the singing nearness of a red-and-black fire, then the cooling like water of a pale, silver-and-gold light that could have been the child of the sun and the moon.

His hand went to the dusty pavement, and the light and the fire were gone. Jigme tried to get up, tried to catch his breath, tried to get ready to run again. But his breath wouldn't come back fast enough. He just sat there, wheezing and coughing.

A lilting voice said, "Goodness me. Never could keep my feet straight."

Jigme coughed in reply.

The voice continued. "Sorry, lad, but I can't say it looked as if you were carrying that for your gran." The fabric rustled on the concrete as the backpack was dragged away from him.

"Please," Jigme said.

The sound of tired, dragging steps got louder. Jigme turned around.

The tourist whose pack he had stolen stood over

him.

"Lawks," the man in black said, grinning. "Such long faces. You look like you're hardly fit to stand." He kicked two chairs out from the table. "Sit down and have a stout. Both o' you."

Jigme gawked. The tourist did too, but finally he shook his head and said, "This... this arse midget just stole my pack."

The man patted the black fabric with a hand that seemed both as brown as Jigme's yet pale as the walls of the city. Puffs of dust leaped off the pack. "Aye, and more credit to him for lugging it this far. What'd you pack, all the dirt in India?" The man motioned to the chairs. "Besides, it's hardly stolen now."

"But it was stolen," the tourist said, "and he stole it. I thank you for stopping him, but all the same I'd like to talk to the police."

"Do you, now," the man in black said, sitting up. "I hadn't figured you for some tourist who only just learned which way his passport opens. But then, you're clearly tired after coming a long way." The man breathed in deeply. "Aye, quite a journey. Tibet. And Mount Everest. You can always tell the place just by the smell o' the grit."

The tourist smirked.

"It's all that sun and cold, you see," the man in black continued. "It tastes like life and death smacking into one other, and it smells like the beginning and the end o' the world."

He breathed in again. "Lots o' places." A pained look crossed the man's face. "Right back to jolly ole Ireland and then some. A man who's seen this much o' the world, I'd figure he'd know things are always a fair sight more complicated than a boy legging it down the street. But it's clearly your first time here. No matter where you've been, nothing prepares you for India. Nowhere else on Earth does the fire o' life burn so bright as it burns here. And I think that now that you've collected your thoughts a wee bit, you're remembering not to expect India to be like home."

The man took another sniff and continued. "Ah, Idaho," he said. "The ole U-S-o'-A. The only thing you can expect about India is that it will be itself. But who will you be? Are you a Yank... or a wank?"

The tourist's breath hitched. *At least I'm breathing more easily,* Jigme thought, tensing his legs as the tourist's gaze locked onto him.

"My name is Jay," the tourist said, "and that pack is all I have in the whole world." He sat in one of the chairs. "Why did you take it?"

Jigme looked at the two men, then at the last empty chair. "Are you going to get the police?" he asked.

"I'm not happy that you stole from me," Jay said, shaking his head. "But I won't get the police. As long as you help me understand."

Jigme sat down.

"Some nourishment will ease this discussion," the man said.

A door opened and a woman came out, carrying three brimming curved glasses of dark liquid topped with white foam.

"Why Jade," the man said, "impeccable timing as always."

Jade set a glass in front of each of them. A flush burned Jigme's face and he tried to hide behind the black beer. When she looked at him, Jigme couldn't bear to look back into her blazing eyes. It was like looking at gods and suns. His attempt to thank her spilled out onto the table as a mumbled jumble of syllables.

The tourist—Jay—stared at her, and she seemed not to be able to look back at him. She started to say something, but instead nearly caught Jay's eye. Jade nodded sharply, turned, and went back inside.

"Who?" Jay asked. "Who was that?"

"That would be Jade, finest bartender in India," the man in black said.

"She's..." Jay trailed off.

"Beautiful," Jigme replied.

"Yes," Jay said, smiling. "She is beautiful. I'll drink to that, um..."

"Aye, we could do with some introductions," the man said. He joined his palms and held his hands in front of his chest. "Namaste," he said. "That's a common greeting and farewell here," he said to Jay. "It means 'the god in me salutes the god in you.' You've already said you're Jay. I'm Faddah Rucksack, but most folks skip the Faddah and just go for the Rucksack." He looked at Jigme. "And you?" he asked.

"I'm Jigme."

"You're what, sixteen?"

Jigme nodded.

"Old enough to know a taste o' reality," Rucksack said, raising his glass. "Strangely met but well met, lads. Now c'mon, raise those pints. There's no such thing as the sound o' one glass clinking."

They clinked and drank. The thick dark liquid was beer, Jigme realized, and it sparkled in his mouth. It also made him sputter and cough, and he set down the glass.

A quarter of Rucksack's beer disappeared, then he said, "No sipping, lad. Sipping is for those damnable sodas you kids drink and that discolored water Americans and Guru Deep piss off as beer. To stout is to quaff. As such." Rucksack raised his glass and Jigme clinked with him again. They each took a long swallow of the black beer.

This time, Jigme smiled as he set down his much emptier glass. A loose, free feeling buzzed inside. The world seemed clearer. Shapes, colors, forms, people, objects, and animals all looked both more distinct and defined yet more connected and unified.

"How do you drink beer this thick in a city this hot?" Jay asked.

"The heat mucks with how you see the world," Rucksack said, "but stout's too real for anything to mess with it. It keeps me seeing what's what."

"You're crazy."

"I at least had the sense to sit down to a pint in this heat," Rucksack said with a chuckle. "You're the one who tried to walk into town in the middle o' a day like a wet wildfire."

"How do you know that?" Jay asked.

"Let's just say that even the roaches will avoid your boots, lad," Rucksack said, tapping his nose. "You could try burning them, but I think the flames would extinguish themselves in protest."

Rucksack's gaze turned to Jay's backpack. Jigme's did too. As the talk paused, Jigme heard a soft rustling sound. Rucksack listened intently, but Jay seemed to be trying to ignore it.

"Now that we're acquainted, to business," Rucksack

said, looking at Jay again. "So, the backpack. Surely you didn't have the crown jewels in there."

Jay smiled. "No."

"What are the crown jewels?" Jigme asked.

"The crown jewels o' travel," Rucksack said. "Your passport, your money, and your tickets. Any traveler worth his pack never keeps the crown jewels on his back. He usually keeps them in a money belt, or some sort o' pouch he can hide under his clothes. He can lose everything else right down to his unwashed skivvies, but as long as he has those three things, he'll be a'right."

Jay shrugged. "That's all true, but it doesn't mean I want my pack stolen. There's still important stuff in there."

"I understand," Rucksack said. The men looked at Jigme. He grabbed his glass and took a long swallow. The more stout he drank, the more the world made sense. And the more he understood what he had to say.

Jigme sighed. "My mother is sick," he said. "That's why I took the pack. We have no money. I gave her medicine but it didn't work. And we have no food."

Jay stared hard at him, saying nothing. *Does he think I'm lying?* Jigme thought.

"You thought you could sell what's inside," Jay finally said.

Jigme nodded. "She's all I have." His eyes burned and he looked away. "No matter how hard I try, she doesn't get better."

Jay took another swig of stout. "I lost my mother," he said. "If I could have prevented it, there's nothing I wouldn't have done either." The gentleness in his voice made Jigme look at the two men again. He saw Rucksack look at Jay too, a question poised in the man's eyes.

But Rucksack turned to Jigme and asked, "What does she need?"

"Doctor. Real medicine."

"Do you know what's wrong with her?"

Jigme shook his head.

"Drink up, lad," Rucksack said, swigging the last of his pint. "We'll come with you and help as we can."

"What?" Jay asked. "Look, I don't even know you, and this kid just tried to steal my bag. Plus, I'm beat. I've been bouncing around the back of a truck for days, from Tibet to here. All I want to do is find the Everest Base Camp, get a bed, and sleep."

Rucksack stared hard at Jay. "You know as well as I do that the road isn't what you walk. The road is where it takes you." Rucksack pointed at the sign hanging from the second story of the three-story building, visible to anyone walking up or down the street. Against a brown-and-black background, a gold outline traced the shape of a silver mountain. Inside the outline, blue as a god's skin, shone the words, "Everest Base Camp Pub & Hostel" in English, with green Hindi characters beneath.

Jay looked from Jigme to the door. Weariness poured from him like waves.

"Don't you worry about the hostel," Rucksack said. "It'll still be there when we get back. Jade'll have a place for you. I asked earlier if you were a Yank or a wank, and I think you've answered that." A grin widened over his broad face, and his white teeth gleamed against his brown skin. "But tell me this, Jay o' the road. Are you a traveler... or a tourist?"

Jay downed the rest of his pint. He turned to Jigme. "Where does your mother live?"

IN THE QUIET of the empty pub, the soft *pthump* seemed loud as a drained steel keg falling on the concrete floor. *Finally,* Jade thought, *something to distract me.* Whenever Rucksack was gone, the pub seemed so quiet lately. She wondered where he, the boy, and the backpacker had gone, but even that had not kept her mind occupied long enough.

The last two hours had been broken up by the chai wallah dropping in. He filled the pub's urn with sugary, milky tea while they talked about how hot it was outside and how thick the crowds were today. The chai wallah had left with a glazed look. Jade realized he'd hardly spoken but had mostly nodded while she rattled on and on.

A delivery of various liquors and some new kegs of Deep's Special Lager made her sweat while she got everything into storage. The exertion made her grateful, but that ended far too soon, and she was back behind the bar, annoyed and distracted with her jangled thoughts.

Next Jade had cleaned behind the bar, reorganized the bottles, and dusted the shelves. With that done, now she was walking around the pub, making minor tweaks to the spacing of every table and chair, rearranging the furniture completely, moving everything back where it had been before, and then starting all over again. To her eye, she had to confess that the pub looked no different, though she tried to convince herself she'd just found a layout that increased standing room by a good five percent.

Then came the *pthump*. Walking back to the bar, Jade wondered what was so important that The Management needed to send a special directive.

She had just reached toward the cabinet when the pub door opened and the backpacker from before walked in.

Her heart sped up again as her voice fell into her shoes, but her mind rebelled. *There's nothing special about him,* Jade thought. *He's the embodiment of average. Average height. Average build. Okay, maybe a little muscle and slenderness from traveling with that pack on his back. The face isn't bad. Good chin. I like the brown hair.* The road had coated him with enough dust, dirt, and grit that it was nearly impossible to tell what color his skin was, but Jade sensed a creaminess and wondered how it would contrast against the olive of her own.

*What business would his skin have being that close to yours?*

She realized the traveler had said something and was waiting for her to reply. Jade hunted for her voice and avoided his eyes. "Bed?" she finally said, the word falling out of her mouth before she realized she was speaking.

A red flush burned through the dust on the man's face. "Um, what?" the traveler said.

Waves rippled through Jade's belly. Her jumbled thoughts crashed into each other. Her voice didn't know how to work anymore, but instinct and years of experience were kicking in. "You need a bed, right?"

"Oh. Bed. Rooms have beds. Yes, a room. I could do with a room. Yeah."

"I've only got dorms. Through there." Jade pointed at a door to the right of the bar.

"No worries."

Reaching under the bar to the board where the keys were kept, Jade took one at random and held it out. His palm brushed her fingertips as he reached for it.

"I'm Jay," he said.

"Jade," she replied. *It's the damn eyes that do it,* she thought, staring at his nose. *They're green as my name, but the gold in there, it's like the man has sunrise in his eyes.*

For a few moments they said nothing, their outstretched arms not moving, their hands barely touching, the bar between them.

"Jade?" His voice quavered. Under the hard edges and the grit of years of travel, there was a softness there—maybe a kindness, even. "Yes?"

"Could you let go?"

Jade looked down at their touching hands. Her fingers clenched white around the key ring. She let go and Jay stepped back slowly. His face was as red as bad wine.

"Do I need to pay you now?" he asked.

"We'll take care of it later," she said. "Go ahead and sign in." She took a large book from under the bar and opened it to a page with only a few signatures. "Name, home country, passport number, signature," Jade said, watching him fill in the information. *He didn't even need to take out his passport,* she thought. *He's got the number memorized.* She followed the scrawl and loops of his "Jay" signature.

They finished discussing the particulars of his stay. Jay looked from her face to the floor. He started to say something but couldn't find his voice. He gave her a quick wave and started walking to the door that went up the steps to the hostel dorms and their beds.

But he stopped when she said, "Oh, Jay?"

"Yes?" he said, lilting with confused hope.

"Be sure to come down for the music later."

The traveler nodded and left. Jade hoped he would take a nap. And a shower. He looked knackered. Jade wondered what he looked like clean.

She stood still for a few minutes, clenching the bar and trying to breathe deeply and calmly. In her mind she was still looking deep into his eyes.

*What did he see in mine?*

"Stupid, stupid schoolgirl," she said at last, turning around and looking at herself in the mirror. "You're a Jade," she said to her reflection. "Not some witless teenager mooning over a movie star or some eejit who just came out with another record." Her eyes blazed like a summer storm and a midday sky.

It wasn't until she glanced at the special cabinet that she even remembered.

Jade opened the door and took out the envelope. The special directives never looked special. Back in her old life, she'd gotten letters from far-flung friends and family who came with more ceremony and decoration. The pale brown parchment was made by hand, as were the envelopes. She knew because part of the training was that each new Jake and Jade must make a thousand perfect envelopes and a thousand perfect sheets of paper. Jade had finished hers in record time.

The Management had said that this exercise was meant to help them understand the importance of process and repetition, of paying the closest possible attention to detail regardless of the task at hand, regardless of experience, regardless of how many times you'd done the same action before.

Jade suspected it was really a way to save on the cost of paper.

Glancing at the pub door and taking a moment to not just hear the sounds but listen to the minds and souls of the people teeming outside, Jade exhaled. The world wasn't coming in yet, so she had nothing to worry about. Jay was just another traveler and she was just a Jade—and that was all there would be to it. She unfolded the paper and read:

```
The new traveler is not just the new
traveler. He and the world must remain
in Agamuskara until the eclipse, so he
can be as a sunrise that never ends.
When the time is right, you must make
him forget himself and follow what he
would never follow.
```

Jade read the letter two more times, memorizing the lines and wondering what the hell it all meant. The Management's missives sometimes held a certain poetic tone. Jade could never decide what was profound and what was just wrapped up in a convoluted mixture of philosophy and high-handedness. Or maybe it was a translation quirk of beings that weren't human trying to communicate with humans. But she'd never seen anything this inscrutable.

She made a cup of coffee—roasted, ground, and poured perfectly in every way. Coffee, she had learned in the training, was the drink of ultimate perception. A perfect cup of coffee, The Management had explained, could help you see the world in the way it was meant to be seen. They had also cautioned that coffee—along with stout, absinthe, and water—could not be influenced by Jakes, Jades, or even The Management themselves. Those safe havens had made coffee Jade's beverage of choice over the years. Every time she needed to ponder, every time a difficult sense of destiny and decision took her longer than usual to determine, she looked through the gently wafting steam of a fresh cup of coffee and found her way.

Today's cuppa offered no insights. Reality was as obscure as the black liquid in her cup, nearly as opaque as GPS.

Jade read the directive again. None of it made any more sense than it had before. What was so special about Jay? Other than the effect he was having on her heart rate, he wasn't very different from any other traveler who'd sought a bed at the Everest Base Camp. And why "the world must remain in Agamuskara?" Agamuskara was a small place in a big world, not the other way around. Besides, the city was crowded enough already without packing in the rest of the planet. And what would make Jay forget himself and "follow what he would never follow" anyway?

Jade shook her head. "You'll figure it out in time," she said to herself. "Do your duty, and duty will show you the way."

For a moment, the memory of Jay's green-and-gold eyes left her mind, and she felt focused on her purpose, on her work, again. A moment's heated rush.

Some sense of attraction. *Well, Jade reasoned, I'm still only human. More or less. No one ever said we couldn't feel a bit of a flush toward someone. Just as long as it doesn't get in the way of what I have to do.*

She started to let the directive fall from her hand, the way she had hundreds of times before. Once it left her person, the sheet of paper would always disappear. No flames or puffs of smoke; as the paper drifted to the floor, you would start to see the floor through the paper, until the sheet had faded away into nothing. Or not nothing. What happened after the paper disappeared, where it went, she did not know; Jade always figured The Management simply moved the sheets into some sort of filing system. Even when managing existence itself, every management had to have an office, and every office had to have its filing.

But her heart beat faster again as she thought of his bright eyes, the long years and hard miles behind his gaze. Jade couldn't let go of the sheet of paper. The directive was seared onto her brain, but the realness of the words on the page pulled at her. For the first time in her career as a Jade, she ignored policy, folded up the directive, put it back in its envelope, and tucked it into her back pocket.

*THE TROUBLE with hostels is the stairs,* Jay thought as his legs wobbled him back from Jigme's place. And hostels always had stairs.

*Well, except that one place in Ireland, but that was an exception in so many ways.*

They could never be grand, sweeping staircases, either—no wide, perfectly spaced, ergonomically correct steps that fit your struggling stride. Hostel stairs were always barely as wide as your pack. With every step, the backpack fabric would rub on the walls, sometimes resulting in a new look for your pack, depending on the quality of the paint. Every time you moved, you barely moved. The friction of wall and pack conspired to hold you still, while you burned energy you didn't have just to get to your bed and collapse.

If the narrow stairways didn't get you stuck, there was always a turn in the steps, some small landing that would make sardines claustrophobic. That always resulted in a few embarrassing moments of shifting back and forth, trying to turn a little to one side or the other, anything to get you free and trudging again.

Due to some twisted law of the universe, Jay had concluded, getting stuck on hostel stairs also compelled someone from an upper floor and someone from a lower floor to need to use the stairs at the same time. Then came the tricky negotiation of who continued on their way first, while the other two hapless travelers tried to squeeze themselves into the wall so the other could pass.

In these inevitable situations, the laden backpacker always lost.

As the first traveler passed and then the second traveler passed, Jay breathed out hard and extricated himself from the wall. His legs shook. His feet throbbed.

There was still one more flight of steps to go.

"Leave the pack with Jade," Rucksack had encouraged him as they went with Jigme. But Jay just couldn't do it. He wasn't letting the pack out of his sight until he fell asleep—and even then, he was seriously considering chaining his wrist to the pack, just to be on the safe side.

*Bollocks*, he thought, in a part of his mind that seemed far away and somehow not fatigued. He tried to ignore that part of his mind, but it persisted. *It has nothing to do with the pack,* he thought. *You just couldn't deal with seeing her again.*

Jay started up the last landing. He was almost to the third floor.

His memories of Jade weighed him down more than the pack and the fatigue. When she'd first come outside, three pints on her tray, one look had washed away every bump, bruise, exhaustion, and hardship of the day. Of the last three days. Of the last five years. Both calmness and excitement had settled over Jay, as his gaze caught her blue-and-gold eyes. Now, their second encounter bewildered him. The air had all but crackled between them. And the brush of their hands? His skin still tingled. *This day has been strange in so many ways,* he thought, *but maybe it will make more sense once I've slept.* He trudged up the steps, trying to put Jade, Jigme, Rucksack, everything out of his mind.

When he got to the door of the dorm room, Jay listened a moment before opening it. Loud arguments, loud hangovers, loud attacks of food poisoning, louder sex, and some particularly loud masturbation had all taught him never to open a hostel dorm door quickly.

Not so much as a snore. *Maybe my luck is changing.*

Jay opened the door and sighed. Not that he'd expected better. Cheap hostels were always packed, and most backpackers felt lucky to be able to lie on their backs. Still, Jay had hoped to be able to turn over in his bed and not bang his shoulder on the bunk above him. Judging by the number of made beds to big packs and general let's-spread-out-a-bit clutter, the dorm was only half-full.

*Thank goodness it's not full-on tourist season.*

Inside the room, Jay counted two rows each of three sets of bunk beds. There was bed space for twelve. The door opened at the long end of the room, and the beds stretched off toward a short wall at the other end, with a doorway cut into it. Backpacks, clothes, and various effects of six travelers covered beds, walls, and floors, but their travelers were nowhere to be seen. They were probably out seeing the fire temples, buying silk, noshing on street foods, and wandering the streets of Agamuskara. They'd be checking out the locals, talking with the locals, and maybe, for a moment in their hearts, feeling like they were locals. *Good for them*, Jay thought. *At least for now I can get some quiet sleep.*

Right across from the door, the first row of beds had an empty bottom bunk in the middle. Dogs pee to claim territory. Backpackers just set down their stuff.

The air didn't smell too rank or stale—a good sign that no one was terribly unkempt, habitually hung over, or regretting eating that dodgy curry last night. However, he would understand if his dorm-mates were all crazy. The green of the cinderblock walls was mint gone wrong, neon past its prime, a bucket of paint rejected by a prison. Stark shadows scrabbled around the walls, making them foreboding and slightly psychedelic. Three bare bulbs hung from the ceiling like travelers who'd stayed in the room too long. Yellow light dribbled like an incontinent cow.

In the middle of the far wall, a thin door opened to the lone loo, and Jay's bladder pulled him toward it. *The budget for building materials must have run low,* Jay thought as he groped for a light.

In the dim glow from the dorm room he could make out the squat toilet, a concrete pad with a rough oval hole cut in it, surrounded by what looked like a dirt floor. After spending so many years on the road, Jay didn't think twice about squat toilets, though he still shuddered at the memory of the toilet at the other base camp, its stalagmite of frozen poo rising from the hole.

Then he realized why this toilet bothered him. *This is the third story of the building,* Jay thought. *So how is the floor dirt?*

Waving his hand high and in front of him, he finally caught the thin string of the light's pull cord. The heavy light of the bare bulb must have been carefully calibrated to look exactly like urine.

Jay looked down. Roaches glared back at him, but they ran from his feet as Jay stepped forward.

As he released the stout and water from the day, a roach crawled up onto the rim of the toilet hole. Something about its waving legs and antennae suggested a taunt, a threat. The other roaches were still, listening, waiting. An antenna waved and then so did the thousands of antennae of the assembled roach army. Jay stared back at the menacing roach general. "Point that somewhere else," Jay said, blasting the roach off the toilet.

The other roaches glared at him with revenge in their tiny compound eyes. Jay realized his ammo had run out. Zipping up, he retreated as tactfully as he could while walking backwards, not taking his eyes off the roaches until the door was shut.

Jay lay back on his new bed and folded his hands under his head. "It'll do fine," he said, grinning as he slipped into a deep sleep.

His body rested, but in his mind the travel never stopped.

In his dream, the white alley glowed, but the dull red door looked like smeared blood. "Hope is inside," Rucksack said. The small backpack that was his head slowly revolved on his neck.

"Hope is dying," Jigme replied. A turning backpack had replaced his head also. Around them, the white walls of the alley faded into a gray mist. Only the red door remained. The air smelled of ash and old fires. "Will you help?"

"I don't know how to help," Jay said. "I couldn't help anyone. I didn't even know they were gone until..."

"I can't open the door," Jigme said, his hands straining at the bolts.

"I can't either," Rucksack said.

"But it's easy," Jay replied, moving between them and touching the door.

Blood cascaded down his feet. Jay was certain his t-shirt was ruined, but he didn't look down. Where the red door had stood, an open doorway showed them the small room where the sick woman lay undecided between living and dying.

Jigme pointed to the frail sticks on the bed and said, "Amma. Say hello, Amma. Please." The sticks had been woven into the shape of a woman, but there was no skin, no breath; this woman was hollow inside. She had no mouth so said nothing. Though there were no eyes, the stick woman seemed to watch them.

"What is her name?" Rucksack asked.

"Asha," Jigme said.

"It means hope," Rucksack said to Jay. "Where there is a mother, there is hope."

"But there is no hope here," Jay replied. "She is empty. Asha is gone. Hope is dead."

Heat welled up in the air around them. The scent of fires grew fresher, hotter.

"She has a fever," Jigme said. "It burns."

Black and red flames flickered around the walls, eating the room from the ceiling to the floor. When the room burned away, the rest of the world stretched out around them. Where the white walls had gone, ash and rubble lay smoking. The sun had been eaten like an egg yolk. As far as Jay could see, a black world smoked.

"There is nothing we can do," Jay said.

"Where there is a mother," Rucksack repeated, "there is hope."

The flames gathered around the bed. "No!" Jigme said. "Don't let them!"

"There is nothing," Jay said. "Nothing."

The flames gathered into a red-and-black crescent of shadow and blood. Sharp points stretched into a grin, then widened over the sticks that were shaped like a woman. The sticks moved. Organs and blood appeared inside. Wicker whitened into bone. Skin stretched over muscles. Eyes opened.

Jade stared at Jay.

"No!" he shouted, leaping forward as the fires lowered.

Her scream went out in a *whoomph* as the mouth of

black flames swallowed her.

Jay reached for her, tried to leap forward, but Rucksack and Jigme pulled at his arms. "The moon told you," Jigme said, pulling Jay away from the black mouth. Flames flickered like shadows.

"The moon told you," Rucksack agreed. "Oh, and now look."

Jay's feet felt wet. He looked down at his shirt, reddened from the blood from when they had come in —only now the blood flowed fresh. Then the pain hit him. He staggered and his knees hit the dirt floor. He touched his chest. His fingers went inside.

"You can touch your heart," Jigme said. "I can't do that."

"Take care not to drop it," Rucksack said.

Jay reached into his chest and pulled out his heart. It beat in his bloody hand: red and pink, swelling and condensing with each empty beat. "This isn't what it really looks like," Jay said. With his other hand, he wiped away the blood. A small world floated in his hand, turning slowly. White clouds swirled, bringing shadows to the brown and green lands within. He could almost hear the waves of the blue waters rise and crash, rise and crash.

The mouth opened again, and the black flames moved forward.

"Run!" Rucksack shouted.

But the world felt faint and hazy like wisps of ash blowing up from a fire. As Jay watched the little world, grayness and blackness spread out from what looked like a miniature Indian subcontinent. Soon, a charred blackness covered the entire globe, swallowing up the colors of the earth and sky.

"Don't let it!" Jigme shouted.

"Why not?" Jay said. "It's just a souvenir."

He dropped the charred little world into the open mouth. Behind him, the backpacks of Jigme's and Rucksack's heads burst into red-and-black flame.

Rucksack and Jigme sank to their knees. Where the packs had been, there was nothing. The pair fell forward.

"No," Jay said. "You were supposed to be there still."

He looked at the black mouth. "Give it back!" he said. "Give it back!"

The mouth grinned widely again then lunged forward until all Jay saw was black.

His head smacked the bottom of the bunk above him when he sat up.

The impact knocked him back onto his bed, and pain washed away the dream. "Aaagh," Jay said to the heavy, hot darkness waiting at the window behind his bed. He touched his forehead. No sweat. If anything, a chill pulsed inside him as he sat up—slowly, carefully this time.

The dream was quickly fading, until he remembered only vague snippets about a fire, Rucksack, and Jigme. "What were we doing?" Jay asked the empty dorm. "Having a barbecue?" He shook the remnants of the dream out of his mind and rubbed the sharp ache out from his tenderized forehead.

Fast-paced music wafted from the floor: the sharpness of whistles and flutes, the clatter-clap rhythm of a drum, and the circular sawings of...

*No*, Jay thought. *No way. I'm in India, not Ireland.*

He kept listening. Then he got a few things

together in his smaller daypack, freshened himself up, and secured his large backpack to the bed.

*It is though,* he thought as he left the dorm and started down to the pub. *It's definitely a fiddle, or I'm not in India anymore.*


THE NOISES MET JAY on the narrow stairs, washing out the rustling coming from his small daypack. When Jay opened the door, the pub was a different world. Silence had been booted into the streets. The world outside had realized its throat was dry and it needed to come inside. Jay couldn't even see the floor, much less an empty chair to sit in.

Different languages whooshed past Jay. He passed by tables of travelers sitting together, Indians sitting together, and Indians and travelers sitting together. Looking around, he identified Australians, Israelis, Swedes, Germans, Japanese, Kenyans, Egyptians, Americans, Brazilians, Canadians, Mexicans, and Scots. The whole world seemed to be at the Everest Base Camp, getting to know each other while swapping stories and clinking glasses.

A wayward foot made him stumble. Two men sitting at a table caught him by the arms and steadied him. Something about their faces seemed familiar, but he couldn't quite place it. "Thanks," Jay said. The men nodded and he continued on.

He hadn't noticed earlier, but where the Everest Base Camp's walls weren't white plaster, every color of the world turned the pub into an atlas and a scrapbook. Scrawled with signatures and well wishes, flags from over one hundred countries hung from the walls. Postcards. Photos. Maps of states, countries. Across from the bar, a large world map hung on the wall. Jay wove and twisted through the crowd until he stood before it. The map was large enough and detailed enough to show not only the world's countries, but also states and cities. Much of the map wasn't even visible, though; it was stuck with pins representing where the patrons came from. Not just travelers but locals too, Jay saw; India itself was covered in pins.

The countries he had visited were also well represented. Ireland alone had twenty pins stuck in and around New Galway and the surrounding country. *Maybe a sign pointed them here,* he thought, remembering the red hair and the white sign of a long-ago memory.

He looked west, across the Atlantic Ocean and the North American continent, until he stopped at Idaho. Other than a couple of pins stuck in Boise, the state was empty. Jay traced the green shape of the state with his finger. *The map is not the world,* he thought. Still, for a moment he expected to see the river there again, or smell freshly sawed cedar in his dad's workshop, or hear the excitement in his mom's voice as she read from another guidebook.

Instead, he remembered the door opening, the rain pouring in sheets behind the man walking in.

Jay lowered his hand. "Maps are dreams, hopes, and memories," he said to himself.

Beneath the frame a clear, covered tray held pins. Jay stuck one in Idaho and turned away before the memories could come back.

On the pub's corner stage, ten people sat in a circle,

playing music and singing. The musicians too were local and foreign, though Indian and Celtic sounds and rhythms dominated. People clapped hands, tapped feet, and whooped as a fiddle and a sarinda dueled, their respective players bowing furiously. Other people called out tunes, and the musicians acknowledged each request with a nod.

Jay trudged to the bar, finally resting his elbows on the polished mahogany. The only person behind the bar was Jade, and she moved so quickly that Jay could hardly keep his eyes on her. He watched her as best he could, fascinated with how regally and gracefully she moved. No glass slipped from her hands. No miscounted change dropped to the bar. No patron even had to repeat a drink order. And Jade never stopped moving. Her every motion was efficient to the point of ruthless yet elegant as a bird in flight.

Now and again, she seemed to blur like a skip, a bad spot in her motion that Jay couldn't follow. Jay chalked it up to needing a beer. She was busy at the other end of the bar, mixing five drinks and pulling a pint of Deep's Special Lager. She bent over to get something from a low shelf. *No rush then,* Jay thought. *I'll just... enjoy the view.*

And then she was there in front of him. Looking irritated.

Jay realized he was a few seconds behind events. "Huh?"

Jade's hand seemed to twitch toward something underneath the bar, but she stopped herself and grinned razors. "I said he's over there. With your pint."

"What? No... Who?"

The irritated look sharpened in her blue-and-gold

eyes. "Let me know when you unpack your brain, backpack boy," she said. "Who do you think?"

Then she was gone, a blur behind the bar again.

At a table in the middle of the floor, Faddah Rucksack lifted his pint to Jay and beckoned to the empty chair behind a brimming stout.

"You look rested," Rucksack said. "Or at least a little less like hell. Now it's time to be restored."

Jay set his daypack under the table as he sat down. He tucked a chair leg through one of the straps and ignored the endless rustle, which was audible over the talking and the music. "I could do with a drink. Thank you."

"After the day you've had, you've earned a pint. Welcome to India, my lad!" The men clinked glasses and drank deeply.

Rucksack set his glass on the table. "It's been quite a path for you," he said. "I think we have a bit in common, Jay o' the road. Could just about figure we were destined to meet. You do like I do. We follow the path we see and let it take us where it's going. Destiny."

"Never was one for destiny," Jay replied. "I choose what I want to do, where I want to go. Then I go there. I make my own way."

"So you just up and came to India."

"Sure. Time for a change. Thought I'd get to know one of the world's most amazing countries. Figured I could see the eclipse too before I skip out of here. It's supposed to be a rare one. Besides, after Tibet I could do with some warmer weather and thicker air."

"I can imagine. But I envy you too. I miss Tibet. I know the dirt o' those mountains anywhere, and that stuff's ground itself into you from your skin to your soul to the fibers and heart o' your backpack."

"You've been to Tibet?"

"I have. As well as Bhutan, northern India, Kashmir and Pakistan. From the Hindu Kush to Assam, I know this country like the back o' my right hand."

"And the back of your left hand?"

Rucksack grinned. "You're smarter than she took you for. The back o' my left hand, that'd be Ireland."

Jay stared at the black leather glove. The left hand was smaller than the right. "What happened to your left hand?"

"Ah, you wouldn't want to hear about that. It's a gruesome tale involving an innovative effort to come up with the world's first piecrust flattener machine. But the way o' it is that I'm from the world's wisest seats o' wisdom, my lad. I'm born of India and the Himalaya—not necessarily o' the country, just the mountains themselves, and the land, the water, and the air. I'm Himalayan by birth, Irish by fortune, and myself by choice."

"How'd you wind up in Ireland?"

"That's a boring story o' youth and a family that had to flee for their lives. Nothing that would interest you. You must be tired, you devil, and I've peppered you enough. Look at this place!" Rucksack swept his arms wide. People sang, danced, played music. Every table was talk, jokes, stories. But Jay's eyes kept going to Jade behind her bar.

"Aye," Rucksack said. "She's something. More than you or even I know."

"Maybe I'll find out."

"Maybe. Few people are more guarded than a Jake

or a Jade, lad. Let that stay right in your mind."

"What does that mean?"

"All you need to know."

"And what are you, then?"

"I am the world's only Himalayan-Irish sage. Now drink up and enjoy."

The stout warmed something in Jay. Rucksack was evasive and full of riddles, but Jay couldn't help but like him. "I've been traveling for five years," Jay said. "Lots of stamps in that passport. I've even added pages. The last two years I've been in Asia."

"Yet this is your first time in India."

"It's a big world. I wanted to see more of it first. Asia... I guess you could say I wanted to save the best for last."

Rucksack eyed Jay over a swig of stout. "At least you're here now. India must seem pretty small beer to a well-worlded lad such as you though."

Jay shook his head. "On the contrary. It's obviously an eventful place, and I haven't even been here twenty-four hours. The scariest part, though, was the gang of cockroaches in the loo."

"How are the roaches?" Rucksack asked.

"I didn't stay long enough to find out how much they charge for protection money."

"There's only one thing for those buggers."

"Don't they say roaches would survive the end of the world?"

"They do. Trouble is, *they* know nothing about Indian booze. Get yourself a bottle o' Ram Rum or some o' that other swill Jade keeps on the bottom shelf. Pour it all over the loo. Corners o' the walls, around and in the shower drain, under the sink, everywhere. Bastards won't bother you again."

"Why? Does it get them drunk?"

"Melts their legs off. Roach can't menace if it can't walk."

"Not exactly a nonviolent approach to one of our fellow creatures, eh, Rucksack?"

"Please. I have too much to do to muck about with being holy."

They laughed. Jay sat back in his chair, looking around the crowded pub. *He's fascinating,* Jay thought, *and he's the best conversation I've had in ages.* He relaxed. Even the noise in the daypack faded from his mind.

Jay nodded toward the musicians. "I've never seen anything like this place," he said. "You could've bet me a year's travel money, and there's no way I'd figure that you could play Indian and Irish music on the same stage."

Rucksack nodded. "The world never ceases to amaze me with how it brings things together. Your fiddler there is playing a mean up-tempo riff on the song o' me heart, 'The Little Beggarman.'"

"And the Indian player?"

"He's playing a sarinda, which in a way is like an Indian take on a fiddle. Or you could say the Irish fiddle is a take on the Indian sarinda. Someone here is probably arguing the finer points."

"What song is he playing?"

"'Bole Chudiyan,'" Rucksack said. "Wonderful hit tune. The title translates as 'My Bangles Spoke.'"

"I'd heard about the interesting songs from the Bollywood films here, but I've never actually heard any."

"They could teach the world a great deal about

what to call things. There's also 'Chand Mera Dil Chandni Ho Tum,' or 'The Moon is My Heart, You are the Moonlight,' and one o' my favorites, 'Mera Man Tera Pyasa,' or 'My Mind is Thirsty for You.'"

Jay drank half his remaining pint. "Nothing like an Indian love story, from what I hear."

"Where you hear that?"

"*India Through the Third Eye*," Jay said. "Big section on Bollywood movies. 'Love transforms,' it says. It transforms so much, a scene can go from the middle of a city like Agamuskara to a man and woman singing in a flower field in Kashmir or dancing around each other with the erotic temples of Khajuraho in the background. The movies are larger than life because India is larger than life. If they seem over the top, it's because they are trying to get at the bigness of the feelings and morals beyond what we normally deal with, what we share and experience in our day-to-day lives."

"Maybe we should write a song," Rucksack said.

Jay smiled. "You're on. How many drinks do you think it takes to write a hit Bollywood song?"

Rucksack laughed. "At least two an hour till it's done. That would give you a helluva tale you'd be dying to tell the folks back home."

Jay's face darkened. "There are no folks back home."

Rucksack's pint arm froze halfway to his mouth. "I'm sorry, Jay."

Jay shrugged and looked toward the stage.

Rucksack set down his glass. "I lost my mum and dad," he said, clenching and unclenching his gloved left hand. "Long time ago, but sometimes it still hurts like it just happened."

Jay nodded and looked back at Rucksack. "Do you think Jigme will lose his mum?"

In the silence between Rucksack opening his mouth and actually speaking, the train of Rucksack's thoughts leaped to another track. "I don't know. I'll keep doing what I can, if the doctors can't do anything else for her. But at this point they have a better shot at healing her than I do. Her malady... there was a time where I could have set her right, just about no matter what it was." He flexed his left hand. "But not so much these days."

Jay let the hyperbole pass him by. "These doctors are good ones, though, right?"

"The best in the city." Rucksack drained his pint. "I have to admit, when I first saw you I thought you might be another Annoyican wanker, parading his Americanness and expecting the world to part and smooth before you. I understood you being mad about your pack being stolen, but you know as well as I do that for a relatively well-to-do foreigner such as yourself, the theft meant an inconvenient day while you replaced your belongings, especially since the crown jewels weren't in there. No trouble at all for you, really."

"What changed your mind?" Jay asked, setting down his emptied glass.

"When you took her to the hospital."

"He what?"

The men looked up. Jade stood over them, holding two pints on a tray.

"The lad from earlier, Jigme, who stole Jay's pack," Rucksack said. "We visited his mum, Asha. I did what I could for her."

"Are you a doctor too, then?" Jade asked

"I'm just a man who does what needs doing," Rucksack replied. "But in this instance I couldn't do much. Asha was thin and feverish as could be, and Jigme explained they couldn't afford any doctors or medicines. Jay stared long at her. Next thing I knew, Jay had arranged transport for Asha and helped her get settled in at the hospital. He said he'd pay for everything."

A red, hot flush crept down Jay's cheeks. "It was the right thing to do, that's all."

Jade locked her eyes on Jay's. "There may be something to you after all, backpack boy," she said, setting down the pints and going back to the bar.

"You didn't have to tell her," Jay said.

Rucksack smiled. "You're going to fit in well here."

"Why do you say that?"

"Some countries focus on the mind, the voice, or the appetite. But India is a country o' the heart. It's beautiful and bewildering. As long as I've been in and out o' the place, I've yet to understand it. Indians aren't perfect. They're no better, no worse than anyone else. But they lead with their hearts. You can tell at a glance. The movies. The dreams. The look in the eye o' people as they walk down the street. And I can tell it about you too. You've got years o' travel on you and hardship from before you ever put on a pack. You're armored in all the thick skin, old scars, and dusty layers that entails." Rucksack raised his brimming pint. "But beneath all that, you've got heart."

The men drank. As Jay lowered his glass, he said, "Rucksack, are you a man who fancies his chances with the ladies?"

One eyebrow went up. "That's a random question."

"Not really," Jay replied. "Behind you, at a table along the wall, there's a woman sitting alone." Rucksack sat still. "Usually when someone says that," Jay said, "the other person starts to wheel around and try to look. Of course, that gives the whole thing away to the person doing the secret staring."

"Let's just say I'm old enough to know better. What's she doing?"

Jay shrugged. "She alternates between reading a piece of paper on her table and looking up and staring at you. I'm guessing she's not reading a menu."

Rucksack's brow wrinkled. "What's she look like?"

"About my age. And hot. Luscious, really."

"You've been sleeping in dorms too long."

Jay smirked. "You asked."

"In case you're forgetting, there's more to a woman than her attractiveness. Is she older, younger? How is she dressed? Where does it seem like she's from?"

"Maybe this would be a good time for you to turn around," Jay said.

"What, and spoil it?"

"No, because she caught me looking. She's leaving."

Rucksack turned around. The woman didn't need to push or shove to make her way through the crowd. She walked with a litheness that could move her between the raindrops of a monsoon without getting wet.

"I can't see her face," Rucksack said. "Where is she from?"

"How am I supposed to be able to tell?"

Rucksack stood, watching the woman until the pub door closed behind her. "Dammit, Jay." He sat down.

"People spend so much time talking about how seeing is believing, only to notice nothing when it counts. You might as well not have eyes."

"You don't have to be such a jackass about it," Jay replied. "Just a pretty lady leaving."

Rucksack looked away for a moment. "You're right. I'm sorry."

Jay nodded, then stood up and walked away. "Jay?" Rucksack said, but Jay ignored him.

No one had yet sat down at the table where the woman had been. Drops of lime-scented water remained in her empty glass. Over the stink of unwashed travelers and sharp booze, the scent of jasmine flowers lingered.

Jay looked at her chair. Nothing.

Then he looked underneath and smiled.

Sitting back down, he explained the glass and the scent to Rucksack. "That was the only trace of her. Believe it or not, some of us have senses other than our eyes."

"That was everything?" Rucksack asked.

"Yes," Jay said. "Except for this." He slid an envelope across the table. "It was empty, but it must have contained the paper she had been reading. Since she was in such a hurry to leave, it must have fallen under her chair."

Eyes wide and mouth closed in a tight line, Rucksack stared at the envelope. Handwritten in black ink that reminded Jay of Hindi and Tibetan scripts, one word stared back: "Kailash."

Rucksack finally looked up. "Did you see her face?"

Jay nodded. "I couldn't say where she's from, though. Long black hair, deep brown skin, brown eyes with hints of amber and black. The closest I could say is she looked Asian, but that's so general it's meaningless. What's going on?"

"I don't know yet. I just have this." Rucksack pulled an envelope from his vest and set it on the table next to the first envelope. The word "Rucksack" was written on it in the exact same script and hand.

"I take it there's a letter in there."

"Not just a letter," Rucksack said, nodding. "It's the reason I've been here for months, waiting, watching, wondering." He stared hard at Jay. At last, Rucksack said, "Can I trust you?"

"You're bewildering, but you've shown I can trust you," Jay replied. "Besides, I owe you one. So yes, you can trust me too."

"Open it, then."

Jay pulled a thin sheet of blue paper out of the envelope. Something about the color seemed familiar. For a moment, his memory flashed back to his arrival in the city and to the strange things he kept seeing out of the corners of his eyes. He blinked and his vision cleared. Written in the same script as the envelopes, the letter said:

```
Rucksack of the World:
Before the eclipse, in the city of
Agamuskara, by the river of the same
name, what began it will end it, and
you will find again Kailash.
```

Jay read the letter a few more times, then set it on the table. "So I take it that may have been her. And who exactly is Kailash?"

"Someone I couldn't possibly meet again," Rucksack replied. "Not in Agamuskara. Not anywhere in this world." Anguish passed over his face, and sadness burned in his eyes.

"Like I told you before, my parents died many, many years ago," Rucksack said. He looked to the door, then back to Jay. "Kailash was my mother's name."


THE MUSIC HAD DWINDLED, and now only a few musicians remained. For the first time all evening, Jade stood still and had a moment to look out over her customers. The thinning crowd revealed empty chairs. The flow had reversed. As quickly as they had come in, the people had poured out of the pub and staggered back out into the world.

Jade hoped their hearts were lighter, their eyes brighter, and their spirits happier and resolved. *Better be, anyway,* she thought. *I went through three-quarters of the stock in the cabinet just calming people's nerves.*

From the first patrons through the door to Jay to the woman who'd left in a hurry to all the murmurs underlying the pub's congenial air, it had been a strange evening.

*Maybe I can chalk this up to the news about the mirror eclipse,* Jade thought, *and how there hasn't been one since The Blast.*

The Blast had happened long enough ago that in some places and cultures the memory had begun to fade. But not in India, where The Blast remained both tragedy and joy, horror and opportunity.

After the explosion had scoured Ireland and

England, the scale of The Blast had terrified India as much as the rest of the world. Nation after nation had suspended wars, negotiated peaceful ends to conflicts, and reduced or even disbanded their militaries. India had joined other nations with shipments of supplies and volunteers sailing to Ireland and Britain to aid the survivors.

With England decimated in the aftermath, its global British Empire had fallen into disorder. Indians still raised many a glass to the nameless hero who had arisen after The Blast, united the country as it had never been united before, and dismantled the British Empire in India, which some of the Brits had started calling, "The Raj." The jewel in England's crown. There had been little violence. Many of the English laid down their guns; they were too scared for loved ones back home to care about fighting, too confused about their place in the world to care about colonies while London burned. After India had achieved independence, the nameless hero had disappeared, never to be seen again. But today, when a mirror eclipse was said to be coming, India still shuddered.

Some flickering shadow, like one caused by firelight, had seemed to hang over the destinies and paths of everyone in the pub tonight. It had been hard to read the intertwining paths of destiny and decision, hard to see as far ahead as Jade normally saw. People expressed uncertainty about this marriage or that job, about a birth or a trip. Life always held uncertainty and indecision, but never had Jade seen it at such a magnitude as tonight.

The first patrons through the door had confused her the most.

Jade glanced at their table. *They'll most likely be the last to leave,* she thought, *the way they're nursing those pitchers of Deep's Special Lager.*

They seemed like two old men who should be arguing on a park bench. They could have been from anywhere, though something in their features reminded her of Rucksack.

Their helixes confused her. Most people's paths wound out like rivers, with a mix of straight lines, bends, and meanders. These men's helixes spiraled, spun, crisscrossed, and curlicued. If she didn't know better, she'd have thought the helixes were playing a joke. Luckily, all Jade needed to do was serve them what they ordered. Whoever they were, whatever their business was, they knew their course and needed no steering from her. Jade was relieved. All the zigzags made her dizzy.

Leaving a table of Brazilians who were traveling around India for three months, a woman came up to order a vodka and tonic. Jade came back to the now. One glance at the woman's helix and Jade added a few dashes of independence to the drink.

The woman had traveled too long with the men and women in her group, and now she was bored, felt she had lost her way. A few days doing her own thing, on her own, and she'd not only enjoy the trip more, but she'd give the group some much-needed leadership.

The woman's eyes lit up when she took a sip. "This is the best vodka tonic ever," she said as she returned to her table.

Jade grinned. When she turned around, Jay was standing at the bar, a small black daypack slung over his shoulder.

Eight pints with Rucksack had hazed Jay's eyes and given him a certain sway as he stood there, but he still grinned when he saw her. She started walking over, but she felt dizzy again, as if the two men's helixes had whip-cracked her about the ankles. The floor didn't seem to be where it should be. She stumbled. Her leg spun out to the side, and she fell forward. Light glinted off of the polished edge of the bar, right where she knew her forehead would hit.

A dull sound stopped the world. Jade stared at the edge of the bar, which was dangerously close but at least not embedded in her head.

She looked up. Jay's hands were holding her shoulders, firmly but not too tightly. He helped her back up.

"Y'kay'?" Jay slurred.

"Yes, I'm okay," Jade replied, trying to hide her irritation and stepping back from his hands. *An entire night of fast movement, never stopping for a moment, no mistakes, no problems, no tripping,* she thought. *But one look at this eejit and suddenly I'm nearly falling behind my own bar?*

"Mm bit druk. C'n y' nd'stnd me?"

"Anyone around Rucksack more than an hour winds up hammered, mate," she said. "It's okay. I speak drunkese." *More fluent than you could believe,* she thought. Drunkese had been a required part of her training. The Management had explained that true drunk talk was not just intoxication but a form of primitive speech that humans regained when their minds were free of inhibitions like high cognitive functions and learned language.

Jay nodded. "Hoz'h'no'druk?"

Jade shrugged. "Wish I knew. I've never seen anyone put away as much stout as he does, but for all the effect it has, you'd think he was drinking decaf coffee." *Sometimes I so wish he would order something else,* Jade thought. *Something I could influence. Maybe then I could figure out more about him...*

More nods. Jay's eyes slipped closed and his sway became like a buoy in an ocean getting stormy. "Um, Jay?" Jade touched his shoulder to steady him.

His eyes opened wide, and his voice rang clear. "Melt their legs off," he said.

"What?"

He nodded and the stout returned to his voice. "R'ck'sk said y' knew 'bout... 'bout... roaches."

Jade laughed before she could stop herself. "They're a way of life around here," she replied. "Just a sec." She came back and handed Jay a bottle full of amber liquid, covered with a black label and large red letters like flames. "Ram Rum. This is the worst we have. It's the same one I use to get rid of the buggers," she said. "Whatever you do, don't drink it. You've had enough. Especially for your first night hanging around Rucksack. To bed with you."

"Mm'kay. Th'ks."

He was still standing there, but Jade sensed a customer heading to the bar, and she started to walk away.

"Jade?"

She stopped and came back over to Jay, relieved to have stayed on her feet this time. "Yes?"

He smiled and nodded. "You... are... a really, really good bartender," he said, slowly and deliberately, as if relearning speech.

"Thanks, Jay. I appreciate that."

"And... and you're really pretty too."

The words fell as fast as a monsoon. Before either of them could say anything else, Jay waved to her and staggered out of the pub toward the stairs that would take him to his dorm. A rustling sound followed him out, and it looked like something in his daypack was moving.

She stood still. *He thinks I'm pretty,* she thought. Then she saw herself in the bar mirror.

"You're grinning like you won a billion rupees," Rucksack said, standing at the bar with an empty glass in his hand.

*I'm grinning like a bigger eejit than you are,* she thought, trying to force the smile away. "He's funny when he's drunk," she replied. The corners of her mouth still poked up. "Another stout, I take it?"

"One more. Man's gotta have his nightcap."

Jade started pouring another pint of GPS. "Are you marinating Jay from the inside out in this stuff?"

"He clearly needed nourishment."

Jade laughed. "Next thing I know you'll be taking him to The Mystery Chickpea."

"I doubt I could keep him away. We walked past it with Jigme earlier, and Asha was the only reason he didn't stop there then." Rucksack leaned forward. "Gotta give that to him. He certainly knows what to be fascinated by," he said with a wink.

Heat tickled Jade's cheeks. "You know travelers," she said. "They can be big flirts."

"And I know Jakes and Jades," Rucksack said. "They act like they aren't people. Especially when they're feeling some emotion that reminds them how human they still are."

Jade looked away to the emptying pub. The door closed behind four people. The Brazilian woman and her travel companions were nursing what Jade sensed was their last round. The two men slowly worked their way through another pitcher. Most of the locals had left; a handful of travelers remained scattered at tables, some deep in conversation, some deep in flirting, some deep in their Guru Deep guidebooks, figuring out tomorrow's adventures. "Did you notice anything weird about Jay's daypack?" Jade said, lowering her voice.

"People like to say I speak in evasions and riddles. I've nothing on you," Rucksack replied. "But since you're insisting, yes. And his large pack too."

"It's almost like he's got a pet in there."

"A traveler's backpack might as well be a dog, but I don't know what's in that pack. Jigme fell on it earlier, and for a moment his hand lay on a bulge where the sound seemed to be coming from." Rucksack thought for a moment. "His eyes got wide. I didn't mark it then. But now... Now I think I will have to ask Jigme about it. What he noticed. What..." Rucksack's voice faded. He seemed to stare at something far away.

"What is it?" Jade asked.

"Nothing yet," he replied. "Just a tremor in my mind. A memory of stories from long ago, told when I was a child. Maybe I'll learn more and something will be relevant. Or maybe my past is just too much on my mind this evening."

"I thought you said you never got drunk."

"I don't. Not on stout, leastways. But that's why I

never touch anything else."

"Liquor is quicker, it's said."

"In me it's just sicker. And don't think I don't know what you're on about. Try to pull that influencing stuff with me, only thing you'll know for sure is you'll be giving the floor a good mop," Rucksack replied. "You'll never see me touch a drop o' booze, other than my stout. No, I don't get drunk. But the stout helps me see clearer, and tonight it seems to have me nostalgic."

"Nostalgia doesn't help us figure out what happened earlier today," Jade said, "but extrapolating from events does." She checked the pint, and as she came back the Brazilians left the pub. Jade smiled a small smile when she saw a glint in the woman's eyes, careworn yet fiery and determined. Other people left too, and soon only the two men and their pitcher of Deep's Special Lager were left in the Everest Base Camp.

"I've been thinking backward from when Jay got here," Jade said. "When he entered Agamuskara should correspond to when we saw the helixes."

"I can see where they would be connected," Rucksack replied. "So, whatever is in Jay's pack somehow, for a moment, made clear the destinies and decisions lying before the world?"

"That's what I've got so far."

Rucksack nodded. "We need to figure out what's in his pack."

"What were you remembering?" Jade asked.

"I thought nostalgia was no help."

"It's not. But you aren't a man who has idle, random thoughts. Maybe I spoke hastily."

"I'll take that as an apology." Rucksack told her

about the woman who had been staring at him, the envelope Jay had found, and his own letter, written in the same hand as the envelope the woman had left behind.

"Kailash isn't exactly a rare name," Jade said, making sure her eyes said nothing additional. "There's an old woman who's been cleaning the pub the last few months, and her name is Kailash. But the same handwriting? And the woman was staring at you? Could she be some sort of relation? Maybe someone who was entrusted with something originally meant for your mother?"

Rucksack shook his head.

"How can you be so dismissive?"

"I was an only child," Rucksack said. "And I had no other family. With my parents dead, there are none left who share my blood and spirit."

"You sound so certain."

"There are many things I'm no longer certain of. But this I know. I know it from bone to earth, soul to sky."

"How can that be? You're not telling me something, Rucksack. If we're going to figure this out... Look, we have to trust each other. You know I'm not just a bartender. And I know you're not just some itinerant drunk who rambles off nonsense that passes as wisdom."

"I prefer to think I ramble off wisdom that passes as nonsense."

Jade set his fresh pint in front of him and grinned. "Jakes and Jades have lots of stories about you, did you know that?"

Rucksack chuckled. "I'm sure your Management

love that."

"They tolerate it. It's like ghost stories kids tell around a campfire. Though if most people saw you, they'd never tie you back to the stories."

"You've got a fierce quick mind, Jade of the Everest Base Camp. You can seem like old winter ice, but your heart blazes. You remind me of my mum."

"That's not something any woman ever wants to hear."

"If you'd known my mother, you'd know what a compliment it was."

Jade stepped back and stared at him. *His heart beats like a person's,* she thought. *He breathes and blinks. He drinks and eats... and drinks. The sun, cold, wind, water, and dust of the world are etched into him like tattoos. He could seem like other people.* Jade stared hard at where his silvery helix should flow out into the world. *Except for this emptiness, this loneliness around him. He is so alive, life burns like a fire in him and hums like a song, but he has no path.* She locked her gaze on his. "Tell me why you don't have a helix," she said.

Rucksack looked away.

"You don't want to tell me?"

"It's not that. It's pretty hard to believe."

"I accept plenty that would be considered hard to believe. It's pretty much a Jade's job description."

Rucksack looked at her again. "I lost my helix—my paths of decision and destiny—when I lost my parents."

"How did your parents die?"

Rucksack sighed.

"I told you," Jade said. "I can believe it."

"Jade, my parents died in The Blast."

"But that... but that would make you..."

"A lot older than I look," he said, nodding. "I appreciate you saying that I'm keeping well for my age."

She stepped back.

"I thought you said you could believe it."

"Just because I can believe it doesn't mean I don't need a moment to let it sink in," Jade replied. She smiled, thought for a little while, then said, "No wonder the letter is so perplexing. Your parents died so long ago, then to be told that you would be reunited with her. But for this to happen today, the same day Jay arrives with something strange in his backpack? The same day you and I see helixes clear as leaves and rivers? These things are connected."

"You're okay with this? Really?" Rucksack drank another long quaff of stout.

Jade shrugged. "It's high up on my list of strangenesses that I've encountered or have learned about, yes. But it explains a lot." She stared at him a moment, chewing her lip. "Rucksack," she said, "did you survive The Blast?"

"Mostly," he replied, his left hand clenched tight. "Sometimes I think I didn't survive enough. Sometimes I think I survived too much." He drained his pint and set the empty glass on the bar. "Do you trust me now, Jade?"

"I heard there was this guy," said one of the two men at the table. "Went to the top of Mount Everest and back in a night."

Rucksack nearly knocked over his glass when he whipped around. Jade stared at the men and their empty pitcher. She'd now and again caught snippets of their conversation. They were like two traveling businessmen who were catching up and swapping stories. *This is the loudest they've been all evening. Lager making them louder?* she thought. Their winding helixes were like existence's practical jokes. *Or do they mean for us to hear this?*

"I know, right? Impossible," the man continued, his indistinct face looking only at his companion. "Takes days to climb Everest. Hell, takes ages just to get to the foot of the damn mountain. Yet here's a tale of some damn traveler who skips up and back in time for tea. They say he didn't even remember it."

The man took a long drink of Deep's Special Lager. "But he was standing on a little rise at Everest Base Camp, the Tibetan side, looking toward the mountain that night. The full moon rose over the slope, silver light shining on the white snow and the gray-black stone. The next morning, they say he was standing there again, only his clothes were ragged and torn. His face was bruised, his hands scratched up. He looked like he'd lost a fight with a pack of wild cats. Thing is, no one had seen him come to bed, but no one had seen him standing there all night either. But it's Everest, you know? Sometimes you hallucinate up there. Low oxygen, high altitude, frigid temperatures. He couldn't have been outside all night. The exposure would kill him."

The second man nodded, but his back was to Jade and Rucksack. "I heard about that too while I was finishing some business in Kathmandu. The stranger the news is, the faster it travels. Even weirder, from what I heard? The guy was clutching an Indian flag, and the flag was covered with signatures. Here's the thing." He tapped the table. "An Indian climbing team had recently summited Everest. And they had left that flag at the top."

The second man took a swig of beer and continued. "People say that when they saw the guy that morning, he dropped the flag and staggered from the little hill to his tent. You'd figure he'd want a long flop. But no. A couple minutes later, he's running out of there, this huge black backpack on his back. Next thing everyone knew, he'd talked to these two guys and hopped into the bed of their truck as they were leaving. Don't know who they were. They could've been from anywhere, you know?"

The first man grinned. "Sounds like what I heard. No one knows for sure what happened or where he went after that. I heard he found something in his backpack that made him run. But I've also heard others say he'd worn out his welcome in Tibet—something about hocking portraits of the Dalai Lama—and the authorities were after him. Maybe a little of both. All I know is that somehow this guy had a flag that had last been seen at the top of the world's tallest mountain. I also heard later that the flag wasn't on the summit anymore. I don't know where he is now or who he is or anything... But I tell you what. That's one hell of a traveler."

"I'll drink to that," the second man said. They clinked glasses and finished their beers.

"What the hell?" Jade said, moving around the bar.

"What else have you heard?" Rucksack said, walking toward the men at their table.

One of the men smiled at Rucksack, then glanced at the bar and nodded once.

A crash behind Jade and Rucksack made them stop and turn around. The Deep's Special Lager tap handle had shot off and was clattering on the bar. Beer gushed onto the floor.

"Don't let them leave!" Jade said. She ran to the taps and turned off the flow. "Who are they?"

Rucksack shook his head. "Wish I knew," he replied. "They're gone."

"We were only turned around a moment," Jade said. "How'd they get out the door that quickly?"

Rucksack's face was tight and grim. "They didn't use the door," he said. "They vanished."

"My new guest isn't just another backpacker, is he?" Jade said.

Rucksack didn't reply. Jade looked at the empty pub, and thought of all the things she hadn't told him yet.


*How much more did it cost him for us to have our own room?* Jigme thought as he looked out the window at the city.

*I wish I could calm down,* Jigme thought. *Maybe then I could sleep.* Instead he stared out the window, trying to make sense of the last few hours.

They had walked by the other rooms. The beds were in rows along the walls, and all seemed to have people in them. At first, Jigme was certain that's where they were going, but they hadn't stopped. After the big wards, they passed an area where nurses bustled. Beyond it, the attendant rolling Amma had stopped. He started to open a door, but then he stood still and looked at Jigme. Kindness softened his smile. "Do the honors, son," he said. "Let your mum in so we can get her better."

Jigme stared at him. His feet froze to the floor. The word "son" coming out of a man's mouth made no sense. Only Amma called him "son." No one else used that word with him.

"It's okay, Jigme," Rucksack said. "You can see her whenever you want. We just have to get her settled in first."

Jigme nodded. He stepped forward and touched the silvery handle.

The cream and brown of the simple room reminded Jigme of cows. To the left he saw rails and buttons, a flat surface that sloped at one end, and beneath it all, a big beige metal platform. "What is that?" Jigme asked.

"That's your mum's bed," the attendant said as he wheeled in the chair that held Asha.

"It's really nice," Jigme said, thinking of how the thin fabric that had passed for a mattress crinkled when the attendant had lifted Amma off her bed.

"She'll be much more comfortable now," the attendant replied.

The car hadn't been able to come down the alley. The attendant couldn't even drive to the street that led to the alley, because The Mystery Chickpea was in the way. Jay, Jigme, and the attendant had left the car at the end of the street, dodging annoyed looks and shouts from vendors and people walking through.

As the attendant unfolded a wheelchair, Jay had struggled the large pack onto his back. He looked like he wanted to fall in the street and sleep. Jigme couldn't blame him. He had held the pack for only a few minutes, and it had been so much heavier than it seemed for its size. It was like trying to carry a person, like trying to carry the world.

*Why would you wear that every day just so you can go places?* Jigme wondered.

"Why don't you just buy things wherever you go?" Jigme asked. "You are rich."

Jay smiled. "I can see where I would seem rich. I buy things when I need to, but I still have to be careful with my money."

"That pack is so heavy."

"It is. After a while, it becomes like a friend. Sometimes it's almost as if it looks out for me. At least lately, whenever I need something, it's always at the top of the pack."

"I'm sorry I tried to take it," Jigme said. "If I were rich like you, I'd travel too."

"Maybe someday you can. Do you know where you want to go?"

Jigme opened his mouth but no words came. *Where would I go? I've never left the city.*

He knew India was a vast country that was part of a world that was vaster still. Jigme knew the alleys and streets of his city, where the bakers had lazy eyes and where the fruit sellers had kind hands. But the world beyond that? "I... I don't know," he finally said.

"I didn't either," Jay said. "The main thing is to go somewhere. Then the world will take you where you need to be."

"Where are we going?" the attendant asked.

Jigme pointed.

"Wow," Jay said. "Whatever that is, it smells amazing. I'm so hungry I could eat cow pies."

Jigme tugged his sleeve. "That's The Mystery Chickpea," he said. "You don't want to eat there."

"Why not?"

"His food..." Jigme struggled to find the words. "It does funny things to you. Amma has told me I was never to go there."

"If his food tastes as good as it smells, it'd be worth a few days of the runs," Jay replied. "I've gotten far sicker on far worse. Man, there was this one time in Kenya, I'd drunk some dodgy water, and I swear I was painting the loo orange for days."

"That's not what I mean," Jigme said. He nodded toward the old man behind the cart. "He doesn't speak. No voice. But it's like he tells you things through the food."

"He's telling me that if a pint of stout is a sandwich in a glass, I'm hungrier for way more than a sandwich. I've had enough beer. I'm ready for some real food now." Jay veered toward The Mystery Chickpea. The old man glanced up, his face hazy behind clouds of steam.

"Wait," Jigme said. "Amma."

Jay stopped. "Sorry. I'll get something later."

They went down the alley. Shadows gathered as the sun dropped lower in the sky. The red door opened, and Rucksack walked out of the room. "She should be okay to be moved," he said, touching Jigme on the shoulder. "I'm sorry I couldn't do more."

Jigme didn't know what to say. No one paid attention to him and Asha. No one helped anymore or even asked how they were. Every day, he went out and tried to do what he could to provide for them, but it was never enough. *We've seen more kindness today than we have in months,* Jigme thought. *I had no words for any of that.*

The hand left his shoulder. "One way or another, lad, she'll be all right," Rucksack said with a shrug. "Who knows. This funny world has ideas of its own. Maybe there's good to come from you trying to take that pack."

The attendant set the wheelchair by the red door, then went inside. "She's so light," he said as he carried Asha out.

When the daylight touched Asha, Jigme thought he saw her shudder, thought he saw the smallest hint of a smile on her lips. But it must have been just his hope, just a play of light and shadow. The attendant set her in the wheelchair. Her head slumped.

"Does she sleep like this often?" the attendant asked.

"She mostly just sleeps," Jigme replied.

The attendant said nothing, but everything in his air and gaze seemed to say, "Poor boy."

Jigme locked up the room, and they all followed the attendant. As they passed The Mystery Chickpea again, Jay wiped drool off of his mouth. Rucksack stared hard at the old man behind the steam. "What is it?" Jay asked.

"Dunno," Rucksack replied. "Something about him seemed familiar."

On the drive back to the hospital, the attendant instructed Jay on the particulars of paying for Asha's care. Jigme didn't understand much of it. He could hardly understand that the man he'd tried to rob was now helping him.

Jigme noticed Rucksack looking at him, as if he'd

been listening to Jigme's thoughts.

"He's got his reasons," Rucksack said to Jigme. "I'd reckon Jay knows what you know: the pain of losing someone you love. He's man enough to get beyond where things began and go instead to where they should be. You should have your mum. Hopefully now you will." For a moment, Rucksack was silent, then he said, "Jigme, where's your father?"

Jigme shrugged. "I don't have one," he replied. "All Amma has told me is my dad was from Tibet, and the mountains called him away from us. That's why she's never seen him again."

"You've never known him."

"No."

Rucksack nodded. "Is that why no one helps you?"

Something hot blazed in Jigme's eyes. "Yes," he said, wobbling his head. "And no. When I was younger, they helped. Our neighbors in the alley said Amma became a spoiled woman, but they did not blame me. They helped sometimes, but they told me never to let Amma know. One day Amma overheard someone telling me my dad was a rich boy from the other side of the city. He got my mum in trouble then died of cholera. When she heard what I was being told, she became angry, said I was being told lies. Then she said many mean things to the other people in the slum. After that, no one could come near us without her saying terrible things, scaring everyone away with her voice. Then they didn't help anymore."

Rucksack started to reply, but Jigme shook his head. The old pain, the old question, burned at Jigme's mind and heart. Experience had taught him the only way to make the pain go away was not to speak or think of it. Jigme looked away and said nothing else.

With Asha settled in to the hospital bed and a cot set out for Jigme to sleep on, the attendant took his leave. Jay and Rucksack stayed a few minutes longer, offering some last bits of help and encouragement. Jay handed Jigme some rupees.

"You know where to find us," Jay said. "For now, eat up and rest. You can do more for your mum if you have a full belly and some sleep."

With a nod to Asha, the men left.

Jigme sat alone by Asha's side, holding her hand for a while. Eventually, he went out for food. When he came back, he did feel better. And tired. Jigme moved the cot next to his mum's bed. "You're going to be better soon," he said, kissing her forehead, then lying down and closing his eyes.

When the sun rose, Jigme woke next to an empty bed.

He sat up and looked around but didn't see her anywhere. "Amma?"

"Good morning, son," she answered, her voice soft as first daylight.

Asha stood by the window, her back to Jigme. The sun rose softly over the city. As the first morning light touched the window, Asha turned around. "I'm better now, Jigme," she said. A silver-and-gold gleam hovered on her skin and her smile. "What do you want to do?"

He couldn't see her until she spoke. Now he saw her clearly and wondered how he had missed her before.

She was better.

She stood, smiling, gazing out at the world.

"We can get treats then go to the park," she said,

the old angry fire in her voice extinguished. "Tomorrow, we will go to Tibet. It is time we were with your father. How does that sound?"

Jigme started to answer. Then he ran to hug her.

The moment they touched, the sun fell out of the sky. His arms wrapped around nothing, and he could not see in the black room.

He started to scream for her, but there was nothing in the room but black, and he could not breathe black. Alone, he clawed at his throat, clawed at the black, but he could not breathe, he could not breathe—

When the sun rose, Jigme woke next to an empty bed.

He sat up and looked around but saw her nowhere in the room. "Amma?" Jigme asked.

It was hard to see in the dark room, as if the very air were black. Jigme walked to the window, wondering why he felt so hopeful when he did so. As he looked outside, dawn had just begun to come up over the city. A red sun rose in fire over a black world.

"Jigme," said the voice behind him. "I need you."

"Amma?" He turned around. Far away in the black void, a red smile burned like coals.

"Where's my mum?" Jigme asked.

The smile said nothing, but it seemed to get bigger.

"Where's my mum?" Jigme asked again.

The smile grew until the room was no longer filled with black but with red fire. His brown skin began to char and blacken. The pain ate into him, etched into his nerves and soul. "Where's my mum?" Jigme asked again, the pain twisting his voice as he yelled.

"Find me," said the smile, "and you will find her." Then all Jigme's world was red and black.

When the sun rose, Jigme woke to feel his hand still wrapped around his mother's hand. She lay as still as when she had been brought in, and the first soft rays of dawn made her face seem peaceful. The light took away the lines her anger had etched, the hollows under her eyes. Asha looked like the younger woman who had laughed, smiled, and played with her son. Then the light's harsh fullness came through the window, and the woman of his memory gave way to the thin, angry being lying still and silent on the hospital bed.

A little later, a doctor came in. "We have much to do to understand your mother's condition," he said. "Could you come back in a few hours?"

Jigme nodded.

"Is there somewhere you can go?"

Jigme shrugged and left the room.

Outside in the early morning light, the dreams returned to Jigme's mind. The memory burned. The city was still so empty. Hardly anyone was in the streets.

Jigme ran, trying to leave the dreams behind.


No matter what crowded country or over-peopled city housed their establishments, The Management made sure that every Jake and Jade had one luxury: a private room.

Jade silently thanked them for that small peace as she turned off the lights and locked up the pub. After such a loud and hectic night, the quietness soothed Jade's ringing ears, heavy feet, and weary mind as she went through the door to the small foyer between the pub and the dorm stairs.

At the end of a short hallway by the staircase, no one ever noticed her room. She didn't know exactly how that worked, only that people didn't seem to realize there was a hallway there.

"I love the flowers with the painting," a woman from Hong Kong had said to Jade once. She pointed at what to Jade was an open hall and what to the woman was a wall next to the stairs.

Jade's room was always cleaner than the rest of the pub and hostel, though the regular cleaning staff didn't know about the room either. Jade knew only that The Management had something separate arranged, but she never saw anyone else come and go.

After unlocking her door, Jade waited a moment before going inside. She didn't quite know how this part worked either, but whenever she turned the key in the lock, the door seemed to take a moment to evaluate her, like a bouncer scrutinizing an ID. Satisfied, the door opened, and she breathed in deeply as she walked in to her haven and closed the door behind her. It locked with more than just bolts. Should anyone ever notice the room of the Jade of Agamuskara, the door was all but unbreakable. No one had ever broken into the room of a Jake or Jade.

The walls were the same cinderblock as every other room, but hers were painted a creamy white instead of rancid absinthe-green. She breathed in the room's quiet serenity. Already something inside her unclenched and relaxed. She sighed when the door latched. A glass of water with a slice of lime waited on the desk, as it always did whenever she came to her room. She drained it and readied herself.

She stood in the middle of the room and closed her eyes. *Time for one last check*, Jade thought.

"In the way people understand it, you can't read minds," The Management had said during her training, "but you can listen to and comprehend the general tone of their thoughts and emotions. In time, you will not only be able to listen to people; you will listen to animals and plants, even to objects. All things have history and understanding. They may not exist in the same sense of time or language, but if you learn how to listen, you will hear what they have to say, and you will understand."

Jade listened now as she did every night, her final check before turning in. As her head lifted, Jade's thoughts and feelings quieted. As they faded away, the Everest Base Camp spoke, and so did all inside.

In a second-floor dorm, a bubbling vengeance had taken hold of someone who had eaten a bad curry. The pale green flames and haze of their feelings were dashed with red. Jade turned her attention away as the poor bugger ran into the toilet again. *I don't need to listen to everything*, she thought. But she did make a note to have the cleaning staff pay extra attention to that loo on their next visit.

In a third-floor dorm, sighs, gasps, and giggles burned bright from a bottom bunk. The guy in the bunk above them was deciding between trying to ignore it and go to sleep, or dump his water bottle onto the happy couple.

The Brazilians were arguing. A silver-and-gold light shone from inside one of them, and Jade recognized the woman from earlier. She must have just explained her plans to go away for a few days on her own. The others were trying to convince her not to, but no confusion muddied the woman's light. *Good on you,* Jade thought.

Gray fogs dotted many of the rooms. Typical, given those people had also just left the pub. A large, thick fog hung like a stale thunderhead in one of the third-floor dorms. She pitied how hung over that person would feel in the morning. Despite that, excitement and electricity arced through the fog in bright red, like lightning in a cloud. *Curious,* she thought, listening more closely.

It was a man. He was asleep but his mind burned with adventures new and friends just made. And it burned with what could only be kissing.

New kissing too, the kissing of first touches of soul to soul, skin to skin, sun to sky, water to earth, direction to path, tonight to tomorrow, hope to forever. For a moment, she felt like she was in the dream, as if she had waded in slowly. The dream washed over her gently, gradually, like waves at her ankles, then her thighs, then...

She opened her dream-eyes and grinned to see who she was kissing.

Jay answered her smile with his own.

Jade opened her real eyes and jumped back.

"Too close," she said, shaking her head, years of training and experience jumping to attention after being caught slacking on the job. "Too close. What are you doing? You know not to get that close."

She walked to the mirror at the desk by her bed and looked deep into her own eyes. "Okay," she said. "He's attractive. There's clearly... something about him. But he is who he is. I am who I am. And the only kissing for a Jade is in someone else's dreams."

More than ever, she wanted to fall into bed, but the job wasn't done. She stood and closed her eyes again. After making sure Jay's stout intake had kept him pleasantly awash in drunken dreams, she turned her attention away from the dorms. Everything there was clearly fine and no different from usual.

Over the rest of the building, she listened. Three men were pissing up against the outside wall. Nothing unusual there. A yellow sparkle in the walls drew her close. A frayed wire hissed and flashed in the wall between the pub and the foyer. *That could start a fire,* she thought, making a note to get it fixed.

Her thoughts crossed into the pub itself, the heart of the building—the heart of the city, some said throughout India and the rest of the world. Even Guru Deep, who famously wouldn't set foot in India, had said in his guidebook that the Everest Base Camp was "the heart, soul, and pulse of Agamuskara, where the rivers of lives from all the world come together."

She couldn't help but feel proud of that.

At this time of night, the pub was usually as quiet as it was dark and empty. Normally, the tables, bottles, walls, and bar all faded quickly, practiced sponges at absorbing emotion and conversation. Not tonight, though. Tonight the pub was awake. Tonight there was too much to absorb. Feeling and intensity filled the pub like water in a flooded basement.

Ancient and new had mingled tonight in ways she had never seen before. She had seen an older gentleman from Bangalore clink glasses with a family traveling from Brazil. He was old. This... entity was ancient. Beyond the usual scope of life. Beyond the age of the city. But what was it?

Over the last few months, Jade had grown accustomed to a slightly off feeling from the pub. That was Rucksack, and from what little The Management had told her about his oddity, she expected the pub to be a bit uneasy with him. Overall, the place liked him. He drank out of a love she didn't comprehend, and with a joy that filled a soul hollowed out by deeper sorrow. The pub tolerated him but didn't quite know what to make of him. Then again, neither did she or The Management.

Jade thought back over the evening. So many people from so many places. So many ages and desires. So many decisions. So many destinies. But as she reflected on the different people in the pub that evening, four stood out.

"That's one of my favorite drinks too," Jade had said to the woman when she ordered a glass of water with lime. "Where are you visiting from?"

"Far away," the woman replied, her accent beyond Jade's recognition. She seemed to be in her late twenties or early thirties. The woman's thick black hair fell in waves over her shoulders, and she peered at Jade with her large brown eyes. Her simple sari looked well made, but its deep brown-and-black was completely unlike the vibrant colors Jade usually saw on the streets of Agamuskara.

"Are you from India?"

The woman bobbed her head. "India. Himalaya. Here and there, you would say."

"Where in India?"

"A small village."

Jade handed over the water with lime. The woman

sat at a table near the wall, and she cast a wary glance at the two men sitting with their pitcher of Deep's Special Lager. A look of recognition, perhaps? *Unusually well guarded,* Jade thought as she tried to listen to the woman's feelings. *The only thing I can tell is she's older than she looks.*

*And she's nervous.*

The woman took out an envelope, opened up a sheet of paper, and read it over and over and over. Jade regularly brought her more waters with lime.

"If you don't mind my saying," Jade said, "you look like you're waiting for someone."

The woman folded the paper and set it on the envelope. "I wait on a dream," she replied. She gazed deeply into Jade; it was like being tested, evaluated, measured. Only when the woman spoke again did Jade realize she must have passed the test.

"Have you ever been presented with something you knew was impossible," the woman said in a voice bright and flowing yet also ancient and sad, "but all the same you had to see if you were wrong—that it could be possible after all?"

*Every day,* Jade thought, *except for the second part.* "Lots of people wait on dreams in a pub. Are you sure I can't bring you something else to soothe your nerves?" Jade hoped she would say yes; a drop of hope and two of confidence would give the woman the steadiness and sight she needed to see through whatever she was anticipating and waiting for.

"Only the waters, please," the woman said.

"We have food too," Jade said. *I can influence food no more than I can water,* she thought. *But it's only right to offer.*

"Yes, that does sound good. Do you know *thukpa*?"

The training took over. "Barley noodles," Jade said, "plus vegetables and meat in broth, right?"

The woman nodded.

"Okay." She started to walk away but stopped herself. "If you need anything," she said, "my name is Jade. I don't want to pry, but if you want to talk, I'm around."

"You are very busy," the woman replied. "Many to serve."

"And always time to help someone who needs it."

The woman nodded. "Thank you, Jade," she said. "My name is Kailash."

"That's a wonderful name," Jade replied. "Like in Tibet, right? Mount Kailash, the holy mountain?"

She smiled. "You know much, Jade. Yes, like the holy mountain. The world mountain, some say. The mountain that moves, that travels the world and tells of things to come, of dreams that are to be real."

"I thought that was Mount Meru. Besides, isn't that a myth?"

"Some would say a myth is only a truth that is not a fact," the woman replied. "Many say that Kailash and Meru are the same mountain, one rooted in Tibet, the other a manifestation that moves throughout the world, in dreams, visions, and plain sight."

"And you are named for it. What do you believe, Kailash?"

Kailash smiled. "I believe that the mountain Kailash sits in Tibet, far away yet close as a dream. Yet since I cannot see it myself, I cannot truly know it is there. So I must believe. But I know that the mountain moves."

"I wonder what it has to tell us."

"Until it speaks, the mountain is silent."

The women looked at each other, saying nothing.

Jade went back to the bar, put in the food order, and then brought it over when it was ready, but Kailash only smiled and nothing. The crowd grew. As Jade served and listened, influenced and directed, she still kept an eye on Kailash, alone at her table. Despite seven glasses of water, Jade noticed, not once had Kailash gotten up to pee. She just read her sheet of paper over and over.

Until Rucksack came in. Jade saw that Kailash kept staring at him.

Jay came down and Jade sent him over to where Rucksack was sitting. The next time Jade glanced at Kailash's table, Rucksack and Jay were looking at the woman. Soon, Kailash was on her way out the door.

*I have much to tell Rucksack,* Jade thought in her room, her mind drifting back to his letter and the matching envelope that Kailash had left behind. A pang of guilt passed through her. *Maybe I shouldn't have acted as if I knew nothing.*

*No,* she thought. *There's much that he'd better start telling me, if he wants me to be more forthcoming too.*

The guilt passed.

Something about the woman seemed ancient, the pub told her—older than the city, older than India. *She is who she seems,* the pub said, *and she is not who she seems.*

*That's not much help,* Jade thought.

When she opened her eyes for a moment, the weariness was nearly overwhelming. The pub's extra intensity had been more fatiguing than usual. After the long day, she needed to get off her feet. Jade sat at her desk next to the bed, ignoring the absence of photos and keepsakes, extra things that would have needed dusting. Her shelves held only files, notes, manuals from her training and from Guru Deep's *The Bartender*.

Jade closed her eyes again and listened to the pub's recollection of the evening.

If the Everest Base Camp were a person, then Rucksack had made the pub merely uneasy, as if it had a touch of vertigo. In comparison, the two loud men had made it violently ill.

From the moment they came through the door, Jade noticed them but saw no need to pay them much attention. Their cockiness said they already knew the world. They knew where they were going when they got there, and their place in the world was wherever they were. Rarely did such people need any help from a Jake or Jade.

But they did need beer. It fueled their big laughs, which rang off the walls no matter how full the pub got. Their laughter deepened the lines around their eyes, though their faces told her they seemed just on the edge of early middle age. Light shone like hazy halos off of their clean-shaven heads and the thick, squarish glasses they both wore. They looked like they could be from anywhere, but Jade suspected they were from India, perhaps even nearby. Their blue button-down shirts reminded Jade of the blue statues all around the city. *Some say there are more gods than people in Agamuskara*, Jade thought.

As the pub filled, Jade noticed that people kept tripping or stumbling around the two men's table, though no one ever actually hit the floor. Sometimes they righted themselves. Sometimes, like with Jay, one of the men caught an arm or helped them regain their footing.

*This has to stop,* Jade thought. She added a dash of Purple #8 to a fresh pitcher of Deep's Special Lager. As Jade set the pitcher on their table, her feet remained steady and never thought once of betraying her.

"Where are you lads in from?" she asked.

"We lose track!" said one of the men in a thick bubbling accent. He laughed loudly and reached across the table to slap his friend on the shoulder. The other man laughed too.

"New Delhi. Varanasi. Everest. Zhangmu. Kathmandu," the second man said.

"You get around."

Their heads bobbed. "We do as we must for what we will," the second man said. "That is the life of those who work for the Office of World Light and Foreign Visitors."

"The office of what?" Jade asked. "That sounds government. Is this a surprise inspection?"

"It is!" the first man said.

Surprise indeed shot through Jade. They'd just been inspected a month ago, and as always had passed. "What are you inspecting this time?"

"Your beer!" the first man said with another laugh. "And it passes twice. Pim, have you ever had such a fine a pint as what is poured at the Everest Base Camp?"

The one called Pim filled their glasses from the fresh pitcher. "No, Mim. They pass! First Class. Highest Muster. Grade A. Prime Premium Select!"

"If you're wanting to put one of those fancy stickers

on the door," Jade said, "I hope it's a bit shorter than all that."

"Fear not Ms. Jade, we would never want to cover up your 'As Seen in Guru Deep's Third Eye' sticker," Mim said. "That itself is most more select than what we humble officers of the Office of World Light and Foreign Visitors can offer."

"Since we have passed such muster with you lads," Jade said, "may I ask a favor?"

"What might that be, Jade of the Finest Pour?"

"I don't know how you're doing it, but stop tripping my customers."

Pim shrugged and pointed to a patch of floor. "Slippery floor is unkind to feet. People come to find themselves, only to find themselves on their backsides if not for us to steady them once more."

Jade's gaze hardened. "I don't know who you are, but I didn't pour my first beer yesterday. No one has ever tripped around this pub like anyone near your table tonight. Whoever you are, whatever your deal is, leave my customers alone. Anyone else stumbles, and I won't care if you work for Shiva. I'll personally boot you out into the middle of the nearest steaming pile of divinity."

Mim and Pim raised their beer glasses. "Of course, Miss Jade," they said in unison.

*Oy,* she thought. *It's like Rucksack and The Management had a lovechild.*

The men sipped their beer, and she started toward the bar.

*At least they'll calm down.*

"Oh no," said a flat, unaccented voice.

Jade turned to see Pim, shaking his head. He

poured his beer back into the pitcher.

Mim's head bobbed. "Oh no indeed, my dear Pim." His accent had also disappeared, and he emptied his glass into the pitcher too.

"Is there a problem, gentlemen?"

"Oh Jade oh Jade," Mim said. "We thought you knew."

"That's a fresh keg of Deep's Special Lager. Knew what?"

"Oh yes," Pim said. "The beer is fresh as can be. But something is off." His gaze tightened on Jade's. "Something that should not be there."

"I'll be happy to get you a fresh pitcher."

"Thank you for on-the-house, Miss Jade."

"Who said anything about on-the-house?"

"Thanking you now for in-advance," Mim said. "The Office of World Light and Foreign Visitors does not require anything, shall we say, additional. Nor would it do you any good to exhaust your precious stores."

Jade stared at the two men. *I could tell them to leave, and never come back,* she thought. *I could tell The Management I need help. I could chance adding—*

"Please pass our compliments to your Management," Pim said. "The service is unparalleled, the servers are attentive, and the served are content."

"We know that you do not know, and that is okay. We of the Office of World Light and Foreign Visitors need none of the additional services provided by the noble Jakes and Jades," Mim said.

"I don't know what you mean," Jade replied.

"You don't know much of late, we know," Pim said. "Even when you don't know what is under your feet, you have a path."

"Who are you?"

"Who are you?"

Jade stared hard. The men's helixes waved like snakes, but not in any way that she could construe as menacing. If anything, it was as if their helixes were... laughing. Laughing at her and at everyone around them. Laughing as if they were telling the punchline to the greatest joke of the universe—and knew that no one else got it.

Then Mim and Pim began laughing out loud. "We will make sure that no one else loses their feet tonight, Jade Agamuskara Bluegold," Mim said. "In return, we request only that our beer be... itself."

*They know my full name,* Jade thought. She took a step back. *There's nothing I can do about this. Could The Management even do anything?*

Resigned, she said, "Your terms are acceptable."

Mim and Pim smiled.

"I'll even give you the free pitcher. I'm just that nice a Jade." She returned to the bar with the influenced pitcher and soon set down a fresh one. After she had taken care of some waiting customers, Jade tried to work out what had happened. *These men know about me, the Jakes and Jades, and even The Management. What could that mean? Why are they here? What is their real purpose?*

A soft *pthump* made her turn.

*Two in one day?* she thought. *You'd think it was my birthday. Have The Management been observing? Will they explain who these guys really are?*

But when she opened the directive, all she got was four words:

`The tricksters are allowed.`

Jade looked up. Mim and Pim saluted with raised glasses. People walked by, but if they were unsteady, Jade knew it was due only to a good night's drinking. The Management said the men were okay. Jade didn't like it, but customers were waiting.

She got back to work.

Jade opened her eyes and was back in her room. The pub shared her questions and her concerns, as well as her begrudging acceptance. The pub also confirmed what Rucksack had said earlier: Mim and Pim had caused the tap to break so that she and Rucksack wouldn't see them vanish. But the pub saw.

And the pub saw more.

The men weren't human. At least not in the way that Jade both was and was not human anymore. Like the woman Kailash, the men seemed to be what could only be described as ancient, though their faces were like an older brother's. But what brought them to the pub—and again, like Kailash, on the same day that Jay arrived?

*Not just Jay,* Jade thought, her weary mind trying hard to focus on him. *Jay and whatever is in his backpack.*

The pub felt its presence but did not know what it was. She only knew that it was both new and ancient. Over and over, the pub called to her. It said the same thing, but she did not understand.

*I'm too tired,* she thought. *Maybe it will make sense once I've had a chance to rest.*

She undressed and lay down. Weariness washed over her. Tomorrow, she would not have to work in the pub, but this would be no day off in the sit-and-relax sense. There was Rucksack to counsel with. There were tricksters to allow. There were mysteries to understand.

As Jade faded into sleep, the pub continued repeating itself. For a moment, her barely conscious mind understood.

Usually, she could perceive only faint feelings from objects and places, even one as powerful and soaked in humanity as the Everest Base Camp. But now, just as she fell fully into sleep, she understood what the pub was trying to tell her.

The pub seemed to be saying, "He carries dangerous, he carries doom. He carries dangerous, he carries doom."

But sleep claimed her, and Jade stopped listening. The pub cried on.

IN THE DREAM the full moon rose over the slope of the world's tallest mountain. As he talked with the moon, he rose high over the camp, over the Himalayas, and up the slopes of Everest itself, which was called "Qomolangma" in the Tibetan: mother of the universe, mother of the earth.

Wind whipped at the rocks and flags, but somehow its cutting chill did not reach him. The moon seemed so close he could almost touch its face. Instead of the wind blowing, he heard a soft mellifluous voice. Then cold, gray, pale air hung in the frosty morning.

He stood on a little hill looking toward the mountain. His hand was out, palm up, as if waiting for something.

A voice, a familiar voice, someone from his tent,

said, "What happened to your clothes?"

*shr-shr-shr-Shr-Shr-Shr-SHR-SHR-SHR—*

The rustling was louder than an alarm clock. It pulled Jay out of the dream and into his hangover. The fog in his mind had broken into a pounding storm, though when he looked out the window, a soft dawn waited.

*Rucksack said stout helps people see clearly,* Jay thought as he staggered toward the loo. The strange night at the mountain made sense now, at least. It must have been an onset of altitude sickness.

The only cure was to get to lower elevation as quickly as possible. *That's why I fled to the dorm tent, packed up, and hopped a ride down the mountain,* he thought. *I just needed to get to lower elevation so I didn't die. That's all. Nothing on the mountain told me to go to India, to the city with the white alley. I needed a change of scene anyway, and India's heat and franticness seemed like just the thing after the high-altitude chill and quiet of Tibet.*

Jay turned on the light in the toilet. In the harsh light from the bare bulb, no roaches menaced. The booze had done its work well, though the air still reeked of yesterday's spicy meals, the sharp tang of Indian rotgut, and a distinct metallic undercurrent that must be the scent of molten roach legs. The combined odor sent a quake through his innards and bent Jay over the hole in the floor, stout and more threatening to come rushing up.

But at least no roaches were glaring at him eye to eyes.

After a few minutes, Jay's stomach decided to stay in place. Shaking, he stood up and saw the tap on the wall to the right. A hot shower was just the thing.

*But I guess I'll settle for lukewarm,* he thought as the tepid-cool trickle drizzled over him. Still, the dust and grit of the last few days sloughed off. His stout-choked pores opened. His clumsy movements became less floppy. Soon, the water didn't feel like a hammer smacking his forehead.

Back in the dorm room, the other beds were full of lumps. If anyone had heard the racket of the thing in his backpack, they didn't wake up. Fellow travelers snored and farted. A boozy fugue hovered over the room like smog. Jay envied them a little. There'd be no more sleep for him, hangover be damned.

Then again, there was a city to see.

*Besides,* Jay thought, *this isn't the worst hangover I've had. It's up there. But it's no reason to spend the day in bed.*

For a moment, his mind flashed back to Austria. He and his dorm mates had staggered back to the room after a night of Vienna lager, boasting grand plans to wander the city the next day. They'd read *Austria Through The Third Eye.* They would walk long circuits and sup in inns, the way the great composer Ludwig van Beethoven had done. However, the guidebook said nothing about how to wander while suffering a skull-rupturing hangover.

Only Jay had gotten up at the appointed dawn hour. As he finished getting ready, head pounding hard but feet itching more urgently, one of the other travelers snorted himself awake. He stared at Jay.

"I'm still drunk and you drank more than I did," the traveler said. "But you're going out there. You... You are the world's greatest traveler."

"I'm just going where I go," Jay replied, but the other traveler had already fallen back to sleep.

Jay wondered where Agamuskara would take him today. Jigme's white alley floated in his mind. "Go to India, to the city with the white alley," he remembered the moon saying that night at Everest.

*Lots of cities have white alleys,* he thought. *Doesn't mean anything. I am where I am, and that's where I am.*

The clothes he expected to dig for were in fact waiting for him when he opened the backpack. Things like that had been happening more and more lately.

The first night with the truck drivers, when they'd stopped in Nepal, Jay was going to rummage for some snacks to share. The food had all but jumped into his hands.

He'd expected a harsh scent to smack him in the face too, from a bottle of whiskey that must have broken after the jostling truck ride down the mountains. But the bottle was intact and waiting. He hadn't remembered wrapping it up, but there it was, wrapped safe as a baby in a couple of t-shirts—one, a favorite since Ireland, said "I Can See Clearly Now" beneath a pair of eyeglasses with silhouettes of Imperial pints for lenses.

Money belt secure around his waist, Jay tucked some cash into the zipped pocket of his more or less green cargo pants. He couldn't resist the russet brown t-shirt he'd found in Austria, with the letters "ID" centered inside the outline of a potato that looked vaguely like his home state.

The fresh clothes made Jay feel more or less human. *What I need now is a hot drink and some breakfast,* he thought, *and I know just where to go.*

As he slipped out of the Everest Base Camp, he saw no sign of Jade or Rucksack, and he smiled. It'd be good to have a day all on his own, just him and his pack and the world. *The way things are supposed to be,* he thought. From his daypack, the thing's noise had settled back down to its usual soft rustle-whisper. As Jay settled the pack on his back, the blunt pain of his hangover lessened.

The young day brightened, not yet blazing and over-bustling but already beyond night's cool and quiet. Men drank hot chai from small cups, wisps of steam rising over faces wrinkled or smooth. From front stoop after front stoop came the *thck-thck* of brooms as women in brightly colored saris swept. No one looked at Jay. There would be time in all the day to sell something to yet another tourist; for now, these few quiet moments were for them and only them.

The moon may have said the city with the white alley, but it hadn't been specific beyond that. Every wall of Agamuskara was white. Jay wandered, but not to Jigme's alley as he'd originally planned. He realized he was walking in the other direction. *A ramble before breakfast, then,* he thought. The rough edges of his hangover still rasped against the city, but it wasn't as bad as he'd expected after all those pints.

A change in the air perked up his step. He came out from the streets to a wide, open space. To his left and right, the road continued. Before him, stone steps had been cut down to the edge of the river. Centuries of feet had worn rounded corners and a smooth sheen into the yellow sandstone. He stood at the top of the steps, looking up and down the Agamuskara. Little boats sat on the shore. People bathed and children played in the river.

*Why are you standing here?* Jay thought. *You got up wanting to go to The Mystery Chickpea and check out Jigme's alley. Why did you come the opposite way instead?*

*I decided to come this way,* he thought. *I always choose where I'm going to go. This is just a change of plans. Where I am is where I'll be.*

Jay walked down the steps to the river's edge. The brown-gray, quarter-mile-wide Agamuskara River ran like a vein from the soul of the world. The waters seemed shallow, sluggish. Jay knelt at the bank and dipped his hand in the water, surprised at the force and power of the flow. He jumped a little and nearly stood up, but it was as if the river had grabbed his hand.

At first, he heard only the sounds along the banks: the gurgles and plinks and shushes of the current, the cries and laughs of the children, the fast speech of the people talking. Then a door opened in the world's sounds.

Bright songs and golden light danced in all his five senses—all glowed. Like scratching away a thin skin, everything in the world around Jay shone with a silver-and-gold light. The light came from inside everyone on the banks, from the boats and the buildings, from the steps and from the river itself.

The river shone brightest, pulsing with the breath and heartbeat of the world. The murky water turned clear. Muddy brown transformed to the bright blue of the god statues all over the city.

Jay yanked his hand from the water and stood with a jerk. Once more, he heard nothing but the quiet morning, still and slow in its waking, kids playing by the water, men and women talking, small waves lapping at the wood and aluminum hulls of the boats along the banks.

He shook his head to try to clear the light out of his vision. The world dimmed, and the skin closed back over the light of the world. Things looked like things again. The river was just a river, murky and brown. Above the water and the city, the hazy pale-blue morning shimmered only with heat.

"Lightheaded," Jay said to himself. "Numbnuts. This is what happens when you sightsee before breakfast. All that beer and now this? You're faint, Jay. You think the moon took you to the top of Everest and gave you a weird little orb. Next thing you know, you're gonna think the sun took you to the top of a building and gave you a tomato."

He ran back up the steps and headed for The Mystery Chickpea.

The city looked like the city again, with only the slight complication that now everything was gods.

From shrines at the mouths of alleys to carvings in massive buildings, all the city seemed built not on stone and brick but on statues, carvings, and paintings. Holding sheaves of wheat, scrolls, human heads, tridents, or sunlight, the figures shone red, blue, gold, silver, black, green, and brown. There were gods small for life's little hopes, and gods large for the universe. The white walls sang with their colors, deeds, and histories, and the gods sang too.

No one else on the street seemed to hear them—or if they did, it must be commonplace enough that none noted it. As he wandered away from the river, Jay realized each statue, carving, and painting stared at him.

As their gazes followed him, the songs changed. Instead of multiple songs in his head, like he had heard during the parade the day before, now every song became the same. He listened more closely:

"White and gold burns to red and black.

"The secret turns and you cannot go back.

"The sun burns dark, the sun burns twice,

"Choose your destiny. Choose your price."

The gods stared and Jay looked into the many fixed eyes. All around him, people went about their morning. No one looked at him or seemed at all to notice that he was there, turning frantically, staring at the buildings and walls.

"You really, really need some breakfast, Jay," he muttered.

He stopped walking, closed his eyes, and shook his head. *Go away, go away, go away,* he thought. The song repeated in his head, but he spoke louder in his mind. *Go away go away GO AWAY!*

He opened his eyes. The buildings and walls indeed were packed with carved and painted gods. But their fixed eyes did not stare at him, and they did not sing.

Jay moved next to a building. After checking for no gods at all on the plaster, he stood with his back against it, trying to breathe deeply and slowly. "Should've gone for grub straightaway," he said. "Who knows what tricks my eyes will be playing on me next."

With another deep breath, he looked around again. The city woke, moved, filled. The streets were fuller now. People stared at him as he walked. A boy came over and said he would be his guide, best places, best price. Another boy approached and said the same thing. Jay shook his head and walked away.

*It's like no one noticed me till now.*

Jay stopped and got his bearings. On the other side of the road, a small archway led to the side street that led to Jigme's alley, and to The Mystery Chickpea. His stomach gurgled. He walked quickly, already anticipating the aromas of spices and broths.

Instead, he smelled old cow flops and the exhaust of a rickshaw that slowly puttered by, asking him where he needed to go, best price, best price.

Jay waved the rickshaw away and stepped into the side street. A cow stood where The Mystery Chickpea should be.

*Now I'm really losing it,* he thought. *All I want is something to eat!*

He'd have to do some more wandering, but he shouldn't have to wander far. Already, he had seen people setting up other food carts, small grills and braziers, and stands for refreshing *lassi* yogurt drinks.

Jay turned to walk back out of the side street. People walked to and fro in the early morning sun. Bicycles and motorbikes, cows and trucks, people on foot, and people in bumblebee rickshaws, all wove in and out of each other's paths. Above them all, weaving through them all, the song called. Instead of just being in his head, he could now tell where it was coming from.

From the end of the alley, the song got louder. He could satisfy his appetite, he knew, but his curiosity would continue to go hungry.

He didn't think about walking. With every step the song grew into a call, steady as a heartbeat. It held him. It drew him. And on he came.

At the mouth of the alley, just as he began to step beyond its threshold, a voice surprisingly soft said, "Jay?"

The voice cut through the song, the only thing he could hear outside the call. But on he stepped. As he put one foot in the alley, a hand touched his shoulder. The song stopped. Jay fell to his knees.

"Jay?" the voice said again, but the morning had turned black and quiet in the dirt.

JADE WOKE in the dark, and the fragments of the dream faded from her waking mind. The dream itself had been disturbing enough, but that was nothing. *I'm a Jade,* she thought. *We aren't supposed to dream.*

Her wide eyes reached for the meager lager-yellow light that trickled in from her window, the last dregs before sunrise. Few were the nights she wished she wasn't alone, but this had just become one of them.

Moving from the bed to the wooden desk chair, Jade clicked on the desk lamp and pulled her knees up to her chin. The chair's cool wood soothed her naked arse and back, but her mind still raced from the dream's fire.

The room's bare walls stared back at her. No photos brought comfort. No knickknacks or mementos. She found no comfort in memory.

It was easier this way, that was for sure. There was no need for pictures. She didn't want to remind herself of people who couldn't remember her. Knickknacks not only traveled poorly; they were just something else to dust. Mementos kept the past important, but the past could not matter to her. *My world is the now and only the now,* she thought. Jade closed her eyes and then opened them. *The only solace is to deal with what's in front of me.*

"And what's in front of me is fire," she said.

Much of the dream had dashed itself to fragments when she woke, but every lingering shard and scene remained hot to the touch. She and Jay had walked through the city, discussing their lives and travels. Jade found herself talking with him as if with a long-known friend, except that something more than friendship crackled between them like a fire. When they finished their walk, back at the inside stairs of the Everest Base Camp, Jade took Jay's hand and led him to her room.

The rest of the dream had shattered. Except for the fire.

They woke in her bed and the world was screaming. As the walls of the room sagged and softened, the silver-and-gold light pouring through the window darkened to a dull reddish-black, as if blood had been mixed into shadows. The door fell to flames that began to move toward them. The window began to melt. The tall rectangle was her way to look out at the world, onto Agamuskara's busiest street, the better to aid the listening.

Now it could be their escape.

Jade jumped toward the window with Jay behind her. But the window melted like wax, the rectangle falling into a sharp horizontal crescent. The red-and-black light bleeding through made the narrow curve look like a smile.

Jay held her hand and said she would be okay.

Flames kissed them. She woke.

As she sat in the chair, her eyes drifted over the notebooks and volumes from her training. "You will find," The Management had said one day, "that you do not dream anymore." And she hadn't. Since the day she'd completed her training and become a Jade, she had not dreamed. She would fall asleep and all would go black.

Until now.

Jade stood in front of the window and peered at the outside world. Another morning went from darkness to hazy-gray in Agamuskara, as it had throughout her ten years in the city. To the few people wandering the waking streets, this wall of the Everest Base Camp had no windows on the ground floor. Looking down her body a moment, Jade grinned. *They're missing quite a show,* she thought. An extended youth and vigor came with the benefits package, The Management had explained. But they'd never mentioned what to do if she dreamed.

Her thoughts turned to the note that she had kept, despite policy. "The new traveler is not just the new traveler," it said, clearly meaning Jay. But what had his arrival caused in the city? And what did it mean for her, when she had both a duty to perform and a growing attraction, a sense of connection, with the very person she had to influence?

In the back of her mind, she felt the stirrings in the hostel. Jay was awake, agitated, and hung over, but he wasn't letting that stop him. Jade was impressed. Usually, people who drank with Faddah Rucksack didn't wake up for a day, but here was backpack boy, getting ready to sightsee.

Often on a day off Jade would let herself stay in bed, sleep longer than usual, maybe spend a casual hour or two gliding her thoughts over the city, listening to this or that of the daily lives of the people who shared Agamuskara. But this morning, there was too much happening. She washed and dressed. She needed to follow Jay, understand where he was going and why, and what it meant for her city.

*I'm the Jade of Agamuskara,* she thought. Jakes served one area for their entire duty, but The Management usually moved Jades around, depending on the times and the need of a particular place. But once when Jade had asked where she would go next, The Management had said simply that they could see only that she was needed the most in Agamuskara. She wondered if they knew why that was or if it was or if they simply had chosen not to tell her. *Jade Agamuskara Bluegold,* she thought. *Is that who I will always be? Is that who I will only be?*

*But I was nearly something else once.*

As she dried her face and dressed, the memory kindled: the churning inside her, the adrenaline as she had walked to the gardens where he had been waiting for her. She did not know for sure, but she felt like she loved him, and she believed that he was going to propose. But she didn't know what she was going to say. She loved him, but she loved her independence. She loved him, but she loved who she was and did not know if a partner, a husband, was something she wanted. She loved him, but she did not know if he was right for her.

Then the dream shifted and she was in the plaza beneath the blue dragon carved into the wall. He had just taken out the box, shown her the ring, and asked her to marry him.

Then the world had stopped, except for her. And The Management. They appeared and gave her a choice. She could go back to the life she was living, forget this encounter with them, and live out her days as an ordinary woman. Or she could become a Jade and help turn the world.

She saw his face again, frozen in time and space, his hand outstretched, a glint of afternoon sun on the gold ring with the inset jade stone. *He couldn't even hear me,* she thought, *and I still couldn't tell him no.* With a nod to The Management, all that old life was gone.

Jade had never asked The Management about him, and over the years she had thought about him less and less.

Until now. Until there was someone else around who sparked similar feelings.

And bigger questions. As Jade finished dressing, she watched lives through the window again. Children in uniforms skipped toward school. Women walking in groups talked about their families, about movies, about the toils of the day.

*Did I choose right?* she thought, standing in her lonely little room, her one luxury in all the world. *I keep the world turning, but what keeps me going?*

The dream was love and fire, and the dream was the need to know. She was where she was supposed to be. Home was a little room and home was behind the bar. Home would never be what lay beyond that man with the ring in his hand. Home would never be Jay. Home was duty and duty was Jade's only true partner and companion.

She left her room and went out into the streets of Agamuskara, following Jay. With every step, she told herself it was all for duty.

Bent women swept stoops, their twiggy brooms going *thk-thk* as the dust flew. Though, as Rucksack said, all that sweeping really sent the dirt on its long northward journey to build the Himalayas. Pots clanged. A bicycle bell *ting-a-linged* its slow way through groggy throngs. Prayers rang.

She stayed far enough behind Jay so he wouldn't notice her, but close enough so she wouldn't lose track of him. The backpacker seemed single-minded as he walked, and Jade knew he wasn't going to turn around. He didn't even pause until he had arrived at the steps leading down to the slow, meandering waters of the Agamuskara. Jade sat at the foot of a blue statue and watched him walk down the stairs. Jay touched the water.

He vanished.

Jade stood up so fast she whacked her head on the statue. For a moment, the blue god seemed to stare at her, annoyed. Then her head cleared, and the statue was just a statue again. She looked back toward the water, and Jay reappeared. At least, he mostly reappeared. He seemed hazy and indistinct, as if he wasn't quite in the world anymore, but she was instead seeing him through the skin of reality, like cloudy glass, and he was in some hinterland just beyond the world where she walked.

As he came up the steps, Jay kept looking around, as if he were seeing something Jade wasn't seeing. No one else seemed to notice Jay at all, she realized, as if he wasn't there. *Can I see him because I'm a Jade?*

On they walked, back the way they had come from, until Jay suddenly stood full and distinct in the morning light again. Jade jumped behind a cart covered in eggs, their white and brown shells glinting slightly. She ignored the annoyed look from its owner.

"You want egg?" the owner said.

"No," Jade replied.

"Good eggs," he continued. "Healthy. They make you shine."

"I don't want any eggs."

Jay started wandering again, and people clearly saw him now. Relieved, Jade started to move away from the cart.

"Shiny eggs," the owner said, pressing one into her hand. "New eggs. Best price for you."

Still warm from the hen, the egg felt fresh as the morning. In that egg could be life, a new chicken that could go on to lay more eggs. Some would become more chickens. *And some, she thought, would become breakfast.*

"No thanks." She gently set the egg back on the cart. Before he could reply or hand her another egg, she quickly walked away.

She couldn't see Jay.

A panic rose in her, an unexpected urgency. She had to follow him, had to find him.

But where had he gone? The old city was so built upon itself that over the centuries it had become equal parts maze and labyrinth. From where Jade stood, eight streets and alleys intertwined. He could have taken any of them.

Every moment meant more steps, more streets, more city between her and him. There was only one thing to do. Jade wandered close to one of the walls, put her hand on the cool plaster, and listened. She didn't normally listen when she was among other people. Too many interruptions. Too many well-meaning souls asking if she was okay, if she needed a cool drink or a moment in the shade. There was no choice now, though. Jade closed her eyes.

The hardest thing about listening for something specific was filtering out everything else. It helped that the city wasn't fully awake yet, and the sleepers and dreamers were easy to ignore. The animals faded easily. With so many concerns and thoughts, ideas and ponderings, feelings and doings, it was hard to determine which people to exclude and which people to hone in on. Yet as she listened to the city, she noticed something. Everywhere she looked, from the streets to the buildings, the city made her job easier. All of Agamuskara seemed to be watching Jay, and it was as if the city itself led her right to him.

She wasn't familiar with the alley where he had been standing, but her years in Agamuskara told her it must lead right to the center, the heart, of the city.

And at the heart of the city, there was nothing for her to sense. The city's white walls ended at a black void, tinged with red like a faint memory of fire. Then she listened to Jay again and heard the song that seemed to be pulling him toward the darkness at the heart of Agamuskara.

Jade opened her eyes and ran.

When she neared the mouth of the alley, Jay wavered where he stood, as if both following and resisting the song that called him. "Jay?" she said.

His only response was to take a step forward.

Near enough to touch him at last, Jade put a hand on his shoulder. He shuddered and fell to his knees. A silence seemed to fall on the alley.

"Jay?" she said again, but he fell forward, landing in the alley. His daypack seemed to wheeze as it compressed onto his back. She started to lean down to help him, and she heard the noise again. *Shr-shr-shr—*

Then it stopped.

Jade looked at his daypack. The little bulge inside had been moving, but now it was still.

A tremor quaked through the ground. Jade swayed back and forth. So did the entire city. After the world settled, the bulge began to move again, and the *shr-shr-shr* resumed its whispering. *That's got to drive him mad,* she thought. *What the hell is in there, anyway?*

Jay was breathing, but his eyes were closed. *Well, he's all right then,* she thought, and reached over to the daypack zipper.

The pack's little teeth had just started to part when Jay's eyes opened. His hand closed around hers, fast but not tight, surprisingly gentle.

When he saw her face, his eyes widened. "Jade?" he said. "Thought someone was trying to nick my pack again."

Whether from the day's rising heat, his falling and passing out, or all of it, she would have expected his hands to be clammy, but instead they were warm and dry. *I thought they'd be rougher,* she thought. The dream rose in her again. The walking and talking, the moment back inside the Everest Base Camp, the fire later—

Jade pulled her hand away. "What happened?" she asked. "Are you okay?"

Jay sat up and brushed the dust off his clothes. "I'm just hungry," he replied. "Haven't had enough water this morning, and did too much wandering instead of getting breakfast first. Dumb traveler stuff."

Down the alley, the white walls stretched straight as far as Jade could see. Eventually, they seemed to bend, but she couldn't tell for certain. A shadow lay far back in the alley. Beyond it, everything was murky and dim, despite the sun angling down and bringing brightness everywhere else.

*That's the heart of the city,* she thought. *But I have no idea what's there.*

"How did you know where I was?" Jay asked.

*Oh crap,* Jade thought. *He can't know I was following him.* "You know traveling," she replied. "Serendipity is everything. I was out, um, talking with a new supplier for the pub's eggs. Happened to see you, thought you looked kind of dazed. Considering the night you had with Rucksack, I wanted to make sure you were okay."

Jay stood. "Yeah, I'm okay. A bit of hangover got to me. Plus, I need something to eat. Thought I'd try The Mystery Chickpea, but it's not here today." He stared at her. "Jade? Are you okay?"

"What?" She realized she hadn't replied.

"You look kinda pale."

"I... You know you should never eat there, right?"

"That's what I keep hearing. Sounds to me like just the reason to try the place."

"Even Guru Deep says not to eat there."

Jay shrugged. "Guru Deep doesn't come to India either. I like his books, but I use them just as much as a guide for what to skip as for what to see. What he doesn't mention usually gives me a good idea of what to be sure to do."

"Look, there's a great little cart down the way, back on the main street. They do amazing samosas. And there's a lassi stall next to it, does the best mango lassi in the city. Tell them I sent you."

"Sent by Jade of Agamuskara, huh?"

Her breath cut off. *He couldn't possibly know that,* she thought. *It's only how he happened to say it.* "I'm just a bartender," she said with an edge in her voice.

Jay took a step back. "Sorry," he said. "Don't know what I said to annoy you. Just meant, you know, you seem like you've been in the city a long time. You know what's what, and people know who you are."

"People don't know who I am," Jade replied before she could stop herself.

"I can see why," Jay replied. "Look, thanks for helping me. But I'm going to chase up those samosas and lassis. Um, see you back at the Base Camp, I guess."

*Damn,* she thought as he walked away. *I should have handled that better.*

She peered down the alley. The white walls brightened as the sun rose, but the shadows far down stayed as murky as before.

She had never seen it herself, but every day she'd been in Agamuskara, someone had spoken of The Mystery Chickpea. It was always around. But not today. Jay took a fall and the city shook.

*None of it makes sense,* Jade thought. *It's like where there should be sun, there's only shadows.*

She turned away from the alley and walked toward the combination of streets that would take her to a small building of little flats. Her mind blazed out over the city, absorbing the different thoughts and reactions to the tremor. *It's time Rucksack and I have a chat,* she thought. *Then we'll take a look at the heart of Agamuskara.*

THE GOD'S EYES seemed so lifelike. Staring into them was like having a conversation with the universe. Jigme looked deeper.

"Cool statue," said a voice behind him. "I don't remember seeing that before."

Jigme jumped and turned around. Jay sipped a lassi. "Have you had breakfast?" Jay asked. "I got another samosa."

"Um, okay."

Jay handed the samosa to Jigme and walked to the statue. He caressed the globe in the god's hand. "How did I not see it before? I mean, it's not like gods just come out of nowhere. Or do they? Maybe it's a little party trick they play on the universe to amuse themselves."

Jigme had lived his whole life in the alley, and he had come and gone from it ever since he could walk. He knew its dirt and its smells, its sounds and the way the light shone on the white stone. But he had never noticed the statue before.

At the corner where the alley met the street, about at eye level with Jigme, the statue stood on a small round pedestal. The wall containing it had been hollowed out so that the statue hid safe inside, flush with the surface. The blue of the god seemed to pulse and shimmer against the white walls. Flawless and unweathered, the god statue seemed like flesh, not marble. In its palm-up left hand, a bluish-white globe lay level with the figure's neck. The god looked not at the globe but at whoever looked at the god. Its right arm was stretched out in front, hand up, palm forward, as if to say, "Stop. No farther."

"It's good you're having breakfast," Jay said, still staring at the globe in the statue's hand. "I waited too long and I saw strange things. Stranger than this. Only none of them had one of these. Why do you think that is?"

As Jigme swallowed a bite of samosa, Jay turned around. A fire seemed to be sparking up in his eyes. An answer tried to jump out of Jigme's throat, but some samosa got caught and he started coughing.

"You don't know either?" Jay said. He shrugged and looked back at the statue. "All the gods around here carry so many things," he said, "but none carry a globe. It's like a perfect little replica of our own little world. Where in your mythology would that even come from? Guru Deep doesn't mention it, and he spends a lot of pages talking about the gods here."

A cough knocked loose the samosa crumbs. Jigme hacked again and swallowed. "Here, have the rest of this," Jay said, handing over the lassi. The fire in his eyes died down.

"I've never seen it either," Jigme said. "But I don't believe in the gods anyway, so what they carry doesn't matter to me."

"You don't believe?"

Jigme shrugged. "People say the gods do kind things, help people. Amma and I spent years asking the gods for help. Asking for my father to come back. Asking for us to live better. Every time we asked, we lived the opposite of what we asked. So I stopped believing in them. There are no gods. There's just a world that lets anything happen but good things."

Jay stepped away from the statue. The fire was gone from his eyes. "There's a time I would've agreed with you," he said. "Not saying I believe in gods. I'm only interested in living the life in front of me, not pondering ethereal maybes. If there are gods, they don't do much. If they're supposed to be in charge of the world and they're this damn lazy, then they don't deserve any consideration. If they're not around, there's nothing to consider. Gods or no gods, there are people, good and bad, and things that happen for reasons we may never understand. Maybe it's like The Blast. Some say we'll never know what really happened that day in Ireland. Maybe it's like our parents. We'll never know why we had to get cut to the core with that deep a love only to have it ripped away."

"Any love I feel, I feel for Amma," Jigme said. "The only love I get in life, I get from her."

"I wish I could say something to soothe that," Jay said, "or fill the void that must be inside you. I won't patronize you with empty words, though, about how love is all around, how life is love, or any rot like that. I thought I once knew a lot, and then found out I didn't. Ever since I've been on the road, all I've learned is that there's so much I'll never know. One of the few things I know is that life is how we deal with the road in front of us. There's always a choice. Even if it doesn't seem like a good one, there's a choice you can make."

"It never seems like I have choices," Jigme replied.

"Or if I do, they're never good ones."

"You'll find your choices," Jay said. "You're strong, Jigme. You'll find ways to be stronger, do more. "

Jigme finished the lassi. "What makes you strong?"

"Going on," Jay said. "My own way. My own decisions. I learned to love my solitude, and I keep my rules simple: Don't get too close. Don't stay too long. Leave when the time is right. Never look back." He nodded at Jigme. "What makes you strong?"

"Hoping Amma gets better."

"I get that," Jay said. "And I hope she does too. Your world will be all the better for it, but whether or not she gets better isn't something you can control. If you want to be strong, you have to find something in yourself that's up to you—not something that's dependent on someone else. What else makes you strong?"

His mouth opened, but there were no words. What did make him strong? He hardly went to school. He didn't know many songs. He only knew one thing. The rush of the hot air on his face, the big laugh inside when he barely missed colliding with someone—

Jigme grinned. "I love to run."

"If it gives you a smile that big, then it must make you very strong," Jay said. "You hang on to that."

For a moment, they stared at each other like brothers. Jigme wondered how long Jay would stay in the city. He couldn't help but like the tourist.

A hot breeze blew out of the alley.

Jay turned and looked toward the faraway shadows. A glint like sparks gleamed in his eyes again.

"Jigme," Jay said, "what's at the other end of your alley?"

"No one knows," Jigme replied. "No one ever goes that far. No one ever goes much farther than our door, and most never even come near that."

"Do you know what it means when people don't go somewhere?" Jay asked, his voice quiet and far away.

"No."

"It means there's a reason to go there." Jay stepped toward the mouth of the alley again. He patted the statue like a dog and grinned at its turn-back-now gesture.

He stepped into the alley. The noise from Jay's pack seemed louder.

"Wow. That was harder than I expected," Jay said, "but easier than before."

"I... I don't think you should go to the dark end," Jigme said.

Jay started walking down the alley. "If you haven't been there, how would you know?"

"It isn't done," Jigme replied, standing next to the statue. "No one goes there. There are shadows there." Even as he said it, Jigme realized how flimsy it all sounded. All his life, he'd heard the whispers about the alley that led to the heart of the city. It was never anything but "It just isn't done" and "Oh it's dark" and "That doesn't go anywhere, so why bother?" But no one else had been there either.

"You told me you wanted to travel," Jay said, glancing back, the fire bright in his eyes. "Traveling starts with what's outside your own door. If you won't go there, how will you be brave enough to go anywhere else?"

*What do they know? All they do is tell me what isn't,* Jigme thought. *Asha isn't good. Jigme isn't worth breath and food. The alley isn't worth going down.*

*They're wrong about everything else.*

"No one else goes there either," Jigme said, "but they all say what's there. Why is that?"

"They let fear get in the way of knowledge," Jay said. "To a traveler, fear is an opportunity to learn."

Jigme smiled and started walking down the alley.

"By the way," Jay asked, "do you know why The Mystery Chickpea wasn't set up today?"

"What?" Jigme asked, stumbling and only just staying on his feet. When he had seen Jade following Jay, he hadn't noticed anything else.

"Yeah. I wanted to have breakfast there," Jay said. "What's the deal with the old man? Holiday? Birthday? Sick off his own cooking?"

"I... He's always been there before," Jigme replied. "Long as I can remember. There's never been a day he wasn't there."

"Bugger. I know there's a first time for everything, but why does that have to happen the day I'm here?"

"I hope he'll be back," Jigme said. He didn't understand why it bothered him so much, but the street without The Mystery Chickpea was a void in the city, like an organ that had gone missing from the body.

"Have you ever eaten there?" Jay asked.

"No one ever eats there."

"That's fine for no one. How about you?"

Jigme had never told Amma, and far as he knew no one else had either. Maybe no one had noticed. But on that day long ago, when he had stepped inside the steam, it was as if a door had closed between him and the world. Jigme could see them, but to everyone outside the steam, Jigme somehow knew they saw only an empty cart and an old man.

"We were very hungry, and I had not been able to find any food for days," Jigme said at last. "I don't know why I even went there. My feet seemed to work for my stomach, and there I was."

The old man's smile had been small, kind, and safe.

"He patted my shoulder. Everyone says he can't talk. He just handed me a bowl and a spoon, and pointed to the two pots."

"Which did you choose?" Jay asked.

"I asked for an egg," Jigme replied. "I don't know why. An egg sounded so good. But instead the old man just pointed again to the two pots. I picked the one to my left, and he filled up my bowl."

"What was in the one on the right?"

"I don't know. Same thing, for all I know. He just seemed to want me to choose for myself."

"When I took a bite, it..." Jigme's voice fell off. The strange sensations rushed back.

"It's okay," Jay said. "It was only food for a hungry boy, right?"

Jigme shook his head. "No. That's the thing. When I dipped the spoon in the bowl, it looked like regular dahl. The broth was broth, and it smelled so rich and amazing. There were lentils and vegetables. The scent itself seemed to speak to me, like it was telling my stomach and my heart how much it was going to help me." Jigme's mind deferred to his stomach and his soul. "But taking that first mouthful, it was like... It was like biting into a conversation."

"What, did the food talk to you?"

Jigme nodded.

"You aren't serious."

*He doesn't believe me*, Jigme thought. *I don't know why I thought he would.* "I am serious, Jay. The food said that when I asked for an egg, the old man had said no because I would have egg enough to come. It said my love was pure but would not be enough. And it..."

"It what?"

"Forget it. You don't believe me."

For a moment, Jay said nothing, then, "Look, I'm sorry. You're right. I've seen some hard-to-believe things over the years. I shouldn't have said that."

Jigme nodded. "The food sang to me."

"What did it sing?"

Jigme closed his eyes for a moment as they walked. The song flooded back:

"He loves to run, but one day he will stand still.

"He will know the world in the city.

"When he burns, he will be the flame in the fire."

"Do you know what it means?" Jay asked.

Jigme shook his head. "That was all the food said to me. After that, it was just soup. I ate it and the man gave me more to take home to Amma. I started to offer him work to repay him, but he just shooed me away."

"Have you been back since then?"

"No."

"You have a mystery of your own to work out," Jay said.

They walked by the red door. The wall around Jigme's home was white, but as Jigme stared, a shadow seemed to darken the red on the door. He stopped. "I don't think we should go any farther, Jay."

"How would you know when you never have?"

Jigme started walking again. They had hardly passed the door when the world seemed darker. When Jigme looked up, the sun was still bright in the sky, yet all around him, the alley's white walls had become grayer. Shadows seemed to grow with every breath. The air seemed cooler too, as if they were in a part of the city that somehow never knew light and stayed always in the chill of just before dawn.

"It's cold," Jigme said.

"Think this is cold?" Jay replied. "You ought to go to Mount Everest. It's so high up, the air is thin and everything is cold. You can be there in the mountains only a couple of days and you start to forget what warm is."

They said nothing more. Jigme ached to turn around and run back to his door, throw it open, run inside, and lock the door. Only Amma was not at home anymore, he remembered. Home was no longer home.

*Run back to the hospital,* he thought. *Go back to Amma's side, stay there until she wakes up. Maybe she's awake already, and feeling better, and wondering where I am.*

Jigme stopped again. He turned away from Jay and the whispering raspy noise coming from Jay's daypack. There seemed to be a glow. It began in Jigme's mind, but its red warmth soon bled out over the alley.

"Leave," a voice inside whispered, "and there is no world. Keep going, and see the world. Keep going and your mother will be healed."

Already he could see down toward the brighter end of his alley, where first lay his old home and then the people beyond and the street and the city. Amma was out there, waiting for him.

But the voice held a promise that sounded as sure as the sun talking about dawn.

Jay said nothing when Jigme caught up.

Mists swirled now, as if the river's morning fog didn't burn off during the day but instead came here to wait out the sun before returning to the water. Jigme couldn't see the walls anymore. He could hardly see Jay, could only make out the strident outline of the man and his pack as they moved forward.

"Scary, isn't it?" Jay said.

"Yes."

"That's usually a sign it's the right thing to do," Jay replied, but his hard voice sounded brittle and cracked.

The mists fell away. A dim gloom of light showed them where they were.

The alley stopped. At its dead end, at the heart of the city, a wall of smooth, glasslike black stone rose to the height of one story. It had no features, except for two statues standing before it with a passage between them. The statues were identical to the statue at the mouth of the alley, and they stood no more than the length of a step in front of the wall.

"Where do we go now?" Jigme asked.

Jay shrugged. "Forward is the only direction I know."

"But there's nowhere to go."

With a grin, Jay pointed to the statues. "It looks like a wall," he said. "But how can we really know until we get closer?"

Fear split through Jigme. "We need to stop," he said, tugging at Jay's arm before the tourist could walk between the statues.

"What's your deal?" Jay said. "We came all this way already. Why stop now?"

"Because we have to!" Jigme said. "We shouldn't go here. It's wrong!" The words made sense from his mouth but not in his head.

"She will die," the voice said again, clear yet harsh in Jigme's mind—powerful but raspy, as if unused for eons. Its ancient echoes burned away everything else in his mind, including his own thoughts. Jigme's hand fell away from Jay's arm.

Jay moved forward. The voice in Jigme's head faded until he could hear himself again. Jigme reached up and grabbed the daypack, right where the fabric bulged. Jay stepped between the statues and touched his palm to the black stone.

From where his hand clutched the daypack, Jigme could feel the thing inside move faster. Its sound got louder too. Then there was nothing inside Jigme's mind but the voice.

"Back to the flame and the boiling sea,
Back to the fire, back to truly free,
Back before life, when all fire was me—"
Something pulsed out of the black stone like a wave sweeping out over the city. Jigme could hear screams and shrieks, fears that leaped like flames from building to building, soul to soul. The force of the wave knocked Jigme and Jay backwards onto their arses. A tremor quaked through the ground.

"What?" Jigme said. "What was that?"

"That song," Jay replied. "It's that damn song again."

Worlds away, the screams faded. In front of them, the stone seemed no different than before.

Jigme tried to get to his feet, but his legs kept

tumbling him back down. Jay didn't fare any better at first, but some desperation seemed to rip through the tourist's body and stiffen his legs.

Jay reached out. The strange fire had left his eyes, but that was no comfort. Now they blazed with an urgent fear.

"I don't understand," Jigme said.

"I don't either," Jay replied. "And you know what? I don't want to. Forget this. Forget Agamuskara. Forget India. I'm out of here."

He didn't look at Jigme. Jay just turned around and ran up the alley. The mists closed, leaving Jigme alone.

Jigme thought about following, but the black stone seemed to sing to him. He stood and stared at it, wondering what had made Jay so afraid.

*Now I know how Amma can live,* he thought as he walked back to the world beyond the heart of the city.

Big as an eclipse's shadow, the understanding brought a grin to his face. Jigme began to run.


THE SHOUTS, offers, and curses couldn't slow Jay's pace. From the mouth of the alley to the street beyond, he ran, daypack bouncing and the thing inside whooshing so fast he wondered if the friction would make it tear through the fabric. Everest burned his mind, as did the parade the day before, with the song that was like setting someone's mind on fire. A grinning flame passed through his vision every time he blinked, so he tried not to. But it didn't matter; a voice like clinking coals in a stove singed his thoughts.

*I'm getting out of here,* Jay thought. *I left Everest in a hurry; I'm going to leave here in an even bigger one. Find a way to ditch this thing, then hop a train to Kolkata, fly to Bangkok, and lose myself in Thai beer. Forget this place. Forget these people. Forget all of it. Just keep going, Jay. Just keep going.*

He was relieved to see no sign of Jade, Rucksack, or anyone else at the Everest Base Camp. Once inside the dorm, Jay locked the door and started packing. He rearranged his daypack, threw a t-shirt over the thing, and refused to look as it floated above the guidebook, snacks, water bottle, and various traveler detritus inside his pack.

Next, he unhooked his money belt and set it on the bed. He took out his passport and the photo. From the cash underneath, he counted out bills and estimated what should be enough for a train ticket east, plus money for food and beer along the way.

As he put the rest of the cash back into the money belt, the photo stared at him. For five years he'd looked at the picture. Now he looked closer. The faces now seemed to frown. But how could a photo change?

"Sorry, Mom and Dad," Jay said. "I have to get out of here."

He tucked the photo back into the money belt, avoiding the glares of his parents, and then wrapped the belt around his lower belly. He glanced at the bed. *Nearly forgot my passport,* he thought. As he reached for it, a knock on the door made him look up.

*Forget it,* he thought. *Ignore them and they'll go away.*

He sat on the bed and waited. There was no use going to the door when he had no idea who was outside. Not Jade or Rucksack, that was sure. It was Jade's hostel. If she wanted in, she would announce herself and then unlock the door if no one opened it for her. Rucksack didn't need to knock with anything but his voice.

*What about Jigme?* Jay thought. *Would he have followed me back here?*

Guilt panged at him like a kicked shin. *I convinced him to go down that alley,* Jay thought. *He was scared, he kept saying we shouldn't, but I hounded him to come. What was all that guff about travelers and fear? I was damn near wetting myself, and I don't even know why. But I had to go...*

Had to go.

Just like Everest. He'd been hauling arse to get out of Tibet before the Chinese police could catch up with him. Instead of cutting south the fast way from Lhasa to the border with Bhutan like he'd planned, he'd set out southwest. A few narrow escapes kept him on that road, fleeing into the Himalayas until he showed up at Everest Base Camp, wondering why the hell he was there. Somehow it had worked. No one had looked at him twice, and maybe the Chinese police hadn't figured he would go to such a place.

But it made no sense to Jay that he'd gone. Then there was that night with the moon and the mountain —and again, the next day, the feeling that he had to go. Had to leave Everest for India. Skip Nepal and go straight into the heat of Agamuskara.

*It's like I'm not deciding anything lately,* he thought. *Something else is doing the deciding for me. And I know what.*

Jay stared at the floating lump in his daypack. The t-shirt spun softly in the air. The thing had gotten slower and quieter again. *I'll chuck it down the loo,* he thought. *Let the roaches have it. Then I'll block off the hole with my Guru Deep India book. Forget India. I don't ever want to see this place again.*

He reached to pull off the t-shirt and grab the stupid floating thing. It spun faster—and the knocks on the door became louder. *Dammit,* Jay thought. *They're still here?*

"Mr. Jay?" said a voice. "Ah, Mr. Jay, thank goodness we have found you."

Jay froze.

"We have come to help, Mr. Jay. Could you open the door, please?"

"Just a minute!" Jay said. If they were still there, they weren't going away. Jay glanced at the windows. No way out through the bars outside. If he was leaving, he was leaving through this door.

But he was getting rid of the thing first.

He reached for the t-shirt again, but what was underneath seemed to know his intentions. It moved out of his grasp, floating over the bed like the ghost of a softball. He lunged forward; his hand closed on nothing.

"Mr. Jay?" said the voice. "Thank goodness we have arrived not an hour too late."

A key turned in the lock.

Quickly looking up, Jay cracked his head on the bed and toppled backward onto the floor.

Dazed, he looked up to see the floating t-shirt waft back down into his daypack. The zipper closed behind it, and the little padlock on the zipper undid itself and then locked the pack shut.

Jay had just gotten to his feet and moved between the bed and the door when the catch clicked and the door opened.

In the doorway, two men in drab olive uniforms

smiled empty courtesy. Something about them seemed nearly familiar, but not quite. They could have been anyone, could have come from anywhere: India, Nepal, China. Something twitched and jangled in a forgotten, blanked-out part of Jay's brain, but he couldn't place them.

The first one said, "Mr.—"

"Jay will do just fine."

The men looked at each other. A shrug. A head bob.

"Mr. Jay," the first one continued, "we are Mim and Pim, no misters required, from the Office of World Light and Foreign Visitors. We hope you have been enjoying your stay in our India, as your pleasure is paramount to us."

"It's... a complex country," Jay said. "But I'm about to head out. Realized I took a wrong turn at Tibet. I should be in Thailand right now."

"India it is, sir, most marvelous," Mim said, "and that you found pleasure and safety here we are so glad."

"You haven't had the last few of days I've had—"

"Chai we have brought you, sir," the second man said, bobbing his head. Jay guessed he was Pim. Before Jay could reply or continue, a hot cup was in his hand. He hadn't noticed either man move. The scent of cardamom and clove widened Jay's eyes, and the heat in his palm brought comfort. The first sip unlocked the daylight in his soul. He drained the cup. Suddenly, India indeed seemed a country of pleasure and comfort. "I gotta say, this is the best tea I've ever had."

Pim's head bobbed. "We take pride in your

pleasure, safety, and comfort, sir."

The chai was hot and sweet. The bright day was full of India's life and loveliness.

*Why had things felt so urgent?* Jay thought. *All that fear and running?*

Jay blinked and glanced at the bed, the ready-to-run packs sitting on the mattress. His passport lay next to them. The warmth of the chai faded as he shook his head. So much had happened today already. No wonder the room looked blurry, and he felt so groggy. But no matter how good the tea was, he needed to leave.

"None out of three ain't bad. Look, fellas, I appreciate the chai and chat, but I've got a busy day of getting out of here. To what do I owe the honor of the visit of the Office of Luminous Travelers or whatever?"

"Only a small matter it is, Mr. Jay," Mim said, bobbing his head. Jay wondered if he could feel seasick while inland. "For your pleasure, safety, comfort, and enlightenment, The Office of World Light and Foreign Visitors cares very much. That is why this bright and wonderful day we have come to you."

"My pleasure, my safety, my comfort, and my enlightenment?" Jay said. "So far, you're none for four."

"Now please and thank you for we should see your passport Mr. Jay." No head bob.

Jay glanced at the bed again and saw only the backpacks. Again, he hadn't seen either man so much as twitch, but Mim was already flipping through the pages of Jay's passport. Jay thought about grabbing it back, but his hands seemed very heavy. Lifting them seemed not really worth the trouble. A tiny, wary part of the back of his mind seemed to shout that he should be wondering why that was. But all he said was, "I have a visa."

The men looked at each other. "Of course, sir," Pim said, his head now still and stiff. "We just must make sure all is correct. Many visas have suffered premature failure due to faulty glue, sir."

"Faulty glue? How hard can it be to make glue stick?"

"We do not know, Mr. Jay. An exalted import from USA was the glue. Many high hopes but sad to report to exalted World Light and Foreign Visitors such as your good self that the glue has trouble doing its job in the heat of India."

"You need to check the glue on my visa?"

"Very good sir," Pim confirmed, bobbing his head in approval. "As bright as your good name you are, Mr. Jay."

Mim stopped at the blue-and-lavender sticker adhering to a page near the end of the passport. Next to the Hindi script, Jay saw the words "Republic of India." Mim held the passport up to the light then low to the floor. He held it as far to the left and the right as his arm would allow. Each time, his gaze seemed to peer between the visa and the page. He lowered the passport with a sigh and did not hand it back.

"Ah, Mr. Jay," Mim said with a deep sadness on the verge of tears. "It is as we feared."

"What are you talking about?" Jay said, pointing to his India visa, stuck securely to the page. "It's not even got a loose corner."

"Sudden glue failure has been a horrible sad

problem, sir," Pim said. "Then like a lost, lost soul visa flutters, and many World Light and Foreign Travelers have problems leaving India."

Jay nodded, figuring out the game, despite the woolly fuzz all around his mind and vision. His eyelids drooped as he wondered how much "new glue" it would take to grease his visa back to its page. "A costly problem, I'm sure."

Pim bobbed his head. "We can easily fix your visa," he started to say, but he frowned and stopped. "Oh, but Mr. Jay, it is worse than we thought! Wrong your visa is!"

"Wrong? My visa is fine. I got it properly. It didn't even cost extra."

Both men stared at him.

"Okay, only a little extra. But the dates are fine!"

"No and no, sir," Mim said. "We are sorry but for you and it are all wrong."

"Look, I get it. Find the dopey Yank. Do a little squeeze. Fine. How much for my visa to be" —Jay winked—"'fixed?'"

"I'm sorry, Mr. Jay?"

"How much?" Jay held up his hand and rubbed his thumb over his first and middle fingers. "Come on. I know the game. *Baksheesh*. Money is the grease that makes the wheels of the world turn, and all that dahl. A few rupees and the glue on my visa will be perfect. So, how much will it take?"

The men exchanged horrified looks. "No, no, Mr. Jay!" Pim said. "We have all we need. It shall be fixed. Wrong your visa is. New better glue it needs. Not your fault. We fix. You no pay. Only wait."

"Wait?" Jay said. Waiting meant staying in

Agamuskara. Staying where that damn alley was. Staying around Jade and Jigme and Rucksack. Each of them kept howling in his mind that they were reasons to stay. Even without them, there was the fire that singed his mind every time his thoughts turned to the alley and the black wall, and it seemed harder and harder not to think about them.

Already in his mind's eye he could see the train station and the long blue line of the Kolkata Very Express. He couldn't wait. He had to leave. Now.

"No. You wait," Jay said, shaking his head. The words seemed to trip and jam in his mouth. "No. You know what?" he said. "That sounds great, just—" Jay lunged forward to snatch his passport back, but his lunge became a stumble.

Something wasn't working right between his mind and limbs anymore. Or vision. The men were fuzzy. They stood right in front of him, so why did they sound like they were down a tunnel?

"All is fine, sir," the second man said. "You and your passport could not be safer, and both fixed soon!"

"The chai," Jay said, his mouth and eyes sagging. "You..." *Drugged me...*

As his vision faded, for a moment Jay saw clearly. A winding light shone from the men, silvery like a chain. But the silver faded like a mask removed, and beneath it their chains were blue.

"You," Jay said. "You look familiar."

He fell.

No hard floor whacked his head though. There was only a soft *flump* onto his bed, as if the two men had caught him then set him down as gently as a baby.

Jay's vision faded, but still he could see hazily what Mim and Pim were doing. Mim set the large backpack on the floor, while Pim lifted Jay's arm and tucked the daypack between his arm and his chest like a teddy bear.

"You are safe," Pim said, patting Jay's cheek. "And you will keep it safe until the time is come."

Mim walked back around the bed and stood next to Pim. The two men smiled at each other and bobbed their heads. Then they seemed to realize what they were doing and stopped.

"Always takes a moment to get out of character, you know?" Mim said.

"I wish we didn't have to be so over the top with the accents," Pim said in flat, bemused English.

"Or all the 'sir' and 'mister such-and-such' stuff," Mim said, his voice crisp as the fresh poppadom cracker bread Jay had eaten with his samosa earlier.

"Though the whole 'Office of World Light and Foreign Visitors' bit never gets old."

"At least it's close to the truth," Mim said. "I could never lie to them, you know?"

Pim nodded. "If only we could tell them the whole truth."

"It'd never work. You know that. It's one thing to be truthful, but if we were outright honest they couldn't take it. And they wouldn't believe us anyway."

"True," Pim replied. "I'm glad we caught him. For a moment I thought the poor chap might conk his head on the floor, and he's had a rough day already."

"Nothing compared to what he's got to look forward to," Mim said. "I don't envy him." He looked at his colleague. "But really, faulty glue?"

"Sorry, I blanked. I had to think fast. The original story wasn't going to work."

"Why?" Mim asked. "Did you think he might recognize us from Everest that morning?"

"Or from last night in the pub," Pim replied. "At least it worked. Besides, the glue is faulty. Gluing a visa into a passport like his, with all that's about to happen? Silliness. Glue is so... ordinary."

"Shall we go fix his passport, then?"

"Yes. By the time we're done, he'll never need a visa again."

Pim closed the door and locked it. Mim and Pim smiled at Jay, and Mim held up Jay's passport like a salute. Then they vanished with a smile, leaving behind only the scent of chai. Despite the sun, the world turned dark as Jay fell asleep.


DOES HE EVER BLINK? Jade thought as she finished recounting to Rucksack all she hadn't told him yet: Kailash and their strange conversation, the tricksters and the note, Jay and the alley.

He'd hardly said a word since she had started talking. When she stopped, Rucksack just breathed in deeply as he sat back in his chair. "I need to think on this a moment," he said, the laughter in his gaze fading.

Deep in thought, he closed his eyes. This troubled her even more. Rucksack sat between her and the window of his small third-floor room, a few blocks away from the Everest Base Camp ("No offense to your fine rooms," he'd told her, "but I prefer to improve my constitution before I improve my constitution."). Yet Rucksack's voice was like dancing. Whenever he spoke with someone and looked at them, he had a way of making them feel they were the most important person in existence. Without his voice or gaze, he seemed to be far away, as if he'd rambled across the universe and slipped back in time ten thousand years.

*Who are you?* she thought.

Since The Management didn't like to speak of it, the Jakes and Jades were left to rumor and speculation. She'd heard the stories that in the world there were men like ghosts who had been cut off from destiny and decision. Usually The Management monitored for these ghosts in all places where a Jake or Jade was stationed. It was said that one ghost had never been seen by Jakes and Jades, since he had first lost his helix, but Rucksack had been sighted for years.

Word had it Rucksack had been involved in the incident in the Hong Kong pub some years back, but The Management were even more silent than usual about what had happened.

All Jade knew was that as a result of the Hong Kong incident, The Management had worked out a way to keep the ghosts out of their pubs, but they had relaxed it at Everest Base Camp when Rucksack first came to Agamuskara. Of course, they didn't tell her why. Yet with the notes coming her way lately, she couldn't shake the feeling that The Management were watching the Everest Base Camp more closely than usual and more closely than they watched other pubs.

*Or maybe they're not watching the pub,* she thought. *Sometimes it feels like they're watching* me.

The sad laughter of Rucksack's eyes flared up when

he opened them. Jade realized she'd been holding her breath. The world seemed to inhale, and so did she. "You back then?" she asked.

With a smile he stood up. "Ah, Jade," Rucksack replied. "You know as much as I do the importance o' thinking things over before you speak. It's like letting a good quaff o' stout wash ambrosia in your mouth before finally allowing admittance to your soul. And you've given me a lot to think on."

"Where should we begin?" Jade asked. "I've turned this over and over in my mind. I know all these events are connected and somehow Jay's at the center of it all. I just don't know which path to take first."

"Aye," Rucksack said. "Especially since we don't know how they wind, or if they go to or away from another in a way that could prove just as vital."

Jade walked to the window, looking out over the city's packed streets. "Rucksack?" she said.

"Aye?"

"How about you run downstairs and we start with Kailash?"

"Why do you say that?"

Jade turned around. "Because she's standing on the street opposite, staring at your window."

The color fell out of Rucksack's face.

Jade ran to the door. "Come on," she said. "Don't you want to know who she is?"

Yes and no wrestled in his gaze, and he didn't move.

"That wasn't really a question," Jade said, firmly yet gently. "You have to find out who she is. No matter where that leads."

"You have no idea what that path could be."

She stared him in the eye. "Neither do you. But do you think you could stand continuing not to know?"

Rucksack had started down the steps before Jade could move.

The hot day greeted them as they ran into the river of people, and immediately they were in the thick of the crowded street separating them from Kailash. Too many people, too much happening in the street, Jade realized too late.

Rickshaws and lorries closed in on them from both directions.

*Nowhere to go,* Jade thought.

Jade looked left. The rickshaw driver's face confirmed he had nowhere to swerve. She looked right. *Thirteen,* she thought. *That's how many small bars are on the grill of this truck.* Its engine stood taller than she was. Even if the driver had seen them, there was no way he could avoid them.

The look in Rucksack's eyes mirrored hers.

*Not like this.*

The breath left her. *Who will miss me?* she thought. As her eyes closed, an image of Jay's eyes passed into her mind.

The shout had to be loud to be heard above the crowd, yet it seemed to Jade that whoever was shouting was as calm and quiet as someone saying good morning.

Seconds passed. Jade opened her eyes.

The vehicles continued on their way, safely beyond both Jade and Rucksack.

A wobbliness whooshed into Jade's legs with a warmth, she imagined, that must feel similar to peeing one's pants. *Will anyone notice when I fall?* she thought.

Rucksack turned. The fire in his eyes seemed brighter than ever, as if fed by a new sense of hope, purpose, and direction. His hand wrapped around her upper arm faster than she could see him move.

"Jade," he said. "If I can do this, so can you."

What fueled the fire in him passed to her. With a breath her legs propelled her forward again. *At least my pants aren't wet after all,* she thought.

The traffic was nothing to them now. They danced through it like a crowded ballroom and didn't step on a single foot. At the other side of the street, Kailash stood still. Her eyes were closed, and she breathed heavily, as if exhausted.

"I'll go up first," Jade said to Rucksack. "Stay here."

"But—"

"Just trust me."

Rucksack stood still.

Not wanting to surprise Kailash, Jade slowed her pace, but the woman's eyes opened.

"I wondered when you would finally notice me down here," Kailash said.

"Are you okay?" Jade asked.

"About as shaken as you," Kailash replied. "That was much harder than it used to be." She glanced at the traffic.

Jade looked too. *Wait,* Jade thought. *Is she telling me that she's the one who shouted, that she's the one who saved us?*

"I'm sorry I left in such a hurry last night," Kailash said. "I thought I was ready, but I was too afraid."

"What are you afraid of?" Jade asked.

"Many things. More than you have time to hear. But the one I am here to face is the one I fear the most."

As Jade looked at Kailash, she noticed a difference in the woman. *Or maybe I just didn't notice before,* she thought.

The face seemed young, but the eyes did not. There was age there. Joy and sorrow far beyond what Jade thought a life capable of holding inside. She thought she glimpsed it in the woman's helix too, strong yet weary, but a fog and a shadow obscured what little Jade could see. "Why do you fear it?" Jade asked.

"I fear for the past. I fear for the future, which hinges on this present. I fear for him. For you. And for the other one. I never thought I would see another in all my days."

"Another what?"

Kailash smiled but it faded just as quickly. Kailash looked away from Jade, toward the heart of the city. Tears shimmered in Kailash's eyes when she looked at Jade again.

"I want you to know, Jade, that I did not want this. Any of this," Kailash said. "If I could go back to the Heart and undo all of it, I would, even if it cost me all I ever loved. I fear I may lose it all anyway. But I did as I did, and I never knew what would happen. Now I am older. I know too much, but I don't know enough to help you as I wish I could. I don't even know if I can help him, and if I can help anyone, I should be able to help him."

Rucksack stepped forward. He and Kailash looked directly at each other. Jade hadn't noticed before, but now she did. Their eyes were nearly identically brown-and-black. So were the emotions churning in their respective gazes. Deep loss and impossible hopes. Regret and guilt. A wish for different times. A sad acceptance of what was.

As she looked from one eye to the other, Jade understood the well from which Rucksack drew his laughter and his bravado. He transformed his grief into gold, a rich happiness that didn't serve him but served to bring out the joy in others, since he seemed not to have any of his own. It was an amazing alchemy, Jade realized. She couldn't help but admire him.

He and Kailash both seemed on the verge of speaking. Then something rocked through the ground, and Jade was looking at the sky.

Rucksack lay next to her. A pebble was pressing into his cheek. Around them, the stunned city had also paused. Screams and crashes shouted into the sky, but they were small sounds against the intense silence that fell over Agamuskara.

Jade could feel it being said already: "Strange things," the city said. "Strange things happening again."

Then Jade realized she was lying on the street. She knew all too well the feet, hooves, and wheels that ground old food, fresh dung, and more into the pavement. She got up quickly and so did Rucksack. He looked behind her. The widening of his eyes, like a punch in the gut, told Jade she didn't need to turn around to know that Kailash was gone.

"What the hell happened?" Jade asked.

"I don't know yet," Rucksack replied. "But I think I know where it came from."

"The heart of the city."

He nodded. "We were going to go there anyway."

They started walking as the city found its breath again. All around them, people dealt with the strangeness of what had happened by deciding nothing had happened at all. But not all of them.

"People are starting to wonder," Jade said.

"Aye," Rucksack replied. "But it's a city resilient against hard lives. They won't wonder for long."

"They will if more weird things keep happening."

"I'll worry when the city worries," he replied, but his flat voice said otherwise.

"We're going to see her again," Jade said.

"You don't know that."

"I do. She may be scared, but she's here. She knows something of what's going on too. It terrifies her but she's drawn to it too."

"Like Jay," Rucksack said.

"Like us, apparently."

"She seems so familiar," Rucksack said.

"You could have been brother and sister," Jade replied, "but you said you don't have any siblings. At least none that you know of."

"I definitely don't have siblings."

"How can you be so sure?"

"My mother told me there were... complications around my birth," Rucksack said. "She and my father never could have had other children."

"I hate to say this, but sometimes people have children with someone other than their partner."

"Believe it or not, Jade, I'm old enough to know that." Rucksack shook his head. "Neither of my parents was able to have children again."

They walked in silence. Jade tried to use the time to think through what had happened and to listen to the city. People indeed were getting back to their days, but the tiniest yellow threads of fear had begun to bloom like anemones.

Agamuskara was a city of gods, and nothing could remind you of that like the solid earth suddenly giving you a good shake. *What do the buggers get up to if they get bored?* Jade thought. *Are they bored?*

As they neared the alley, Jade realized what was most different. The walls here, from some of the city's oldest buildings, seemed to have pulled into themselves like a scared child curled into the fetal position. *I need to understand this,* she thought, *but how?*

The idea scared her. It would be so hard, so draining. The walls were old. Even though she wanted to hear what they had to say, they would be reluctant to talk.

*But I have to,* she thought. *I have to listen to the walls.*

She and Rucksack were nearly to the alley when Jigme came running toward them. His strange smile seemed like it was someone else's mouth, swollen to the wrong size, as if something inside him was growing and wanted to burst out. When Jigme saw her and Rucksack, he stopped.

"I told him it wasn't a good idea, but he said it's what travelers do."

"What?" Rucksack said.

Jigme explained about the alley and Jay's decision to leave Agamuskara.

"How long ago did he run away from you?" Jade said.

"Not long," Jigme replied.

Jade looked deep into the teenager's eyes, but he turned away. Jade thought she saw his cheeks flush red. "Are you okay?" she asked.

He bobbed his head. "Mum will be okay," he said. "I know it now."

"Go see her," Rucksack said. "I'll come by later."

Jigme ran off toward the hospital, the strange smile back on his face.

"We have to get to the hostel," Jade said. "Now."

"Why there?"

"He's still got to pack. But there's no way Jay's leaving us." She spoke from a sense of duty, trying to ignore the strange anger boiling under her words.

"No way he's leaving," she said. "It's time we got some answers. It's time we saw what's in that pack."

THE FOG reminded Jay of the down comforter he'd slept under as a boy. When his mom woke him for school, the smells of coffee and toast would float in like quiet birds. His dad would always be sitting at the kitchen table, drinking coffee while they all talked about the day ahead.

*It's so nice being back here,* Jay thought. *It's good to be home.*

His dad set down the paper and said, "What do you want to be when you grow up?"

Jay started to answer, but a knock tore a hole in the fog. His mom and dad faded away.

*Can't it just be quiet again?* Jay thought. *I like being under my comforter. It's cozy. It's calm.*

Voices outside the fog said something that reminded him of his name. He squeezed his teddy bear closer. Where did the comforter go?

A rattle of metal on metal opened his eyes. The fog

was gone. His boyhood room vanished back into memory. He was in his bed in the Everest Base Camp dorm room. The teddy bear turned out to be his daypack, tucked under his arm.

A key turned in the lock.

Jay tried to jump off the bed, but most of his body was still asleep. When he tried to swivel on his arse to put his feet on the floor, he succeeded only in falling back onto his thin pillow. His daypack fell on his face. *Why do I feel so hazy?* he thought, setting the pack on the floor. *And what the hell am I doing here anyway? I thought I was sightseeing today. Who's here?*

The door opened.

Jade and Rucksack had each tried to come in the door first, and now they were stuck in the doorway, glaring at each other while also looking at Jay. Something in their eyes seemed to say they were trying to make sure he wouldn't vanish on the spot.

"Jade," Rucksack said, "could you just back off and let me through? We'll never get in here otherwise."

She turned slightly and gave Rucksack enough of a shove to pop him back out into the hallway. "Ladies first," she said, laughing and stepping like a dancer into the room. When she looked at Jay, her lighthearted smile brightened. Then it faded as she breathed out and closed her eyes, as if relieved the room wasn't empty.

"I don't remember being here," Jay said. "What's going on?"

Rucksack rubbed his belly as he walked into the room. "What's the last thing you remember?"

Jay shrugged. "I was talking with Jade. Then I went to get some breakfast."

A wary glance passed between Jade and Rucksack, and Jade's face softened. She sat next to Jay on the bed. "What did you have for breakfast?"

A fog blanketed through Jay's mind again. *Why do I feel so groggy?* he thought.

"Samosas. And a lassi," he said at last. "Wait. That's not right. I was really hungry, so I got two samosas. But I only ate one. Oh. I ran into Jigme. We were looking at this crazy statue that had appeared at the mouth of the alley where he lives. I gave him the other samosa."

He started to say more, but a spark in his mind burned up the fog. The rest of the morning shone brightly again. He told them about the alley and the weird quake and the strange men who had come to his room.

"My passport!" he yelled, standing. "That's it. Those guys took my passport. I have to find it. Otherwise I'll never get out of here!"

A wary look passed between Jade and Rucksack again. "Why do you keep looking at each other like that?" Jay asked.

"We understand you're scared," Jade said. "It's been beyond a weird morning for you. But there are things we need to talk about. Things we all need to understand. And things you need to show us."

"I don't know what you're talking about," Jay said. "Look, it was great meeting you both. You're cool people. But I've decided I'm not digging Agamuskara. Or India. I'm heading to Thailand and lay low for a while. I appreciate that you're worried about something, but I need to find my passport. Or head to the embassy to get it replaced. I need to hit the world and see the road."

Rucksack shook his head. "We'll get the passport sorted. Jade and I will help."

"Great!" Jay said. "Let's go!"

Rucksack closed the door. "Let's talk about your daypack first."

Jay sat back down on the bed. "Black nylon. Has a twenty-liter capacity. Been run over by two bikes, one motorcycle, three rickshaws, and one truck. Has one main compartment reached through a locking zipper," Jay said. "I'm pretty sure you can get knock-offs anywhere from here to Lhasa. We can talk about it more on the way to the embassy."

"Sorry Rucksack wasn't more specific," Jade said. "It's time you showed us what was in your pack, Jay."

"I don't know what you mean."

"No, you don't," Rucksack replied, his voice soft as the click of a spring coiling closed despite an intense power locked up in it. "And it's high time you bloody did."

"You know what it is?" Jay said, shutting his mouth quickly. *You said too much,* he thought.

"I have a suspicion. If I see it, I can tell you if I'm right," Rucksack said. "And I can tell you what it is."

"You mean you'll actually explain?" Jay said. "It won't be all witticisms and evasions?"

Rucksack grinned. "Explanations galore, as many as I can spare."

"Then we can start hunting down my passport?"

Jade nodded, though she seemed to be trying not to glance at Rucksack. "I'll go with you to the embassy myself, while Rucksack hits the streets."

"I don't know how I got it," Jay said, pulling up his

daypack and resting it on his thigh. "I can't seem to get rid of the thing. But I don't know what to do with it. Before the two men vanished, they said something about me taking care of it until the time came. I guess this must be what they meant." With a deep breath, he unzipped the pack.

Jay hadn't touched it directly, skin to world, since the first time he saw it in his tent at Everest. As his hands wrapped around it, careful so as not to bruise the clouds, a golden song rang in his mind, sung in a language he did not know yet somehow understood.

He pulled the thing out of his pack.

The words and tune rang softly yet Jay could have heard them anywhere, from a mountain taller than Everest to the very core of the world. The air shimmered as if made of golden afternoon sunlight.

Rucksack and Jade shone with gold and silver, black and brown, green and blue. Rucksack's eyes were like the voids of existence and possibility, where worlds were made and unmade. Jade's eyes were their own suns. As he gazed at her, at the twining lengths streaming from her, he saw him and her, the world...

Jay felt his feet leave the floor. Was he really floating between floor and ceiling, earth and heaven?

Then a shadow of red and black poured over his vision, and the shock made Jay fling his hands over his face, palms open and empty. The song collapsed. The colors vanished. Jay fell to the floor, landing on his arse and smacking his head on the bed frame.

Around him, he saw stars and haze as a dull ache passed through his head. Jade and Rucksack stared, and Jay looked where they looked. The ache faded as he stared.

*I was so intent on getting rid of it, so scared of how impossible the thing was,* he thought. *I never let myself see how beautiful it is.*

In between them, about the size of a small cabbage, a globe floated.

Jay recognized the continents from all the maps he'd studied over the years. Asia, complete with the Indian subcontinent, stared back at him. Clouds floated over the land and the oceans rippled, their colors contrasting sharply. As the little globe turned, part of it shimmered in bright daylight, and part of it slumbered under night's dark blanket. Golden points of light twinkled against the black continents.

"Is that..." Jade started to ask.

"Yes," Rucksack replied. "It's the world."

RUCKSACK'S FACE fell faster than a glass knocked off a table. "Jade," he said. "Someone could show up here at any moment, and we could do with some privacy. Since the pub is closed, is there any chance we could continue this discussion over a pint?"

"You want a drink at a time like this?" Jay said.

"It's actually a good idea," Jade replied. "As Rucksack likes to point out, nothing makes the world clear like darkest beer. You could do with seeing a bit more clearly."

"What about you?" Jay asked.

"I don't actually drink," she said, shaking her head. "It's a... company policy thing."

Jay raised an eyebrow as he shut the globe back into his daypack.

In the empty pub, Jade turned on the lights, poured

pints of GPS for Jay and Rucksack, and made herself a cup of coffee.

Rucksack took a pull from his pint. "Let's see that world again."

Jay pulled the globe out of his daypack and set it above the table, floating in between the three of them. The little world spun slowly and silently. Jay told them about Everest, the strange impossible night, his fleeing to India, and his various attempts to get rid of the globe.

"I don't understand," Jay said. "How is something like this even possible? And why me?"

"It'd take someone far wiser than me to explain how it's possible," Rucksack said. "But I said I'd tell you all I can, and that's what I'll do. Just give me a moment to figure out where to begin."

Jade stared hard at the globe. *This is what the world looks like from space,* she thought. *If I were standing on the moon and looking back to Earth, this is what I would see, only bigger. Is this little world populated with teeny tiny versions of us and everyone else in the world? Do they have any idea that they live in a traveler's backpack?*

*If this is the world but in miniature,* Jade thought, *then what are we living and walking and traveling on?* She looked at the ceiling. *How do I know we're not living in a backpack too? A cosmic pack, flung around the universe by some itinerant being, some itchy-footed god who now and again takes us out and looks at us like a souvenir?*

"It's been a long, long time since there was one of these around," Rucksack began. "They're rare beyond belief. When one appears, it means big changes for the world. The appearance is striking. It really is like a wee world, though as I understand it, it's more just a visual reminder."

"A reminder of what?" Jade asked.

"That the world is at stake," Rucksack replied. "Every bit of it, from land to life."

They all stared at the globe, then Rucksack continued. "You'll find something like this carved and depicted all over the planet: a small world, floating over a person or a group o' people. Though it's not really a world. In any language, culture, or mythology, it's always described as an egg, but the proper name is *dia ubh*. That's me native Irish. It means 'god egg.'"

"Eggs crack," Jay said.

Rucksack nodded. "And eggs contain a force of life, though in this case it's far more than a tasty breakfast. When a dia ubh opens, it shines a great golden light. At that time, the world stands on a razor's edge. If a force o' good and love stands within that light, great kindness and learning happen in the world. If a force o' evil and hate stands within that light, great destruction falls. When a dia ubh opens—and before you know it, this will open—the world's destiny has brought us to a moment of decision."

"What kind of decision?" Jay asked.

"The choice is what the choice always has been and always will be," Rucksack said. "Life or death. Continuance or final destruction. Yes or no."

"The egg," Jay said. "The dia ubh... It brought me here, didn't it?"

"I think it did, Jay."

"I suddenly wanted a change of scene, but I hadn't been considering India until I arrived here. At least, something was considering India, but it wasn't me." Jay drank more of his stout. "Do you know when the dia ubh will open?"

Rucksack shook his head.

Jade looked from one man to the other. "I can guess," she said. "We're having an eclipse in two months."

Rucksack nodded. "Aye, that's our most likely time."

"Why did this come to me?" Jay said. "I'm just a traveler. I'm no saint. I'm no hero. I've never done anything of note or merit. At one time I was just a working guy in Idaho. Then... Then I started traveling. I've eaten with the locals, haggled for souvenirs, paid unofficial fees for visas, and drunk oceans of beer in various countries. That's all I've done. There's no reason for something like this to come to me."

As Jade looked from Jay to Rucksack, a light seemed to catch fire in the brown-and-black eyes. "Merit does not always play into the world's decisions," Rucksack said. "The greatest loves and choices often come from the unlikeliest people. One day they find themselves on a path they didn't know they were taking, and they simply do the best they can. Sometimes life's best hope is the most improbable chance."

"This came to me because I was such an unlikely choice?"

"It doesn't always happen that way. But in this case, I would say so."

"Am I supposed to be the one who stands in the light?" Jay asked.

"It could be," Rucksack said. "But that isn't for certain. For all I know, you could have been nothing more than the most convenient way for the dia ubh to get here. We probably won't know for sure until the day it opens."

"What happens to the person who stands in the light?" Jade asked.

"Many things can happen," said an ancient voice behind them.

Jade and the others turned around. An old woman stood by the mahogany doors at the front of the pub.

"The light brings out the person's truest self, amplifies it, and makes that all of who you are. Some say it can make gods. Some say it can destroy the world. All these things are probably true."

*What the hell is she doing here?* Jade thought.

The old woman had a wrinkled face and a stooped back. Jade stared hard at her now. When the woman first came to her, her helix had looked normal. But now it was obscured from Jade's sight, as if by a cloud or a haze.

Adrenalin tapped into Jade's body. Her mind tightened in on itself. *Stay focused,* she thought. *There's enough impossible and crazy happening here without the Jade of Agamuskara losing her cool.*

"Those doors were locked," she said, her voice flat, despite her pounding heart. "And it's not your day to clean."

"They are still locked," the old woman replied. "Your Management can continue to feel proud of their security. But there are things in this world older than locks. Older than The Management. And there are ways into a place other than doors."

"I should've asked for references," Jade replied.

"Who is she?" Rucksack asked. "How do you know her?"

"Remember when I told you an old woman named Kailash had been helping me with the cleaning around here?" Jade said. "Faddah Rucksack, meet Kailash. Kailash, meet Faddah Rucksack and Jay."

"Not the old woman you thought I was," Kailash replied as she hobbled toward the table.

Jade blew out a sharp breath. "I do prefer truthfulness when people work for me. You said you needed extra money and asked me for work."

"Why would you think I was lying?" Kailash said. The playfulness in her steady tone made her sound younger. "In this world, one can always do with extra money, especially when you're an old woman who doesn't know how long she has left in this life. But being truthful is not the same thing as telling an entire truth."

"Are you here to keep an eye on the pub?" Jade said. "Have you been watching me? Did The Management send you?"

"No, no, and no, Jade Agamuskara Bluegold," Kailash said. "I've known The Management for a long time, but they did not send for me, though they are perfectly aware that I'm here. They just clearly did not see a need to inform you. As for what I've been watching?"

Kailash locked her eyes on Jay. "I've been watching for you. Waiting for you to finally become curious about the dia ubh. It's about time you started being more accepting of the things that have happened to you, and of the things that are going to happen to you. I've been trying to get you to do that for years."

"What are you talking about?" Jay asked.

"I'm named for the world mountain," Kailash replied. "The mountain that moves. The mountain that is bigger than Everest, though some say I am Everest, am Qomolangma, the world mother. But I am not Qomolangma. I am only Kailash. I am old, if not quite so old as the world mountains. But Kailash is the mountain of the soul, the axis around which the world turns, that sits in Tibet and shares my name. The mountain that is small enough to fit in your dreams, and that you have seen in every mountain range and behind every stretch of hills ever since you started traveling."

"That's an impressive speech," Jay said, a smirk growing on his face. "Are you going to talk as long as a mountain is tall?"

"You certainly thought the mountain was impressive in Ireland," Kailash replied. "It wasn't only the white sign that surprised you so."

Jay's smirk vanished.

"The mountain has followed you everywhere," Kailash continued. "The full moon has spoken with you. You carried the dia ubh, just like you were asked to do. Thank you."

Jay shook his head. "How do you know about that?"

But Kailash talked over him, and he fell silent. "To speak only of Jay is not enough to convince all of you. After all, I'm just an old woman who showed up unexpectedly," she said, looking from Jay to Jade. "But tell me, Jade Agamuskara Bluegold, has any day of your life been more important than the day of the blue dragon?"

The pulse of Jade's adrenalin flashed into a flood. She saw it all again: the strange gardens, the blue dragon carved into the wall, the outstretched hand where the ring's blue-and-green stone glinted in the afternoon light. And then the world had stopped. *The*

*Management appeared,* Jade thought, *and I chose duty over love.*

"No," Jade said. "Everything in my life changed that day." Wetness stung her eyes and she looked away.

"Two out of three is very good," Rucksack said.

"I'm glad you approve, my dear boy," Kailash replied. "You are wily and not easy to impress. You are old too, I know, but compared to me you are still a child. I have failed only twice of three times, though. Your disbelief will not be my last failure."

Jade dried her eyes and turned back to the people in the room. *I've never seen anything like this.*

She stared hard at Kailash. The longer Kailash spoke, the younger her voice sounded. The old woman's dark brown skin reminded Jade of earth and trees, with hints of sunset and gold. When she was young, Jade realized, she was beyond beautiful. Even now, as Jade looked at her, the old woman didn't seem as old as before.

*Did I simply get caught up in the idea of her being an old woman?*

"Never made claim to being the most ancient slightly-not-human in the world," Rucksack said, staring hard at Kailash. "But you're not yet rocking me with your specialized knowledge."

Kailash smiled. "Maybe because as you aren't sure who I am, I am not entirely sure who you are either. How can you be who you say you are when everyone knows Faddah Rucksack died in The Blast?"

Rucksack held her stare. "My parents died in The Blast, along with millions of others. If you want proof of who I am, I can tell you that my father died first. I thought I could shield my mother with my body, but the way she screamed... Before the world went black for me, her scream was the last thing I heard."

"That does sound like Faddah Rucksack," Kailash said. "If so, there's something you can tell me."

"What's that?"

"What did your mother wear around her neck that day?"

Rucksack replied without hesitation. "I still see it in my mind every day. Around her neck was a silver-and-gold necklace with a simple pendant of a rare jade that shimmered both blue and green. She always said—"

"She always said," Kalish interjected, "that this rare jade was found only in the Heart of the World, deep in the Himalaya, where she had grown up. The necklace was lost after The Blast, just as she was lost to you."

As Kailash spoke of Rucksack's mother, Jade saw that the woman now looked like a mother herself. Her face had smoothed over, but lines of worry and laughter were lightly etched around her eyes and mouth. Her breasts seemed full of milk. Kailash's back was no longer stooped under the weight of time. She stood like a queen. A fire burned in her brown-and-black eyes.

Rucksack said nothing, and silence fell over the pub. At last, Rucksack looked at each of them, and he stared again at Kailash. "You know who we are. Who are you?"

"You're not ready yet," Kailash replied. "I am sorry I have to come to you now. I had not wanted to reveal myself, but it was destined to be otherwise. I will tell you only that I am here to help and that if we are to survive what is to come then we must trust one another."

"What changed?" Jade asked.

Kailash nodded at Jay. "He carried the dia ubh past the guardian—first yesterday and now today too. He should not have been able to pass at all. There are old protections there that should have prevented this, but they did not work. The guardian was there to prevent passage of anyone who sought to wake the Smiling Fire, and that was our failure."

"But Jay walked down the alley today," Jade said.

"No," Kailash replied. "He first walked into the alley yesterday."

Rucksack nodded. "Asha."

"Yes," Kailash said. "When he came to the alley, it was with concern for another in his heart. The protections could not stop him because his intent was pure. But his pure intentions could not prevent what happened, though he did not intend it. All these years and it all is undone by an accident."

For a moment, Kailash seemed old again, weak and bent. But with a breath the strong mother reappeared.

"The Smiling Fire felt the presence of the dia ubh, the first to arrive here in many generations," she said. "It woke hope in his flaming heart. Even now I can feel him gathering strength."

"What are you talking about?" Jade asked. "What is this Smiling Fire?"

"When the world was new, born in fire and heat, there was a being that lived in the world. How he came to be, I don't know. But he dominated the world, bent its forces to his will. He wandered the world and had a grin that was as of flame. Nameless, he became known as the Smiling Fire."

Jay sat up. "Isn't that what 'Agamuskara' means?"

"Yes," Kailash said. "The Smiling Fire made the volcanoes pour lava. He made the seas boil. He made the sunlight blaze over the world. He craved all fire, and he hungered for it to burn in himself and only for himself. He succeeded, too. He had things exactly as he wanted them. Until the day life appeared."

"I've heard similar stories," Rucksack said, nodding to Kailash. "All life has a spark to it, a fire o' its own. You, me, everyone. Every bacteria and bovine. Everything. And our little fires, when they first started burning in the world, weren't the Smiling Fire's. Whatever that first primordial goop was that came to life in this world, it was like dunking the Smiling Fire in the coldest part of the Arctic Ocean. He wasn't as warm anymore. Beyond that, he was furious that there was a fire o' life outside his control."

"So, let me get this straight," Jay said. "From the beginning of the world, there's been some sort of devil thing that ruled the world, hated living things, and wanted all the fire of life for itself."

"I wouldn't call him a devil," Rucksack said. "Brings too much religious credence to someone who was really just a non-mortal feckin bastard with a mean streak."

"Every time we've learned of life nearly going extinct due to volcanoes, asteroid impacts, you name it," Kailash said, "that being was behind it. He strove to extinguish all life."

"But you say 'strove,'" Jade said. "Is this being no longer alive?"

"If only," Kailash replied. "For eons, the Smiling Fire has battled life, seeking always to take back control of all the fires of life. Sometimes he has come close, and life has hung on by the barest thread of existence. Always life has rebounded. Eventually, humans began to flourish. As you may know, for many generations humans wandered the world. Thousands of years ago, this region was one of the first parts of India to be settled by nomads. They made their home here, along the river in what would in time become Agamuskara. They were peaceful people but hardy.

"Like many others, they had encountered the Smiling Fire before. As life proliferated and endured, despite his attempts, life kept getting stronger. And he kept getting weaker. But the Smiling Fire still could strike out. Yet for many years, there was no sign of the Smiling Fire. Those early settlers hoped they could now tend their crops and animals in peace, and raise children in a world where life was no longer constantly under such a threat."

"But it never goes that way," Jade said.

A sorrow fell over Kailash's eyes. "No, it doesn't. One day in the village, beneath the dark light of a mirror eclipse, the Smiling Fire appeared. A tall slender figure he was, as if your longest shadow had stood up from the ground. Wreathed in black, as if his clothes and flesh were made of smoke and shadow, he murdered dozens of villagers, consumed them and their fires of life, before the alarm was even raised."

"And this happened here?" Jay asked.

Kailash nodded. "Not far from where we are now, just outside of the main city. Back then, a woman and a man led the village, and they quickly gathered together everyone who had survived. You see, over the years, humans had learned much about battling the Smiling Fire, and people knew powers then that are long forgotten now. Humans could sense when life became precarious, but so great had been the Smiling Fire's concealment and silence that none knew the growing threat against them until it was too late. That day in the village, all learned that over the long years the Smiling Fire had regained enough of his former power to once again threaten the world. He came to strike the first of his last blows against life. The village was life's only chance. If the Smiling Fire killed the villagers—especially the woman who was pregnant and soon to give birth—then the Smiling Fire would be powerful enough to destroy all life. And this time, he would succeed."

Kailash paused a moment, closing and opening her eyes as if some great pain and sorrow were washing over her. Jade studied her carefully. She began to look even younger. And there was no doubt now. Before their very eyes, Kailash's appearance had changed. There was even something familiar about her.

"The Smiling Fire surprised everyone that day," Kailash said. "No defense held him. He swooped in fast, beyond the eye's ability to follow. Soon he held the woman leader against him. A heat radiated from him, like a walking volcano. Once he had consumed her fire of life, and the growing spark of the child inside her, he would be unstoppable.

"The villagers were helpless. The man leader looked long at her face, and a rage of love burned in him, but he could not help her. The woman leader too was helpless. The Smiling Fire was stronger than life. He stood tall, one arm like a shadow wrapped around her swollen belly and his other hand pressed against her head like a sun. Behind her, his mouth opened and he made ready to devour her. And then," Kailash said, laying her right hand over her stomach, "the woman's unborn child kicked at the Smiling Fire's arm."

Jade's gaze went to Rucksack and Jay. Jay sat straight and wide-eyed, like a child at a campfire listening to a story. But Rucksack was pale, and his hands clenched the tabletop. His glass was empty.

"If you've never felt a baby kick you through the womb," Kailash said, "it is quite a surprise. It surprised even the Smiling Fire. His hold on the woman loosened. And she, feeling not only the threat to herself and the world but the threat to her unborn child, turned and struck with a ferocious love.

"It was a desperate blow, but it was her only chance. The world's only chance. Her baby's only chance. She called up the old powers but also her hopes for herself and her beloved, her hopes for her child, her love of life and the world. She aimed as best she could at the Smiling Fire's chest, and her aim was true. She reached through, plunging her hand into smoke and shadows. She clenched her fingers tight and pulled. When her hand emerged it was as if she held all the fire and light in the world. The Smiling Fire sagged and she caught him. On his knees, he looked up at her. A chill came from him, as if he were made of ice.

"'For all you burn,'" she said, "and for all you do not know, I pity you and your empty, hungry smiles.'

"'This world is mine,' he replied. 'You stole it from me!'

"'This world is ours as well as yours, but you want

all of it only for you.'

"'The heat! I must have the fire!'

"'The fire is not yours. The fire is not ours. The fire of life belongs to itself. We belong to it, not to you.'

"'So... cold...'

"'Cold you must remain, as long as you believe this world is for you and for you alone.'

"'Kill me, then. So cold. Kill me.'

"But the woman shook her head and said simply, 'We are not you.' She leaned down and kissed his forehead. He slumped onto the ground, which despite the heat in the day felt cold as the Himalayas. Then she stood tall, looked at her hand, and smiled. She raised her arm and opened her fingers.

"A small globe, the first dia ubh, floated in the air. At first it looked like the world. Then, under the gray light of the mirror eclipse, the dia ubh itself turned gray and a crack ran down it.

"The dia ubh opened, and warm, golden light poured down on all who remained. The woman, the man, the surviving villagers—even the unborn child. Many things changed in the world that day, but especially us. We no longer aged as normal people. We were not gods, but in many ways we could act and live as gods. In each of us, our purest essence of self shone forth, and we were remade in that image," Kalish concluded.

"What happened to the Smiling Fire?" Rucksack asked.

"Jay has seen it," Kailash replied. "The black wall at the heart of the city. From the ground we raised obsidian, the black glass made from the world's fires. We made both a temple and a prison. A temple where the Smiling Fire could be remembered. That was my first failure. The world has forgotten. There are songs sung by those who do not know what they mean. A river and a city carry a name that should be writ like flame on the soul. But these memories have fallen out of us or burned to ash.

"But inside the temple, we dug deep into the earth, past the crust that sustains us, and into the molten rock that flows around the core of the world. There, we made a chamber of obsidian, with a black pedestal where the Smiling Fire could lay. We had no desire to kill him. Killing and destroying were all he knew and all he was. It may be that even then, weak as he was, we could not destroy him totally. We knew only that we were changed, and we feared that killing the Smiling Fire would be the first step on a path to becoming like him. In time, we hoped that perhaps this being of fire and hatred could find a way to coexist with life and love. We laid him on his pedestal, and but for one message we left him to the smooth black walls, deep in the earth, where he could still feel warmth."

"What was the message?" Rucksack asked.

Kailash smiled. "A reminder," she said. "I carved the words myself: 'Life belongs to the world, and the world belongs to life.' Then we shut him in his prison. But that has been my second failure. Either his penitence or the presence of a dia ubh could allow him to leave his prison and go inside the main temple above the ground. Now he is in the temple. I can feel his dampened fires, his chills, his hatred. There is no change in him—only the desire to resume where he left off, to try again, to find a way to succeed this time."

"This is the greatest story ever," Jay said. "And you were there."

Kailash shrugged.

"You couldn't be," Rucksack said.

Jade understood. "You've spoken for a long time," she said. "Let me get you a glass of water with lime."

The mother had become younger, but the metamorphosis had stopped. Her figure had tightened and the lines around the eyes had softened. Before everyone stood the woman who had fled the pub the night before and had vanished before Jade and Rucksack earlier.

The scent of jasmine filled the air.

"I am thirsty," Kailash said, "and I was there in the village so long ago, under the mirror eclipse on the day the Smiling Fire fell but was not vanquished." She touched her stomach again. "You see, Faddah Rucksack, you never remembered me from when I was this young. I may have never found my pendant, but on the day of The Blast, you did save me. Just as those long years ago, when you saved not only me, but the world—and all before you were even born."

"THERE IS NO CHANGE. I'm sorry. She may simply need more time. She has not been here long. But we cannot yet say if she will ever wake up again."

The doctor squeezed Jigme's shoulder as he left, but the doctor's face recoiled with surprise when he looked Jigme in the eye. The door closed, leaving Jigme and Asha alone in a dim room full of deep shadows.

Jigme pulled a chair over to his mother's bedside. Her hand had a fire inside, yet at the same time it felt cool as wet stone. The elation from the alley still held a grin over Jigme's face, but as he looked at his mother, that grin, that elation seemed smaller now, less sure. The powerful certainty that had all but flown him here had faded the moment he saw his mother, as unmoving as the statues all over the city.

The doctor's words echoed in Jigme's mind. He squeezed his mother's hand. "I believe you can come back, Amma," he said. "I would give anything to help you come back."

He sat back in the chair and watched his mother. Time passed but he did not follow time. The room darkened but he turned on no lights. *Rucksack said he would come,* Jigme thought. *Why isn't he here?*

A deep longing welled up inside. *Speaking with Rucksack must be what it's like to speak with a father,* Jigme thought. *I wish he were here. The world seems so much bigger and brighter when Rucksack is around.*

But there was no Rucksack, and his mother was as a shell.

In time, as shadows consumed the room, Jigme let himself slump back in the chair. He still held his mother's hand as his eyes closed.

The alley no longer had white walls—or rather, the walls held the memory of white but no longer could show them as white. The shadows had consumed all the light and brightness here too. Only the black wall at the end of the alley seemed real now; the rest appeared as insubstantial as a burning dream.

The two statues stood as silent as Asha lay. The gray globes seemed to hover just above the hands that no longer held them.

When he was here with Jay earlier, Jigme had been so afraid, but he no longer understood why he'd been afraid. Jay had been brash, and he did not know what he had done. Jigme understood now. He stood between the statues, reached out his hands, and touched each globe, all the while staring ahead at the black, featureless wall in front of him. It had already begun.

Jay had changed the world.

The alley and the statues vanished. Even the black wall was gone. Vertigo passed through Jigme. *Where am I?* he thought. *There's nothing here. It's like I'm nowhere.*

His vision began to adjust, and he realized the black wall wasn't gone. He saw more black walls, a black ceiling, and a black floor with a rectangular hole in the middle. The chamber glowed with a red-and-black light like coals in a campfire.

*I've gone where Jay couldn't,* Jigme thought. A spark of excitement flared in him. *Who's brave now, Jay?*

*The black wall isn't gone,* he realized. *I'm on the other side now.*

The walls of the dim room were as featureless inside as they were outside. The floor showed no lines of age, wear, or stonecutting. Other than the hole, there was only a continuous sheet of black stone. It was like he was walking on a void. The ceiling was a starless night from which there would be no dawn.

*What is this place?*

Jigme moved forward.

*But I didn't walk,* he thought. *I hadn't moved...*

Still he shuffled, not conscious of moving, as if his body and mind were wrapped in the grasp of a powerful force.

"It has come," said a voice that wasn't Jigme's.

*Who's here?* Jigme said—or thought he said. *I can't actually speak in here,* he realized. *I have no voice. Only thought. What does it mean to have no voice?*

"It has freed me. It is time."

A wall got closer and closer as the shuffling seemed to speed up. Just before the wall, the shuffling stopped. Something raised itself. Jigme guessed it was an arm, but it was indistinct, as if made of shadow and smoke. At the end of the arm, something raw, red, and black reached out to touch the wall.

A doorway, tall and rectangular, opened out onto the world. Jigme glimpsed the alley again. The backs of the two statues were before him now. The world outside the chamber seemed dimmer, farther away, as if the very walls were shrinking back from the thing in the doorway. A deep, rasping noise reminded Jigme of someone taking a deep breath. "Life steals the fires," said the voice, like steel scraping rock, like wood popping as it burned. "But the fires will be mine again."

The creature lifted what seemed to be a foot, raw-fleshed and swathed in shadow and smoke. It took a step over the threshold and touched down outside the black walls.

"Free again," said the voice, with a noise that seemed at once like laughing and coughing.

All around Jigme, triumph swelled like a new flame, bigger than the Himalayas, a pyre ready to burn the world.

"'Life belongs to the world, and the world belongs to life,'" said the voice. The laugh rasped louder. "But both belong to me."

Jigme wondered what would happen when the wave of flame crashed down and flooded the city like a river wild and swollen.

The creature started to step over the threshold into the outside world. But as it did, a chill crept into the laugh and froze it into silence.

"No," said the voice.

Around Jigme, the flame shuddered. A chill swept through the chamber. Jigme shivered.

"The cold!" shrieked the voice. "Colder! So much life! My fires. It has stolen them all!"

The world shifted again.

*No, not the world,* Jigme thought. *The creature. It's falling. It's as if the world is killing it. It said "life," but how can life suck the life out of another living thing?*

The creature tottered forward, its frail body careening over the threshold. *If it falls out of this place and into the world,* Jigme thought, *it will die. Life will kill it.*

He didn't know why, but he thought only of leaping backward, of tugging and pulling the creature with him, back inside the chamber. The creature kept falling.

*It doesn't matter,* Jigme thought. *He's going to die and I can't save him.*

Something shifted in the creature's fall. Instead of landing outside in the alley, the creature fell backward into the chamber. The doorway closed. The creature lay on the floor in a ragged pile, writhing and twisting like smoke in a breeze.

"The cold!" he shrieked. "The cold!"

The shriek became a wail, but the wail soon faded into a sputtering cough. *Last breaths,* Jigme thought.

*He's still dying.*

Jigme's thoughts turned to his mother, all but lifeless in her hospital bed. *I would do anything to save her. Isn't this pitiful creature also worth saving? What has he done, other than want to walk outside? There's only me,* he thought. *Only I can save him. But how?*

He stared at the creature. It thrashed less and less, weaker with every moment. *I'm not in his mind anymore,* Jigme realized. *I'm standing next to him.*

A feeling surged through Jigme, like power and responsibility, strength and maturity.

*Purpose,* he thought. *This is how purpose burns.*

With the thought came the understanding. With the understanding, Jigme found his voice again.

He kneeled on the ground next to the writhing, shrieking smoke.

"I will help you," he said, reaching out his hand. All his fears were ash. All his hopes blazed higher than the flame that for a moment had seemed bigger than the Himalayas. Jigme touched the creature. He felt his strength, the fire of his life, siphon into it.

The thrashing stopped.

*Did he die?* Jigme thought. *Did I fail to save him?*

Grief and relief moved through Jigme, distinct and raw, yet each also resisted the other.

Jigme was overcome with lightheartedness. The dark place swirled. His vision faded in and out.

When the world came into focus again, the chamber was sideways. He had been standing, Jigme realized, but now the floor was cold against his cheek. His strength continued to pour into the still creature.

*Am I dying too?* Jigme thought. The world seemed to fade. Jigme's self felt like it was passing from his life, his body, to the creature.

Then the world snapped back. Jigme opened his eyes but could barely move. The world was firm again. Strength trickled into him. He sat up. A chill ached in the hand that had touched the creature.

Smoke and shadow no longer writhed and swirled. *I feel so weak,* Jigme thought. *Was I not enough?*

He waited, staring.

Nothing moved. He started to look away.

A red-and-black smile began to gleam.

Like the door of a furnace slowly rising, a thin curved line shone out. Then the line grew taller, brighter, and wider. The heat from the smile seared Jigme's skin, and a strange burning smell came from Jigme's eyebrows.

Jigme sat on his knees, afraid to look up. The creature rose, tall, slender, wrapped in shadow and smoke. The curved line of fire seemed like both a blazing smile and an impaling stare.

"You will serve," said the same voice, rough and rasping yet stronger now.

Jigme said nothing in reply, only felt the corners of his mouth stretch. As the grin widened, his skin and muscles burned from the tension, as if he were smiling too big for his face.

A faraway voice, gentle and warm, said, "Jigme?"

His smile continued stretching. Just when he thought the pain of it would make him cry out, the black walls, the hole in the floor, and the fiery smile all vanished.

Jigme opened his eyes, not sure how much time had passed or how far he had moved. *Too much light in here,* he thought. He closed his eyes tight again.

"Jigme?" repeated the voice.

He opened his eyes once more and kept them open. Morning light poured into the hospital room. His hand tingled as if he had touched something freezing, but the only thing he was touching was his mother's hand, which he still grasped tightly.

"Jigme?" he heard once more. The voice sounded both strange and familiar, as if known but not heard for so long he'd begun to forget.

He looked to his mother's face, into her wide, bright, open eyes.

Asha smiled.


As Jade locked the door behind Rucksack and Kailash, the click reminded her that she was now alone in the pub with Jay.

She turned to see him standing behind her, looking at her. A fire flared through her body. The shock of it nearly made her look away, but instead she held his gaze.

*So much life blazes in those eyes*, she thought, *and right now there's so much happening to him. To me. To us.*

She could all but see it, the big weight of the world that had fallen into his pack. *I don't know the how of it all —this Smiling Fire, The Mystery Chickpea's absence, Jay's stolen passport—but Rucksack and Kailash and I are part of it too. There's so much I should say to reassure Jay. Tell him that yes, this is all overwhelming, but... But what?* she thought. *Yes, it's overwhelming, but he has so much to rely on? What does he have to rely on? His backpack? Rucksack? Me?*

*Yes. Maybe he has me.*

"Are you okay?" Jay asked.

"Me?" Jade replied, but nothing followed. No witty bartender repartee. No one-liner. Nothing.

"I know I'm pretty freaked out right now," Jay said. "I've hardly been here twenty-four hours, and it's like my entire world has changed. But you look more scared than I feel."

Jade nodded. "We just saw a woman grow from old to young before our eyes. It turns out you're carrying some sort of divine egg that accidentally woke up an ancient evil that wants to wipe out all life on the planet. Rucksack and his mother are not only ancient; they're not quite human yet not quite gods."

*And I really, really like looking in your eyes,* she added but managed not to say. "It's a lot to take in." *And I'm a Jade,* she thought. *Weird is my world. But this is beyond me. Can even The Management cope with this? Or is it beyond all of us?*

"When you haven't seen each other in nearly two centuries," Jay said, "how long does it take to catch up?"

Jade chuckled. The fear blooming in her seemed smaller, less potent, less overwhelming. *He can make me laugh,* she thought. *I like that.* "Who knows when we'll see them next."

"Who exactly is Rucksack?" Jay asked.

"Clearly more than either of us understands."

"True," Jay replied. "I can't help but really like the guy. There's something about him... like... like a brother."

"Do you have siblings?" Jade asked.

He shook his head.

"He's not like what a brother is," Jade said. "He's

what a brother should be."

Jay's eyes widened. "So, you're not..."

"Not what?"

"You know." Redness crept over Jay's face. "Involved. You and Rucksack."

Jade grinned then sputtered. A huge laugh burst out of her. No chuckle, this time. She doubled over, as belly laughs rolled out of her. Tears welled up and fell on her cheeks. *Did I just slap my knee?* she thought.

"Is that a no?" Jay said.

Jade nodded. The laughter slowed to a trickle then faded out. "That's a no," she replied. "Rucksack is fascinating, and there's a fair bit we have in common. We're more like siblings and colleagues. But romance? No. It'd be like dating my brother."

"A really, really, really older brother," Jay said.

The laughs poured out of her again. When she looked up, a bright hope glimmered in Jay's eyes.

"I have an idea," he said.

She cleared her throat and tried to reassert her usual resolve. "Does it involve leaving town?"

He shook his head. "I can't leave without my passport."

*Oh crap,* she thought. *He's going to want to go out and hunt for it now. And he has no idea what he's dealing with. I don't even understand these Mim and Pim guys. He could have a dozen god-eggs in his pack and he wouldn't stand a chance. What a... What a man,* she thought. *Can't he see the way I look him in the eye? Can't he tell that he makes me laugh and how rare that is?*

Jay shook his head again. "I want my passport back, but I'm not going to find it tonight. Tomorrow I can look for it. Maybe it's tied up in all this other weirdness. No, I was thinking of something else."

"Okay." *Smarter than I gave him credit for,* she thought.

"The pub is closed tonight," Jay said. "We've had a day beyond crazy. Could I... Could I buy you dinner, and we just... you know, stay here, talk, have a bite to eat?"

She smiled. "That sounds perfect." They stood closer. In the pub light, his eyes reminded her of dew-covered grass in early morning sunlight. *He really makes me laugh,* she thought.

"I," he said, a quiver in his voice. "I'm not asking you out or anything."

*Bugger that,* Jade thought. Her fingers brushed his hand. "Maybe you should be."

Jay moved closer. "You're a tough woman to read," he said. "Strong. I can see where a lot of men would be scared as hell of you."

Jade took another step forward. "Are you scared of me?" *His lips look really soft,* she thought.

"I am," Jay said. "You are a little scary. I've never known anyone like you."

Now they stood only a few inches apart.

"My dad once told me it takes a strong man to love a strong woman," Jay said. "If I've learned anything from the road, it's that fearing something is a chance to become stronger."

He leaned forward. His lips were so near. Jade realized their eyes were closing.

A soft *pthump* made them open their eyes and step back.

"What was that?" Jay asked.

*What the hell do they possibly need to tell me right now?*

Jade thought.

"Jade?"

"Oh," she replied, her mind trying to work again. "Something behind the bar must have slipped." She touched his arm. "You're right about dinner," she said. "Let's freshen up a little first. You bring the food. I'll do the drinks."

He opened his mouth, but Jade ended his protest before he could speak. "I insist," she said with a grin. "My pub. My rules. And I make the best drinks in Asia. Whatever you want."

"Okay then," Jay said. "Your best single-malt scotch."

"How do you take it?"

Jay leaned in close again. "I thought you were the best bartender in Asia." A small smile curved up his lips. "You tell me."

"You're on," Jade replied. "See you soon."

Jay went out first, through the side door and up to his room. Jade lingered a moment, staring at the special cabinet. She thought of the note in her back pocket, and defiance swept through her. *It's my day off,* she thought. *You can bloody well wait.*

After freshening up in her room, Jade decided to change clothes. She took the note out of her pocket and read it again:

```
The new traveler is not just the new
traveler. He and the world must remain
in Agamuskara until the eclipse, so he
can be as a sunrise that never ends.
When the time is right, you must make
```

him forget himself and follow what he
would never follow.

*Maybe it's time to let that go,* she thought. She set the note on her desk and waited.

The paper remained.

*No,* she thought, *you disappear. You always disappear.*

The paper stubbornly continued to exist.

Jade shook her head. *You're not going to worry about this right now,* she thought. *You're going to get ready to have dinner with Jay.*

She looked away from the paper and opened her small closet. She flipped through her bartender's white button-down shirts, a two-piece *salwar kameez*, some t-shirts, pants, skirts, the sari, and...

*Ah,* she thought. *What every traveling woman needs.*

If the black silk dress had feelings, it would have been mad at her for neglect. Jade tried to think of the last time she'd worn it, and she cringed at how long it had been. But time had been merciful. The dress looked fine and it smelled softly of the sandalwood sachets she kept in the closet. She put the dress on in front of the mirror.

The flowing silk moved with Jade—not tight, but fitted just enough to accentuate her curves. The A-line skirt flared out above her knees, and it swished with every move of her hips. Bare up to the cap sleeves at her shoulders, Jade's golden-brown arms shone in the light. The front of the dress dipped into a slight V-neck.

She wore no make-up and shook out her hair so that it lay loosely over her shoulders. Looking closer at herself in the mirror, Jade knew her body had hardly changed in ten years, but how she looked at herself, how she felt in her body had changed.

Jade knew her movements were strong and precise, capable and powerful. But sensual? Aside from some rumors about Jake Bangkok, Jakes and Jades weren't exactly known for being romantic. The solitude, the apartness, the sense of duty all had a way of leeching away one's attractiveness or sense of sexuality.

*I haven't tried to look like this in a long time,* Jade thought. *Will he notice?*

After slipping on a pair of strappy black short heels, she went back into the pub. Jay hadn't returned yet, but he probably wouldn't be much longer.

She stopped.

Her gaze went to the top shelf behind the bar, where the best liquors were kept. She looked, comparing what she saw to how the shelf had been stocked before.

*Ah.*

The bottle of scotch hadn't been there before.

Its simple label barely covered the clear glass and amber liquid, which was renowned as the best single-malt scotch in the world. When a special circumstance didn't leave time for their usual distribution, The Management delivered something like this from out of nowhere. Once, she recalled, a bottle had appeared before her very eyes while she was standing on a stool and dusting the top shelf. The shock had nearly made her fall.

After taking down the bottle, Jade's gaze went to the cabinet.

*There's no way they sent this as a good luck token.*

The note was as simple as before. Jade often

wondered which directives came on the paper she had made during the training. She was certain this sheet was one of hers; something about the patterns and layers of the fibers pulled at her memory. But all that fell away as she read:

```
The traveler must forget himself and
follow what he would never follow. The
heart is not the path.
```

*As strange as the first,* she thought as she read the lines again. Clearly it was time for Jay to follow the right destiny that was before him. He seemed on it already, with so many circumstances conspiring to keep him in Agamuskara until the day of the eclipse. But there was more.

As she read, her surprise and unease grew.

Usually, The Management gave nothing but their vague, somewhat poetic, somewhat awkward instructions, leaving the Jake or Jade to supply the correct influence. It was unusual for them to send a recipe, much less one so specific.

Her eyes got bigger as she read. She was to combine three elixirs for his drink; usually only one was needed.

*I've never had to combine more than two before,* she thought. *What the hell is it about this guy?*

She decided to keep this note too, folding the paper and tucking it down the front of her dress.

Part of her mind tugged her to think more about the line, "the heart is not the path," but she ignored it. Duty was duty. A Jade was a Jade. And a Jade was duty.

"We serve because we love," they had said during

the training.

*There is no question of disobeying,* Jade thought. *We obey because we love. To disobey would be as futile as telling our hearts not to beat.*

But it no longer seemed that simple anymore.

*At least,* she thought, *it used to be that way for me.* She stared at the note. *Why is this right?* She shook her head.

*It's right because it's what must be done.*

Jade took down a small tulip-shaped glass—the best way to present the scotch's aroma—and poured in the exact amounts of each of the three elixirs in the order specified by The Management. After putting away the elixirs, Jade set the glass down on the bar next to the bottle of scotch.

*What will this combination of decision and destiny do to Jay?* she wondered. *What path is it keeping him on? What effect will it have on his traveling, on that look in his eyes?*

A knock on the outside door made Jade look up. *Whatever happens, we've still got tonight,* she thought. *The rest is destiny.*

She poured a dram of scotch into the glass, followed by a slight trickle of water to bring out the aromas and flavors. Then she unlocked the door.

"Whoa," she said.

Jay had never exactly seemed cleaned up to her before. Haggard when she first saw him, slightly defatigued last night, and showered but hung over today, the globetrotter had always carried a rumpled look. But some soap and a razor had scraped away all the grime and exhaustion. The man shone.

Hints of creamy skin, bronzed by wandering days in the sun, glowed on his clean-shaven face. Jade wondered how smooth his cheek would feel under her hand. Even after going into the dusty air of the city in the evening, his scrubbed skin gleamed, and his short hair accentuated his cheekbones and his bright green-and-gold eyes. The long-sleeve black shirt he wore had some wrinkles and rumples to it, sure, but she could tell he'd smoothed it out as best he could. His khaki cargo pants were devoid of so much as a grease splotch on the knee or dried mud on the cuff.

"You beat me to it," Jay said. "You look incredible."

"So do you, backpack boy," she replied. "Sometimes I forget how well a traveler can clean up."

"It's the shirt. An English guy I once met told me every globetrotter needs one black button-down shirt. It'll smarten him up for just about any special occasion."

Jade showed Jay into the pub and locked the door behind him. He set a bag on a table as she poured herself a glass of water with lime. "I was just getting our drinks," she said.

*Oh the hell with it.*

She poured a second scotch and brought the drinks over.

"How do I take my scotch?" Jay asked, glancing at the bottle on the bar and nodding his approval.

"With three drops of water. Just a touch to help the aromas bloom."

"That's how my dad took it too, and I've never drunk it any other way. You truly are the best bartender in Asia." He looked at the two glasses. "I thought you didn't drink?"

Jade shrugged. "It's my day off. I figured I might as well have one nearby. In case I felt like it."

"I still can't wrap my head around everything that's happened today," Jay said. "But looking at you, somehow things make more sense." Jay picked up his scotch.

*This is it,* Jade thought. *The moment his life changes. The moment he firmly puts himself on his path, on his destiny. I don't know what that is. I just know that it must be.*

Jade's stomach twisted. Adrenalin pumped through her. *I'm following orders,* she thought. *What's wrong?*

"Here's to you." Jay raised the glass to his lips. Breathing in the scotch's aromas, he readied for the sip, the amber scotch almost shining near his lips.

"Wow," he said, lowering the glass slightly. "That aroma is perfect. You really brought out the vanilla notes. It might be the world's best scotch, but now you've made it a beautiful drink." He smiled. "All the better to drink with a beautiful woman."

He brought the glass to his lips again. The scotch rolled toward his mouth.

"Wait!"

Jay shook his head and sat back, just before the scotch touched him. "What's wrong?"

"Sorry," Jade replied. "Silly mistake." She took the glass from his hand and moved hers over. "I prefer it neat, and I just realized I'd given you mine."

"Oh. No big deal."

*Very big deal,* Jade thought. *I can't do it. His heart isn't the path? Since when is the heart not the path? Why shouldn't it be?*

"To the rules," Jay said, raising the uninfluenced scotch. He smiled. "And more importantly, to breaking the rules."

*You have no idea,* Jade thought. No, she wasn't

supposed to drink. But that was an on-duty rule. Off the clock was a gray area. Not encouraged, not expressly permitted, but not prohibited either.

She raised her glass to his with a *tink*, and they drank deeply.

Drinking someone else's influenced drink, though?

*I might be off the clock*, she thought, *but I still took this directive upon myself. Jay's now having the perfect, uninfluenced scotch I originally poured for myself, and I'm drinking someone else's destiny—his destiny. What does that mean? Sure, it's happened before. Someone got a drink order mixed up or swapped drinks with someone, and there was nothing anyone could do about it. But a Jake or Jade drinking someone else's decision and destiny?* She thought hard to remember whether this had happened before, but no other times came to mind.

She waited for the impact. The scotch warmed her like Indian sunshine all the way down, but that was no different from any other scotch. After they lowered their glasses, they looked into each other's eyes. Jay seemed content not to say anything. She felt the same. And she didn't feel anything else. No great magnitude of existence. No shift in the order of things. No sense of changing direction. The world seemed the same.

"Oh," Jay said. "Dinner. Let me get that out before it gets cold."

Jade got them two Deep's Special Lagers. *He noticed nothing,* she thought. *I don't feel any different.*

Was it that simple?

*Just because I drank his destiny doesn't mean I've taken his path for him,* she thought. *I'm not him. It can't work the same. Maybe it doesn't work at all on someone else. Maybe that combination of elixirs is so specific because it can work only with one person, as a protection against mistakes—or, well, other occurrences. By me drinking it, it's canceled itself out. I just can't do it. Not to him. If The Management want Jay on a particular path that badly, well, they'll just have to sort it out themselves.*

*I like him too much.*

As they ate chicken and vegetables over rice—expertly spiced and cooked, with oven-fresh *naan* breads on the side—they gradually began to talk more. Jay spoke of his travels, and Jade talked about her years in Agamuskara. She thought about trying to explain more, but she couldn't do that either. He'd taken on so much already today.

She realized Jay had asked her about her family. "I had a lot of siblings," she said. "Brothers and sisters."

"Big household," Jay said. "Happy family?"

She shrugged. "It was all too overwhelming for my parents, I think. Like they'd gotten more than they'd bargained for. They could be very strict."

"Is that why you can work the way you do?"

"What do you mean?"

"Watching you is like watching a poem move," Jay said. "You're like a dancer. There's this focus to you, this strength in everything you do. I guess it sounds to me like you learned to live in your own mind, listen to what mattered, shut out the rest. A way to deal with the chaos you grew up with."

"It's not something people usually understand," Jade replied. "But that's a good way to put it."

"Do you keep in touch?"

"Things got really bad at one point," Jade said. I left home when I was thirteen. I've been on my own ever since."

"That must have been really difficult."

"At times. But I survived."

"Not what you expected out of life, though."

She shrugged. "What's to expect? Life is what we live. Decision, destiny, it's all still one foot in front of the other, all through our lives."

Jay nodded. "I like that. We never know entirely what will be before us."

"What about your family?" Jade said. "They must miss you."

Jay lowered his gaze. "There's no one to miss me. I started traveling five years ago. I'd never planned to. I... I had to. See, I grew up about as average an American as can be, in a small town in Idaho with a river running through it. I never wanted to go anywhere else. I was an only child. My parents wanted more, but after me they couldn't have another. Mom never explained why. My parents and I were very close. After school I started working, got a house not far from where I grew up. It was just me and them, and we'd have dinner together a few times a week. Dad and I would work on each other's houses. I'd take Mom out for errands or mom-and-son dates. We'd all get together and play board games, drink wine, and talk for hours. I was never much for friends, and I didn't really date." He sighed. "I can't remember the last time I talked about all this."

Jade touched his shoulder. "I'll get us another drink."

"My mom and dad were the best people I've ever known," Jay said. "Dad was a lawyer, and an honest one. Everyone in town looked up to him. Mom was a teacher, and she was the heart of our home. She was so vivacious. She read travel magazines. She played violin and ukelele. She liked to tell me she wanted to play 'Somewhere Over the Rainbow' on the uke on every continent before she and Dad died."

"They traveled?" Jade asked.

Jay shook his head. "They wanted to. They were planning to. Dad was going to work a few more years, take an early retirement. While he put in long hours at his law firm, my mom clipped photos, read guidebooks, and planned itineraries after school."

Jade came back with two more scotches, both uninfluenced. A corner of The Management's note poked her chest.

"One evening when I came over for dinner," Jay continued, "Mom and Dad were beaming when they opened the door. When I looked behind them, I saw why. On the wall in the living room, they'd framed and hung a huge map of the world. Mom had stuck purple pins in every continent. 'Our retirement-around-the-world,' she called it. She was so happy and Dad was excited. They weren't planning some quick posh luxury vacation either. Over dinner that night, Dad told me about how they were planning to climb Mount Kilimanjaro in Tanzania. Mom told me about riding elephants in Thailand, and the abandoned Angkor capital city in Cambodia, the old stone buildings now thick with jungle. They spoke of the wild, fierce North Atlantic, and the Scottish Hebrides islands there—the strong, reserved, kind people who lived honest and closer to the earth and sea. They spoke of music in Vienna and Incan cities in Peru. Their eyes were wet with tears when they said they wanted to ride the train across all of Russia, from

Moscow to Vladivostok on the Pacific coast. They wanted to stand in the Australian Outback and watch the sun rise and set on the massive red face of Uluru.

"Dad figured they'd have enough saved to travel the rest of their days if they wanted. Not lavish travel, mind. They talked of hostel dorms and public transport in Europe, of looking for where the mothers took their children to eat in India. They wanted not just to see the world but to become friends with as many people in as many lands as they could in the years they had left."

"Didn't you want to go too?"

Jay laughed. "Funny thing is, I didn't. I was happy where I was. I liked my job. I liked my home. I was living a quiet, content, nondescript life in a quiet, content, nondescript bit of true-to-heart Americana small town. I figured if anything, I'd be like Mom and Dad. I'd work and live. Maybe find a wife and raise a family. Maybe not. When I was older and retired I'd look at the whole travel thing. If I was even interested. As far as I was concerned, Mom and Dad had more than earned their dreams, their excitement, their happiness. I hoped that one day I would too."

"I don't understand, though," Jade said. "You're here, not there. Why didn't they get to travel?"

For a moment Jay looked away. When he looked at her again, his eyes glistened. "They died."

Jade took his hand. "I'm sorry."

He nodded. "It was my twenty-fifth birthday. We were meeting at my favorite restaurant. It was raining hard that day—so hard there were concerns about flash floods. I waited. But they didn't show. After an hour, a sheriff's deputy came in. It's a small town, after all. He and I had been in high school together. He knew where we'd be, what day it was. He said my parents' car had been found in the river, half submerged and banged up against a bridge pillar. Mom and Dad must have been swept away. We searched for days. I took time off work. I helped dredge the river. I roamed the forests. I called police departments from there all the way to the Oregon and Washington coast. We never found their bodies, but there was no way they had survived. Mom and Dad were declared dead."

"Jay..."

He cracked a fragile, tense smile. "Funny thing is, Dad being a lawyer, all their affairs were in perfect order. The house, vehicles, everything was paid off. They didn't have so much as credit card debt or an unpaid magazine subscription. I was the only beneficiary on their life insurance policy, and they left everything—travel books, the map, the house, their money—to me."

"So you have a good bit of travel money."

He shrugged. "Yeah, but I work a lot too. I like to earn my money. I grieved hard for Mom and Dad. I still carry their picture in my money belt. After a few months, I knew what I had to do. I quit my job and I sold both our houses. I sold anything that didn't mean anything to them or to me. Then I took the map and the guidebooks and promised Mom and Dad that since they never got to see the world they loved so much, I would do it for them.

"A year after they died, I left Idaho. I've never been back. Everyone understood. It was a son's way to handle his grief and honor his parents. Now I've been all over, doing the things they wanted to do, and having a few adventures of my own. I keep doing all I can do to honor their memory. And I've learned so much. I can't believe I never wanted to travel. Now I can't imagine ever stopping. I guess you could call me a traveler and a globetrotter, but really, all I am now is their wish to see the world."

Jay looked like he was holding back tears. Jade squeezed his hand. She said nothing. Just watched him. Just thought. No matter how gentle or funny or comforting or crass, nothing she said would keep this rare fragility. The first word from her mouth would close up his heart tight and perhaps add locks. No words could bring Jay closer to her or prove he could trust her or show what she felt for him.

Her own doubts and turmoil pulled at her, the calls of roads not taken and the grass-is-greener regrets of the paths she treaded. Just as she had no way to comfort Jay with words, she had no words to voice her shared grief, her confusion, her regrets, her wishes for home, a different life, an open heart, a warm touch, a comfort by her side. Jade had nothing to say.

So she kissed him instead.

*Now, this seems like destiny,* she thought. His lips were as soft as she'd wondered, and so were his cheeks under her hands. His hands were gentle yet strong as he held her.

There was no pub. There was no Management, no destiny, no decision, no spinning little god eggs or ancient evils or strange inscrutable tricksters. There was just them: Jay and Jade, travelers and a destination, a journey they no longer had to wander alone.

When at last they moved apart, they said nothing. Jade held Jay's hand tight in her own and he squeezed back. They stared into each other's eyes.

"I don't know what this could be," Jay said.

"I don't either," Jade said.

"I want to find out."

"Me too."

They kissed again.

Later, after more kisses, more words and relief and hopes, Jay helped Jade tidy up their dinner plates and glasses. Then, after many final kisses, he went up to his dorm, to dream of their plans of a sunrise ride on the river.

As Jade stood behind the bar, Jay's kisses still fresh on her lips, she tried to think only of Jay, of what they might have together.

Tomorrow there would surely be repercussions. Tomorrow there would surely be another note from The Management, a rebuke, a punishment. Hopefully, she could explain. Hopefully, there would be a way to convince The Management that Jay could just remain a traveler, that there was no special destiny that needed him. Surely it didn't have to be Jay. He'd done enough. He'd lost his parents already. Shouldn't that be enough for anyone? Couldn't he just travel in peace, honor their memory, and live some simple pleasures of his own? And couldn't she be there with him?

She wondered what that would mean. *Am I thinking of resigning?* she thought. *Whenever this is all finished and he can leave Agamuskara, won't I want to go with him? Of course I will. But I can't be both a Jade and his love. I can only be one or the other. I've been a Jade for a long time, just as Jay has traveled for his parents' memory for a long time.*

*Maybe it's time for both of us to live some different reasons. Some different passions. Maybe it's time we found a different happiness.*

A knock resounded through the front door.

"Even your bloody knock sounds like a laugh," she said.

The moment Rucksack and Kailash saw her, their big smiles got even bigger. Rucksack took a bounding step inside and wrapped his arms around Jade, lifting her off the floor and spinning her around.

"What?" Jade said, slightly dizzy. "What's going on?"

"Ah, Jade," Rucksack replied, setting her down. "We had to tell you right away."

"Did you see Jigme and his mother?" Jade asked.

Rucksack shook his head. "No time. It will have to wait till tomorrow. Besides, this is more important."

Kailash closed the door. "Mim and Pim found us earlier."

"The two who stole Jay's passport?"

Rucksack nodded. "As we were coming back here, they appeared before us, smiling and bowing. Said they were glad we found their letters helpful."

"They set it up to bring the two of you together," Jade said. "Curious. But why would they do that? Can they be trusted?"

"Probably not," Rucksack said. "But as far as I can figure they can be believed. For now, that will have to do. What they told us gave me hope. We can beat the Smiling Fire. Things are already on course to defeat him."

"That's incredible!" Jade said, elated. She hugged Rucksack, and Kailash too. *The ancient evil was no match for us,* she thought. Hope surged inside her.

*Maybe Jay isn't needed at all anymore.*

It made sense. Maybe Rucksack and Kailash were the key. After all, they helped bring down the Smiling Fire before. And Rucksack hadn't even been born yet. *Now he's, well, he's whatever he is,* Jade thought. *So Jay's not needed after all. If he's not, then maybe I'm not either. We could just leave. Go off together. Get to know each other, get to know what we have, what we want, what we can be.*

"So, things are okay now?" she said. "Jay's done what he needed to do?"

"Things are okay because Jay is staying in the city," Rucksack replied.

Jade's soaring hopes plummeted.

Even if Rucksack saw any sign of her sudden despair, he kept talking. "That's the key to everything. As long as Jay is here when the eclipse happens, we can beat the Smiling Fire." He reached into his pocket. "They gave me this. Said it was all they could do for now, and they asked me to keep it safe, just in case."

He took out a small, dark-blue booklet.

"Just in case of what?" Jade said. "This is Jay's passport. They claimed they needed to fix it. Did they?"

Rucksack bobbed his head. "Depends on what you believe 'fixed' means. Remember how Jay had told us all the places he's been?"

"He talked about all the stamps, visas, and stickers in his passport, yeah."

Rucksack held up the passport and opened it to the identification page. Jade saw Jay's photo, place of birth, and other information. Then Rucksack flipped through the rest of the pages.

All were blank.

"They wiped out his passport?"

"We don't know why," Rucksack replied. "They just said they weren't done yet."

"Why do they want you to keep it?"

"I don't know that either, but I don't have much choice."

"That doesn't matter. It's not ours. It's Jay's, and we should give it back to him."

"It's not his destiny," Kailash said.

"But it's his passport." The destinies clashed in Jade's head, from Rucksack's and Kailash's words to the scotch Jade had taken from Jay before he could take in the path The Management had said he needed to take. But fighting back was the new destiny, born in Jade's heart the moment she and Jay had kissed so short a time ago. A new future, a new life, a world to see, a person to get to know. But where could that life exist?

"You said that maybe Jay just was the best way to get the dia ubh to Agamuskara," Jade said. "Can't his role be done? Why does he have to stay here?"

"Ah Jade," Rucksack said. "That's the most amazing part o' it all. I can't say I understand as why, but that's not me place. For whatever reason, the world has made its choice. Jay's not just a traveler. Unless the world and all life be destroyed by the Smiling Fire, Jay must stand in the light when the dia ubh opens."

"But surely you or Kailash would be far better choices."

"I wish it could be so," Kailash said. "But the power I was given did not include that destiny. It was all we could do to imprison the Smiling Fire with the power we had, all the while knowing and fearing a day like this may come when life hung in the balance again."

Her gaze softened. "That's not the full truth, though," Kailash said. "I've never been able to balance love and power, Jade. Not truly. I've always tended to power, and the problem with that is I have become less and less human over the years. I see only the big picture, as they say. I don't see details anymore. I don't see things like love and compassion. I have protected the garden of life, but I no longer care to smell the flowers. I could stand in the light of the dia ubh and become more powerful than ever. I could then destroy the Smiling Fire. But I would become him, Jade. The power would ruin me. Once I destroyed him, I would never stop. I would become as terrible a fate for the world as he is."

"Surely Rucksack could though."

"My son is a hero of old, if not *the* hero of old," Kailash replied. "He is recovering more and more of himself. My son is not only life; he is love."

"But sometimes," Rucksack said, "I love too much to do what must be done." He shook his head. "I would not be able to destroy the Smiling Fire. I could maybe imprison him again but no more. And while the Smiling Fire exists, life will never be safe."

Rucksack shut the passport and put it back into his pocket. "Do you understand, Jade? It has to be this way. There has to be a balance, and Jay's got it. He loves the world. He loves life. That's why they chose him above all others. Jay's got a lot more to look forward to than cheap dorm beds—no offense intended, o' course. He's not going to be as he was. He... He's going to become a god."

The scotch, the kiss, the destiny, so much swirled

in her mind and body that Jade was finding it hard to stand up. She opened her mouth to say something, to snap at Rucksack and Kailash, to tell them to go away and take their legends with them. But no words came.

"Jade?" Kailash said. "Are you all right?"

"Thank goodness you're all here," said a voice near the bar.

Everyone turned to see Jay standing in the pub, pulling closed the door to the stairs and dorms. *Did he hear any of this?* Jade thought.

"What's wrong, Jay?" Rucksack asked.

"I didn't know what to do," Jay said. As he walked over he took his daypack off his shoulder and unzipped it. When he touched the dia ubh he cringed, as if the contact were painful.

"It happened after I left here, Jade," he said.

"Left here?" Rucksack said.

"We had dinner," Jade replied. Kailash studied her with a gaze that indicated that she understood everything Jade hadn't said.

"I wanted to see the dia ubh again before going to sleep," Jay said. "But it's different. When I took it out, well, see for yourselves."

He held up the dia ubh and took his hand away. As before, the world was lit with the sun, its white clouds, brown and green lands, and blue waters shining. In the dark parts of the world, such as India, all lay serene under night's soothing blanket. At first, all seemed exactly like before, but Jay was right; it was different. The small globe floated but not smoothly. It shuddered and flickered. Every time it did, Jay cringed and winced.

"You're connected," Jade said.

"I guess so," Jay replied. "It hurts. Why does it hurt?"

Rucksack and Kailash said nothing. *Are they not going to tell him?* Jade thought, her feelings for Jay surging with anger. *It's his own destiny. Shouldn't he know?*

She started to open her mouth to tell him everything. But another part of her mind, trained and experienced from years of being a Jade, rose in her thoughts too. *Yes, it's his destiny,* said the voice, calm yet compassionate. *But destinies aren't stories to tell. They're decisions to live. It's not our place to give that away.*

Jade said nothing. You didn't tell someone their destiny. You just gave it to them and let them figure out the rest. That was the only way it worked.

*But I don't want it to work.*

"Jay," she said, "there's something you need to know."

Jay looked at her. "What?" he said. He then winced and gasped. He said no more but his mouth hung open. His eyes bulged wide. He yelled, his pain filling the pub and making everyone wince.

Silent again, he fell to the floor. Jade rushed to him and held up his head. He was barely conscious.

"It's starting," Rucksack said, staring with a mixture of fear and excitement in his eyes.

*No,* Jade thought. She didn't want to, but she looked away from Jay, to where Rucksack and Kailash were staring.

The dia ubh still hung there, but not as before. The white clouds, the green lands, the brown lands, the blue seas—all were gone. A gray, featureless rock, smooth as an egg, floated in the air between them.

The dia ubh jerked and wobbled. For a moment longer, it hung in the air then fell to the floor.

A sharp crack made Jade cover her ears. She looked to Jay, her eyes wide.

"Huh," Jay said, his voice tired and ragged. "I liked it better when it was pretty."

Then he passed out.

# II

"I'VE NEVER heard you do that before," Kailash said.

"Do what?" Jade replied.

"Sing."

"I wasn't singing."

"And I was born yesterday."

Jade said nothing, but Kailash's reply made her look more closely at Rucksack's mother as they walked through the city toward the Everest Base Camp. No, Kailash hadn't been born yesterday, but until recently she'd looked hardly any older than Jade. Two weeks after Jade had met her, though, Kailash's young, maidenly appearance seemed to have matured, deepened, changed.

When you were as old as Kailash—however old that was—did you still mind if someone mentioned that you were looking older? Jade decided not to ask. "Okay," she said, "I was singing. A little."

"You're always singing and smiling lately. I'm glad your time with Jay has been so good for the both of you," Kailash replied. "It seems that if you aren't working, you're off somewhere in the city with him."

*It was true,* Jade thought. From the early morning wanderings through the narrowest back streets and alleys of Agamuskara to that afternoon at the edge of the city, studying the carvings on the erotic temples and winking at each other, all her time had been spent either at Everest Base Camp or with Jay. Sure, when she was working he was off with Rucksack, looking in on Asha and Jigme or hunting for Mim, Pim, and his passport. But these last two weeks with Jay had brought a happiness she hadn't realized she'd forgotten how to feel.

Maybe lately he was spending a little more time on this passport quest than he was with her, but that was probably just a mistake. What mattered was how close they'd gotten, how happy they felt.

*I haven't been this happy since...* The image of a man from long ago, his bright eyes similar to Jay's, cut off Jade's thoughts. She never knew what had happened to him. Her abrupt departure, all those unanswered questions, were the only things she knew right now that could pull down her happiness.

"A girl's entitled to a bit of bliss," Jade said.

"Oh yes, oh yes," Kailash replied. "I would never disagree. But you chose not to be a normal girl. How long can that bliss last, Jade? What will happen once the mirror eclipse falls and the dia ubh opens?"

"We don't even know for sure that it'll be a mirror eclipse. Could be just a regular, boring eclipse. Just because you and Rucksack keep saying Jay's destiny has to be this one thing, doesn't make it so."

"True. So what does make it so?"

*I do,* Jade thought. *But I refused to serve him that destiny. We got each other instead.* "Jay could make it so," Jade replied. "If he wants. If he chooses. But maybe he won't. Maybe something else will change. Maybe you're wrong and it's not going to happen at all the way you think."

"It wouldn't be the first time. I don't claim to know the future. I just read where things are going. Perhaps we should tell him then. Doesn't Jay deserve to know what the world wants from him?"

"No," Jade replied. "I agree with Rucksack. There's no use in telling Jay yet. Soon. But not yet." *It'll spoil everything,* she thought. She and Jay were together and falling into whatever people fall into when they like being with one another. Even The Management seemed to have changed course. Despite her refusal to follow their instructions, there had been no reply, no retaliation.

Had they just decided to let it go, to let her have this happiness?

As Jade and Kailash rounded a corner, the sign for Everest Base Camp came into view. "We're meeting Jay and Rucksack at the hospital, right?" Jade asked.

"Yes, in an hour. That's when Asha is being released."

"Good. I just need to pick up something, and we

can go over there."

Kailash nodded. "Does it bother you that Jigme doesn't seem happier about his mother's recovery?"

Jade stopped at the heavy mahogany doors. "What do you mean?"

"The boy is different of late. There's disquiet, like something is burning in his mind. Some question, some doubt. I don't know," Kailash said. "But of late he seems unhappy. I would have thought that this time, when his mother seems to be getting better, is when he would be the happiest we've ever seen him."

"He's a teenage boy. Who knows what all is happening in him." Jade unlocked the door. "Do you mind waiting out here? I won't be long." Kailash bobbed her head and Jade went inside, closing the door behind her.

The broken table still needed to be cleared away, but she would do that before opening the pub later. She thought back to the fight, how abruptly it had blazed out of nowhere. Nothing in the two Indian men, locals, had suggested violence, nor had any twining tendril of their helixes warned her.

*Maybe I missed it,* Jade thought, but she dismissed the thought as quickly as it shot through her mind.

One mention of the disappearance was all it had taken. Within a few minutes, angry words had become shoves and blows.

Jade had immediately gone from the bar to the middle of the fight. Her presence was enough of a shock to make the men pause, giving other patrons the chance to pull them away from each other and hold them still.

"What's going on here?" she had asked.

"He says that the one who disappeared won't be missed!" said one of the men. "My son is gone! Where is my son?"

The other man said nothing.

"Do you have children?" Jade asked him.

The quiet man nodded. "A daughter," he said. The pain in the words told her he was admitting that his child was at risk of vanishing too.

"You will sit together," Jade replied. "You will speak to each other of your children."

The men glowered.

"You don't have to," Jade said. "You can also choose to leave here and never come back."

The men said nothing. Their eyes were still angry, but they did not argue with the Jade of Agamuskara.

With healthy dollops of understanding and peace added, Jade set hot drinks in front of them. When next she checked, the men went back and forth from pride and laughter to the sadness of parents sharing fear, loss, and lack of control.

The men had met as enemies, but they left as friends.

None of it should have happened to begin with, though, she knew. *What was this disappearance?* Jade thought. *Is it the only one, or have others been disappearing too? Clearly, it's rattling the city, and even the pub isn't immune.*

*What will I do the next time something like this happens?*

Jade wondered if she should be helping Rucksack and Kailash more. While they deepened their understanding of the Smiling Fire and the dia ubh, she was off kissing Jay.

Then again, no one had any indication that

anything had changed at the black temple at the heart of the city.

*It's all okay,* she told herself again. *It's not as bad as we feared.*

But beneath the rush in her blood and the thrill when she kissed Jay, the questions beat at her as constantly as her pulse.

The visible helixes, burning out like singed paper.

The dia ubh turning gray and lifeless, no longer floating.

A child gone.

And Jay's destiny.

*His damned, damned destiny,* Jade thought, *which I should be bringing about, not averting. Love has no place in decision and destiny. Or do decision and destiny have no place in love?*

A soft *pthump* made her turn and face the bar.

The Management hadn't sent a note in weeks. Jade went over to the phone, which never rang, and opened the special cabinet.

She tried to think only of the night ahead, though. After the pub closed, she and Jay were meeting for a drink. *Just the two of us, just like that first night,* Jade thought. *After that, we're going back to my room for the first time. I've got more than a black silk dress to show him tonight.*

Jade grinned, imagining the hours to come. She reached for the note inside the cabinet.

As she read, all thoughts of the night drifted away like ash.


```
We have been long in discussion, Jade
Agamuskara Bluegold. What you have
```

```
done was wrong for a Jade to do.
Another would have been dismissed
immediately. But because we understand
the lonely rigors of your role and
because of your long service, we
present you a choice:

Love is not the traveler's path.
Influence him with the mixture below.
Remain a Jade. You will be forgiven
and rewarded.

Continue resisting your duty and the
needs of the world, and you will cease
to be a Jade.

You have three days to choose your
destiny.
```

Jade read it again and again. The paper crinkled and crackled like the cone that had held the *bhel puri* she and Jay had shared yesterday, smiling as they passed a spoon back and forth, crunching puffed rice and tasting the sweet tang of vegetables spiced with tamarind sauce.

"I'm getting used to this," Jay had said.

"To snacks?" she had replied, grinning.

His face had remained serious. "To us."

She had said nothing. Tears stung her eyes now.

*Did I know?* she thought, staring at the crumpled note in her hands. *Love or duty? The Jade of Agamuskara or a Jade who is no longer a Jade? Who am I? Who do I want to be?*

The bar shelves broke Jade's reflection. Her blue-and-gold eyes shimmered, wide with fear and a sadness that loomed like a hole she could fall into and keep falling.

*A life with Jay, or the life of a Jade?*

But what was the worst that could happen? Whenever a Jake or Jade left, either from resigning or from being sacked, The Management always let them choose new circumstances to move into, or as they called it, "revision." No one had to just pick up where they were leaving off. Usually, people took a new direction in life, often with family, a lost love, or some other path that may have been. If they wanted, they could have their memories of their service removed, but most didn't do that. They treasured their old selves, like old photographs occasionally taken out of a dusty box. They always chose health and wealth. No former Jake or Jade, far as she knew, ever wanted for life's basics.

The Management knew they asked a lot from their Jakes and Jades. In return, no matter the circumstances, they always offered a healthy severance.

*The worst that can happen is a new life,* Jade thought. *I'd never want for anything. Jay and I could go anywhere, do anything, for as long as we wanted. I'll age but I'll be healthy. Maybe that's not so bad.*

Flowing through her mind was the potential of what could be. *I don't have to choose yet,* Jade thought. *I have time to figure this out. Maybe there's a way to do both and be both. Maybe I can appeal to The Management somehow. There has to be a way around this destiny, a different path for him. For me. For us.*

She closed the cabinet, folded the note, and tucked it into her pocket with the other two notes.

*Why didn't I know right away?*

Jade breathed in deeply, arching her head back and closing her eyes. When she breathed out she lowered her head and looked straight in front of her. There'd be a way. The Management had to know there were other options. She would figure things out with Jay and this supposed destiny looming over him, her, and the city. "Jade or not," she said. "I'm still me."

She stepped outside, squinting at the harsh light as she locked the door.

"Are you okay?" Kailash asked. "You seem flushed."

"I'm okay," Jade replied. "Just rattled over that fight last night. I have to get back in time to get rid of that broken table."

"But you got what you needed?"

"Oh..." *I forgot,* Jade thought. "We can just go," she said, turning and starting to walk in the direction of the hospital. "It wasn't the right thing after all."

"No more song?" Kailash said.

Jade didn't reply. Kailash said nothing else, and Jade didn't like a word of what the other woman wasn't saying.


ASHA TOOK her first steps on her own, and everyone cheered. Her feet shuffled a short distance from her hospital bed. She smiled but looked down at her feet, surprised that they were stepping and that she was moving them.

"It's been so long," she said, her face still gaunt but filled out slightly from over two weeks of regular nourishment.

"A step at a time, my lass," Rucksack said. "No rush. The world's a better place just seeing you up and about again."

Jigme glanced at Rucksack, who was standing next to Kailash to the left of the door, and at Jade and Jay to the right of the door, their hands intertwined. *They're all here. Together,* he thought. *For Amma. For me. They all smile so big, so bright. They all look so happy.*

Somewhere deep inside Jigme, a little boy wanted to jump and cheer, spin in circles, hold his mum's hand, and gaze at her with wide eyes.

But every time Jigme tried to let that happiness flow through him, something leaped up inside him and burned away all the cheer.

He tried to smile as big and bright as everyone else, but the corners of his mouth would barely stretch upward. His face felt thin, as if his skin had been replaced with cheap paper.

*Shouldn't this make me smile?* Jigme thought. *Shouldn't I be happier? Just a few weeks ago I felt so alone. Now Amma's come back. It can be me and her again, the way it used to be. The way it should be.*

Asha took another shuffling, unsteady step forward. Jigme managed a smile. This one seemed a little stronger. She looked up from her feet and caught Jigme's gaze.

"You're doing great, Amma," Jigme said.

He glanced at Jay, whose nod confirmed that the bill was paid. They could leave anytime. He and Amma could go home, thanks to the hospital, the doctors, and Jay.

"Yes," said the rough voice in the back of Jigme's

mind, "you can go home. You can enjoy your sweet mother's company again. But remember, boy, your mother is not walking because of the hospital. She isn't awake because of these doctors. And all the money from that fool is no more responsible for her walking than you are for the sunrise. You know why she's able to move around again."

Heat rose in Jigme's mind. *Yes,* he thought, his memory trying not to turn back to it. *I know why.*

A hand on his shoulder made the heat fade. Amma's hand. She stared at him, kind and hard. "Son?" she said. "Are you okay?"

"It's so hard to believe this is over," Jigme replied. "That you're okay again." The memories pushed at him, but her eyes on him, her hand touching him— the memories could not make him look.

"I'm getting better," Asha said. "It will still take some time, but I will try hard, Jigme. For you. I will get better."

Jay looked over at the doctor, standing in the far corner of the room. "Were you able to determine what got her so sick?"

The doctor shook her head. "We tested for everything we could. All we know is that she had nothing contagious."

"Will it come back?"

A shrug. "Hopefully not. I can't say with any certainty if she'll relapse. Any signs of a recurrence, any malaise, any listlessness, please come back immediately. We'll do what we can. It's been a most strange case, and I hope you have a full recovery."

Kailash stepped forward. "How about the rest of us wait out front, so Asha and Jigme can have some time alone? Asha, once you're ready, we'll take you home."

The door closed behind the others. The moment it clicked, Asha smiled bigger than Jigme had ever seen before, and she leaped straight into the air.

"I'm better!" She landed without a sound and stepped forward to hug him. "Oh, Jigme, I'm sorry to have put you through so much. Will you forgive me?"

"I'll always forgive you, Amma."

"Are you angry? It's okay to feel angry. Your mother wasn't here for you. That will never happen again."

Jigme shook his head. "It wasn't easy. But my friends have helped." *And I have found other ways to make you better.* His thoughts flashed to the temple.

Asha hugged him tightly to her. Jigme was surprised at how much strength was in her frail body. "Be careful, Amma!"

"Oh, I won't hurt you," she said, giving him a squeeze around the ribs.

"I don't want you to overdo it."

Asha smiled. "Oh Jigme, I couldn't overdo it. Not now. Never again." Something flashed red in her eyes. "I came back strong. I came back to be the mother you need me to be."

*She's really okay,* Jigme thought.

Now he smiled.

Asha stepped back toward the bed, where her best sari, bright red with black accents, lay waiting for her. "I'm going to get dressed," she said, pulling the curtains closed. "And then, my son, we're going home."

*Home.*

Jigme wondered what home looked like now. Since the night Asha had awakened, Jigme hadn't been back to their small home in the alley. He'd slept in the hospital room. The only time he left was when he returned to the alley, walked past the red door, and went to the black temple. Lately, the dim temple had begun to feel almost like home.

Once Asha came out, sparkling and elegant as her sari's subtle silver-and-gold threads caught the light, they walked down to the hospital lobby and then outside, into the midday air and light. This time when everyone smiled, Jigme managed a grin more easily. Jay led them all to waiting taxis.

"Son," Asha said, "do the honors. Tell the man where we're going."

"Home," Jigme said. *Wherever that is now.*

He then gave the driver the details he needed to get them home. A few miles and countless horn honks later, they stood around the red door, which Asha insisted that Jigme unlock. When the door creaked open, a musty smell wafted out—the smell of hot dust, unaired bedding, and stale sick breath.

"I'm sorry," Jigme said, blushing. "I should have cleaned."

Asha shook her head. "It will be good for me to clean," she said. "Because of my illness, our home was not what it should be. Together, we will make it a better place. Okay?"

Jigme nodded. *Just like what the Smiling Fire says,* Jigme thought. *It will all be a better place.*

"It will be a lovely home," Kailash said.

"All in due time," Rucksack added.

Asha stared at each of them. "We'll start immediately," she said, taking a step toward the threshold. Pride flared in her eyes, and Jigme again saw the old strength in her, the mother who could twirl around while she held him over her head. Asha stepped over the threshold, regal, back straight.

Her foot caught the splintery wood and she gasped.

"Amma!" Jigme yelled, but she was falling before he could even step toward her.

Dust puffed off the floor around her body inside the dim room. A dull smack knocked the smiles off everyone's faces.

Jigme stared at the hair on the back of his mother's head. She didn't move.

A cough rose from the face he couldn't see. Asha wheezed, trying to breathe air back into her lungs.

"Must've knocked the wind out of her," Jay said, stepping forward. "Here, let me help you up, Asha."

Jigme jumped between them. "No!" he said. "I'll help her. She's my mum!"

Jay stopped. "Okay. I just wanted to help."

"You've helped enough," Jigme said. He leaned down and put his hands under Asha's shoulders. "Amma? Mum?" She looked at him with pain in her eyes. "I'm going to lift you up. Can you help me do that?"

She nodded. As they stood, her wheeze deepened back into something resembling breath. "Such... a good boy," she wheezed. "Always... such a good boy."

"Are you okay?" Jade asked.

Asha nodded. "Silly... So silly." She coughed. "I caught the step wrong."

She stood upright with Jigme next to her. His eyes felt hot and anger burned in his gaze. *Why do I feel mad at them?* he thought. *They're only trying to help.*

"They are a help you don't need," said the voice.

"It's time for them to go."

"Would you like us to help you clean?" Kailash asked. "Help you get settled back in?"

When Asha shook her head, Jigme thought he saw a red glint in her eyes. "Thank you for your help and your kindnesses," she said. "But I think it would be best if Jigme and I had some time alone in our home, just mother and son."

"We'll come back around later," Rucksack said. "We're nearby if you need us."

"Thank you," Asha said. "You've done so much already. I'll get stronger. I want to get stronger. Good-bye." With a small smile that stabbed the corners of her mouth upward, Asha closed the door.

"Amma?" Jigme said. "What now?"

Weak light collided with the dust in the stale air.

"Now we wait," she said, her face half in shadow, half in the watery light.

"Wait for what?"

"Wait until we know they are gone." With that, Asha stood still, her eyes locked on the closed door. Jigme tugged her hand and continued to speak to her, but she did not reply.

Once a few minutes had passed, she looked away from the door. "They're gone now," she said.

"Are we going to clean?" Jigme asked. "Would you rather rest first? You don't want to do too much on your first day home."

"You're wrong," Asha replied, stepping forward into the light. "There is much to do." The red glint shone brighter in her eyes now. Fiercer. "Starting with you leaving."

"Leaving? But we only just got home. Where are we

going?"

"Not me," Asha said. "You."

"Me?"

Asha nodded. "My strength is as his strength, son. If I am not to be as I was, then you must help him."

"How? I don't... I didn't mean..."

"I know. But it's okay. You didn't know, and neither did he. That's why what you did, even though you meant to do nothing, was so right. It made him strong enough to make me strong enough to come back. Don't you want me to be able to stay here, with you?"

Though he nodded, tears burned Jigme's cheeks.

"Then you must go," Asha said. "He is waiting. He knows what you must do."

"To help him," Jigme replied. "I don't want to go."

"To make him stronger is to make me stronger," Asha said. "I must tell you the truth, my son. I am not better."

"But you came home!"

"I am strong while he is strong, but his power is not fully returned. Not yet. Not for a while to come. If he is allowed to weaken, then I will weaken too. If I weaken... he will live forever but I will not. He may fade but he can come back. If I fade, as I was fading before you helped him, then I will die."

"Amma, please..."

Asha nodded. "I know it's hard. But isn't your mother worth it?"

The tears kept coming, but Jigme choked out a small, "Yes."

"That's my son," Asha said, kissing Jigme on the forehead. Her lips burned.

"When will he be strong enough?"

Asha said nothing. The glint faded from her eyes. Jigme began to think she wouldn't respond. Then the red flickered again.

"He will be strong enough when he tells you to bring me to him," she said.

"It's the only way?"

"Whatever he tells you is the only way."

Outside, the world was still in midday. Around their small room all seemed dim and gray, like pale light under stormy clouds. Jigme stepped into the alley.

"Son?"

He turned and looked at his mother.

"I know you'll make me proud."

Asha closed the door. For a moment, Jigme looked longingly toward the living end of the alley, where mothers cooked, where children played, where lives were being lived in the bright light of the day. Jigme turned the other way and returned to the black temple.

"I DON'T UNDERSTAND the problem," Rucksack said, wiping the last bits of grease off his fingers, "though clearly it's so vexing it's put you off your samosa."

*The samosa should have looked tasty,* Jay thought as he stood against the wall. He and Rucksack were just outside the flood of people wandering the city's busy streets in the afternoon heat. The samosa's warmth permeated Jay's right hand, and he looked down at the small pasty, its warm weight promising a spicy delight of vegetables, potatoes, and chickpeas. The scent of chickpea dough, fried in nut oil, had pulled Jay by the nostrils to the man's cart.

Jay sniffed in the aroma of the carrots and peas, simmering beneath a cloud of steam. After a morning of looking over half the streets in Agamuskara, they hadn't even eaten lunch before meeting up with the others at the hospital.

Now, with Jade getting the pub open, with Jigme and Asha back home, and Kailash doing, well, doing whatever Kailash did, he and Rucksack could get back to what mattered most: hunting the city for Mim and Pim. It was as if Jay could sense his passport. Somehow it always seemed near, though they had yet to catch so much as a glimpse of Mim and Pim.

By the time they began churning through the busy streets again, Jay's stomach protested like horns in the city's daily traffic jams. Holding two fingers up to the man at the samosa cart, Jay began to drool, not just for the food but also for his favorite part: the haggling.

The past couple of weeks in the city had been just the sort of exercise he needed. Lots of walking and lots of negotiating over the prices of gifts for Jade, meals, and rides all over the city. The haggling had always been one of Jay's favorite parts of travel.

"It all comes down to who wants it more," someone had told him so many years and passport stamps ago. "If you want it more, they will win. If they want you to buy it more, you will get the price you want."

The man at the cart wrapped each samosa in a small square of newspaper. Jay stared at the wrapper as grease absorbed into today's news. From the photo, it looked like some story about the sun. The newspaper was fresh, at least.

"Jay?" Rucksack asked. "Are you okay?"

"He charged me four rupees," Jay replied.

"Quite a bargain you struck." The straight line of Rucksack's mouth made it clear he had overdone the haggling.

"That's the thing. I didn't strike a bargain. We didn't haggle."

"What do you mean, you didn't haggle? It's not as if he gave you the local price straightaway."

Jay bobbed his head.

"He charged you the local price? No haggling?"

"I couldn't so much as express my outrage at his prices."

Jay thought about the exchange again. Bringing forth his mastery of international language, Jay had arched an eyebrow and rubbed the tips of his thumb and index finger together in the opening salvo. *How much?*

Instead of asking forty rupees—a far more typical price for the foreign traveler, from what Jay had come to understand from previous samosa purchases and from talking with other travelers at the Everest Base Camp—the man had charged Jay what he would have charged a local.

"It's just not done," Jay said. "I was going to counter with ten rupees. Not that he would accept that, of course, but there's a process to this—a time-honored tradition of someone trying to get extra money from the bloke who clearly isn't from around here. I respect that tradition. It's a thrill, even. I love telling someone their prices are outlandish and then walking away."

"Aye," Rucksack said. A nostalgic wisp brightened his eyes. "He lets you go a few paces, then he shouts, 'Wait my friend! Wait my friend!' You come back, of course. That's how it's done. And he's clearly happy that you understand the rules and he can engage in a proper transaction."

"It's not like these fresh-faced backpackers you get nowadays," Jay said. "All wet ink behind their passport stamps. They would've just left, denying both people a chance to talk about his kids and how expensive good fresh ingredients are nowadays."

"Even if he's not buying good fresh ingredients," Rucksack replied. "Then he would've said his usual price is sixty, but you're a guest. Special price for you."

Jay nodded. "So, of course I'd counter with twenty, knowing full well he's talking poo."

"Anymore so, you could pat his words into a cake, chuck it on a wall to dry in the sun, and burn it for cooking later," Rucksack said.

Jay shrugged. "I tried to tell him to charge me more."

"You didn't try to speak Hindi, did you?"

"Eventually. At first I think I told him he had chickens on his ears. After a few goes, he understood that I was trying to make him charge me exorbitantly so we could agree a fair price like gentlemen. But it's like he had decided the rules didn't apply."

"What do you mean?"

"I don't know what he was signifying," Jay said, "but it's like he traced a triangle in the air, then a circle, then he pointed at me and just said again, 'Four rupees.'"

Rucksack frowned. Outside the throngs of people, a cow wandered toward the two of them.

"What's wrong?" Jay asked Rucksack. "I thought it was just some sort of weird local blessing, like I've been seen enough or seen with Jade or something, so I was getting the local price. That's why I finally just caved in and gave him the money. I tried to sneak in extra, but you know what he did?"

"No," Rucksack said. "He didn't."

"He gave me change."

"It's just not right."

"It's like it's all been getting easier lately. The traveling. The day to day. I'm used to travel being hard. I like travel being hard," Jay said. "Now I'm being charged differently. Everyone is deferential to me. It doesn't make any sense. I'm just another foreign guy with a backpack—no one special."

"Has there been any change in the dia ubh?"

Jay sighed. To his left he saw the cow, its eyes dull yet bright, as if saying it knew something important, only it wasn't going to let on. With his samosa in one hand, Jay brought around his daypack with his other hand, unzipped it, and held the black fabric open so Rucksack could peer inside.

The dia ubh sat like a gray rock.

Rucksack shook his head. "So much to tell you," he said.

"Tell me about what?"

"We'll get to it. Eat up. Let's keep looking."

Jay zipped the pack closed and put it on his back. He held up the samosa, and his stomach sent up something like a cross between a growl and a cheer. "I guess I am still hungry," he said, opening his mouth to take a big bite of samosa.

His teeth closed on nothing.

"What the?" Jay said.

Rucksack's eyes were wide as he peeled the

newspaper off the samosa. "Sorry, my lad," he said, "but we don't want this damaged."

Rucksack held out the naked samosa, and Jay reached for it.

The cow didn't even slow down as it plucked Jay's samosa from Rucksack's hand, munching slowly as it wandered away.

Jay realized his mouth was hanging open. A stream of drool washed over his chin.

"We'll get another one in a minute," Rucksack said. "If it'll make you feel better, I'll do the haggling. In the meantime, well, I'm sure you can hold out a wee while longer."

Jay sighed. "This had better be good. What's so important?"

"Today's paper," Rucksack said. "I hadn't gotten to see it yet, what with today's excitement." He read quietly for a moment, then said, "Damn, damn, damn."

"What's the big deal?"

"Confirmation." Rucksack shook his head. "I knew there was a slim chance it wouldn't be. Maybe there still is. But even if there is, I can't give myself the luxury o' that frail wee hope anymore."

"What are you talking about?"

"In about a month and a half, there's going to be an eclipse."

"Right," Jay said. "Agamuskara's supposed to be the best place to see it."

"You're in for a real bloody treat," Rucksack continued. "Today's paper has confirmed that the eclipse is going to be a mirror eclipse."

"A what?"

"Aye," Rucksack said. "It would make sense you

wouldn't know. They're bloody rare. Last one that happened in recorded history was... was the day o' The Blast."

Rucksack seemed to hesitate. Jade had mentioned something about The Blast always bothering Rucksack. Jay wondered why that would be. *Then again,* he thought, *I could know Rucksack for a thousand years and probably still know only a fraction of who he is and what he's about.*

Rucksack took a deep breath and continued, his left hand squeezing into a fist. "A mirror eclipse happens under very particular conditions. The eclipse must be total—a complete blackout o' the sun. And there must be clouds."

"If there are clouds," Jay said, "how can you see the eclipse?"

"That isn't understood," Rucksack replied. "The eclipse still appears in the sky, as if it were lower than the clouds. You look up and there it is: big black and gray clouds. You'd think a storm was brewing that could break the world like crushing an egg in the hand. Right there with all that boiling storm, there's this big black disc o' the sun. And it's not like other total eclipses, where maybe you still can see just a wee outline of light, silver-and-gold lining, around the black. Oh no. This is the total o' total eclipses. No light at all. Total dark."

"So how can it even be seen?"

"That's why it's called a mirror eclipse. Next to the black disc is a second disc. This one burns bright as noon o' the brightest day o' the year. The light is both gold and silver, and it shines as if it could light up not just our wee world but the entire universe."

"So there are two suns, one dark and one light, beside each other, burning in the sky?"

Rucksack nodded. "It's said that on days like this, the world can choose dark or choose light."

"What did the world choose the day of The Blast?"

"The world chose both, Jay, but that's a story for another day. It's not important right now."

"You were there, weren't you?"

"Another day."

"Why won't you talk about it?"

"The past is called the past because it is past. We are dealing with what is happening now, and that is far more important than days gone by." Rucksack sighed. "I have so much I have to tell you, Jay. And it's time. Beyond time. I should've told you right away."

"What are you talking about?"

"Come on, Jay," Rucksack said. "It's not just prices that have been bothering you. You've heard it too."

"Heard what?"

"You aren't fooling me. You've heard it in the pub. You've heard it when you walk down the street. Sometimes now it's accompanied by a pointed finger or a direct look." Rucksack shook his head. "There's a story out there, running loose as a wild animal. A man went up and down Mount Everest one night by the light o' the full moon, as easy as walking down the street to get a samosa. And you know who this man is, don't you?"

Jay's eyes narrowed. "No, I don't."

Rucksack traced a triangle in the air, then a circle, just as the samosa vendor had done. "Yes, you do," Rucksack said. "We have to talk."

"Let's get that samosa first," Jay said. "I'm

famished."

"Jay!" Rucksack shouted. "Mim and Pim—"

"Are around here somewhere. I'll see if they're hiding behind the samosa man."

"No, Jay. There they go!"

Rucksack took off running. After a moment, Jay followed, cursing under his breath, stomach rumbling.

Mim and Pim's heads bobbed in the crowd. Everywhere they ran it was as if the world opened a path for them then closed it for Rucksack and Jay. Hard as it was to keep sight of them, much less catch up, Jay still sensed that they had his passport.

*It's close,* he thought. *Closer than I could have hoped.*

For days they had searched, chasing any little scrap or hint. *The one time we see them,* Jay thought, *it's by surprise! Maybe it's just in one of their pockets, and this is all as simple as reaching out and just plucking it away.*

Jay turned right when he saw the other men do the same. They came to a familiar side street.

And Jay nearly stopped chasing them.

The Mystery Chickpea was back.

Jade had speculated about its absence. Sometimes Jay thought Kailash was trying to find the old man who ran it. And now the cart was back, as if it had never left.

*No time to dwell on that,* Jay thought. *Get your passport back,* he reminded himself, to his stomach's annoyance. *Then you can eat the man out of every drop and scrap of slopple he's got.*

Mim and Pim ran down the alley where Jigme and Asha lived. *I always wind up here,* Jay thought.

He kept running. Then he saw Rucksack, breathing hard but no longer running. He was knocking on a red door. Asha's door.

Jay stopped next to him. "Where are they?" he said.

"I don't know," Rucksack replied. "I followed them then had to dodge a couple of people. When I came around and could see down the alley again, they were gone. It's as if they disappeared from right outside Asha's door." He knocked again. "Asha?" he said. "Are you here? It's Rucksack. Can I talk to you?"

No answer.

"Maybe she's resting," Jay said.

Rucksack stared at the door, as if trying to see through it. "Maybe," he said, stepping away.

"We nearly had them," Jay said.

"Who knows what we nearly had," Rucksack replied.

"Maybe we should keep going down the alley."

"They're not down there, Jay. I would've seen them running."

"Maybe they're at that temple."

Rucksack shook his head.

"What makes you so sure?"

"Why do you want to go to that place again?"

Jay stepped back. His stomach growled. A faint feeling crept over him like insects crawling. Too much running on an empty stomach.

"We will find them," Rucksack said. "We'll get your passport back. It's not lost. I know it. But there's nothing else for us to do today."

"What now?"

"Get something to eat," Rucksack said. "And Jay..."

"What?"

"Tomorrow, at dawn, let's you and me go for a boat ride."

"That sounds very romantic and all, but I am taken."

"There's so much you need to understand. Best place won't be in the streets. Too many distractions. Too many people listening. Meet me by the boats before the sun comes up."

"You'll tell me everything you know?"

"We don't have that kind of time," Rucksack said. "You'll have to settle for all I can tell you. But I do believe you'll be satisfied."

Jay started walking back toward the mouth of the alley. "Okay, Rucksack," he said. "I trust you. After all, isn't that what friends are for?"

"Aye, Jay," Rucksack replied. "Aye indeed."

They wandered in silence for a little while. As the mouth of the alley drew near, Rucksack said, "You're going to go there, aren't you."

"Of course I am," Jay replied. "I'm famished. A cow stole my samosa, and if I don't eat there now, for all I know The Mystery Chickpea will disappear again before I get another chance."

"I can't dissuade you, can I?"

"Guru Deep and his guidebook couldn't. The other people at the hostel couldn't. Even Jade couldn't."

"You do understand, though, don't you?"

"Yeah. Everyone thinks the place is food poisoning central."

"Have you ever seen anyone eat there?"

"No. All the better."

"I can't tell you what to do, of course."

"Of course," Jay said. "But this place is famous. Or infamous. Or both. But I have to know. A lot of people say things that wind up being wrong. I can only know something for certain if I find out for myself."

"Why?"

"Because it's here. Because it is famous and infamous. Because it was gone and now it's back. Because it really fascinates me and if I didn't get to eat there, I know I would kick myself for it later. That's why."

Rucksack sighed. They reached the mouth of the alley. "I'm going to talk with my mother. We have much to discuss."

"Okay," Jay said. "Meet you for a pint later?"

"Or ten."

"Oh, I have to be good. Jade said she has something special for me tonight." Jay grinned.

Rucksack frowned again. "More than I want to know," he said. "I'll see you later."

He left before Jay could reply. *Why does everyone seem to have a problem with me and Jade?* he thought. *We make each other happy. Shouldn't that be enough for Rucksack and Kailash? Sometimes it's as if they don't want us to be together.*

Jay shook his head and started wandering toward the clouds of steam rising all around The Mystery Chickpea. *I admit,* he thought, *it doesn't seem the likeliest of loves. But there's something there that we can't deny. Shouldn't deny. And why should we? I can have Jade and still be a traveler.*

Behind the steam, the old man waited. The folds of his white clothes wrapped around him like a robe. The shining white fabric was as clean as if it had just come from the laundry.

Jay glanced down at the three bubbling pots. Fresh and dried splatters covered the pots and the top of the cart. *How could someone who makes this sort of slopple be so clean?* he wondered.

The old man's dark face was patchworked with wrinkles and lines, yet it had the smooth suppleness of a younger man's face. If not for the white beard that wound down to the old man's chest, the face would have seemed not ready for shaving. His brown-and-black eyes reminded Jay a little of Rucksack and Kailash. Behind the beard, even, it seemed as if there were similarities in his face.

*Maybe they're from the same region,* Jay thought.

Jay waited but the old man wouldn't ask what he wanted. Finally, Jay remembered: he can't talk. Jay pointed at the three pots. "One of each, please."

The old man nodded and served up a bowl.

Jay's stomach rejoiced as he ate. At last, a meal! He felt like he'd hardly started the first bowl before it was empty. The second bowl went just as quickly. Finally, after the third bowl, Jay felt full again.

*Why can't you speak?* Jay thought. *And how are we going to haggle?*

"No charge," the old man replied in Jay's mind, as clearly as if he'd spoken out loud. "And I cannot speak because that which gives also takes."

Jay blinked. *Did I get so hungry I started hallucinating again?*

The old man nodded and smiled.

*If you really can speak in my mind,* Jay thought, *then tell me how you gave the soup such a creamy texture.*

"Some butter stirred in at the finish," came the reply in Jay's mind.

*So you can talk.*

"I can think," the old man said. "That's usually far

more important than talking."

"Who are you?" Jay said out loud.

"I am the man who sees," said the voice in his mind again. "I could see or I could talk. That was my choice. I chose to see."

"But you're talking now. Just in my head. Which is pretty weird, in case you were wondering."

"I learned to talk in my own way."

"How?"

The old man pointed at the pots. "To cook is not only to feed."

"You're telling me that you're communicating with me through what I ate?"

The old man smiled. "I'm an honest cook," said the voice. "I'm sorry about that."

"What do you mean?" Jay said. "And where have you been the last couple of weeks? I've been dying to try your food."

No answer.

"You said you were honest."

"I only tell the truth," said the voice. "Unless I prefer not to speak."

"What, you take a holiday? Get sick off your own cooking? Wait, maybe I don't want you to answer that last one."

"No and no." The voice paused. "I was taken out of destiny's way."

"Destiny's way?"

"I'm very sorry for all that is going to happen to you, Jay of the world," said the voice. "You seem nice enough. And earnest. Don't see enough of that these days. It's a shame you have to choose."

"Choose what?"

"The choice of every traveler. The heart. Or the road."

"You know what I say?"

"What do you say, Jay the traveler?"

Jay grinned. "When given a choice, sometimes you have to take both."

"Well, then, you sound quite decided."

"Glad you can concede that."

"Of course," said the voice in his mind. "Just as I concede that the ground can just as earnestly decide that the lightning will not strike it."

"You're saying what I choose doesn't matter."

"What you choose matters. All choices still lead to your destiny, but one destiny can have many outcomes."

"Why do you look like Rucksack?"

"I knew his father. A long time ago."

"How long?"

"Long enough to know what fire feels like when it smiles."

Jay had a feeling in his mind, as if the voice were pulling away, fading. "Wait," Jay said. "What do you mean by that?"

No answer came.

Jay stared at the old man, who stood behind the simmering pots yet somehow seemed miles and years away. No answers came from the brown-and-black eyes.

His full belly felt strangely heavy as Jay left The Mystery Chickpea. The long day's chases suddenly weighed on him as he walked slowly back toward the Everest Base Camp.

*I'd better rest up,* he thought. *Jade said it was going to be a long, long night.* "And I don't care what some weird voice in my mind says," Jay told the city. "I don't have to choose Jade or the road. Dammit, I choose both."


JAY SLID IN CLOSER, his foot knocking the table where they sat. They giggled then went back to kissing. His hand lightly squeezed Jade's inner thigh through her dress, stoking a heat inside her that would make the Indian sun seem cool as winter.

Jade kissed him more deeply, and he opened his mouth to hers.

His breath caught as she slowly traced her fingers up and down his thigh through the thin fabric of his pants. The wooden bench creaked in the empty pub.

*Does my bed creak?* Jade thought. *I guess we'll find out.* She smiled as they kissed. *It's going to be a good night,* she thought. *A long, loud, hot, good night.*

A heat blazed from the top of her head to between her thighs. Jay's hand brushed slowly up her right side, just grazing her breast as he wrapped his arms around her back.

For a moment they stopped kissing, and she stared into his eyes. "Your eyes are as jade as my name," she said.

"Fitting, isn't it?"

"I can think of something else that'll be fitting," she replied, moving her hand and smiling when his eyes got wide.

It was nearly enough to keep the rest of the thoughts away.

But not enough.

She kissed him again.

Her long, tense night in the pub had been filled with more low, scared talk about a new disappearance. The Mystery Chickpea had returned that morning, but people kept saying that later in the day, after serving a customer, something in the nearby alley had gotten the old man's attention, as if beckoning him.

Some said the moment he left, the pots stopped simmering and the steam disappeared.

The cart remained, but the old man never come back.

As if that wasn't enough, no matter how much she tried to ignore it The Management's note burned at her. The words looped in her mind: "Love is not the traveler's path..."

Jade kissed him harder. "Jay," she whispered then nibbled at his ear, making him gasp. "Let's go to my room."

She leaned away, staring hard and bright into his face. *What will he look like in the morning?* Jade thought. *What will it be like to wake up next to someone?*

Jay's eyes shone back at her. *I still have time,* she thought.

"Jade," he started to say, his hand stroking her face. "Jade..."

His eyes widened. All the color fell out of his face.

"Jay?"

"Oh... no..."

He clenched his mouth shut. Jay jumped onto his feet, looked left, looked right. Panic rose in his face. He scrambled past Jade, knocking her against the hard wooden back of the bench. Coughing, she tried to get her breath back.

Jay sprinted toward a door that was not the door to the hostel rooms.

The toilet.

Moments after he ran through the door, the sounds reached her ears. Wet splatterings, grunts, whimpers, and heavings. Jade sucked in air and made herself stand up. She breathed fast. Desire fell out of her like beer from a spilled pint. "What's going on?" she said, walking toward the door.

The understanding stopped her. *He went to the bloody damn feckin Mystery Chickpea*, she thought. *He ate loads of that slopple. And tonight—our first night—he gets food poisoning.*

*Lovely.*

She smoothed her hands over her thighs, which now felt like nothing more than muscle wrapped in skin.

After a few minutes, Jay staggered out of the toilet, his face gray. He stood in the doorway and would not look her in the eye. Behind him, the reek of diarrhea and vomit seemed to bring all the city's open sewers together into the pub.

"I'm sorry," he said.

"For what?" she said. "For ignoring all of us? For eating at the worst place in the city?"

"It was really good," he said. "And it was there and I was hungry. I guess that wasn't a good idea after all."

Anger started to burn in her. "Is that all you're sorry for?"

"Of course not," he said. "Tonight... Tonight was going to be amazing. Except that I ruined it."

Jade shook her head. "All we can do now is get you better." *What am I going to do with him?* she thought. *He looks so weak. Is he going to be okay in the dorm?*

Jay trudged toward the door to the stairs. "I've been here before, you know. Sick. This already seems like it'll be the worst I've ever had. But still, it's not the first time I've eaten the wrong thing. I'll head to my bed. I'll manage."

He opened the door and stopped, then turned and looked her in the eye as he leaned against the doorframe. "I'd love to kiss you," Jay said. "I'd love so many things to be different right now. Including that my mouth is so gross that the last thing in the world I want to do is get it near the most beautiful woman I've ever known." He shook his head. "I'll make it up to you. I promise. Good night, Jade."

He started to walk out the door.

"Wait."

Jade walked over to him, turning off the pub lights and locking the door behind her. "You don't have to be alone. You look horrible, but I've smelled worse. It's not the night we had in mind, but I'll look after you. Someone has to keep an eye on you."

"I can't say I'll be any fun," Jay replied. "After a night with me, your room is going to reek like the bodies burning on the banks of the Ganges."

"If it's any motivation, I sleep naked."

Jay smiled, though it seemed to take half the energy from him. "Jade," he said, "my wonderful Jade. I want to say yes. But it's for the best. Go to bed. Sleep. Forgive me, if you can. Maybe peek in on me in the morning—make sure I'm not drowning in a pool of my own bad decisions."

He squeezed her hand and trudged up the stairs. He didn't look back.

When he was out of sight, Jade stared at the floor. Tears burned her eyes.

She went to her room but she hardly slept. Thoughts of duty and love battled in her mind and heart.

In the morning, the sun came up the same as it always did. She stood at the window, listening to the city, listening to the Everest Base Camp, listening, above all, to the traveler on the third floor. Between bouts of staggering to the toilet, Jay had slept as well as he could. Throughout the night, his dorm mates thought of nothing but getting out early to flee the stench in the room, though a couple of people were making sure to check on him.

Once she was ready, Jade stopped by his room and let herself in. Some people had already left; others still slept and wouldn't know she was there. She kneeled by his bed. "Jay?" she said.

No response. He lay on his right side, his left arm stretched down over his legs, which were straight as sticks, the left leg lying on the right. His head rested on his other arm.

"Jay?"

She lay her hand on his cheek, his breath warm on her palm. *At least he's sleeping now,* she thought. *Though I wish I could've gotten to look in his eyes again. Or do I? If he didn't want to be with me last night, what does he think now?*

Jade leaned forward to kiss his forehead, but as her lips neared his skin, she stopped. *I don't want to wake him,* she told herself. *He needs to rest.*

She set a flask of cooled, sweetened, uninfluenced tea by his bed, along with a small bowl of cooled plain rice. Without looking back at him, she left the room.

In the pub, she cleared away the last remains of their drinks, of the beginning of what was supposed to be...

"Oh stop," she told herself. "Just stop. The night didn't turn out the way you expected, but the day still brings the duty you have."

With a deep breath, she dove back into her tasks, preparing the pub while making herself a small breakfast. Her thoughts of Jay, her feelings for Jay, she tucked into a far-back part of her mind. It wasn't time for those right now. There was much more to do than dwell on love and disappointment. She turned her thoughts instead to the disappearance, to the shadow of fear that had fallen over the city.

*I've been too distracted,* she thought. *Not helpful enough. Not diligent enough. Time to change that.*

A knock sounded on the front door. Jade started pulling a pint of GPS. The beer settled as she opened the door with a smile, but as Rucksack and Kailash came in, their faces were tight and hard.

"What's going on?" Jade asked.

"Jay should be here too," Kailash said.

Jade shook her head. "Good morning to you too. Jay's not going anywhere. Got food poisoning from The Mystery Chickpea."

"So that's why he didn't meet me this morning. We were worried," Rucksack said.

"Do gods get food poisoning?" Jade asked, a rough edge to her voice.

"Probably not," Rucksack replied. "But he isn't a god yet. For now, he's still a man. Well, mostly a man."

"Mostly?"

"Later," Kailash said. "We need to be in the city."

"It's the disappearances, isn't it?" Jade asked. "Is it true that the old man from The Mystery Chickpea is gone?"

Rucksack nodded. "His cart was still there this morning. He never took it away, the way he normally does. No one's seen him since Jay ate there."

"I take it the police have no leads?"

Rucksack's shrug said that any attention the police were paying was misdirected. Kailash looked away from the two of them, her eyes distant and hard.

Jade handed Rucksack his pint. "You'd best drink quickly then."

"Nothing makes a hard day easier like a quick drop," he replied.

"Did Jay say anything about The Mystery Chickpea?" Kailash asked.

"No," Jade replied. "He wouldn't really talk about it, except to say that it was amazing. Before..." Her thoughts flashed back to the kissing, the way he touched her. "Before he got sick."

"A pity. Perhaps I should speak with him before we go."

Defensiveness rushed through Jade. "He's resting. He needs to be left alone."

Kailash shook her head. "The things happening here are too important for us to be delicate with Jay because of a stomachache."

"No," Jade replied, taking a step forward so she was close to Kailash, staring her in the eye and blocking her from entering the hostel.

"You have no idea how easy it would be for me to go past you," Kailash said, glaring sharply.

"Maybe out in the wide world, where you're older than all the city put together," Jade replied. "But not here. I'm the Jade of Agamuskara, and this is my pub. My rules."

"Really?" Kailash replied. "And here I thought you were just an employee taking orders."

"Mum," Rucksack said. "Jade. Enough."

"Are you taking her side?" both women demanded.

"No," Rucksack said. "And yes. You're both right, and you're both focused on the wrong thing. We're leaving Jay be. And Jade's right. Her pub, her rules. Even you or I couldn't budge that door open if she or The Management didn't want us to."

"Interesting," Kailash replied. In a blur, she walked past Jade and went over to the door. She grabbed the doorknob but the metal didn't turn. The door didn't so much as rattle in the frame, but stayed as still as a mountain.

"No one comes in here without my leave," Jade said quietly. "And certainly no one interferes with my guests."

An angry fire in her eyes, Kailash came back over. "Do you know why people are so afraid of The Mystery Chickpea's food?"

"Because after one bowl you may need to remodel your bathroom?" Jade replied.

A small smirk pierced Kailash's cheeks then was gone. "I told you what happened the day the Smiling Fire came, the day the first dia ubh changed us."

"Yes," Jade said. "You became... Well, whatever you are."

"The man who runs The Mystery Chickpea was one of us."

"Mum?"

"I'm sorry I hadn't told you yet, son," Kailash replied. "Another story for another time."

Rucksack drank his pint, a sullen silence on his face.

*Like mother like son,* Jade thought.

"He had been wounded by the Smiling Fire," Kailash continued, "but not killed. His body healed, but his name had been burned away from his memory, from our knowledge, from all existence. Along with the loss of his name, he lost his voice. For thousands of years, he has never spoken again, and he has never known who he is. Not even the dia ubh could return that to him. But to compensate, he gained sight—sight beyond seeing, sight that is far, long, and true. Over time, he learned to express his wisdom through cooking. There is... There was... no finer cook in all the world. The warnings you hear about The Mystery Chickpea, the lies that even Guru Deep spreads—"

"What does he spread other than lies?" Rucksack said, finishing his pint.

Kailash ignored him. "It's not food poisoning they fear. That's just an excuse, a rationalization people use to scare themselves away. What they fear is the unavoidable truth gained from eating that food, and what it means for one's life."

"That's why you want to talk to Jay," Jade said. "You want to know what he learned."

Rucksack shrugged. "Maybe he's already learning it. Maybe it's just being... expressed... in a different way."

"Perhaps you're right," Kailash said. "I'll leave him be. For now."

"Do you know why the old man was gone?" Jade asked.

"I fear it was because of me," Kailash replied, "but I can't know for certain. It's as if he were hiding something from me. But I don't know what. Or if that's the case. I don't know where he went or why he came back. Maybe we'll find answers if we go to his cart." She walked to the pub's front door, glaring at Jade. "May I open this door, Jade Agamuskara Bluegold?"

"Here, allow me," Jade said. She opened the door, all the while returning Kailash's glare.

Standing in the doorway were two men with everywhere faces, wearing tan pants and white button-down shirts. A strange darkness lurked beneath the fabric of their shirts, but that had to be the trick of light and shadow. There was no mistaking the fear wide in their eyes, their trembling hands hanging in the air and apparently about to knock.

Jade and Kailash broke off their stare.

"What the hell are you doing here?" Jade said.

"Mim!" Rucksack said, nodding to the man on the left. "Pim!" He set his empty glass on the bar. "Well, call the gods a bunch o' bloody bastards. To what do we owe this honor?"

Jade studied the men's faces. The jovial mischief she'd seen before was gone, replaced by a timid paleness. "What's happened?" she asked.

"The alley. The Mystery Chickpea. The black temple."

"We know," Rucksack said. "Maybe you should stick to pranks. You're rather bad at news."

Mim shook his head. "We know what's causing the

disappearances. We know what happened to the old man."

"What happened? How do you know?" Kailash replied.

"Please come with us. We'll show you."

"Come with you?" Jade said. "You stole Jay's passport. You blew up one of my taps. You've been leading Jay and Rucksack on a wild goose chase around the city. Who do you think you are that we should trust you?"

"We know who we are, Jade Agamuskara Bluegold," Pim said. "Do you know who you are anymore?"

She said nothing.

"It must be so difficult to be both on the scales as well as the scale itself," Mim said with gentleness. "I almost don't envy the dilemma you try not to face."

"Almost?" *What the hell do you know?* Jade thought.

Mim nodded. "Even if the consequences seem frightening, love is an option for you. Sometimes I wish that was an internal struggle that could threaten to tear me apart."

Jade stepped between the men, into the bright morning sun. Its heat was a pleasant touch after all the harsh words from everyone in the pub. "You still haven't answered me," she said.

Kailash and Rucksack stepped outside and pulled the door closed. Mim and Pim turned to face each other. "We must?" Mim said.

"We must," Pim replied. "If you don't trust us after this, we understand. We'll leave. We won't interfere anymore."

Mim shrugged. "Might as well, really. There won't be anything to interfere with."

The men turned so they stood side to side. They unbuttoned their shirts down to just above their bellies and pulled the fabric aside. Standing together, side by side, it was as if together their burns formed a single image of a smile. Ragged red, pink, and black flesh started at an opposite point on each man's chest, arcing down like a scythe blade from a mere dot of red to a black wasteland, three inches at its widest.

"He's returned," Mim said.

"We suspected," Kailash replied, her voice low and soft, as if to conceal a tremble. "But we weren't certain yet."

The blackened flesh shone like obsidian in the bright sun. Jade's stomach turned and she looked away. "We'll go with you," she said, breathing deeply and forcing her breakfast back down.

All the way to the alley, no one spoke. The Mystery Chickpea still sat empty, quiet, devoid of even the slightest bit of steam. "It looks so ordinary," Jade said, touching the cart's splintered wood and peeled paint. But there was nothing beyond the wood. No voice. No feeling. No memory.

"Like everything else in this world," Kailash said, "the greatest always look the most ordinary."

"Why is that?" Jade asked.

"They're too busy doing," Rucksack smiled, "to worry themselves with putting on a show. Can you tell anything?"

Jade shook her head. "What voice this had, left with the old man. There's nothing for me to hear."

The old man's absence was heavier, more noticeable than his presence had ever seemed. *I never ate there,* Jade thought. *Not once. Though that's probably for the best.*

*I didn't even try to speak with him, though I saw him all the time. Now he's gone.*

Jade saw Rucksack's stare. "You can feel it, can't you?" he said.

She nodded. "Feel it. Hear it. It's everywhere."

Mim and Pim looked at each other. "What is?"

"The fear. The loss," Jade continued. "If the old man was part of the city's beginning, the city feels his absence as if part of Agamuskara itself has been cut away. The city is remembering what lies at its heart."

"The black temple," Rucksack said.

"The Smiling Fire," Kailash said.

"Do we have to go down the alley?" Mim asked.

"Not today," Jade said. "I just need to listen to it, and I can do that from here."

"That's a relief," Pim said, laying his hand softly on his chest. "The closer we get to it, to him... these burn. It's like they're going to catch flame."

Kailash held up her hand. "I don't know if I can heal you," she said, "but I can help."

"No, you can't," Pim said. "Not any more than he could consume us. And for the same reason."

"And what reason is that?" Rucksack asked.

"You really don't know, do you?" Mim replied.

"Know what?" Kailash said.

"Whenever you've seen us," Pim replied, "we can see the question in you: 'Why do they look familiar?'"

"The answer is simple," Mim said. "We used to live among you. In the village."

Kailash's eyes widened. "No!" she said, staring closely. "But you—I know you!" She shook her head. "But how can it be? You were among the first to die."

"And he did kill us," Pim said. "Mostly."

"The dia ubh changed us too," Mim said. "Well, mostly the dia ubh."

"Mostly?" Kailash said.

"We aren't fully alive," Pim said. "We aren't fully dead. We have our own role to play in this world still. That's why we're here. That's why we do what we do. Right down to letting Rucksack and Jay spot us yesterday. But when they chased us to the alley, we don't know what happened. We neared a red door then all went dark. When we woke, we were inside his temple."

"The black temple at the end of the alley?" Rucksack asked.

Mim nodded. "'You have to be awake,' he said to us. 'You have to be aware.'"

"Did he know who you were?" Rucksack asked. "Did he sense his own lost power in you?"

Pim shook his head. "Whatever he is, he has forgotten so much of the fire that he remembers little of what he once was or what his strength once was. He sips raindrops and believes he drinks oceans."

"We had nowhere to flee to, no way to fight," Mim continued. "His mouth opened, red and black and somehow larger than his actual being. He approached us. The air was so hot it burned. And then he... Then he tried to take it back."

"The fire of life," Kailash said.

Pim nodded. "It's like he wanted not to eat us but to consume us, body and soul, mind and fire. He tried." Pim looked at his torso and grimaced. "How he tried. But you could say it was as if we gave him indigestion. The fire of life is what he wants, all of it, back under his control. But the fire of life is not the fire that burns in us. He leaped away, as if in agony. In the confusion, we were able to flee. Perhaps he feared us. We do not know but we were able to find a door and return to the city."

"Did it... hurt him?" Jade asked. "Weaken him?"

"I don't think so," Mim said. "He is weak, he is afraid, but he is gaining strength and courage. Even afraid, he is as a threatened, cornered animal. He knows now that life is all but completely and forever out of his control. He knows that he has but one chance to regain his former strength, one chance to take back the fire of life."

"He knows about the dia ubh?" Rucksack asked.

"Yes," Pim said. "But that's not all. The old man was there."

"Alive?" Kailash asked.

Pim shrugged. "No."

Pain rang through Jade, and she saw the same grief etched into the faces of Kailash and Rucksack.

"We always stopped by when we were in Agamuskara," Mim said. "Just because you're not fully alive doesn't mean you can't enjoy some of the best food in this world."

Rucksack sighed. "The Smiling Fire took the old man from The Mystery Chickpea?"

"We don't know why he left," Pim said. "We just know that he was in the temple and that the Smiling Fire had consumed him. By being in the presence of Jay and the dia ubh, that knowledge now passed to the Smiling Fire. All that knowledge, all that sight... if the Smiling Fire has consumed it and absorbed it, he now sees all the world. He sees the future ahead—what he must do and when he can do it. He knows the mirror eclipse nears. He knows he needs the dia ubh. And he knows about Jay. Jay is in danger."

"We're all in danger," Rucksack said.

"Jay worst of all," Mim replied. "The Smiling Fire knows Jay needs to be there when the dia ubh opens, so the Smiling Fire can kill him. It's not just the light. Jay's blood, his soul, already influenced by the dia ubh, combined with the mirror eclipse and the opened dia ubh, will restore the Smiling Fire to all his former power. And more. He'll destroy the world. He'll burn all life to cinders and then eat the cinders. The world will be nothing but ash and his smile again."

Jade walked over to the walls at the mouth of the alley. She touched her left hand to the white stone. Instead of warmth under the hot sun, a shivering coolness ran through the rock. "It's as if the very walls of the city are terrified," she said. No one replied. She closed her eyes and bent her head, listening to the walls of the city.

The walls saw and heard everything, after all, and always had. These first walls of Agamuskara had been erected years after the black temple's significance had already begun to fade to an oddity, a mere strange formation at the heart of the city, before falling out of memory entirely. The walls heard the songs and stories fade. So many years, so many tales and feelings, so many lives, all absorbed into the stone's memory.

No faces. No sense of identities. To the long, slow life of the stone, distinguishing human faces and lives was as incomprehensible as a person trying to distinguish raindrops during the monsoon.

She could sense some things though: a young

woman, an old man, children chasing a running child. And newer memories. She focused harder.

The young boy followed the older boy. Both were wrapped in purpose and confusion, doubt and fear. The feelings were so fresh. The younger boy followed the older boy down the alley. But only the older boy had come out again.

It had to be the first disappearance.

Next was the old man. He was one of the few things older than the walls, if not older than the stone itself. The wall remembered him for that.

A sudden fear, a sadness had pulled him away from the cart yesterday. But it was more than that. It was concern. Protectiveness.

*He left out of love,* Jade thought, *but for who?*

The old man crossed into the alley. Then all was a fog from which he did not emerge.

*No,* Jade thought. *Not a fog. Smoke from a Smiling Fire.*

The old man faded. Now Jade saw something else. More children came down the alley, but not children who lived there or nearby. Children from around the city. Going down the alley.

Not returning.

*It didn't seem like a memory though. It was more like... a vision,* Jade thought. *Am I being shown the future, or what the future could be?*

Jade opened her eyes and pulled her hand away from the wall.

She heard a voice say, "Jade?"

Turning, she saw Kailash staring at her with deep worry in her ancient eyes. *She looks more and more like an older mother,* Jade thought. She told them what she had seen.

"What do we do now?" Kailash asked.

Jade stared down the alley, looking away from all of them. The tears were starting. Too many lives. The children. The old man. The love she did not know or understand.

*The love I cannot have.*

"We need to get Jay feeling better," Jade said. "Then Rucksack is going to tell him everything."

"What about you?" Rucksack said.

"What's happening here is beyond me. Beyond my heart. Beyond what I want. There's only one thing for me to do," Jade replied. "I'm going to do my duty."

"What do you mean?" Kailash asked.

*Love is not the traveler's path,* Jade thought.

"Another story for another time," she said, walking away from the alley, back toward the pub, alone.

JIGME RAN. The crowds parted fearfully, as if he were a runaway truck. No one bumped into him. No one tripped him. No one who knew him or knew of him sneered at the boy with no father, the boy with the mother who had done wrong.

*And what wrong had she done?* Jigme thought. *Without a husband, she brought me into the world.*

They could all burn. Burn like the old man had. It had been hard to find the courage, but the Smiling Fire had guided him. From there, Jigme had simply gone back to the living end of the alley, watching from behind a wall as Jay had finished eating and left.

A strange longing shone from the old man's dark eyes, as if he badly wanted to tell the tourist something but could not. When he looked away, the longing in Jigme's stare had caught him.

Then Jigme had turned down the alley, and the old man had followed. He had even followed Jigme into the temple, without a doubt, without a flinch.

It wasn't until they were inside that things had become difficult.

The old man's bright eyes had widened when the Smiling Fire loomed over him, and his face contorted with deep terror. Yet he did not try to run. He did not beg or plea. He trembled with fear but soon the old man's face changed.

It was as if he were remembering something long forgotten, something that gave him courage and some sort of peace. The Smiling Fire said nothing, only gathered its strength. Moments remained before the old man would be less than ash.

The old man raised his head and stared into the twin coals of the Smiling Fire's eyes. He smiled brighter than the flames looming above him. Then he looked away and locked his gaze on Jigme.

The old man looked at him as if he were trying to say something.

The Smiling Fire lunged up.

Old yet vibrant, quavering with separateness and longing, the words came into Jigme's mind.

"I'm sorry."

Jigme stared deep into his thoughts, which opened like new days inside his mind. There was so much the old man had to say, so much he suddenly wanted to tell Jigme. Why now? After all these silent years, why nothing till now?

Jigme saw all the times he'd walked by the cart, feeling the brown-and-black eyes staring at him. Not even the day he'd eaten there had the old man tried so hard to communicate with him.

Now came the cries, the memories, the stories, all surging toward Jigme's mind like a once-trickling river now swollen with spring rains and winter melt. So much to say. So much to understand.

One word came racing toward him—not yet distinct, but Jigme focused on it, tried to understand...

The Smiling Fire crashed down like a wave.

"No!" Jigme cried, but it was all too late.

The flood dried up. The thoughts vanished.

Jigme was alone again.

Shards of what he had almost learned fell around him and disappeared, unknown and lost forever. A black cloud filled the temple, yet all was so silent. No screams. No words. No sound at all.

*He was trying to tell me something,* Jigme thought with sadness and longing, *but I couldn't understand in time.*

The cloud faded. The Smiling Fire reappeared and stood before Jigme. He seemed to glow in his red-tinged darkness, as if with fullness and happiness.

"You have done well," the Smiling Fire said. "He was one who long ago defied me, and the time for my revenge had come."

The smile became bigger. The temple seemed hotter. "Much of my old strength has been returned. Yet now I understand."

"What do you mean? Why did you have to kill him?"

The Smiling Fire walked away from Jigme. "Because he stole the fire from me. Yet as if in recompense, I see so much more now. I see so far. He has given me new eyes. Others stole too, as he did, but most of them are dead. Their fires are amongst the world and will be easy enough to recover."

Tears sprang into Jigme's eyes, but he didn't understand why. "I thought you sent him away."

"Oh, you mean the child?"

Jigme nodded but he would not let his memory return to that day, so recent and so raw.

"I've done as I said," The Smiling Fire told him. "The child has gone to the better place I described."

"To the school?"

"Yes. The school. Far north from here. Near the mountains," the Smiling Fire said, his words halting and full of pauses. Sometimes Jigme felt like a finger was poking at images in his mind. "He is still on his way. But he will... He will send you... letters. I can feel his excitement, even now."

Jigme's fears faded in the lull of the words. The child who had followed, now had gone on. It was okay. The old man was different. He stole. He had to be punished. Shouldn't there be punishment for those who stole so much? It had to be right. But so much had happened.

Weariness fell over Jigme.

"May I rest now?"

The Smiling Fire raised a hand. "There is no time for rest. There is only getting stronger or getting weaker. If you rest, I will fade. If I fade..."

Jigme nodded, ignoring the tiredness that had fallen over his body. "What must I do?"

With a wave of the Smiling Fire's hand, images passed into Jigme's mind, along with that feeling again of something poking at his thoughts. He saw children, smiling and running, eyes large and bright, blazing with the fire of life.

The smile widened. "That is what I understand now. The children, Jigme. The children are everything. Bring them. As many as you can. The ones like you. Alone. Desperate. Hungry. I will... I will help them all."

"Just like the first child?" The child's name tried to sound in his mind, but Jigme made it go away.

"Yes. When the time is right, it will be your turn too."

"To go away to the school?"

"With the other children."

"But Amma..."

"She will be... proud... of you," the Smiling Fire said. "She can go there too. You can learn again. You will have fields and hills to run around in. Green. Full of life. Isn't that what you want?

Jigme saw it too, as clear and vibrant as if it were a memory and not a dream. Cold streams ran over grassy hills. In the distance rose the peaks of the Himalayas. One mountain stood above all others. He ran and ran and ran, through the crisp morning air, ran with the other children, all smiles and fast breaths. When he returned, there was Amma, cups of hot chai waiting, and tales of each other's day...

"It does not have to be a dream, Jigme," the Smiling Fire said. "It can be your life. But only if I am strong again."

*It can be my life...*

The words and images resounded through Jigme's mind as he ran through the crowds in the dusty, hot street, the sun high. He'd run to a farther side of the city, far from the alley, far from the streets he usually roamed.

Starting farther away would make it easier, the Smiling Fire had explained.

The cries from the people at the market stalls rang around his ears. Where there were market stalls, there would be people with money buying. There would be people without money seeking, and many of them would be children.

*Money,* Jigme thought, patting his pocket. The unusual weight there was the weight of endless possibilities, and all because of the Smiling Fire, the riches he'd given Jigme before returning the boy to the outside world. Jigme went up to a stall, haggled over the price of sweets and finally gave over some of the coins in his pocket.

The hardest part, he knew, would be to find the lone child, the child who had no one to miss him.

Many of the children had their own groups, all tied to an adult who took what they received from begging or theft. There would be no way to lure one of those children to the temple. But a child alone...

Even here, some suspected who Jigme was. Many of the children stayed away. When they saw him, wariness flickered in their eyes.

But there would be one. There was always one.

The little girl stood against a wall and stared with hungry eyes. Grime covered her face. Her brown dress was torn in spots, frayed in others. Flies buzzed around the muck that covered her feet.

*She can't be older than eight,* Jigme thought, walking toward her, making sure she'd seen him before he opened the bag of *gulab jamun* and popped one of the sticky fried balls into his mouth. The sweetness of the milk, cardamom, and butter rang through him so intensely it almost stung.

Jigme turned and put his back to the wall, standing next to her and chewing. Waiting.

The little girl's gaze stuck to him. When at last she looked from his face to the bag, he smiled and held out the bag to her.

Tentatively, she raised her hand then backed away. Jigme stood still, smiling gently. He looked from her face to the bag. "Go on," he said. "I know what it is to be hungry too."

She plucked two pieces of gulab jamun from the bag and stepped away, as if afraid he would change his mind and snatch them back. She shoved both pieces into her mouth, eyes widening as the flavors hit.

"They're good, aren't they?" Jigme asked.

She nodded.

"You don't have anyone?" Jigme asked. "No brothers or sisters? No parents? No gang?"

She shook her head.

"My amma was really sick," Jigme said. "She almost died. But she's better now. It was lonely."

He held up the bag. The girl plucked out two more.

"She is making dinner. Would you like to eat with us?"

The little girl chewed, her eyes locked on his. Long, silent moments passed.

Then she nodded.

Jigme stepped away from the wall and started back through the market toward the alley. The little girl followed, eventually walking beside him. He told her his name. She didn't tell him hers.

Once they came to the alley, Jigme smiled and said they were nearly there. The girl squeezed his hand.

"Noorjehan," she said.

"Light of the world," Jigme replied. "That's a pretty name."

*And what was his name?* Jigme thought. *That boy, following me to the alley.*

But Jigme would not let the boy's face or name come to his mind, would not look or hear. *I just brought him into the temple and left when the Smiling Fire said to leave.*

With Noorjehan behind him, Jigme came to the red door and opened it. Inside, the small room was so different from when he'd last seen it, as if a different world had moved into the space.

Asha had lit lamps, swept the floor, dusted all the surfaces, changed the bedding. The only thing that had not changed was the dirt on the windows. It was as if Asha had darkened the windows, covered them with layers of ash and soot. No sunlight came into the rooms, dimming what otherwise might have been bright.

Jigme ignored this, noticing instead how different the rooms smelled. Instead of mustiness and sickness, incense wafted through the air, suffused now with the scents of earthy nuttiness of cumin seeds toasting in a hot pan and the sharpness of sliced chiles.

"Amma?" Jigme asked. "This is Noorjehan. Can she come for dinner?"

A smile appeared on Asha's face, though to Jigme it was not the smile he remembered from earlier days. A hungry fire blazed up in her eyes.

"Hello, Noorjehan," she said. "I am Asha, but you can call me Amma too." She nodded at Jigme. "Of course she can stay for dinner."

Asha pointed at a bucket in the far corner of the room. "I'm sure you would feel better, Noorjehan, if you cleaned up. Jigme, you wash up too."

The dim corner was darker than the rest of the room, and in the shadows it was easy to forget the world beyond the red door and the dark windows. As he and Noorjehan washed away the dirt and grime of the city, Jigme hardly heard the knock at the door.

Asha motioned for them to stay where they were.

"Who's there?" Noorjehan whispered. Fear spiked her voice.

"Shh," Jigme said. "No one has to know where you are."

Noorjehan smiled and sat down behind the bucket, as if trying to hide.

Asha opened the door. "Ah, Rucksack, Kailash," she said, standing in the doorway so they could not see past her. "How nice of you to check on us." Coldness lay over her warm words.

"Is everything okay?" Kailash said. "We keep hearing of strange things happening around the alley lately."

"Everything is okay," Asha replied. "And what is India, what is Agamuskara, what is life but a series of strange things happening?"

"Is Jigme here?" Rucksack said. "We've been worried about him. I'd love a chat."

"Jigme is out. You know boys," Asha said. "They must roam and run. I will tell him you asked about him."

"Asha." Kailash paused, as if deciding what to say next. "Do you know what lies at the far end of the alley?"

"Nothing anyone needs to see, I'm sure," Asha said. "I wouldn't know."

"Does Jigme know?" Rucksack said.

"Jigme knows his mother is well again. Things will be different now. I can't talk any longer, I'm afraid. I'm getting dinner ready, and he will be home soon."

"May we wait with you?" Rucksack asked.

"I'm sorry, but no. I do not yet feel our home is ready for visitors."

"Another time, then."

"I don't think so."

"Excuse me?" Kailash said.

"I appreciate all you've done for us," Asha replied. "But please, respect the wishes of Jigme's mother. He has had a difficult time. It is time for me to make recompense, to give him the mother he has needed. You have been truly kind. You were there when I was not. We do not want to inconvenience you anymore."

"Asha," Rucksack said.

"No!" Asha's voice burned hot and loud. "This is my home. Jigme is my son. Leave him alone, see him, speak to him, no more! Leave us alone!"

Before either Rucksack or Kailash could reply, Asha slammed the door and locked it. "Asha?" came the cries, along with more knocks. "Asha?"

But Asha only turned around, her eyes and smile blazing. Eventually, the sounds faded. Rucksack and Kailash left.

Noorjehan and Jigme walked back to the middle of the room. "Is everything okay?" Noorjehan said.

Asha smiled bigger and laid a hand on the girl's cheek. "Oh, sweet girl," she said. "It will be."

* * * * *

ON THE FIRST DAY, Jay left his bed only to stagger to the toilet, and he left the toilet only to stagger to his bed.

With his head between his knees, Jay continued attempting to master the fine art of vomiting and crapping simultaneously into the same hole in the floor.

As usual, he failed.

*I no longer have intestines,* Jay thought. With trembling hands, he filled bowls of water to rinse the vomit into the toilet hole.

*My guts have been replaced by a bunch of pissed-off snakes.*

Every time he puked, some part of him remained aware that he was emitting a strangled cry, as if he were trying to yell after having the breath punched out of his gut.

*The other people in the dorm must think the roaches are torturing me,* he thought, shaking his head. Thin, yellowy bile dripped off his chin and onto his knee.

*No, everyone knows good and well I did this to myself.*

The roaches had all run away within moments of his coming into the loo. Sometimes he thought he saw them hiding in a crack in the bile-colored plaster or trembling under the sink. *How bad is it when the toilet roaches are afraid?*

The rest of the day was a hazy mix of fitful not-quite-sleep, attempts to nibble the rice and sip the tea by his bed, followed by another mad dash to the loo, arse cheeks squeezed like a failing dam. The dorm mates were kind, making sure he was okay, leaving a banana or cooled tea.

Jay knew Jade had been there. Her scent lingered

until the latest bout of vomit burned it out of his nose.

Kailash hadn't been at Jay's bedside but Rucksack had. He'd sat by Jay's bed for what had seemed like hours, staring, his elbow on his knee, chin resting on his gloved left hand.

Little was clear about the first day, except for the fear on Rucksack's face.

Rucksack said nothing until he left. "There's no sick worse than slopplesick." His right hand squeezed Jay's shoulder. Warmth passed into Jay from the ancient man. "I only wish I could tell you the worst is over."

On the second day, Jay tried to get a pint.

The rice had stayed down, as had the tea, which was sweet with a slight salt tang. The trips to the toilet had grown less frequent, though Jay mostly stayed in bed. With every dash to the loo, something more than sickness was falling into Agamuskara's sewers.

Every time he came out of the toilet, something seemed different. When he stared at his face in the mirror, his skin was waxy and pale, almost bluish. He looked into his eyes, wondering what was changing.

*Delirious,* he thought. *Back to bed.*

Later, awake in the empty room, he opened his daypack, took out the dia ubh, and rotated the lifeless globe in his hands. *Rucksack tells me there's something so important about this,* he thought.

The dia ubh could have been a large rock, polished to a smooth, featureless perfection, or the moon, its pocked surface healed. Nothing about it seemed important anymore.

*They told me I was just lightheaded.* His mind went

back to that night in the pub, after the first kiss, when the dia ubh had changed. *And no one's said anything since.*

*What am I not being told?*

Jay shook his head and returned the dia ubh to the daypack, zipping it closed and locking the zipper with a small padlock. Behind it, his backpack glared at him.

"What?" Jay asked. *Must be the sickness,* he thought. *Some confusion from the heat.*

But he couldn't shrug off the idea that lately his backpack never seemed to be quite where he'd left it. It didn't seem as if anyone had rummaged through it or taken anything. But how else could it have been moved? And why did it seem like the pack was always staring at him? Ever since he and Jade had begun going out, the pack had become sullen, as if the habitat of a sack of nylon stuffed with smelly clothes had given rise to emotions.

Without knowing why, Jay patted the top. "You've always been there for me," he said. "It's like forever we've been on the road. You've always had my back. Literally, I suppose. I guess I haven't been paying enough attention to you lately. There's been a girl."

The backpack stared, its sullenness slightly lessened but clearly still irritated.

"She's special," Jay continued. "She's amazing. I keep thinking there could be something with her, something more, something... that lasts for a long time."

He shook his head. "Sometimes I don't know. There's so little I know about her. She doesn't talk about her past. She hardly talks about her time here. She works all the time, but she doesn't talk about that either. She doesn't have hobbies. She just works and makes occasional time to see me. I think she's into it. Into us. She is. I'm sure. I just wish I could shake the feeling that she's on holiday. What do I do when her vacation is over?"

The pack gave the slightest hint of a smile.

"I knew you'd understand," Jay said.

Tiredness crept over him. Jay lay down on the bed and stared at the pack. "It's been a long five years," Jay said. "It's nice to not feel lonely."

His smile disappeared.

"I'm not saying you aren't great company. It's just, sometimes I need human company too." Jay sighed. "Thing is, I finally get all this human company. Affection. Friendship. Then I get this itchiness again, like my soul and my feet won't feel okay until you're on my back and we're wandering somewhere unknown. What is the world but a place full of friends you haven't met yet? That was always so exciting. So many places just waiting to become memories. Maybe someone like me shouldn't be in one place."

The backpack grinned.

"Figured you'd like that," Jay said. "We need to move on. Find the passport—we're close, I know we're close—and see what Jade wants to do. If she came with us, would that be okay with you?"

Jay waited, quiet, his breath ragged from all the talking.

The backpack just sat there.

"You're going nuts, mate," Jay said with a chuckle. "Talking to my backpack. I've gotta get out of here for a while."

Tiredness lay over him like a heavy blanket, but Jay

shrugged it off. He pulled the backpack to him. The fabric rubbed up and down his calf as he rummaged.

"Need a clean shirt," Jay said. He pulled out random clothes, sniffed, then chucked each thing to the end of the bed. The small clothes pile rose like a little mountain.

He pulled out his last t-shirt, black as stout.

*Yes!* he thought. *Perfect!*

Jay reached into the pack again and pulled out a pair of tan khaki pants that looked only slightly dirty.

Dressing and then closing the pack, Jay went into the toilet to slap some water on his face and hair. "I think I've had enough of you for a while," he said, staring at the hole in the floor. "I'm going for a pint. Don't wait up."

The backpack glared as he closed the door and headed downstairs.

*It's like walking into a different pub,* Jay thought.

Empty tables, empty chairs. A few drinkers huddled over glasses and bottles, but the conversation was low, strained, and tense. The stage area was empty of musicians packed tightly in. Though it was weird to see the pub so lifeless, Jay also couldn't help but feel relieved at how easy it was to walk around.

*I'm hardly staying upright as it is,* he thought. His weary feet and wobbly legs questioned his decision to be vertical.

Rucksack was at his table with a full pint of stout in front of him, but his jovial, welcoming smile had stayed home. Across from Rucksack, at an empty chair, sat another full pint.

"You can always find yourself in a pint of GPS," Rucksack said, nodding approval at the text on Jay's t-shirt. "But, Jay, can you keep one down? You look like hell, and I would know."

"Tired of being in my room," Jay replied. "It's getting... weird up there."

"I had a feeling you were going to have more gumption than sense," Rucksack said as Jay fell into the chair.

"You haven't been talking to your backpack for the last hour," Jay said.

"Good conversation?"

"One-sided." Jay looked at his pint. Would it stay down?

"Maybe you don't know how to listen."

"Come on, Rucksack," Jay said. "Even for you, that's strange."

"Lot o' weird things in this world, my lad." Rucksack took a swallow of stout. "Such as how, while I wish you were still in your bed getting better, I'm glad you're here."

"What's going on?"

"Two things. If you're feeling good enough to start getting around, then at dawn I'd like us to take that boat ride."

Jay nodded. "I'll feel better. Good enough to stagger down there, anyway. Tired of being cooped up." Jay smiled. "But there had better be some answers. No evasions or murky talk."

"Whatever you want to know," Rucksack replied. "If it's in my power to tell you, I'll tell you."

Jay took a deep breath and picked up the pint. "What's the second thing?"

"Kailash is gone."

With the glass nearly to his lips, Jay stopped.

"She left Agamuskara this morning. So did Mim and Pim." Rucksack reached into his pocket and slid two envelopes across the table. "These were tacked to the outside of the pub's door last night. Jade gave them to me this morning."

*Jade.* Jay picked up the envelopes and looked over his shoulder, to where Jade stood behind the bar. Instead of her usual blur of motion, she stood still and stared at a small sheet of paper.

*I didn't even say hello,* Jay thought. *What the hell am I doing?*

After a small sip of stout, he waited. *Oh, just feck it,* he thought.

The next mouthful left the glass much emptier. For a palate that hadn't tasted anything but tepid tea, cool rice, and hot stomach acid for two days, the beer poured through him like a spring bubbling up after a long drought. Stripped of the spices and flavors of India, his palate for the first time really tasted the stout. More importantly, his mind and soul opened up to the beer.

*Rucksack always talks about stout as reality in a glass, as if it's more real than the real world itself,* Jay thought. *For the first time, I understand.*

With another swallow of stout, his world began making sense again.

*What the hell am I still doing here?* Jay thought. *It's time to be moving on. I'm a traveler. For me the world is either memory or anticipation. My world isn't standing still. It isn't routine. It isn't the same places and faces over and over again, day after day after day. I need my passport, and it's close, I can feel it. I need to know what's going on with Jade. And one way or another, I need to get out of this city.*

"Jay?" Rucksack asked. "Are you okay? I ask o' course out o' interest for your good health, but also out o' self-interest. I'd prefer to drink my stout, not wear yours, particularly after it's traveled through you twice."

*It all makes sense now,* Jay thought as the stout suffused him. *I know what I need to do.*

"I'm okay," Jay said with a nod. "Just had to wonder for a minute there what was going to happen. This has been a brutal bit of food poisoning, but it's clearing up quickly."

Jay opened the envelopes and read the notes. "So," he said, after laying aside the sheets of paper. "They're terrified of this Smiling Fire thing and think it's awakened."

Rucksack nodded. "It's after them. He nearly destroyed Mim and Pim. They got away, but that doesn't mean he wouldn't try again."

"They think that by leaving the city, he can't get them, and that will slow him down or keep him from getting stronger."

"Yes." Rucksack's face drew tighter and harder, like a bow ready to fire an arrow around the world.

"You're worried about your mum," Jay said. The men drank more beer.

"For the longest time, we thought each other dead. We find each other here," Rucksack said. "And get torn apart again by this damn thing. The trouble with being me is there's always trouble. Keeps me from getting a lot done."

"She must be worried too. For you. For the world. No wonder she didn't tell you where they were going."

"If she doesn't want to be found," Rucksack said, "I

won't be able to find her."

"It must have weighed on her pretty badly," Jay said. "She even looked older these last few days. With Mim and Pim gone too, how are we going to find my passport?"

Rucksack drained his pint. "I suppose so," he said, standing up. "I'd best be off. I need to get my thoughts in order."

"Oh. Okay."

"Rest up, Jay." Rucksack nodded to the bar. "And for heaven's sake, if you're going to make such a big deal o' being with her, at least say good night before you go back to your room."

Heat bloomed on Jay's cheeks as Rucksack left.

After drinking the rest of his pint—and paying close attention to what his stomach was going to do with all that heavy reality—Jay finally felt it was safe enough to approach the bar.

Jade finished serving some drinks. "How are you feeling?" she asked.

"Been better," Jay said with a shrug. "Been worse."

"I've checked on you."

"I know. Thank you."

"Jay—"

"Jade—"

They looked away from each other. A customer came up to the bar. "I have to, you know," Jade said with an indifferent shrug.

"I know," Jay replied. "Always dutiful. Look, I'm starting to feel better. A good night's sleep, I'll be good as new. See you tomorrow, okay?"

Jade nodded and walked away.

Back in his room, Jay was too tired to undress. As

he dozed off in bed, he could've sworn the backpack was smiling.

Deep in sleep and long after midnight, Jay dreamed the door of his room opened. A lone woman entered, carrying a tray with a small glass on it. She set the glass by his bed and left. The door clicked softly as it closed.

Jay woke.

*It was only a dream. It had to be.*

Still, he looked down. A glass of scotch, the best single-malt in the world, sat on the floor by his bed.

*That was nice of her.*

On the third day, Jay drank.


JADE SHUT THE DOOR that separated the pub from the hostel. Her hands trembled so hard she had trouble turning the lock.

Finally setting the bolt, she turned and pressed her back against the door, eyes closed. Her heart beat so hard and so fast it sounded like an urgent knock. But there was no knock in the empty pub.

Jade clasped her hands together in front of her. For a moment she wished that she didn't know so much about the world. Then that she had some god to pray to.

*Don't cry,* she thought. *Don't you dare cry.*

She felt the pub listening to her. Its shock at what she had just done reverberated through her senses. Even though the pub disagreed with her, its presence, its companionship, still comforted her.

"I had to," she said, opening her eyes. The bright lights above the bar reflected off the bottles and the shiny black plastic of the phone that never rang, leaving her and the rest of pub in darkness.

It had all made sense then. But now, having set the drink by his bed, knowing he would drink it...

She felt Jay's mind as he stirred from sleep. Down every drop went, into his body and soul.

His future.

*None of it makes sense anymore,* she thought, but it was too late for sense or nonsense. All that remained was choice. And consequences.

She saw it all in her mind again. Jay's eyes burned at her while she made herself not look at him, staring instead at The Management's instructions on the sheet of paper. *How to make Jay a travel god,* she thought. *How to set him on the path that takes him away from me.*

Once the pub closed for the night, she stood alone behind the bar. The three bottles of ingredients surrounded the double Scotch in a triangle. The sheet of paper lay beside them.

Jade unstoppered Green #2 and Black #11. Holding them over the glass, a thick drop bulged from the end of each bottle. Simultaneously, each drop fell into the drink below.

Her sob surprised her so much she nearly dropped the bottles.

"This is his destiny," she said. "It's not about what I feel or what I want. It's about what must be."

Picking up the third bottle, the thick drop of Gold #1 shone like a miniature sun. The drop glistened as it started to slide from the top of the bottle.

*Once this is in the drink,* she thought, *it's ready.*

*Am I?*

There would be a glow like a flash of golden daylight. Then it would fade and there would be only the drink. And all that came after.

*Once he drinks it, destiny will be as The Management said it must be.*

Like the sun coming down from the sky, the drop began to fall. Like a gold thread, a thin tendril connected the drop to the bottle.

The thread broke.

The drop fell.

Inside her mind and heart, duty and love fought each other. Jay's face flared. His green-and-gold eyes shone as he looked at her. And the future burned black and red. Then nothing. Only ash and a fiery smile.

*It must be,* she thought.

*What must be?* she answered.

Jade's right hand swept over the glass. Thick yet light as air, the drop splattered on her palm.

*What am I doing?* she thought.

Jade washed her hands and emptied the glass down the drain, along with a thick stream of water, enough to dilute and neutralize the power of the drink and the elixirs.

*I can't love him,* she thought, *but I can't let him go blindly into some destiny just because someone says he must.*

Jade faced the open cabinet, shining with its unknown light.

*So I'll set him free instead.*

Jade took out all the bottles cland set them on the bar with the others: Gold #1, Green #2, Gray #3, Red #4, Brown #5, Yellow #6, Blue #7, Purple #8, Orange #9, Silver #10, and Black #11. She poured another double dram of the best single-malt scotch in the world.

Then, one by one, she added a drop from each bottle.

Like the elixirs from their bottles, tears threatened to drop from her eyes. "I cannot influence him to love me," she said. "He must love me out of his own self. If I influenced him to love me, I could never forgive myself. And I would never be happy. Everywhere we went, every time I looked into his eyes, I would feel the question burning: does he love me because he loves me or because I influenced him?"

Drop by drop, she made the drink, and she knew the other choice was just as impossible.

"I cannot influence him to become the god The Management want him to be," Jade said. "If they want him to be what they say he must be, if he is our best chance to defeat the Smiling Fire, then he must also decide that destiny. We can't steer him. We can't influence him. A god cannot be a puppet. Neither can a person."

The final drop came from the bottle of Black #11. Destiny in a bottle, The Management had explained. Dangerous and difficult, Black #11 was the elixir that had caused problems in Hong Kong years ago.

As she returned the bottles to their cabinet, a sound like whispers bubbled from the drink. A disc of rainbow light grew softly. It surrounded the glass. The colors changed, fading one into the other. The whole shone more brightly with each shift. Blue, green, silver, black, brown, gold. The colors all phased into white, more brilliant than the walls of the city in the full noon sun.

When the colors faded, the glass seemed like nothing more than an ordinary glass of scotch.

*Does it feel like a rainbow is coursing through the blood in his veins?* Jade thought, staring at the empty tray, her mind listening hard to Jay as he drank.

The phone rang.

All thoughts of Jay vanished. The phone's black handle felt oddly cool in Jade's hand and against her face.

"Jade Agamuskara Bluegold," said the voice of The Management, low and hollow in her ear. As usual, they sounded like three beings speaking in unison, yet one voice that was somehow layered. Every layer seemed sad, woven with a disappointment deep as the world was old. "We gave you a choice. Had you but listened, all would be well, and you would be rewarded and exalted above all."

Fear welled up and her heart beat faster. She closed her eyes and breathed, then opened them again. A glimpse in the mirror showed the hardness of her face, eyes wide and shining, ferocious and terrified.

"When given a choice," Jade replied, speaking as evenly as she could, "sometimes the best thing to do is take both."

"You disobeyed. Twice. You have influenced not only yourself, but you influenced the traveler in a way he should not be influenced."

"My influence was not out of love," Jade said. "Nor was it out of concern for his future or well-being."

"You lie."

"You know I do not."

The Management was silent.

*What will they do to me?* she thought. *Where will I go*

*back to? Who will I become?*

"He will not love me unless he chooses to love me," Jade said. "He will not take on this destiny unless he chooses it himself. I didn't just take both choices and give them to him. I gave him a third choice."

"The All and Nothing," The Management said. "That combination is to be used only under direct orders and supervision from us. It has been used only two times in all of history."

"Three," Jade said. "Now it's three. I guess you can add that to the lessons, along with your description of my fate, the fate of what happens to a Jade who disobeys."

"You have altered the future in a way that could mean there is no future."

"I gave a person the freedom to decide his own destiny."

"You have condemned the world to ash. You have delivered us all to the Smiling Fire."

"You don't know that. The future isn't written like some book where you can skip to the end. Even I know that and I'm just a Jade."

"Some futures are clearer and more definite that others. Your betrayal has destroyed us all." The Management paused, as if to take a breath, though Jade knew they didn't breathe. "And you are no longer a Jade."

A pain stabbed through her and she closed her eyes. *I knew it could happen,* she thought. *But I never thought they'd do this over the phone. They always appear. They are always with the Jake or Jade when it happens.*

*I betrayed them so deeply they won't even sack me in person.*

"Jade Agamuskara Bluegold," came the voice of The Management, so cold now her skin and muscles hurt where the phone touched her flesh. "You are no longer the Jade of Agamuskara. You are no longer the Bluegold. We strip you of your powers and of your duties. Your benefits are ended. Effective immediately, you are no longer a Jade; you are merely of the name Jade, as you were when you came to us."

"What about," she began, terrified of their reply. "What about my life?"

Again, a pause.

"You are as you are. You will be what you will be, in such time as you have left before the Smiling Fire murders Jay, is restored to his full power, and consumes all life. Your life will receive no revision."

"I am as I am?" The shock made her voice shake. "No change?"

"From now on, you will age as a normal human. You may never enter one of our pubs again. You have until tomorrow night to remove your personal effects from the room." A clacking sound came from the special cabinet. "The power of destiny and decision we strip from you. The cabinet is locked. When this call ends, you will leave the pub and return to your room. You will never enter the pub again."

"I live my life... as it is right now?"

"That is your punishment. As one grace for your time of otherwise exemplary service, we will not age you to the years that have passed. But you will not be able to choose the life you come to next."

"But... But even if you sack a Jake or Jade, you've said so yourself, they still can choose the life they go to after their service."

"We said we have the right to allow you to do so. We never said we had an obligation."

The words ripped her breath from her. Images tore through her: the ring in the outstretched hand, the loud house she'd known from birth, full of pain and...

*Where will I go and what would I do anyway?* Jade thought. *I would never go back to my family. The one I left I can never return to. What else do I have but the life that is right in front of me, here in Agamuskara or wherever else I might go in the world as I am?*

Tears rolled down her face. *What the hell do I do now?* she thought. *Without my duty as a Jade, what am I? Who am I?*

"I'm sorry," she said. "I'm sorry. Don't sack me. Please. Punish me. I accept whatever you deem right and necessary. But this is who I am. It's all I am. Please, let me stay."

"Your destiny and your decisions are beyond us now, Jade. Thank you for your service. We are sorry that this is how it was to be." The regret in the voice stung. "Good-bye."

With a click, the line went silent.

Jade set the phone on the hook. She pulled and pushed at the cabinet, but just as they had said, it was locked.

As she stepped over the threshold between the pub and the hostel, a hum in the air made her turn.

She tried to step forward again but could not cross back into the pub. The air itself hardened like a wall. It darkened, blackened, until she could not see into the pub anymore.

When Jade pulled the pub door shut, it locked with something more than turning bolts.

Then she noticed the deep silence. It was as if a limb had been cut away. She touched the door to the pub, thinking about the space beyond: the bar and the glasses and bottles, the tables and chairs and walls covered with maps and memories. She knew it was all still there, but she couldn't hear it anymore.

"I'm sorry," she said. Her fingers tightened on the glass of the door. The emptiness around her had weight, hard and sharp and dark. Jade walked down the hallway, past the illusion at the staircase, and into her room.

*For the last time,* she thought, closing the door behind her. *Wait.*

Jade turned the doorknob but the door didn't open. Nor would the window. *Trapped,* she thought. *Trapped until I'm packed and ready to leave here forever. I'm alone now.*

She stared at the ceiling toward Jay's room. *I can't hear him anymore,* she thought. *Even that's gone.*

Jade closed her eyes, wishing and hoping and even praying. *Choose me,* she thought. *Please, choose us.*

Then she opened the closet and drawers and began to pack. Tears fell on papers and clothes as Jade prepared to leave behind the Jade and live now as only as herself.

WAS THERE A STREET left in Agamuskara that did not wear his footprints? Dull pains stabbed Jigme's toes, heels, shins, and knees.

Jigme limped along the alley. For the last time in three days, the black temple receded behind him. Three days of running, seeking, convincing, returning, and going out again. After bringing the last child to the temple, Jigme's legs had collapsed and he could hardly stand.

*I can finally go home,* he thought. *I've done enough and he is pleased. I can rest.*

Jigme wondered if Asha would be awake. She needed the rest, but he doubted she would be asleep. Every day she had been more and more anxious, as her early strength waned and she became more tired yet could not sleep.

*Not that I can sleep either,* Jigme thought.

A distant fire always glowed in his mind. Jigme saw it the most when he tried to sleep. Saw that and the children. Their faces showed suspicion and trust. They were always afraid when Jigme left the temple, just as the Smiling Fire came toward them.

The Smiling Fire's need had been great, and Jigme had brought him what he needed. To every corner of the city he had run, seeking out children like Noorjehan. *Like the first boy,* Jigme thought. *Never a name, he has no name, if he doesn't have a name, he doesn't, he isn't—*

"He isn't anything to worry about," came the rasping yet comforting voice in his mind.

All of the children were healthy and well. They had been alone, unnoticed and not missed. Now, because of Jigme, they were on their way north to fresh air and freedom, to days of learning and playing, days of full bellies and soft beds.

"Soon," said the voice, "you'll be with them."

As Jigme neared the living end of the alley, the absolute quiet in the back streets of Agamuskara told him it was around two or three in the morning. *All the city sleeps but me,* he thought.

Before him, deep shadows made the red door seem murky and dirty. Jigme unlocked it and went inside. A lone oil lamp burned with barely enough light for Jigme to see in front of him. Still, he could make out where Amma lay, a lump on the mattress, her breath raspy and uneven.

"But you were getting better!" Jigme cried.

"Jigme," she said, quiet yet rough. "My son, my son, I'm sorry, I'm sorry. I'm not myself."

"It's okay," he replied. "We got you better once, Amma. We will get you better again." He kneeled by the bed and held her hand, feverish and fiery yet cold and clammy.

"Have you eaten?" she asked.

He shook his head. "There's been no time today."

"You look so thin." She stared at him and touched his face. His cheekbone protruded so sharply that he worried it might cut her hand. "But you ate yesterday."

"No," he replied. "Or the day before. The need was too great, the city so big. So many children to bring him. I have to make you well again. I can only do that if he gets what he needs." *And I haven't been hungry,* Jigme thought. *I can't eat. When I look at food, I see only the children. When will they arrive? When will I get a letter? I haven't even heard from—don't say the name!—and surely he's there by now.*

Asha squeezed his hand. "Such a good son," she said, but then she coughed and went rigid.

"No!" Asha shouted. She looked at Jigme again, her eyes wide and fierce, protective and afraid. Without the redness and shadows he had seen in her gaze lately, her eyes were so dark and clear.

"This is wrong!" she said. "This is all wrong! Get out of me. Get out of my son!" She went silent, as if listening to some distant voice. "No more!" she shouted. "I'd rather die!"

Again, she seemed to listen to something far away. Then she closed her eyes and went limp. Tears and sobs shook out of her. "But I will not leave him alone."

She pulled Jigme toward her, wrapped her arms around him. "I will not leave you alone, my son. Never. You will always have me. You will always have my love."

"Mum?" Jigme asked. "What's wrong?"

"It's too late," she replied. "I was too weak. I could not help, I could not stop it. I'm sorry, son. I've done you wrong. He…"

Her back arched. Asha rose from the bed until only her head and feet touched the thin mattress.

Jigme fell backward. Asha collapsed onto the bed and was silent, her eyes closed, her chest hardly rising.

Jigme sat on his knees and moved to the side of the bed. "Amma?" he said.

No reply.

"Mum?"

Asha's eyes opened. She looked at Jigme, then rose and sat. "Son," she said, her eyes gleaming red and black, her voice rasping and harsh. "How many more can you bring?"

Jigme shook his head. "There can be no more. I'm so tired. People suspect now. So many children, so quickly. I could hear the whispers as I brought the last child. They don't understand and they are wary. If I try to bring another, I may be caught."

"You must bring one more."

Something hot pressed at Jigme's eyes. All he could feel was the weariness in his legs, his feet sore from pounding over kilometer after kilometer of the city, nearly without halt. "I can't."

"I am not strong," said the voice in her mouth, becoming softer, gentler as she spoke. "If I am not strong, I will die."

"Mum," Jigme said, shaking his head. He reached for her hand, but she pulled away. Something inside him tore. "I'm so tired. I can't do this anymore."

Asha lay on her back. "Then you kill me," she said, her voice harsh again. She stared at the ceiling.

Every cell and muscle in Jigme's body begged for rest. But he saw the pain and weariness on his mother's face.

*What is my own pain compared to hers?* Jigme thought. *What is my own compared to the Smiling Fire's? At least I can go about freely. They're both so trapped. All they want is to be well.*

"If you want us to be well," Asha said, "then bring one more."

"The last one?"

"Yes."

Deep inside, from his toes to his head, strength trickled into his muscles and spirit.

*Just one more,* he thought. *Surely I can do that, if it's to make her well?*

The weariness faded. Not completely, but enough.

Jigme stood. "I will bring the last child."

Asha smiled and squeezed his hand. "I knew you would not disappoint me."

A chill cut through the alley as Jigme closed the red

door behind him. Even in the center of Agamuskara, few lights lit the dark. Above the city, dark clouds crowded out the stars. Jigme walked through silent streets. Around him, people slept on the pavement, in doorways, on top of carts. Families huddled close. He could take no children here.

*How far can I go?* he thought. *I can't go to the far corners of the city. I feel stronger but I must be smart. I must be fast. For Amma.*

At an intersection he stared down the different directions. "I don't know where to go," he said. His strength flickered. Weariness stabbed his legs again.

"Just surrender," said the voice. "Just follow the darkness."

Jigme turned right. The clouds were thicker over that part of the city, and for blocks he wandered, staring into doorways, looking down side streets. Adults. Families. No children alone.

The weariness grew. *Am I going too far away? Will I make it back before I collapse? What if I make a mistake?*

The thoughts scratched at him, a seeping fear that made him want to crawl into a doorway and sleep.

*All he wants is to be better,* Jigme thought.

"And the children are better too," said the voice. "Think of that. Tonight a child from these streets will go somewhere better."

The strength came back. Jigme passed another alley.

Behind the statue of a god lay the huddled body of a sleeping child. No one was near. No one would know.

Jigme kneeled by the child. He had no thoughts, no plan. Something else was guiding him now. The boy was thin and small, skin like paper. He seemed to rustle when Jigme touched him.

"Who are you?" the boy said, his voice heavy with fatigue.

"Don't be afraid," Jigme replied. He looked into the child's eyes. He was dirty, but his clothes weren't ragged. They looked new. This wasn't a street child. Jigme smiled. "They'll be so relieved you're okay."

"Amma?" the child said. "Appa? They know where I am?"

"I was sent to find you, and I've been looking everywhere, all day. It's a big city to find such a little person in. But I've found you. It'll be okay. We can go now, if you'd like."

The boy nodded and got up. The statue of the god did nothing. *There's nothing to do,* Jigme thought. *The boy is safe. He is going somewhere better. Parents or not. Mum and Dad. A dad, even. Isn't he lucky. I wish I knew what it was like to have a dad.* The jealousy felt like flames.

They wandered back to the main street. Jigme turned them toward the alley.

"This isn't where I live," the boy said.

"We aren't going there," Jigme replied. "Your parents had learned that you may be in this part of the city. They're waiting for you."

Finally, they reached the street near the alley. "What's your name?" the boy asked.

"It doesn't matter," Jigme replied.

The boy stopped. "What's my name?"

Jigme looked at him. "We're nearly there."

"What's my name?"

"You'd rather hear it from your amma and appa."

The boy took a step backward. "Where are we going?" he said loudly.

Jigme walked toward him. "We are going to where you need to be," he said, grabbing the boy's arm.

"No!" The boy kicked Jigme's shins and knees. "No!" he shouted, struggling as Jigme grabbed him. "Let me go! Let me go!"

Murmurs reached Jigme's ears.

"People are waking up," said the rasping voice. "If they see..."

Jigme pulled the boy forward and curled his right hand into a fist. A power flowed into his arm and the rest of his body. The impact of Jigme's hand on the boy's head reverberated through his arm, making it feel dull and dead. Pain bloomed through his fingers as if something had broken.

The boy cried out once, but the blow to the temple dropped him. Unconscious, he collapsed. Hand screaming, Jigme caught the boy before he fell to the street.

More voices. People were up, looking around for the trouble. Soon they would look down this street.

*What am I going to do?* he thought. *I'll be caught!*

"If you're caught," said the voice, "she dies."

Jigme looked at the child, his breathing slow but steady, eyes closed. He could have been sleeping again. Hand screaming as he squeezed, Jigme picked up the boy and draped him over his shoulders, behind his head. The boy was heavier than Jay's backpack, and Jigme felt more tired than ever. He ignored it though, the tiredness in his legs and the pain from the boy's kicks. The mouth of the alley enveloped him.

But not quickly enough.

Cries followed. Someone had already come into the street. Someone had seen.

The cries brought other people. Jigme heard their footsteps pounding down the street and into the alley. *The noise will wake the people who live here,* Jigme thought. *What if I'm seen by someone I know?*

No voice replied.

He looked toward the main city then down the dark alley. The boy felt heavier with every moment. *What if I were caught?* Jigme thought. *At least it would be over.*

*Over for Amma.*

Jigme poured all his energy, all his soul into his legs. *Run,* he thought. *Run like you've never run before.*

His tired legs carried him down the alley toward the red door. Behind him, closer now, the people ran too.

Jigme ran faster, the child's limp limbs bouncing. *So heavy,* he thought. But there was the red door. *Soon we'll be inside and this will be over.*

*No it won't,* he thought. *Someone will see me take the boy inside. They'll know it was me. Everyone here hates me and Mum. They'll kill us. Plus, if we're surrounded, we'll have no way to get the boy to the temple.*

With a cry Jigme stumbled and fell to one knee. He tottered under the child's weight, about to fall. His knee hit a stone, and pain blazed through his body.

People were getting closer.

Jigme stared at the door, thought of Amma inside. "Get up," he said. "Get up."

With every inch his knee threatened to buckle. The child nearly pulled him over, but Jigme fought back. Trembling, he stood up again.

His fingers were made of broken glass as his hands squeezed tight around the child. His knee swelled. But the voices were close now, too close. Jigme ignored the pain and began to run again. He limped slightly from his knee, but he ran past the red door. Above the alley, the clouds were thicker and blacker. A fog swarmed down.

He smiled at the cries from the crowd—even more so at the absence of the sound of their footsteps. *They were next to the red door,* he thought, *but she is safe. No one has seen my face. They do not know it is me. And none will pass into this part of the alley.*

Jigme ran. Despite the thick fog, he trusted his footsteps, knew that nothing would obstruct him. He ran down the alley, between the statues, and into the temple.

The warmth inside made Jigme realize how cool it had been outside. The Smiling Fire beamed. Something in his grin seemed almost proud.

Jigme set down the child, who was still unconscious.

"Soon you can return," the Smiling Fire said. "Tomorrow I will do as I promised. Sleep now, child, then return to her. And then, Jigme, the time at last will have come for you to bring your mother to me."

Jigme smiled as he sank down against a black wall. *I've done it,* he thought. *It's over. Amma will be healed.*

He ignored the sounds and drifted into sleep. There was no burning or screaming. He would endure just one last nightmare before waking into a brilliant new day.

* * * * *

IN THE WEAK LIGHT of the foggy, just-dawned morning, the blood on Jay's shin shone with a strange brightness.

"Walking around the boats is easier than walking through them," Rucksack said. "Though you've made our choice easy. We'll take this one."

Jay rubbed his shin through the tear in his thin cargo pants. "Why?"

"It knows you now." Rucksack pointed at the bright red smear on the faded brown-and-black metal of the long, shallow boat. "A boat that knows your blood will take you anywhere safely."

"You say that like you're being serious."

"There wasn't exactly a luxury charter service when I first went to Ireland," Rucksack replied. "I got to the boat in a bit o' a hurry. Already had blood coming out aplenty, so I left a bit on the hull as I got aboard. Lots o' boats left that day, and we were halfway there when a terrible storm blew up around us. Our boat was the only one that made it."

"I don't see how we're going much of anywhere today," Jay said. "This fog is so thick I can hardly see in front of me."

Rucksack was quiet for a moment. "Just feck it," he said finally. "We need to be off."

At the river's edge, the fog embraced Rucksack, as if he had slipped into another world, but his voice rang clear and strong. To Jay, it sounded like Rucksack could have ordered the Indian subcontinent to plow into Asia and create the Himalayas.

"You know who I am and why I'm here," Rucksack said to the fog. "Now enough with the buggerin' theatricals. Clear off."

Slowly at first and then in a hurry, the fog thinned and cleared. Jay's skin warmed in the dawn light.

"Did you really just do that?" Jay asked.

"It would've cleared eventually," Rucksack replied. "But we don't have time for eventually. There's a lot you need to know, and we need to get away to do this properly."

Jay took some rupees from his wallet and tucked the money under a rock at the spot where the boat had been sitting. He stared at the bills, counting in his mind, and then added a few more. "That should more than make up for any temporary distress," he said, going to the side opposite Rucksack. The murky waters of the Agamuskara wet their ankles as they pushed the small boat into the river.

"I'm glad you're better," Rucksack said as he settled in, facing downriver and taking up the oars. Jay stared at the city and set his daypack on the floor of the boat, between his knees.

Rucksack nodded at the pack, but Jay shook his head. "No change in the dia ubh," he said. "Gray and lifeless as ever."

Soon they were making a brisk pace with the current. The river's cool, wet morning air filled Jay's lungs and soul. "I feel like a new man today," he said.

"Up for a wee hike?"

"Where are we going?" Jay asked. "And remember, you promised me straight answers."

"I did at that, didn't I?" Rucksack grinned. "Right, then. In return, though, I expect you'll have enough o' an open mind to accept them. We're going to a wee place I know. Can't get there by car. It'd take too long to walk. Hence the boat. Technically, this place is at the city's northwestern outskirts, but you'd think you were in the middle o' nowhere. It's greener, cooler, with a bit o' small forest and a hill."

"I saw a hill when I first entered the city," Jay said. "It was off in the west."

"That's the one," Rucksack said. "I used to go there as a boy. The top o' the hill is as calm as a pub at dawn. No staring eyes, no listening ears. Just you and me and the world. I'll tell you all I can there."

Jay nodded and glanced down at his red t-shirt. An image of the Buddha faced forward while sitting on a small boat and holding a paddle. Above it, in large black letters, were the words, "life is but a dream." The wooden plank where he sat was hard against Jay's arse. He shifted around, trying to get comfortable. The boat swayed.

"Take a bit o' care," Rucksack said. "You don't want to fall in."

"No kidding. Amazes me how dirty this holy river is. Still surprises me how often dirtier means holier."

"Any eejit can dress himself fine and talk about being divine," Rucksack replied.

"Sounds like Guru Deep and those orange suits of his."

"A perfect example." Rucksack snorted. He rowed faster. "If you want to see holy, really holy, you show me someone who's half in to his last breath, covered in ash and shite, and still shines through all o' that with a light that makes the world worth keeping on. That's a trick I don't think Guru bloody Deep could pull. But it's all I know o' holy, and it's all I know to be worth a damn." Rucksack eased off the oars. "Sorry. Something got my wind up. No, the main reason I want you to be careful is a river like the Agamuskara is a tricky one. A lad like you falls in, who knows where you'll wind up."

"Well, after the river hits the Ganges to the east," Jay answered, "you'd eventually reach Kolkata and then the Indian Ocean."

"Physically, sure, that's how the river flows."

"Let me guess," Jay said with a laugh. "There's an invisible river that flows in a different direction."

"Right," Rucksack said. "In one direction. And here I thought I was going to tell you something you didn't know. The eastern flow is only a physical manifestation of the river. The real Agamuskara, the river behind the river, flows north, up into the Himalayas."

"I could point out that rivers don't flow uphill," Jay said, "but I've seen too many weird things over the years, especially since I've been here." He shook his head. "I know what you're saying shouldn't be possible, but I also know it's not possible; it's actual."

"It's a weird one, I'll grant you that. It's not the only one either. Other rivers have both their physical course and their actual course. If you followed the Agamuskara's real course, you'd arrive at a place, way deep, called the Heart o' the World. Ever hear o' it?"

"In stories," Jay replied. "It's the sort of thing you hear in a hostel common room after everyone's had a bit beyond their fill of guitar tunes and cheap red wine. People say the Heart of the World's some sort of Himalayan utopia, where everything is perfect and everyone is happy."

"Amazing the wisdom that gets passed along as legend," Rucksack said. "Then again, myth is the best camouflage for the real. Heart o' the World exists, Jay.

It's where Mum's from. And when the time came for me to join the world, it's where I was born."

"If it's so perfect, why did Kailash leave?"

"She was among the first with a true wanderlust." Rucksack smiled with a wistful look in his eyes. "Mum wanted to see the world. She soon learned that the world is not the Heart. In time, I think Mum came to understand that she could not change the world as it was, so she decided to become part o' the world as it could be. There's more, o' course. Much o' it I hardly understand. She was going to explain." His voice trailed off.

"But then she was gone."

"Aye."

The men said nothing else. Jay watched the city thin out, the buildings getting smaller and sparser as Rucksack rowed. Soon there was no city to see, only small white, squat blocks set back a few meters from the water. Past those, only trees and grasses covered the riverbanks. Yet Jay could sense that somehow they were still in Agamuskara.

The boat bumped against the shore. On the far side of a patch of forest, the lone hill rose high in the morning air. The men hauled the boat out of the water and stowed it against a tree. After a few moments of silent staring, Rucksack smiled. "Right, that'll stay put. Off we go."

If there was a path, Jay couldn't see it but Rucksack clearly could. The weariness of his anywhere face faded with every step over the hard ground, with every breath of the clear air, fresh and moist from the river and the trees growing all around. *It isn't a forest like home,* Jay thought, recalling the vast woods of the US

Northwest, oceans of green stretching beyond what the eye could see. Jay wondered how much of Agamuskara's forest now existed only in the city's buildings.

The morning sun wove green and gold through the leaves of the trees, landing warm and alive on Jay's skin. The silence enfolded him, soothing and relaxing his body and mind.

They were deep in the trees when Jay finally understood why they had come here.

*There's no one else here*, Jay thought. *Seems like the first time in years I've been somewhere that hasn't been packed with people. But now I'm out in the middle of nowhere.*

The path soon sloped upward and narrowed. As the trees thinned, Jay saw they were going up the hill. It rose sharp and steep out of the ground, more like a mossy potato standing on end than some gently sloping wave in the earth.

Rucksack looked back at him, saying nothing, but the question in his eyes was clear enough. Jay answered by returning his stare. *Yes, I'm up for it,* Jay thought. *I'm up for anything.*

Depending on which part of the world they faced as they wound counter-clockwise up the narrow path, they could see the forest, Agamuskara the river, Agamuskara the city, or the plains that rolled off toward the north. *I'm only separated from all that scenery by not jumbling my feet,* Jay thought, questioning his bravado. But he continued following Rucksack, trying not to fall behind.

The walk had been quiet. Neither man spoke, preferring instead to look out from the hill or down at his feet. The air was still again, warmer as the sun rose higher. The exertion made Jay sweat harder and harder as they climbed the high hill. *We've got to be over five hundred feet up by now,* Jay thought as he wiped the sweat from his forehead with a bandanna. As usual, Rucksack seemed dry as a desert.

In shadows on the shady side of the hill, a sound almost like giggling brought a slight coolness, as if the temperature had lowered a degree or two. Near knee level, a thin stream of water trickled out of the earth, making the path damp and muddy.

Rucksack slipped.

His gloved left hand shot out, but the withered hand couldn't grab onto anything. Losing balance, Rucksack's legs went out from under him as he spun around. Empty air waited to catch him.

Jay shot forward.

Reached out quickly and desperately, Jay grabbed his friend and pulled him away from the edge. They slammed into the side of the hill, the earth damp in Jay's face for a moment. The impact made Jay bounce backward. His feet left the ground. The empty air beckoned again.

*Great,* he thought. *Is it my turn now?*

Rucksack's arm came up. Both men pressed each other into the damp earth, breathing hard.

"Thank you," Rucksack said.

"Friends don't let friends fall off hills," Jay replied.

Rucksack's rumbly laugh pealed over the world. "They don't indeed," he said, clenching and unclenching his left hand. "Useless shagging thing. Sorry about that." He nodded. "Up we get."

"How high is this thing?"

"Nine hundred ninety-nine feet. Technically

speaking, a hill as opposed to a mountain."

"So we've got only, what, a couple hundred more feet to go?"

Rucksack shrugged.

*I don't know if I believe you,* Jay thought as they reached the top of the hill, maybe a hundred feet later or five hundred or a thousand. Hands on his knees, Jay bent over, breathing hard.

Rucksack seemed no more winded than he would have been if they'd walked to the pub for a pint.

Jay coughed and stood. "I hope it's easy to keep fit at your age," he wheezed.

"You'd be surprised," Rucksack replied. "But I'm sure the shock will fade with time."

"What do you mean?" Jay said.

Rucksack plucked a water bottle from a pouch on Jay's daypack and held it out. "Have some water first. Get your breath back."

Jay drank deeply then poured water over his head. Goosebumps puckered his neck and back. "That's better," he said. "It's like I feel alive again."

"The best thing life can do is get on with living," Rucksack replied. "Might as well feel refreshed in the process." He looked out over the world. "Many's the time I wondered why I was as I was. Mum and Dad never wanted to tell me, even when I came o' age and began doing, well, what I used to do. Now I know."

"Is this your way of telling me things?" Jay said.

"I'll give you answers," Rucksack replied, "but I'll do it my way."

He looked out at the world then back to Jay and continued. "Mum pulled the Smiling Fire's power out as a dia ubh. When its light fell on me, unborn, the fire o' life itself was put into me. It changed me, Jay. If it hadn't, who knows what I would've been? Maybe it was destiny or something chosen in that decisive moment. Maybe I was just going to be an ordinary child who would've grown up to live and die as an ordinary man."

"I can't imagine there being anything ordinary about you," Jay said. "Maybe that's the point. It was both your destiny and your decision."

"I could say the same thing about you."

Jay shook his head. "What, because I travel? When I began, it was to honor my parents' dreams, their memory."

"Why keep on now?"

"It was hard at first," Jay said. "There was a point a couple of years ago when I thought seriously about settling down. In Ireland, actually."

Jay looked off toward the north, over the flat plains and beyond to where, in his mind's eye at least, the Himalayas would rise over the earth. "Travel came to be part of me," he said. "I realized I love it more than being still. Even when it's hard or scary or uncomfortable, I love the thrill of the road. Travel is an ultimate love. To see the world is to see yourself reflected everywhere you go. Yet it's also about letting both the world's light and darkness shine into you, show you things about yourself that you never knew. Above all, I came to see what was inside me: this special, boundless, shining love for the road, for the world. I learned I held it inside like this precious jewel. I held it close and no matter how dirty and dusty I got outside, that jewel, that love, stayed gleaming and pure."

The men stood side by side and stared out over the plains. Jay wondered about the world beyond the city, the vastness of India, the depth of its land and people, the length of its history and life. *This country is alive like no other I've ever known,* he thought. *So varied yet so cohesive. I've never felt so alive as I've felt here.*

*How did I not notice the mountain before?*

It bloomed from the edge of the horizon, looming like a moon over the flat plains. Even from this far away, Jay could see the gray-brown rock of the sides of the mountain, the same hues he'd seen in the Himalayas.

"Jay?" Rucksack asked. "Are you okay?"

"I guess I'm just confused," he said, but another part of his mind yelled at him and fought for control of his mouth. *You aren't confused,* it said. *You know what this is.* "Mount Everest is the world's tallest mountain, right?"

"Why do you ask?"

"I'm having trouble understanding how I'm seeing it here. You'd think it'd be set too far back in the Himalayas to be visible. Plus, we're too far south to see even the foothills."

Rucksack peered toward the horizon. "Humor an old man," he said. "Where exactly are you seeing this mountain?"

Jay pointed. *You'd know it anywhere!* screamed the part of his mind he kept trying to ignore. *The blasted thing's been following you since Ireland.*

"I need you to understand something," Rucksack said. "You're right."

"About what?" Jay said. "That it's weird that you can see Mount Everest from here?"

Rucksack shook his head. "You're right that you aren't seeing Everest. And I think you know that."

"That mountain is huge, Rucksack. The summit looks like it's touching the sky, like it's the roof that holds up the world."

"The mountain is huge. I can't even see it, and I know it's huge. But I don't have to see it to know it's there or to know what it really is." Rucksack sighed. "You began to travel because o' what happened to your parents, but you continue traveling because it's who you are. Your travels revealed that. The world is in your blood, in your soul, Jay. Seeing the world is your reason for being. It's who you are. It's no wonder the dia ubh came to you."

"You're talking like now there's some special destiny that I'm deciding," Jay said.

"You wanted answers," Rucksack replied. "I'm going to remind you o' that and something else: the price o' demanding answers is being strong enough to accept them."

Rucksack swept his arm over the world. "The mountain you see, the mountain that is the true largest mountain, is Mount Meru."

"Meru. Another name for Kailash. It's real too?"

Rucksack grinned. "Mount Meru is just as real. Even more real. All reality, all existence, comes from Mount Meru. No wonder it's been following you around, though the fact that you can see the mountain at all is what's most amazing."

"Following me?" Jay said. "How do you know that?"

"Mum and Mount Meru are connected. I don't know the how o' it, but I know the what. She told me how she's followed you, in her dreams, seeing you in

Ireland and onward as you've made your way east. You coming to Tibet, to Everest, you getting the dia ubh and bringing it to Agamuskara, where the Smiling Fire has awakened and is a threat again—these things are no accident. This is destiny at work."

Jay gripped the straps of his daypack. "I decide my life."

"I don't consider the two mutually exclusive. Your destiny is to decide your life. But the decisions you've made have brought you here. Your destiny wasn't just to carry the dia ubh, Jay. You've stayed in Agamuskara, with a mirror eclipse ticking closer and closer."

"Then what's my destiny?"

Sadness and hope mixed in Rucksack's eyes. "It may as could be argued I should've done this sooner. I'm sorry I haven't. The only thing harder than living destiny is talking about it, especially when the path is so difficult, and the person involved has become a dear friend."

Rucksack sighed, as if steeling himself for what he was about to say. "On the day o' the mirror eclipse, Jay, the dia ubh will open. It will shine with a brilliant, golden light. If what Mum and I believe is true, then the Smiling Fire will have regained enough strength to break free o' its prison. It will stand in that light, regain its full former strength, and destroy all life on the planet."

"No!" A heat washed over Jay's face. "That can't be right. I've carried this damn thing all this time, only so it can help destroy the world?"

"That's the destiny," Rucksack said. "You, me, Jade, Jigme, everyone you've ever known, everyone you haven't met yet, will all be reduced to ash. The world will go from lush and living to burnt and dead."

Jay saw them all. All the people he'd shared time with over the years, friends from school and from growing up, a flash of red Irish hair, Jade and her brilliant eyes. He saw them all. Then he saw them all burning.

"There has to be another way," he said. "I can't let that happen."

"I'm glad to hear you say that," Rucksack said. "Because there is one other way. But only one."

"What is it?"

"When the dia ubh opens, instead o' the Smiling Fire standing in the light, you must stand there."

"What happens to me?"

"The dia ubh will transform you. You will no longer be human. You won't even be like me. You'll become a god, Jay. The divine wanderer, here to save the world, here to save all that lives and loves."

*A god.*

The two words crashed through Jay's mind, knocking over thoughts of his future, thoughts of his loves, thoughts of what it was to be a living, breathing person.

"What, like, all-powerful and living forever?" Jay said.

"Somewhat," Rucksack replied. "Gods are almost but not quite either of those, despite what some religions would tell you. Generally what makes a god is becoming the total personification of what you truly are, the pure form o' what matters most at the core o' the core o' your being. You live what you love, and what you love lives through you. As for living forever, you won't age or get ill, and it'd be damn near impossible to injure you. But not totally impossible. You have to have a world, for example. Gods come from life. No life, no gods."

"Funny," Jay said, "I've seen more gods than rice around this city. Shouldn't they be banding together in some sort of big divine army to put this smiling thing down? Bust into his temple and take him out while he's not at full power?"

"If only it worked that way," Rucksack replied. "The Smiling Fire is the only god to have existed outside o' life on this world. He's not the same as other gods. He can't be killed in the sense that mortals think o' it. Every other god could stop everything they're doing—which is a lot more than you might think—team up against the Smiling Fire, and they would still lose. They're not the right kind of gods."

"Why would I be the right kind?"

"You are the world and the world is you. It's no accident or coincidence that the dia ubh starts out looking like a globe. The fire o' life is the world itself. You don't have to have seen every corner of existence to be every bit of it. Besides, ultimately, you aren't the only one who makes decisions. The world makes choices too, and the world chose you. You are the champion, Jay. You are the guardian. If you stand in the light o' the dia ubh, you become the one thing that can destroy the Smiling Fire. You become the one thing that can save us all. I suppose the only question is, do you decide to accept your destiny?"

"Do I have a choice?"

"Believe it or not, yes, you do. I'm not saying the alternatives are nice. You can choose not to stand in the light and let all happen as I've said it would. Or you could stand in the light but then do something else—not destroy the Smiling Fire, I suppose. You could leap off this hill right now, and who knows what would happen. Destiny is not the only path, Jay. It's only the most likely one—or, in cases such as this, the preferred one."

"The alternative being all life in the world destroyed."

Rucksack nodded.

Jay looked out over the hill. The plains below alternated between brown and green. Behind them, the white walls of Agamuskara shone in the sun, a brilliant light of life and humanity, all existence in a microcosm of India. Beside them, the brown ribbon of the Agamuskara river flowed. Jay for a moment thought he saw past the illusion. Instead of seeing a muddy river cutting east, Jay saw the clear, bright, and blue river flowing north toward the mountains, toward the Heart of the World.

"The road forever," Jay said. "Forever the road. That's what I always liked to tell myself. And now here it is. I could become a god, save the world, and never stop traveling. There's something to it."

He pulled down his daypack and unzipped it. The dia ubh was light in his hand and cool to the touch. "But there's got to be a catch," Jay said, staring at the dia ubh. "There's always a catch."

"You'd have to survive," Rucksack said.

Jay looked up and asked, "Why isn't it you?"

"What do you mean?"

"You don't talk about it directly, but it's like you were some sort of superhero. I get that something went wrong. You aren't as you were, but still, why not you? Why me? You're already practically a god because of one dia ubh, why not use this one to finish the job? You'd be a much better choice."

"It doesn't work that way. I am who I am, Jay. There's more for me beyond this. At least, that's what Mum's told me. Helping you to your destiny, she said, was a way to help me regain my own. I think this job, as you say, has come to you precisely because you are just an ordinary person but one who loves the world and its roads and ways with all his heart. Love and power usually do best with those who don't seek them out but instead accept them as the brilliance and burden that they are."

Jay looked down at the dia ubh's smooth, gray, featureless surface, turning it in his hands, then stopped.

"It's like there's the tiniest little scratch on the surface," Jay said. "Like a small crack, no thicker than a hair—that's what I thought it was at first. Here, see for yourself."

Jay tossed the dia ubh to Rucksack, softly but too high.

*Not a very good throw,* Jay thought. *Oh crap! Is it...*

The dia ubh went off to Rucksack's left, toward the edge of the hilltop and the big drop beyond. Rucksack leaped up, but the dia ubh bounced off his left hand. Rucksack twisted and shifted, his hands moving in a blur. He stumbled back to the ground, fell to his knees at the edge of the hill. The dia ubh rolled to a stop and rested in the palms of his hands.

"That was close," Rucksack said.

"Sorry," Jay replied, walking over. "I don't know what I was thinking." He saw a small shape on the ground. "Oh, you dropped something." He leaned down to pick it up.

Jay's face smiled back at him from his passport information page.

Rucksack rushed to his feet. "Jay..." he started to say.

"You had it?"

"They gave it to me and—"

"And you kept it? You didn't give it back to me? How long have you had this?"

"There's a reason, Jay."

"There's no reason. You promised me straight answers."

"They gave it to me the night the dia ubh changed."

Jay stepped backward. A heat and tightness burned in his face and body. "All this time," he said. "For weeks we've run around the city, chasing after Mim and Pim so I could get my passport back. So many times I thought we were close, as if I could sense that it was near. And it was. It was in your damn pocket the whole time." He flipped through the blank pages. "What have you done to my passport? What happened to all my stamps, all my visas?"

"I didn't do this," Rucksack stammered, his eyes wide and afraid. "They said something about fixing it. I needed to hold onto it for a while. You needed to stay in the city—"

"You lied to me," Jay said. "You were helping them."

"No." Rucksack shook his head. "I was helping you."

"You were helping me only because it meant helping yourself." Jay closed his passport and put it in his pocket. "I get it now. You kept me in the city because of this damn destiny. This dia ubh crap, this smiling bonfire thing." He shook his head. "And I nearly believed it."

"Dammit. Jade was right. We should've—"

"Jade knew too?"

"Wait, Jay," Rucksack said. "Let's calm down. I can explain this. I know how this must seem. It's hard to understand. Yes, I lied. I had to lie. You have to be here when the dia ubh opens."

"Choice?" Jay said quietly. "Decision? It's up to me? Bull—"

"It's up to you!"

"You took my choice from me the moment you lied." Jay zipped his daypack and put it on his back. "I'm done," he said. "Done with you. Done with this city. I have my passport back. I don't care what you have to say or what you fear. There's no big boogeyman waiting to set fire to the world. There's just the scared talk of a lost, broken old man with a useless hand. Stay away from me, Faddah Rucksack. I'm leaving Agamuskara. Don't ever let me see you again."

Before Rucksack could say a word or plead for Jay to discuss this over a pint or anything, Jay turned and ran down the hill. He thought he heard Rucksack shout his name, and something about the world burning, but he didn't stop or slow down. He just ran faster.

*I don't care anymore,* Jay thought. *Nothing but lies. And he's probably lying about all this too. Just for whatever it is that he's trying to do. He betrayed me.*

*So did Jade.*

*I'm going to the Everest Base Camp,* Jay thought. *I'm*

*packing up and leaving. Before I do, I'm going to look Jade in the eye and ask her to tell me the truth.*

Jay didn't run for the boat. He could feel in what direction the city lay. He'd walked only a few kilometers when the dirt path turned to cracked asphalt.

Wherever there were roads, there were taxis. He'd hardly set foot on the pavement when he smelled the acrid exhaust and heard the rumbling buzz of a small engine. The yellow-and-black bumblebee pulled up next to him.

"Everest Base Camp," Jay said. "No funny business. I know the way. And believe you me, the fare will be worth the while."

As they entered the city center again, Jay stared at the buildings and the streets. He took in every detail, every texture of the plaster, every dung pile in the street, the colors of all the saris on the women, the way the children laughed as they chased the rickshaw.

*This is the last time I'll see any of this,* Jay thought. *Once I leave Agamuskara, I'm never coming back.*

THE DRAWERS AND CABINETS stood empty, the interiors now dark voids she would never reach into again. Jade had bared and cleaned every surface, and the room was as fresh as if it had never been lived in.

The open window let in the harsh afternoon light and the city's reminders of the sounds and smells of the outside world, but inside the air loomed dark, stuffy, and heavy. The little room had never looked full, but now her pending absence washed over the walls and floor with a lonely emptiness.

*This was my home,* Jade thought. *This room, the pub, this hostel. This was my world. I knew every inch and breath of it. Now I'm leaving. But how do you learn to live in a different world?*

Her backpack lay on the bed, fuller than she expected, but not so full it wouldn't hold the occasional memento and souvenir. Its pale green reminded her of the stone of her name, of Jay's eyes, of pale seawater. She cinched the compression straps a little tighter around the pack, making it more compact.

"Now this is my world," she said.

Jade turned from the pack to the desk. The three notes glared at her.

*How much of who I am was really just what I was told?* she thought. *For so long now I've done what I was directed to do. I always thought I was so capable, so strong and fast, but really I was just good at taking orders, good at living the life demanded by sheets of paper.*

She read the first note again:

```
The new traveler is not just the new
traveler. He and the world must remain
in Agamuskara until the eclipse, so he
can be as a sunrise that never ends.
When the time is right, you must make
him forget himself and follow what he
would never follow.
```

"Will he follow his heart?" she asked as she moved to the second note:

The traveler must forget himself and
follow what he would never follow. The
heart is not the path.

"You're wrong," she said. "There is no path but the
heart."

*The Management I served so long and capably,* she
thought, *I ignored their instructions. Did I betray them? Or
did I choose instead to follow the guidance of a greater
power? And what is that greater power? Who do The
Management serve? Who do I serve now? Love? Myself? The
world? Something else?*

She read the third and final note:

We have been long in discussion, Jade
Agamuskara Bluegold. What you have
done was wrong for a Jade to do.
Another would have been dismissed
immediately. But because we understand
the lonely rigors of your role and
because of your long service, we
present you a choice:

Love is not the traveler's path.
Influence him with the mixture below.
Remain a Jade. You will be forgiven
and rewarded.

Continue resisting your duty and the
needs of the world, and you will cease
to be a Jade.

    You have three days to choose your
    destiny.

"I choose not to control or to be controlled," she said. "I choose to be free." She looked from the desk to the open window. The world outside seemed different now—bigger, darker, harsher, louder, more mysterious.

*There's so much I can't hear anymore.*

"I may no longer be a Jade," she said, taking a deep breath and keeping her voice as level as she could as she addressed the world outside the window. "But I don't have to be. There's no world tougher than me. I can do this. I can do this."

*I hope so, anyway.*

Then she heard a rapping noise and a voice, loud and harsh.

"Jade!"

She walked to the door and listened. "Jade!" came the shout again, followed by more rapping.

Jay's voice. *But he's not knocking on my door,* she thought. *He doesn't know about my room.*

She realized he was in the foyer. *He must think I'm in the pub,* she thought. *That's the door he's knocking on, probably wondering why he can't just go in since the pub should be open.*

Jade knew she had to go to him, but if she left her room, she wouldn't be able to return. Then she smiled, staring at the door.

*Or can I?*

Standing in the hall, Jade held her breath as she listened to the door whisper closed then stop before it could latch. *It's time,* she thought, taking a deep breath.

*Time to choose my destiny.*

She wondered what it must have looked like to Jay, the way she apparently walked out of the wall and the painting. He stood with his mouth open, a syllable standing like an ice cube on his tongue, his hand stopped a couple of inches away from another knock on the pub door.

*Oh backpack boy,* she thought, *I have so much to tell you. It's a good thing we have the whole world and all its time to discuss it.*

*Well,* she thought with a small grin, *if and when we get the opportunity.*

Then she stopped. The grin was gone from her face. He wore his large black backpack with the smaller daypack zipped onto it.

"You're leaving?" she asked.

"I put some money under the door," Jay replied. "It should be more than enough to cover my bill."

Only then did she see how fierce his eyes looked.

*Don't let him say more yet,* she thought. *It'll all be over if you do.*

"Come with me," she said, stepping back through the illusion of the wall.

Jade held her breath. What if the strangeness of what she'd done, and his curiosity about it, weren't enough? What if he just shook his head and left?

She exhaled only when he stepped through the illusion and stood in the small hallway leading to her room. She walked to the door and opened it fully, then picked up her large backpack from where it had kept the door from closing.

*Keep him off balance,* she thought. *I don't know what he's angry about, but I have to keep him curious enough to listen.*

"What the hell is going on?" Jay asked, following her into the room.

"Once I leave this room and that door closes behind me," Jade replied, "I can never go back. It's a world that I'll be shut out of forever."

"Does this have something to do with the pub being closed?"

She nodded. "I did something I wasn't supposed to do, and I refused to do something I was supposed to do. For that, I've been sacked. I'm no longer a bartender. I'm no longer..." *Tell him,* she thought, *tell him everything.*

"I'm no longer a Jade."

"A Jade? What, you have to go by a different name or something now?"

She shook her head. "Jake or Jade is usually just a title, and we put our names aside while we serve. Luckily my actual name is Jade too."

"What did you do?"

Jade stepped forward and took his hands. "I chose you."

"Those must be some strict policies about dating customers."

"I wasn't just a bartender, Jay. As a Jade, I work for a group called The Management. I'm one of hundreds of people all over the world called the Jakes and Jades. We're bartenders. More or less. But really what we do is help The Management direct the course of destiny and decisions for people. We've existed for hundreds of years. We use drinks to influence people's decisions. The Management had a destiny they were determined that you should follow, and it was my job to make sure you followed it."

"And that's what you didn't do."

"I couldn't. The night we first kissed, when I took your scotch, it wasn't because I had mixed up our drinks. It was because I was... I was a good soldier, following the orders I'd been given. I originally was going to do what I was told, but instead when I took your drink, I took that destiny away from you. Since I'm not the person it was intended for, though, nothing happened. It was inert. Your destiny—what they said was your destiny. I just couldn't. I didn't want you to be steered and driven. I wanted you to make your own decisions. I freed you, Jay. I freed you because I was falling in love with you."

"You chose me over this... work?"

"I chose for you to make your own decisions. Now you're leaving. I hope in time I'll understand." She pointed to her backpack. "I have to leave here today. The pub is shut to me, and it will be locked and closed until my replacement comes—maybe a new Jake, maybe a new Jade, or one called from duty somewhere else in the world. I'm hoping that you would like me to go with you. My life has been this work, Jay. Until you. I want to be with you. Share the world with you. If you'll have me."

With cheeks puffed out, a large sigh whooshed out of him. "Can you explain something to me?"

"Anything," Jade said. "I know it's a lot to take in, but I'll explain everything I can."

"I'm hearing that a lot today," he said. "All this time I've been here, drinking all those pints of stout, you've been... You've been messing with my destiny."

She shook her head. "It's not every drink I serve,

only particular drinks for a particular person. And we can't influence stout. It's somehow immune to us. That's why it's all Rucksack drinks."

Jay's eyes flashed. He let go of Jade's hands. "Rucksack knows about you?"

"I don't know how he learned about us, and it's not something The Management ever discuss. But far as I can tell Rucksack's intentions are good. He's just trying to find his own way back to a destiny he lost long ago."

"Yeah, so I understand. Lot of destinies around this town."

"Jay?"

He looked past her then walked to the desk.

*Oh crap,* she thought. *The notes.*

She turned around, staring at Jay, but he didn't look at her again until he'd read the three notes.

"What are these?" he said.

*Tell him,* she thought, *tell him all.* "The Management's instructions to me. About you."

"But you didn't... influence... me?"

"No. Stout is immune. Like I said, I took the scotch that would have influenced you."

His eyes widened. "What about the scotch you left by my bed last night? Did that do something to me?"

"That scotch is why they fired me. Instead of doing what they said, I broke their influence. It's called the All and Nothing. The person who consumes it can no longer be influenced by The Management or by the Jakes and Jades. It's like a... like a vaccination. You have to understand, Jay, I did this to free you. Make it so you could follow your heart, wherever that leads."

He held up a sheet of paper. "But this says the

heart is not the path."

Jade shrugged. "I say they're wrong."

"Do you think you know my heart?"

"Not as well as I would like." She tried to smile but found it too difficult. "I'm hopeful though."

"Hopeful that I'll choose you."

"But not over travel. You can have both, Jay. If you want to see the world, I'll go with you. We know we have something special here, something amazing as the world. We owe it to ourselves to see it through."

Jay closed his eyes tight. When he opened them again, the fierceness had returned. "How do I know that?" he said. "Everything else has been a lie. Why not this too?"

"A lie? I've never lied to you."

Jay reached into his pocket. Jade gasped when she saw his passport. "Did you know that Rucksack has had my passport this entire time?"

Jade started to speak again. Instead she looked at the floor and nodded.

"And you also knew that there's all this hubbub about me having some destiny to become a god? All this weirdness with the dia ubh and the smiling bonfire boogeyman thing?"

Again, she could only nod.

"So, for these last few weeks, you've known all along that I was on a wild goose chase and that Rucksack wanted me to stay here to be part of this supposed destiny."

It wasn't a question, but she nodded. "Jay—"

"How can I be with you when you lied to me? How can I be with you when you buy into the same destiny crap as Rucksack?"

"But I don't," Jade replied. "I told you, I freed you from that."

"You can't feel a need to free me from something unless you believe it's real."

"I did this for you," Jade said. "For us. I went against everything I've known for the last ten years. I gave it all up to be with you."

"No," Jay replied. "You gave it up for a roll of the dice."

"I gave it up for what might someday be love. Do you love me?"

He stepped forward, his eyes locked on hers. "How can I love someone I don't trust?"

"You can trust me."

"No, Jade, I can't." Jay reached up and tightened the shoulder straps on his pack. "If I've learned anything during my time here, it's that the only thing I can trust is the road. If I stop, trouble catches up to me. I'm going now. I'm leaving all of this, all of you, behind. You're right. We had a chance. We had something special. But you didn't just decide against your work when you lied to me. You decided against whatever we might have been. There is no more us."

Before she could say anything, Jay had unlatched the door and was gone.

She took a deep breath. The notes crumpled as she stuffed them in her pocket. Jade grabbed her pack, swung it onto her back, and ran out the door. It latched behind her with more than just locks. This time when she emerged from the wall, she felt a change in the air, as if behind her the illusion of the wall had stopped being an illusion.

*No turning back now.*

Jade opened the side door that led out into Agamuskara. *Find him,* she thought. *Follow him.*

But Jay had moved quickly, and already she couldn't see him among the crowds and the many streets. The loud buzz of the outside world pummeled her, and she could no longer isolate the individual voices that had guided her for so long.

He was gone and she had no way to find him.

A soft click made her swing around, the heavy pack swinging her off balance and making her stumble. "No!" she said, grabbing the latch, trying to open the door. But the Everest Base Camp, best pub and hostel in India, refused to open for her.

*I don't know where to go now,* she thought, unhooking her pack and sitting at the outside table. *Who am I now? What do I do?*

No matter how much she asked, how deeply she looked or listened, she found no answer, only hot tears that she couldn't stop from rolling down her face.


THE LAST TENDRILS of orange cloud faded as the sun set, but the looming black wall removed all thoughts of the darkening sky, of sunshine and bright days.

Jigme tried to get his breath back, standing stooped from the exertion of getting here, but even breathing was a hard labor now. He choked back tears, and at last no more came to take their place.

Asha slipped again, barely standing even as she leaned against her son. Jigme tightened his hand around her shoulder, and the pain from his broken fingers made him gasp. Something seemed to grate in his leg as he shifted to take more of her weight. His swollen knee pressed so hard against his pants that he wondered whether the pressure would tear fabric or flesh first.

"We're almost there, Amma," he said. "Soon you will be truly healed, and everything will be better. I promise."

She didn't reply. Her drooping head lolled. Jigme couldn't tell if her eyes were open or not. She'd been barely conscious ever since he had returned to their room, just before the first glints of dawn brought light back to Agamuskara. There had been no rest when he had returned, only fear of the people of the city learning what he had done, only fear of taking his eyes off Asha as she lay in and out of weak consciousness.

*Amma's dying,* he thought. No tears followed.

*I have to get her inside, get her to him,* Jigme thought. *But I have to get my breath back first. I'm barely standing. Just a moment more.*

Jigme looked up, past where the black line of the temple gave way to the darkening sky. Only the slightest gleam remained.

*Is my father still alive?* Jigme wondered. *Did he die long ago?*

Looking down at his mother, Jigme kissed her head. "You're all I have," he said. "I can't lose you too."

The darkness ate the last gleam of light in the sky.

With a final breath, Jigme forced away all pain and weariness and started walking them forward once more. Asha stumbled when they passed the statues. Jigme didn't know where he found the strength, but he caught her, lifted her up so her body lay across his outstretched arms, her limbs and head dangling. Her weight had faded with the sunlight. She was so much easier to carry now. Ragged, slow breaths rasped in and out of her as the entrance to the temple appeared before them. Jigme stepped forward, crossing a foot over the threshold.

"Turn around!"

Jigme froze. The cry in his mind echoed then repeated.

"Turn around!"

The voice reminded him of his own. But it was also clearer, bolder, yet old, full of fear and worry.

"You can still leave here, leave him, and never return to this place," said the voice. "This is your last chance. Leave, Jigme. Let life happen as life will happen. Let him fade. Do not take her to him."

"Who are you?" he said.

"One who wants to help," the voice replied.

"You are too late to help," Jigme said. "She is nearly dead, and this is my only chance to save the one person who cares about me."

"Do you really believe he's going to help you? Help her?"

"I don't even know who you are," Jigme said. "I have no reason to listen to you."

The voice said nothing else.

With another step forward, Jigme and Asha were inside the temple. The entrance sealed as it normally did, yet something seemed different.

The air felt hotter than Jigme had ever known it before. Sweat beaded on his face. He carried Asha forward, toward the center of the temple. In the red-and-black glare, a long, low block of black rock rose from the floor. Despite the dimness, the obsidian's faces and edges gleamed sharp and bright.

"Lay her there." The Smiling Fire's red-and-black eyes emerged from the darkness behind the block. More of his shape became visible. Jigme could just make out the shadows that covered much of his face, the ragged thin limbs, the darkness that hung off of the Smiling Fire like robes made of night, smoke, and storm clouds.

In his right hand, the Smiling Fire held a long, thin knife, black and shiny as the obsidian of the temple. Jigme took a step back. "What's that?"

"Fear not." The Smiling Fire tucked the knife into his robes. "It is not for you."

Jigme nodded and realized he'd been holding his breath. He kissed his mother's forehead then gently set her on the block. "Will it hurt?" he asked.

"Not for long."

Below the eyes, the scythe-like smile widened. Jigme had never noticed before, but the red-and-black grin looked more like a tunnel than a mouth, deep and endless, covered in sharp points.

"Will we then go where the other children are?"

"Yes."

The Smiling Fire spread his arms over Asha then leaned down. His grin stretched and yawned wider.

"Why haven't I gotten any letters?" Jigme asked.

The Smiling Fire stopped. "Letters?"

"From the children I brought to you," Jigme said. "I thought they would write, but there have never been any letters, and you don't say anything about how they're doing."

"Stupid child," the Smiling Fire replied. "The

children are dead. The fires they stole have returned to me."

"Dead?"

"I do not understand these schools and letters, these flowers and grasses that give you such hope and happiness in your mind." The Smiling Fire glared at Jigme. "They helped you bring me what I needed, but they are not useful anymore."

"You killed them?"

"You know what I did. You have known from the first. You chose to try to believe something else."

"No," Jigme said, feeling the truth of the rasping words inside. *I've always known,* he thought. *From the first I took here, poor child. He's dead. Poor... Don't say the name! Don't ever say the name!*

"It is time for you and your mother to return your stolen fires to me. Once I have your fires, then it is only a matter of time until the fires of all the world come back to their rightful owner. Soon it will all be over."

"Amma!" Jigme shouted. "No! Mum!"

"Jigme?"

Her soft voice for a moment made the temple brighter, tamed the heat of the air. Asha looked up at the Smiling Fire. At first fear blazed through her face with a grief and sadness that almost made the temple cold. But as she stared into the eyes of the Smiling Fire, she calmed down. The fear faded. Slowly, with a shudder that almost seemed like a laugh, Asha began to smile. She turned to Jigme.

"My son," she said. "My beautiful son. I should have been there for you better. I'm sorry."

Behind her, the mouth of the Smiling Fire opened

wider. "Return the fire to me," he said.

She looked at him again. "You'll have it in a little while," she replied. Some hope filled her face, her eyes, her voice. "But you can't keep what isn't yours."

"It is all mine. It always has been. As you will now learn." The Smiling Fire began descending again.

Asha turned back to Jigme. "It's okay, son," she said. "Do not be afraid. Run, if you can. Know that I love you. I forgive you. And I will see you again. Your father—"

Her words cut off. The fiery grin covered her, head to toe, voice to soul. Darkness became all Jigme could see.

When the Smiling Fire rose, the obsidian block was empty. He stepped forward, rose over the block, and moved toward Jigme. "Her fire is mine. The mother is no more. And now, it is time for the son. You will have your reward now, Jigme. Death. Finality. An end to all those things that pain you."

Jigme looked behind him, saw where he had entered the temple. No doorway opened. He hobbled to the entry, felt along the stone for a latch, a crack— something he could use to open the way out. He longed for the world beyond the black temple, for every ounce of existence and life.

*Better the pain than this,* he thought.

But there was no way out, nowhere to run. Jigme turned around. Something in his leg snapped.

Fresh pain ripped through his body and mind. *I couldn't run now anyway,* he thought.

He slipped to one knee.

"Amma," he said, "I'm sorry. I was wrong about everything. I lost you. They're all lost. Because of me."

He saw her face. He saw all their faces.

The tears came back.

The Smiling Fire stood over him now, and his heat seared Jigme's face and skin. He winced. *My eyebrows are gone,* he thought. The flesh of his nose began to char.

Jigme stared into the eyes of the Smiling Fire. "I love you, Mum," he said. "I want to make it right." He looked deeper. "I'm sorry," he said. "All of you, I'm sorry."

*I hope that counts for something,* he thought, staring into the red-and-black blaze.

Fire happened.

When the fire was gone, so was Jigme.

The Smiling Fire rose, his mouth shrinking to its sharp curved grin.

"At last," he said, raising his arms.

The black temple exploded.

Barely visible against the dark night, shards of obsidian burned as they rained back down.

Surrounded now by the night over Agamuskara, the white walls of the city dimmed and tried to shrink away. The Smiling Fire felt all life around him, all the stolen fires. But they did not steal from him now. They never would again.

"You are all coming back to me," he said, moving forward into the alley.

Where he walked, the ground smoldered.

He sensed it before him, the sleeping promise of the dia ubh.

"With you, it begins," he said.

The Smiling Fire moved forward into the world, wondering how long it would take to burn the city to the ground.

NIGHT HAD FALLEN, and when Jade woke she realized she had no idea how long she had been asleep at the table outside Everest Base Camp. Her numb legs and arse certainly weren't telling her anything other than they weren't awake yet.

As the last tendrils of light faded from the sky, she looked at the quiet, bare streets. It was only just past sundown, but the city was more deserted than the middle of the night, when at least there were people sleeping outside.

Even without her Jade abilities, she sensed some fear, some foreboding, everywhere. Every soul in Agamuskara wanted to hide.

She shifted back her chair and reached down for her pack. Her hand swept through empty air.

Her pack was gone.

Jade shook her head. *That was everything I own,* she thought. Her eyes opened wide. *My passport. My cash. That was all in my money belt.*

*Which I had stashed in my pack until I was ready to leave.*

*Now I really don't have anything but myself,* she thought. *No ID. No money. Nowhere to go and no way to get there.*

*What the hell do I do now?*

Near the end of a street, a shadow appeared. Jade sat back in her chair, watching the shadow grow larger as it came toward Everest Base Camp. *No one even woke me to ask about the pub,* she thought. *How long have the streets been so empty? And who the hell is coming toward me? Should I even be afraid?*

The figure moved fast, fading in and out of sight as it passed by the occasional light, suddenly now all but floating along the side of the hostel.

It was coming toward Jade. Fear rose in her and she started to move her chair back so she could stand.

"Oy! Jade!" Rucksack shouted, coming to a stop at the table. "I'm so glad I found you. We may be too late, but we have to move fast. It's Jay. He's, Jade, this is hard to say, but he found out I had his passport. He got mad and—"

"He's gone." Tears welled up again, but Jade forced them back. *I've cried enough for the next ten years,* she thought.

"When did you see him?" Rucksack pulled out a chair. "Tell me fast, while I have a sit. Believe me when I say it's been a hell o' an afternoon getting back here."

"I don't know how long it's been." She quickly told him all that had happened, from The Management sacking her to packing to Jay leaving.

"The bastards did what?"

"I disobeyed orders and influenced Jay so he could never be influenced again."

"Wait," Rucksack said. "This was your doing? You know what's coming, what Jay's role is supposed to be. And you allowed him to steer himself away from it?"

"The world will have far better chances if it can be saved by someone acting of his own free will."

"This is bigger than all o' us. This isn't some blind coercive destiny, Jade. This is destiny and decision working in unison—or at least it's bloody well supposed to be. But if Jay's left Agamuskara, he's left the world to this fate. Because o' you."

Jade stood. The metal chair sounded oddly muffled when it fell to the cement walkway.

"Because of me?" she said, anger rising in her voice. "Who's been here for months, wallowing in his stout? Who glommed onto Jay the moment he arrived, believing every bit of what his mummy said about destiny? And who not only hung on to something that wasn't his, but then, however the hell it happened, managed to let Jay then find out you've had his passport all this time the two of you were supposed to be hunting for it?"

Rucksack's chair fell over as he stood up. When it hit the ground, the sound seemed impossibly big, as if the chair had not so much fallen but exploded. "Always heard you were the best o' the best, the Jade o' Jades. Hell, you never knew it, but I was there the day you were chose and chosen."

"What?"

"I'll never forget the certainty on your face. You didn't hesitate to go off with those hooded wanks, leaving your man—ring in his outstretched hand, and him feeling like the world's biggest eejit. You were supposed to be the one whose sense o' duty never wavered. But look at you now. Sacked. All your stuff nicked. Alone. Full o' doubt and fear and worry. And all because you didn't do what you were supposed to do. Because you just had to fall for someone you weren't supposed to have. This didn't happen because o' me, Jade formerly Agamuskara Bluegold. This happened because you put yourself above your duty."

"I chose love."

"Love was never an option. Unless you want a planet that has a striking resemblance to the universe's biggest ash heap."

"If destiny's destiny, what does it matter? It's not like we have choice."

"Oh, we have choice." Rucksack reached into his pocket and slammed the dia ubh onto the table. The sound was like flames crackling far off in the distance.

"We have this. Jay abandoned the dia ubh," Rucksack said. "He's gone and it's here. Your decisions have thrown the entire world off the rails and into the fire, Jade."

"All this time I thought you'd be helpful," Jade said. "But you're just in this for yourself, for some days gone by that you can't have anymore."

"And I thought you'd live up to who you are. Or who you were, rather."

"I've had it with you," Jade said. "I may have nothing. I may have nowhere to go, but I'll be damned if I'll have anything else to do with you and your laugh and your beer and your damn accent."

Jade reached for the dia ubh. "If I can't have Jay, I'll just keep this as a souvenir."

But her hand closed on empty air. In a blink, the dia ubh was gone.

"Where is the one you call Jay?"

The rasping voice stopped Jade's breath. She and Rucksack stared at each other, mirroring the same shocked eyes and slack mouths. Slowly they each turned.

Neither had seen the shadowy figure come down the dark, empty street. Now she and Rucksack saw the dull glow of fires burning in the distance, burning outward from the heart of the city. Smoke already choked the clouds from the sky and smothered the cries of fear and pain that rose out of the dark.

Jade stared at the figure before them, but a dull, dark red glow obscured its face instead of illuminating it.

A shadowy hand held the dia ubh in front of its body.

"Jay is gone from your reach, old enemy," Rucksack said. He nodded at the dia ubh. "That will do you no good now."

"Old enemy?" the Smiling Fire replied. "I have enemies only for a moment. Then there is nothing left of them but ash."

"Oh, we go back a long way," Rucksack said. "Though it did take only a moment for me to help ruin you. But I suppose you could say we've never been formally introduced."

"I have all I need now," the Smiling Fire said. "Whoever you are, it doesn't matter. Your lives are finished." He held the dia ubh with his hands and raised it high.

A sudden heat made Jade sweat. Her skin felt seared.

Behind her, she heard a click and a creak.

She turned her head. The Everest Base Camp's front door was opening. In her mind, she heard the pub cry out to her: "Run!"

She grabbed Rucksack's hand. "Come on!"

As they dashed inside the Everest Base Camp, the door slammed shut behind them.

"I thought you couldn't come in here anymore," Rucksack said.

"So did I," Jade replied. She ran to the door to the hostel. "If the pub is willing to break the rules so we don't die, I'm not going to argue."

"Fair point," Rucksack said.

A sound made Jade look back. The front door splintered, smoldered, blackened, and vanished in a cloud of ash. A heartbeat later, the Smiling Fire stepped through it and into the Everest Base Camp.

"Where are we going?" Rucksack said as he followed Jade into the foyer.

Jade pulled the door closed behind her. *If the front door couldn't stop him,* she thought, *this one certainly won't.* She shook the doubts out of her head. *Shut up. Doubt later. Live now.*

"Okay, Rucksack," she said. "Now jump through that wall."

"What?"

"Dammit, Rucksack!" Jade shoved him with all her strength.

*If The Management won't let us through,* she thought, *at least he'll be the one to bounce off the wall.*

But Rucksack sailed through the illusion. Jade leaped behind him.

They ran down the short hallway, and Jade pulled open the door to her former room. When she closed it behind them, the door closed as it always did with more than just locks.

"Where are we?" Rucksack said.

"This used to be my room," Jade replied. "It's virtually impregnable. The Management make a Jake or Jade's room so it's a fortress, cut off from the rest of the world. You have to know it's here to get to it, and even then you can only come inside if the pub or The

Management let you. There's no way the Smiling Fire can find us here. Even if he did, there's no way he could get to us. We're safe."

"You mean we're trapped in a small room with someone we're furious at."

"Better than being on fire."

"A moderate improvement, aye."

They fell silent. No sounds reached through the void beyond the door.

The quiet moments fell and lengthened. A small hope flickered in Jade.

*Maybe he couldn't find us,* she thought. *Maybe he left.*

The first blow made the door rattle in its frame.

The hope winked out.

"Jade?" Rucksack said.

"He's more powerful than I would have expected," she replied. "If this is him before the dia ubh opens, he's already more powerful than the pub, even more powerful than The Management."

"I don't know how," Rucksack said, "but he was powerful enough to free himself from the temple." He sighed. "Jade, we can't stop him."

"Then until we can figure out a way, we'd better run like hell." Jade unlocked the window.

As Rucksack followed, the door blackened and fell to ash. The Smiling Fire stepped into the room.

"You humans are so interesting," he said. "You've come so far since I last walked the world. You've given me so much more to burn."

Jade tried to push the window open, but it stuck. "Stupid gods," she said, hitting the sash. "Always thinking you're so damn powerful." Rucksack pushed with her. Finally, the window opened and they raised it as high as it would go.

The Smiling Fire raised the dia ubh over his head. "Not so damn powerful," he replied. "All powerful."

"He's trying to open the dia ubh!" Rucksack shouted.

The blast of heat came again, hotter this time. Jade smelled singed hair and fabric. *What is it going to feel like to burn?* she thought. Fear sapped her strength and will.

For a moment, nothing happened. The Smiling Fire held the dia ubh, and his red-and-black grin became wider. Then, dark as the Agamuskara night, a crack appeared in the gray featureless surface.

"Go!" Rucksack shouted, pulling Jade into the window opening. "Dammit, go!"

A light exploded from the dia ubh, and the world turned white.

Somehow, as if she were suddenly floating bodiless above the city, Jade could see the Everest Base Camp on fire. The roof fell in. Liquor bottles exploded. Flames leaped up from the polished bar. Hostel beds briefly became perfect rectangles of fire. Oddly, though, she couldn't help noticing, all the roaches seemed fine. The voice of the pub pulled at her, screaming in her mind.

Dying.

*Where's Rucksack?*

Something pushed her. Something pulled her. Something seemed like someone holding her hand.

The burning heap of the building collapsed in on itself like a black hole forming in the world. The life burned and melted out of the Everest Base Camp, finest pub and hostel in India, former home of the

Jade of all Jades. As the last thought from the dead pub fell silent, Jade too stopped seeing, listening, feeling.

*Some new life,* Jade thought, fading as the world turned red, dim, and black.


THROUGH THE SMALL TICKET WINDOW, the ticket attendant smiled and asked, "Destination?"

Jay coughed, trying to get his breath back after the running, the taxi flagging, the traffic jam, and the more running, all to make sure he could get to the train station before anyone caught up to him. Late afternoon sun glinted off the glass. Jay wondered if Rucksack was back in the city center yet.

"Somewhere," Jay said. "Anywhere. Everywhere."

"Those are not on our route," the attendant replied. "Destination?"

Jay looked at the people behind him in line and wondered where they were going. They could all see him at the window or in the window's reflection.

He smiled and turned back to the attendant. "The person in front of me," Jay said. "Where did he buy a ticket to?"

"Kolkata."

"Then that's where I'm heading. Kolkata. One third-class ticket. One-way."

"Our second-class and first-class cars will be more to the comfort of a tourist such as yourself," the attendant replied. "Sleeping berths, air conditioning, included meals. And only a small bit more for a tourist such as yourself."

"This traveler wants a third-class ticket," Jay said. "I

don't need comfort and that car is going to the same place as the fancy ones."

The attendant bobbed his head. Jay dug money out of his pants pocket, and the attendant handed over the ticket with a shrug. Printed in black ink on light blue paper, the Hindi script reminded Jay of dancing or of the flames of a campfire.

"When does the train leave?" he asked.

A smile arced up the attendant's face. "Five minutes."

Jay ran to the platform.

Panting, he came to a stop by the empty track. No train. A large crowd stood still. The clock said he had made it just in time. Jay nodded to a nearby family. "Has the Kolkata train left?"

They bobbed their heads. "Five minutes," the man said, smiling.

*India,* Jay thought. *Seems the entire world happens five minutes from now. After five minutes have passed, though, things have a way of still being five minutes away.*

He shook his head. *I'm half surprised Jade hasn't caught up to me already. And if Rucksack's back in the city, surely he's figured out I'd head to the train station. They could be here any minute. They could be here now.*

He looked around as best he could, but if they were there, Jay couldn't see them. His shoulders relaxed as he took a deep breath.

"Mr. Jay?"

He whipped around. Jay stopped walking, but his backpack kept going and he stumbled.

"Never easy to walk around with a house on your back," a second voice said.

Jay righted himself. Mim and Pim stood in front of

him.

"What do you want?" Jay said. "Here to steal something else from me? Or are you trying to find your accents? You certainly don't sound like the same two guys who drugged me and nicked my passport."

Mim smiled. "You're right. We're not in character, as we were before. We are simply and totally ourselves."

"Well aren't I just bloody honored," Jay replied.

"You do not understand, Mr. Jay," Mim said. "Soon I believe you will, but soon is not the same as yet."

"I'm sure yet is only five minutes from now."

Pim grinned. "We understand why you are angry with us, with Jade, with Rucksack. We came to say we're sorry."

Jay had prepped himself for anything: a battle of wits, evading their strange words, dumping their drugged tea. Maybe there'd be a sprinting chase or even a fight. But the apology threw him off balance more than his backpack had.

"You're apologizing?" Jay said. "Let's drop the games and pretexts. How about you just tell me what you're really here for."

"We are here to apologize, Mr. Jay," Pim said.

"Why?"

"Because we have existed a long time," Mim replied. "We know how important it is for someone to be in control of his own life. We too were working toward the destiny you now know about. It would have been better if we all had been honest with you."

"And if you hadn't stolen my passport?" Jay snorted. "What were you doing to it anyway? Why are the pages blank?"

"It is all to do with the destiny," Pim replied. "We truly were fixing it."

All those weeks the tiny lightweight blue booklet had chained Jay to the city better than a ball and chain. He'd kept his passport in his pocket in case the attendant wanted it, but the man hadn't asked. Jay took it out now and flipped through the pages.

*I've treasured it,* he thought. *Crown jewels indeed. Passport. Tickets. Money. Jewels of a different coin. Riches of a different value.*

*Chains that can make a traveler into a prisoner.*

When he looked up again, Jay knew his smile could have outshone the Indian sun. "Here," he said, handing the passport to Mim. "If it's so important to this destiny, you can have it. Where I'm going, I won't need it anymore."

"Jay?" Pim said, concern in his eyes. "This is part of you."

"That's why you took it," Jay said. "You knew I wouldn't leave the city until I found it. But in trapping me, you set me free. I'm never letting anything hold me down, hold me back, like that again. This is yours now."

"Your destiny is crucial to the world."

Jay shrugged. "So are my decisions. You keep wanting me to choose to stay. I choose to keep going. To see all I can see and never stop again."

"What about Jade?"

"I'm sure she'll be just fine."

Mim stared at the track. "We could do something, you know," he said. "Break the train. Cause every bus in the city to stop working the moment you come near it."

The grin came back, even bigger this time. "You could," Jay said. "But you won't. I'm leaving and you won't stop me."

Pim put his hand on Mim's shoulder. "You're right, of course," Pim said. "You've made your decision, and we won't try to dissuade you. Thank you for the passport, Jay. It's good to have it back, as we still have much to do. We'll keep it close. You never know when you may want it back."

"That would suggest we'll meet again someday. We won't."

"As you say. Best of luck."

The train hissed and squealed as it pulled up. With a resigned smile, a bow, and a bob of the head, Mim and Pim vanished into the confluence of people rushing on and off the train, crowding and pushing for the doors. Jay walked slowly.

*I feel light,* he thought. *I've traveled so long, I don't even need the crown jewels anymore. It's time to free myself.*

When he set a foot on the step up to the train car, excitement shot through him. *I haven't felt this excited since I first left Idaho. That's how it's going to be from now on. Wherever I want to go, whenever I want to go there, I'll go.*

Jay glanced at his ticket and turned left. Farther up the train there would be cars with comfortable seats, benches that became beds, air conditioning, even luxurious rooms. *I could afford any of them,* Jay thought. *But money can do other things.*

With a grin, he knew what to do.

Raised voices met him in the dim third-class car. Everywhere, men pointed at filled seats, raised defensive arms from where they sat, and argued over who should go where.

*I'll stand from here to Kolkata,* Jay thought. *I don't need to sit.*

As he adjusted to the din, Jay realized that although no one argued in English, he could understand what everyone was shouting.

*It's like the day I first came to Agamuskara,* Jay thought, *when that parade passed by and I was touching the dia ubh through my pack. All those voices made sense, just as these do. But I don't have the dia ubh anymore. Finally it isn't following me. It feels like it's set me free.*

He made his way to a bare patch of wall. His pack seemed to squirm as he set it down. "What's your deal?" Jay said. "Thought you'd be happy finally being out and about again."

Around him, the loud voices continued. Jay thought about the men in the car—no women to be seen, no children—and wondered what their lives were like.

The noise stopped. All the men had settled in to their seats or the spots where they stood, and all arguments were completed. It reminded Jay of a story Rucksack had told him about how in India people did only what was necessary at the time. Jay shook his head and the memory went away.

Some of the men stared at him. This was understandable, given that Jay's was the only non-Indian face in the car. He looked around the car at the faces, then stopped.

The man sat at the center of the opposite wall of the train car, surrounded by an emptiness that no one would cross. A blue turban covered his head, and he wore loose white robes, leaving only his hands and face visible. The face was smooth, with almost feminine features, and the hands were graceful yet hardened from years of rough work. Gray-blue eyes shone like stars, somehow brightening the train car.

Jay couldn't tell if he was Indian or where he was from. He didn't have the anywhere face that Rucksack had. He must be in the sun a lot but wasn't from here. Before he realized it, Jay was halfway across the car, and he stumbled as the train lurched into motion.

"You must be a traveler," the man said with a voice soft and young, old and hard all at once.

Jay nodded. "Thanks for understanding the distinction."

The man smiled. "What is your good name?"

"Jay."

"Where are you from?"

"Idaho, in America."

"Annoyica?"

"America."

"Ah, yes," the man said. "Good place. Loud but good. What do you do?"

"I live the world."

The man stared at Jay's t-shirt. Jay looked down too. He hadn't noticed it when he had put on the shirt as he packed his things and got ready to leave Everest Base Camp. Overall, the fabric was pale blue, yet it had the barest hint of green. A brown-and-black outline of a hand stamp, like what had pressed many of the visa stamps in Jay's passport, seemed to hover over an outline of the planet.

*I don't even remember where I got this shirt,* Jay thought, *but it's fitting.*

"That is a most interesting occupation," the man said. "Are you married?"

"No."

The man nodded. His smile faded and he said nothing more.

*Did I fail some sort of a test?* Jay thought.

Then the smile came back. With a wink, the man reached behind him and opened a rectangular case that was smaller than a suitcase but larger than a briefcase. "Would you like a drink?"

"That's the best thing anyone's said to me all day."

With a blur, the graceful hands opened the case. Soon a clear bottle filled with an amber liquid, almost golden, was in Jay's hand. "What is it?" he asked.

"My own recipe," the man replied. "Medicinal. Stimulating. Inspiring. And tastes good too."

"No hooch like homemade hooch," Jay said, raising his arm and nodding to the man. "As long as it's not a damn pint of stout."

"Pardon me?"

"Never mind," Jay said. "It's not important. Will you join me?"

"Would that I could," he replied. "I myself don't drink but I find that carrying a bottle or two always helps me find friends on these long trips. It can change your world, a good newfound friend."

"That's one way to put it," Jay said, tipping back a long swallow.

Soon other men came over, some taking a pull from the bottle, some bringing out bottles of their own or food or instruments. *It's like a mobile Everest Base Camp,* Jay thought. *Just a little while ago they were arguing. Now we're all talking, drinking, laughing, swapping stories. This is how it can be for me for the rest of my days. I'll take it.*

He glanced behind the half-circle of men. Alone and propped up on the opposite wall, his backpack sulked in darkness. *If I didn't know better,* Jay thought, *I'd swear it was mad at me for being here. But why? We're travelers. Traveling means leaving Agamuskara and moving on. It'll get over it.*

The talk went on and the clacking of the train wheels joined in the conversation and camaraderie. Outside the small windows, the sky darkened as the train made its way east. As the hours went by, Jay realized, the food and drink never ran out. Every time they emptied a bottle, another appeared.

"You have seen much of the world," someone said to the man in the robes. "Tell us one of your stories."

The man nodded. "I have not seen as much as I would like, and there is much I will never see. Much of what I have seen pales before the bright, shining moments of your own lives. But if there is one story that I must tell, it is something that happened not to me but near me, to someone else. I was but fortunate to have been in the area at the time."

Everyone drank in his words. Jay glanced behind the men again. His pack seemed to be standing straighter, as if anticipating yet listening to a story it already knew.

"My life takes me far," the man said at last. "Recently, I was in the shadow of Qomolongma—Mount Everest herself, mountain of the world. The moon was full that night, shining silver and gold in the cold thin air of the Himalayas. I had stepped out of my tent to have a cigarette and gaze at the mountain as the moon rose high above it. Between my tent and the vast plains and hills that lead to the foot of Qomolongma, there was a small rise at camp—not even a hill, just a small rounded slope where one can gain a better vantage. I thought about going to it, but I also sought solitude on this trip, and someone already stood atop the hill.

"This person and I watched the moon rise up from the valleys and mountains, as if it rose from out of the Heart of the World itself. She was full and bright, big as the mountain. I have seen much beauty in this world, my friends, but never have I seen anything as beautiful as this."

Twinges of pain poked Jay. He realized how tense and stiff he was, no longer enraptured by the story but terrified. *No,* he thought. *It can't be.*

"I looked from the moon to the man, standing on the little rise at the edge of Mount Everest Base Camp. The darkness around him lightened, and then I could not take my eyes off him."

*This didn't happen,* Jay thought. *You didn't see this. Please, you didn't see this. You couldn't see something that didn't happen.*

"All around the man, the darkness became moonlight, and the moonlight became as a gentle hand, lifting the man off the hill and taking him to Qomolongma herself. I watched until I could no longer see the man. I never saw his face, but as far as I could tell, the mountain carried him all the way up to the summit of Qomolongma. That is all I know. That is all I saw. Whatever the moon and the mountain had to say to the man, I do not know. But oh, how I wish I did. And oh, how I am glad to have seen such a moment of magic on a moonlit night by the mountain of the world."

The man fell silent. No one else spoke. All of the men sat as still as children before a teacher.

Jay stood and left the car.

In the vestibule between train cars, the evening air hung hot and wet but no longer blazing. The wind of the fast train washed over Jay as he held onto the rails of the open doorway at the side of the vestibule, half-standing, half-hanging out of the train.

*That didn't happen,* he thought. *It was just a story. A story I've left behind, just like the rest. No more Jade. No more Rucksack. No more legends. No more destiny. I'm free.*

He stared into the darkness as the train rushed through the night. What lay at the end of the line but another city, more pubs, more sights to see already pawed over by throngs of Swedes, Israelis, and Australians, all carrying their dog-eared Guru Deep guidebooks? More taxis and hostels, more questionable food and water, more touts...

*No more,* Jay thought.

Clouds had gathered over the countryside. The air felt damp, heavy, and charged. Off in the blackness, flashes of brown lightning made the world shine. For a moment, the skin of existence had faded away, revealing something beneath, like an everlasting brilliance.

*Why bother with another city or another country?* Jay thought. *Countries aren't sealed and separate. We just act like they are. But we're connected to the it. And the it is the everywhere. Since we're connected, I can go anywhere.*

Lightning flashed again. *What's out there,* Jay thought, *beyond the narrow vein of these tracks? There are fields and villages and places that will never know the mention of a guidebook.*

He walked back to the car.

"Are you all right?" the man asked.

Jay nodded. "Needed some air. And now I need another drink."

More drinks, jokes, stories, songs. Jay told his friends his good name and that he wasn't from anywhere. He was just a traveler and the road was his home. He was not married, and his occupation was to live fully being alive. Laughter and affection glowed from the train car.

Everyone talked about their new friend Jay.

*I can go anywhere,* Jay thought. *I need nothing but myself and my backpack. Nothing else...*

Taking another swig of a new bottle—*How many fit in that case anyway?*—Jay decided the time had come.

For all the years he'd traveled, Jay had never reached into his money belt in public view. Usually, he'd gone into a toilet when he needed to get out a ticket, his passport, or some more cash. Out of sight, out of mind was everything when it came to the crown jewels.

Jay reached around to his right hip and unbuckled the strap that held the money belt in place. Pulling the pouch free, he held it loose in his hand. Thousands of rupees were inside, as were hundreds of US dollars. He thought too of the plane ticket, the fare paid that could get him emergency passage on any plane at any time.

"My friends!" he said, holding up his hand, packed with money. "I don't need this anymore! May it help your dreams come true!" He threw wads of bills out among the men.

Then he reached into his money belt again, pulled

out his emergency ticket, and nodded to the man across from him. "Didn't you say you wanted to study abroad?"

*Wait,* Jay thought, *he hadn't said anything. The hooch must be messing with my brain.*

But the way the man nodded, Jay knew it was true.

Jay handed him the plane ticket. "Here. Go. Live your dreams. Live the world."

"But you, sir?" the man said. "Are you living your dreams?"

Jay shrugged. "I've got one foot in front of the other, and I've got a world to see. That'll do me fine."

The men roared and clapped Jay on the back. He handed out money and dreams like a god among men. *I'm traveling again,* he thought. *No, I'm really traveling for the first time. I was a tourist. Now I'm a traveler. I can go wherever I want. Be whoever I want to be. Tell whatever tales I want to tell.*

When the money belt was empty of the crown jewels, Jay took out the photo of his parents and tucked it in his pocket. "You'll still be with me," he said. "Always."

He looked at the flimsy dirty nylon in his other hand. "But it's time we parted," he said, dropping the money belt to the floor of the train car.

Outside, lightning flashed brown-gold in the heat of the subcontinental night.

As the men began to talk excitedly about their plans, Jay gradually shrank back out of the circle. He slipped his pack onto his back, grateful it was cooperating again.

The man in the robes stared as Jay walked to the door. For a moment their eyes locked, and the man's gray-blue gaze seemed to crackle. They nodded at each other, saying no more. Jay left before the man could ask the question he knew was burning at his mind.

Jay walked out between the train cars, swaying with the weight on his back and the motion of the train, holding the railing as he watched the lightning flash over the countryside.

"This is all we are," Jay said to the world. "A moment's flash, a brief spark against void and nothing. But in a brief flash, I can go anywhere. And I will."

In his mind, Jade and Rucksack flashed, but he pushed back the thoughts. *Look ahead,* he thought. *Never back. Never again. What's behind is what no longer matters.*

"Wherever. Whenever," Jay said. "Why, I could jump from this train, have no idea where I am. Ah tomorrow, what a mystery! What an adventure!"

Jay decided.

"What an adventure!" Jay said to the lightning. If he ran fast enough, across the dark, unknown fields, could he catch the lightning, maybe haggle a ride?

The train would run on and on, to the known and done. Behind Jay, all he'd known. Before him...

Jay braced himself, waiting for the lightning. The sky flashed bright against the black. For a moment, Jay could hardly see. Blue and green flecks dotted his vision. His pack felt heavier than ever, as if trying to pull him backward.

He ran forward anyway.

From the speeding train, Jay jumped into the unseen world before him.

For a moment he flew.

Man of the world. Man above the world. The backpacker of all time. Jay the legend. Jay the myth. Jay of the road. All the world, all his past fell away, dregs of a life long since drained. He stared toward the sky.

Then his pack twisted, and Jay was turning every which way in mid-air, limbs loose and confused as he began to fall.

*Where am I looking now?* Jay thought. *Where am I going? I'm falling. How far away is the ground? What if we're traveling over a bridge? Or along a gorge? What if there are rocks below?*

He flailed in the air as he tried to right himself. He turned around and around in the air. But no matter what he did, the weight of the twisting backpack kept him off balance.

Lightning struck.

Jay saw the flash in the same moment he heard a crack. The thunder, the only thunder this whole night, split the sky from the earth, split past and present and future, split Jay from himself and the world.

The sound faded but the lightning did not.

Jay realized the lightning had hit him. Fire and blue pain, fire and a silver void, fire and a green oblivion, fire and a shimmering gold, pain and pain and pain.

Unable even to scream, all Jay could do was fall.

His burned body broke upon the brown-and-black earth.

The train clattered on toward Kolkata, leaving behind it only the silent night and a traveler who lay still.

# III

UNDER THE HEAVY GRAY-AND-BLACK CLOUDS, two bodies lay in rubble that had once been the white walls of Agamuskara. The blackened walls and charred bones lay jumbled together with burned wood, plaster, skulls, and ribs. Here and there, flecks of white showed through, a futile reminder that there had been a time before the fires—a time when the bones were part of people who lived, who breathed.

Who loved.

The fingers were part blackened flesh, part bone. But in death the two bodies had held hands. On one of the hands, the gold ring was warped from the heat of the flames, but it flashed in the meager daylight. On another left hand nearby, more gold glinted.

How long had they shared that love? How long had

they worn those rings? When they knew they were going to die, what comfort did they take in knowing that at least they would leave this world together, just as they had wandered through it?

A tear fell on a ring.

The woman stood before more tears came, but as she stepped her foot brushed the body. Ash fell away and blew off as a hot wind crashed through the street.

Blue shone.

The man leaned down and pulled the postcard free. A large script in the top left corner of the card said, "Godhpur... Go find yourself!" The famous blue-and-gold sandstone buildings of the city shone out from the photo covering the rest of the card. Compared to the black ruins of Agamuskara, Godhpur might as well have been in another world.

"It's incredible," the man said. "The rest is ash yet this survived." He turned over the card and read out loud, "Godhpur brought us to marriage, but you brought us together. Here is a photo of our wedding. Thank you."

The words flew through the woman's memories, past the agonies and horrors of the last month, through the fog of the days that were lost, past all that had happened before the night the fires came, back to the simple sunny day when everything had changed.

Rucksack leaned down and dug through the ash with his gloved left hand. Part of the photo had been burned away, and the bottom edge was ragged and iridescent. She took the photo from him and stared at the bright eyes, the warm smiles of the newlyweds. They had been so glad they had found each other in such a random heartless world.

She could feel him staring at her. "Jade?"

The tears came back. "That was for me," she said, shaking her head. "Do you remember the day Jay arrived in the city? These two came into the pub. I was to bring them together and I did. They'd only just met, Rucksack. Now they're dead. Because of us."

"No," Rucksack replied. "They're dead because o' the Smiling Fire."

"We should have prevented it!"

"I don't think we could have. We still don't even know how he became strong enough to escape."

"We were helpless then," Jade said. "We're helpless now. For nearly a month we've been running around this city, trying to help people, but all we do now is find charred bones and burned buildings. Agamuskara is dead, Rucksack. So is everyone in it. The mirror eclipse is three days away, and the Smiling Fire has the dia ubh. We might as well be walking corpses."

Despair hung between them like a body in a noose. "I can't do this anymore," Jade said, looking at the photo again. "Whatever keeps you going, I don't have it. It's not in me." *The eyes in the photo see only the long future in front of them, the possibilities and choices,* she thought. *But all that had waited for them was a fiery death.*

Rucksack's smile was soft as he took her hand. "Now you look at me, Jade Aga—"

"Don't." She looked away from him. "That's not who I am anymore."

"You are who you are," Rucksack said. "But suit yourself. Look at me, Jade."

"We should have run away," she said, "like Jay did."

"But we didn't," Rucksack replied. "Because we stayed, we have saved hundreds, if not thousands. The people we saved have saved others. The Smiling Fire has decimated the city. He has destroyed the buildings and carts as much as he has killled the people and animals. Everything is gone. Oh, to be sure. We mourn every death. We mourn every destruction. And we add it to a big feckin bill. He will pay for all he's done. Those he murdered will be avenged. I don't know the how or the path anymore than you do, but I tell you true, Jade o' herself, the Smiling Fire will fall. While we still breathe we will take that bastard down and help all we can along the way."

Jade met his gaze. "That's more like it," Rucksack said. "No matter how much he's burned—and by now it's safe to say he's burned damn near the entire city—as long as we live, we are not helpless. Overpowered and outmatched, completely. Likely to fail, without a doubt. But against all odds, we are also alive. Life is opportunity. As long as we're alive, we have a chance."

Rucksack squeezed her hand. Courage and hope spread through Jade with gentle warmth. "Just because you give me a dose of your courage doesn't mean it will last long," she said.

"Do you feel braver?"

Jade nodded.

"I gave you nothing you didn't already have," Rucksack said. "I just got the other stuff out o' the way." He nodded at the photo and the card. "Keep these. Remember those people. Remember what was, because it can be brought back. Cities can be rebuilt. People can be reborn, in this life, in another. As long as life lives, he's going to fall."

Jade put the photo and card in her pocket. "We should keep going," she said, continuing down the street toward where the alley used to be.

As they walked, Jade thought back over the last few weeks. She had woken up in Rucksack's flat, bruised and scraped up but alive and healing quickly, to Rucksack's surprise.

*At least my Jade healing hadn't left me yet,* she thought.

The day she woke she had ignored his protests, gotten out of bed, and gone out into the city with him. What tears she had, she had left sputtering on hot rubble. She'd been unconscious for three days. While she was asleep, the city, her city, had been little but panic, fire, death—and Rucksack.

He didn't say a word about it. But as they found survivors, tended the wounded, and helped people leave the city, every person stared at Rucksack with awe and gratitude.

The stories came to Jade from person after person. The smiling fires were coming, they would say. There was nowhere to run. Then he was there. Suddenly, somehow, we were safe before the flames caught.

Or, our son and daughter were trapped inside. The building started to collapse. Then he appeared, rushed inside, and came out with them, alive.

Or, as he walked through the city, all the animals— down to the last dog and cow—followed him through the rubbled streets until they ran free across the fields and plains to the north.

Or, he stands on the hill and watches the city. His tears make the grass grow. When the cries rise up with the flames from Agamuskara, he comes as if flying. The air roars like a tiger. The flames flee as if the ocean had come for them.

Rucksack. Bumbling, stout-swilling Rucksack.

*There's more to you than I'll probably ever know,* Jade thought. *Turns out that when there's a crisis, though, you turn into steel. You're loud, evasive, and annoying, but you're a bloody hero.*

And Ruckack and Jade forgave one another. The arguments and anger from when Jay had left, they let them go. There were more important problems to deal with.

They stopped for a moment. As Rucksack looked around, he seemed to be listening, seeing, and feeling much farther out than what he could perceive with his physical senses.

"It's as I thought," he said. "The Smiling Fire is on the far outskirts of the city. He's probably got another old whiff of Jay from when he carried the dia ubh. That'll buy us the time we've been wanting." He smiled at her, as if they were out for a pleasant morning walk, then started off again.

*He's always like that now,* she thought. *Not once have I seen him despair. How does he do it? These last few weeks, he's pulled me along with him, never the other way around. He's always found a reason to smile. He's always found a way to make me laugh. He's kept me strong. I just leech off him.*

Rucksack looked at her and asked, "Did I ever tell you why I don't drink anything but stout?"

The question surprised her.

"Other than to keep people like me from influencing you?" Jade replied. "I always figured you just really liked it. And no beer tastes better than free beer, after all."

"Aye, that helps. Some have joked that if you cut me, I'd bleed black. But the main reason is despair."

"Other drinks make you despair?"

"Hard liquor affects me differently from other people. I lose my will. I lose my hope. A shot will make me seem like I've drunk half a bottle. A bottle would..." Rucksack shook his head. "Let's just say there are things in this world that would be all the better off had I never touched a bottle. It was a hard lesson learned."

"Why are you telling me this?"

"After the Smiling Fire destroyed the Everest Base Camp, I woke on the other side o' the street from the pub, groggy and unscathed but for a scratch on my arm. I couldn't find you. I searched for hours, Jade. I shifted hot rubble that would've burned the flesh off a regular man, trying to find you. But the only thing I could find was a damn bottle o' single-malt scotch that had somehow survived the explosion."

"Why haven't you ever mentioned this?" Jade said. "What happened when you drank it?"

"I stood awhile, holding that bottle, smelling the sharp whisky inside." A hunger shone in Rucksack's eyes. "I wanted to down it, world be damned. That damn Smiling Fire was going to have his way after all. He had the dia ubh, the only person who could stop him was gone, and you were likely dead. There was no hope in me. When there's no hope inside, you might as well fill the void with any alcohol that comes to hand—the stronger the better. I tilted my head back and lifted that bottle to my lips, ready to upend it down my throat. Maybe this time I'd be able to drown myself."

She could picture him standing there, the fires crackling around him, smoke rising from the rubble of the pub and hostel, bottle raised. A battle raging in his soul.

"Maybe I'd finally learned my lesson, Jade," Rucksack said. "I took that bottle and poured some o' the scotch on my scratch. When I looked up, I saw a hand. There you were, behind and under some rubble, not moving, but when I got to you I could tell you were breathing. If I'd taken a drink, I wouldn't have seen you, and who knows what would've happened."

"I can say you definitely have my gratitude."

"No, Jade," Rucksack replied. "You have mine. Seeing you alive filled me with new hope. Filled me with strength and power. It was the closest I'd felt to my own self in a long, long time. I don't despair, I won't despair anymore, because o' you. If you think I'm giving you strength or hope, I'm not. I'm just paying you back."

"Thank you," Jade said. Inside, hope welled up. A new strength bloomed. "If you can do that, maybe I can too."

They smiled, passing by a pile of rubble that was almost a small hill. Their smiles quickly faded.

Rucksack said, "Isn't that—"

"Yes," Jade replied. "I'd know that paint anywhere."

The red door's color was tinged black with soot. Out of all the walls and doors of the alley, only this remained intact and standing. Even the building that had surrounded it, and Asha and Jigme's room behind it, was gone.

"Jade," Rucksack said softly, "can you still do that listening thing your lot do?"

"Technically speaking, all my Jade abilities should be gone by now."

"I'm willing to test the actual beyond the technical," Rucksack replied. "Maybe this can tell us some o' what we don't know."

"I'll try, but no promises." As if she were about to knock, Jade stepped close to the door and laid her hand on the wood. "It's cold," she said. "All these fires. How can the door be cold?"

Rucksack stood next to her and touched the door as well. "Maybe that's what you can figure out."

Jade nodded and closed her eyes. She began to listen for the story that the door needed to tell.

When she stepped away, her eyes were wet. The red of the door's paint then faded to gray. *Every time I think I've run out of tears,* she thought, *some new horror shows me more.*

The door fell over, cracking into fragments when it hit the rubble where Asha's bed had once been.

"What was it?" Rucksack asked.

"It was them," Jade answered. "Jigme and Asha. They worked together. We thought they'd been acting strangely, but I never could have imagined..."

"Worked together how?"

"They brought children to him, Rucksack. And they brought the old man from The Mystery Chickpea. Jigme and Asha took them all to the Smiling Fire. That's how he got stronger. And then, that night, Jigme led Asha to him too."

Rucksack's eyes flickered. *Please don't lose your hope and strength,* Jade thought. *If you lose yours, there's no hope for mine.*

"Then they're dead too," Rucksack said. "We couldn't save them after all."

"There is nothing to save," said the shadow rising

from the rubble. "Their fires have been returned where they belong."

Rucksack stared hard at the Smiling Fire. "Good sneaking," he said. "I didn't see the slightest glimmer of you returning."

The Smiling Fire stood in front of them. "You have stolen many fires from me," he said.

"I have an aversion to people being burned to death."

"A temporary reprieve."

Rucksack shrugged.

"You smell of him," the Smiling Fire said, looking at Jade. "It is fortunate you did not die yet. You will bring him back."

Her fledgling hope flickered, and her newfound courage faltered. "Run. Burn. Die," said the fear and despair deep inside her.

But something deeper turned into steel.

Jade stared into the red grin, and she understood what had to happen. She smiled back.

Then she punched it.

The Smiling Fire staggered backward.

"Jade!" Rucksack shouted.

"Run!" she replied, aiming a solid kick between the shadows of the Smiling Fire's legs. "The last thing he needs is you, Mr. Fire of Life. Get out of here. Stay alive. Help others. Find Jay."

"I can't let you—"

"It's my turn to save you, Faddah Rucksack. Move your arse. Don't you dare let me go unavenged."

Rucksack ran.

The Smiling Fire rose.

"Damn," she said. "I figured balls would've been too

much to ask for."

Jade stared into his red eyes. Something flickered.

*Everything depends on whether or not he's going to do what I think he's going to do.*

"So," she said, "am I right?"

He grinned. The last thing Jade saw was a hot, red shadow.


THE SMILING FIRE tried to open the thing again. When first he had stolen the thing and tried to open it, the rush of power had been almost like the first days, the hot days, the old days. That power had set so much of the city ablaze, even though the thing had not opened. He had been so angry and that had fueled more fires. The city smoked and smoldered now. Gone were the colors and the sounds, the crowds and songs, the foods and life. All was black. All was ash. All was empty and dead.

But no more fires burned in Agamuskara. At first he had not noticed. Now he understood. All that strength, all that fire, was still only temporary. It was all only temporary.

*Except for all the death,* he thought. *That was permanent.*

Now the Smiling Fire understood that the eclipse was like a key for the thing, the dia ubh. The mirror eclipse was one key, but the dia ubh needed two. Jay was the other. The light of one. The blood of the other.

After taking Jade, the Smiling Fire returned to where the temple had stood. The sharp black shards of obsidian glittered all around the rubble. The vast field of smooth bright glass made it seem as if the ground was now the sky. He watched the clouds move over the black glass, over the chunks of charred rock, wood, and bones.

*Except for Jade,* he thought. *There's no sky where she is.*

The large block of obsidian was the only thing of the temple prison that the Smiling Fire had not destroyed. With Jade in one arm, the Smiling Fire shoved the block aside with his free arm, revealing the hole that went down deep into the earth, into the chamber under the world, where the Smiling Fire had been forgotten.

He still couldn't quite understand it. For a place where the Smiling Fire had been imprisoned, had hated for so long, lately he returned here more often and stayed longer. Now it seemed the Smiling Fire cared more about conserving his power than about scouring the city.

And he wouldn't have to worry about finding Jay. His mind made it clear: once Jay knew that Jade had been captured, he would come to the Smiling Fire.

Usually there was no light here but a red-and-black shadowy flicker, dull as a constant headache and hot as a furnace. Behind him, just out of sight, there now seemed to be a silver-and-gold glow. But that couldn't be. A noise buzzed, sounding like a particular word. But that word couldn't be. The noise couldn't be. He ignored them.

Jade slid like water onto the stone slab in the chamber. Her breathing was deep and slow, her eyes closed. At least she was still alive.

How he wished he could talk to her. Say he was sorry. But he had no mouth here, and no tears that he could shed for all the wrongs he'd done.

The noise came again. So did the word.

"Jigme."

That could not be.

He fled.

The voice reminded him of a kind old man. But there could be no kind old men here. This was hell and hell did not cater to kind old men. Hell was for people like Jigme. People who believed lies, even when deep down they knew the truth. People who brought children to their death. People who helped free something that only wanted to murder and destroy.

Jigme no longer knew how long he had been awake or how long he had been... away. He only knew that he would make himself watch. Since he had figured out what he was, he had watched the world through the Smiling Fire's eyes. He would not let himself turn away from the explosions and the fires, the people running and falling.

*I did this.* The thought never left him. It was as constant and real as the body that once surrounded his soul.

*This is all my fault.*

*I got what I deserved.*

*But I won't turn away,* Jigme thought. *I did this and I will not turn away. That is the least of what I owe.*

He remembered the sufferings and hardships he had known in life, but they were nothing compared to what he knew now. *Hell is to be trapped and helpless,* he thought. *Hell is to see the consequences of your actions, regret all you've done, and have no way to make things right.*

Sometimes he wondered where he was. If the Smiling Fire had a soul, did it now contain Jigme's?

Did Jigme's soul somehow rattle around in the body, the form that the Smiling Fire maintained, powered by the fires of life he had burned away from the living? Jigme never came upon a wall or a boundary, never found a place where he could not continue. Still, he knew he was trapped. The world was out there. Life was out there. In here was nothing but void and darkness, the heat of flames, a hollow blackness, and the silence that came in the absence of the living.

Except now there was the silver-and-gold glow again, following him.

He moved faster, trying to fly away, trying to hide.

When Jigme had first awakened here, he had recalled only his body's agony at being burned away, and his soul's guilt, rage, and sadness at watching his mother die. He had floated, unaware. Only when the sounds of fire and screams came did he realize he could move—or at least direct his thoughts in a way that moved his soul around wherever he was.

But the glow moved faster.

Before Jigme could react, it was in front of him. Now it was no longer just a soft glow; it was big and bright as the sun, and it shone silver-and-gold.

Jigme tried to flee another direction but found he could not. There was suddenly nowhere to go. The glow was in front of him yet all around him.

*I'm trapped,* he thought.

"Jigme," said the glow, with its kindly-old-man voice, "you are not trapped."

"I'm dead," Jigme said. "I'm trapped in the hell where I deserve to be. Are you here to finish me?"

"No," said the voice. No longer did it sound like an old man. The voice was like a woman's, like...

"Amma?" he said. But that couldn't be. She had been burned up and was no more. *Just like me,* he thought. *And I'm here.*

"That's right, son," said the voice. "It's your amma. I'm here."

"I killed you," Jigme replied.

"The Smiling Fire killed me by taking advantage of your hope and despair. My body is no more. But I am here."

*I've been tricked before,* Jigme thought. *Look at where that got me.*

"Prove it," he said.

"Ask me something only I could answer," came the reply.

Jigme thought past all that had happened over the last few weeks, before the temple, before stealing Jay's backpack, before... He had it.

"What happened that day when the tourist slipped on the banana?"

"The tourist didn't slip on a banana," came the reply. It almost seemed like Jigme could hear her smiling. "The monkey stole a camera out of the tourist's backpack, and the tourist chased the monkey. Then the tourist slipped on tomatoes that had fallen out of a cart, and he landed in a pile of cow dung."

"And what did you say when I told you this?"

"'I hope the monkey took a picture of such a soft landing!'"

The memory came back to Jigme, as vivid as if it were happening in front of them.

"Amma," he said. "I'm sorry."

"As am I. This is my fault, son, not yours."

"I believed the lies. I brought the children."

"And you did so because it was acting through me. You did so because you thought it was the only way to save me."

"I have done much wrong."

For a moment there was silence. Then Asha said, "We both have."

"Why am I here?" Jigme asked. "There have been no other voices until you. Everyone he took, they are gone."

"You are here because we saved you, as I was saved."

"But I'm not saved. My body was burned. So was yours. Just like everyone he's killed, everyone I brought. I don't deserve to be alive, Amma," Jigme said. "I deserve to be no more."

Something about her words troubled him.

"Wait," he said. "Who's we?"

When the voice came again, it was the sound of the kindly old man. "You never knew me as well as you should have, Jigme," he said. "And you never heard me speak. I lived so long in silence, I never thought that in death I might be restored to my voice. I suppose it's fitting that my voice returns from the one who took it from me."

"Who are you?"

"I ran The Mystery Chickpea, Jigme," he said, "though even here I do not know my name again. That will only come back to me when I pass on. I should have prevented this."

"You just served food," Jigme said. "You were always there."

"I wasn't. I never should have left. Something came to my attention that seemed more important than my duty to guard the alley that led to the black temple. But when I arrived where I was directed, I was told it was all a ruse—part of a larger, more crucial destiny. Despite the haste with which I returned, I was too late. But there still was one thing I could do."

"You died too," Jigme said. "I killed you."

"No, Jigme," the old man said. "You did not kill me. I went willingly. I chose the fire."

"Why?"

"To save you. To save your mother. To save all I could."

"Jigme," Amma said. "They are here. Those the Smiling Fire took as he took us, their souls have been protected. They are guarded now. Their bodies are gone but their selves are here."

"What will happen to them?"

Silence. "We don't know," Asha said. "There is much we don't know. But while they live, there must be a chance for something better."

"This is all my fault," Jigme said. "But I can't do anything about it."

"This is our fault," the old man said. "And above all, mine. None of this would have happened had I acted differently toward you and your mother." He paused. "I must explain. I lived a long life, longer than mortal men, because I served a sacred duty that came to me when the Smiling Fire was first imprisoned. I was to watch, to guard. But I was to exist alone, apart from those I protected."

"I remember always seeing him when I first came to Agamuskara," Asha said. "He was old and silent. There was much I did not know about him. But I knew enough: he was a great man. Anyone would know that just by tasting his food."

"Your mother never should have believed I didn't care," the old man said. "You never should have believed that in this world you had no options or no hope. Perhaps I could have left my duty or passed it on. Instead I have failed you again and again. But I will do all I can now to give you another chance."

Jigme tried to make sense of what he was hearing. "You can't be," he said.

"But of course I am, Jigme," the old man said. "I am your father."


THE MOON, the voice, and the mountain faded. At first all was dark again, dark as a moonless night. The words. There had been so many words. They faded too, but he remembered it was time to open his eyes.

So he did. A white blur met him. When that faded, he looked out at the world again.

The first thing he saw was the backpack, sitting there like it had begrudgingly remained by his side.

"Are you still pissed at me?" Jay said.

The backpack didn't reply, but something in the folds and creases of the nylon made it seem relieved he was alive.

Jay tried to sit up. Pain shot through his torso and legs. His arms buckled when he put weight on them, and he fell back onto the thin pillow at the head of the narrow bed. The bed was pushed against the back corner of the room, whose walls were whiter than those of Agamuskara. On the wall across from him, the eyes of the blue-skinned Hindu god Shiva stared at him from a poster.

Jay chuckled and returned the stare. "Some god, huh?" he said. "Can't step off a train without falling. Now I can't even get out of bed."

He scratched his nose. Then he stared at his hand.

"Exposure," said a voice, old and crackling yet surprisingly strong. "Plus, there was a while where you were hardly breathing. Combined, it's given your skin a blue tinge. Temporary, I'm sure."

Standing in the doorway at the far corner of the room, the woman looked even older than she sounded, yet she was regal in her silver-and-gold sari. Her skin was wrinkled and her back was bent, but strength and authority flowed from her. The way she held her walking stick, Jay had a feeling she could crack skulls if she wanted.

"How long have I been here?" Jay asked.

"Not long enough and too damn long," she replied. "You've been unconscious for over a month. Good thing too. You also have multiple fractures to your ribs, arms and legs, so I'm glad you had the decency to spare me the screaming-in-pain part of all this."

"I'm sorry to have been such an inconvenience," Jay replied. "But thank you for taking care of me." *She may have tended me all this time,* he thought, *but she doesn't seem happy to have me here.*

"You were never convenient," she said. "But I must admit I had hoped you weren't going to do anything so stupid."

"You don't know who I am."

"No, you don't know who you are, but that's what happens when you keep trying to kid yourself." She sighed and walked into the room. "Nonetheless, you only just woke up, and your injuries are still extensive.

I'll forgive you for being a bit slow, but I'm afraid there's no patience to accompany my sympathy. We don't have time for you to go on sitting around being broken."

She pulled a chair to the side of the bed and sat down. Dull pain rumbled through him when she patted his hand, making it hard for him to keep his head clear. He groped for an answer but nothing made sense. And when nothing made sense, sometimes you just had to grab the first bit of nonsense that came to hand. He looked her in the eye. As wrinkled as her face was, her eyes were bright, clear, and brown-and-black.

"Kailash?" he said.

"Thank goodness," she replied, smiling. "I feared I was going to have to recount all the dreams you've been having, all the conversations we've shared in your mind over these last few weeks. Wondered if there'd have to be a code word or an answer to some secret question. 'What does snow on Everest look like under the full moon?' or some nonsense like that."

"Glad I could spare you the trouble."

"A drop compared to the ocean you've brought me."

"They lied to me," Jay said. "Why would I have stayed?"

"Oh yes, a fine time to get stroppy," Kailash replied. "You were afraid of the road in front of you, so you legged it. The stout is always blacker in some other pub somewhere else. How'd that work out?"

He had no reply.

"The night Mim and Pim brought me to you, you were lying all broken and ragged by the train tracks. I damn near left you there." Kailash shook her head. "I'd forgotten what it was to be so angry. That's part of the trouble. I've forgotten a lot of things lately. Of course, for me 'lately' is what you would call centuries. I like to think I still remember quickly, even if I can't seem to do much else very quickly. It was one thing to *be* old, Jay, but this is the first time I've ever *felt* old. Fortunately, those lads were still strapping enough to carry you back here."

"You would've let me die?"

"Some would say it's a mercy you didn't deserve," Kailash said. "By fleeing Agamuskara, you made the end of life all but certain. I could say it's better you died then than get swept up in the decimation that will come when the Smiling Fire regains his full power."

Jay started to protest, but the dreams in his mind flickered. Through the pain, images flashed that were far worse than the aches and stabs from his broken body.

"I thought he was still imprisoned?"

"So glad you're no longer arguing that all this was falsehood and fantasy," Kailash said. "If you did, I'd just whack you with my stick." She tapped it on the floor twice, with twin cracks that made the floorboards wince.

"He's free, Jay. I won't go so far as to say because of you. Something else was happening that we only just learned, and we learned it at a great cost."

"What's happened? And..." Jay said. "And what about Jade and Rucksack? Are they okay?"

"It does these old bones good to hear you ask about them," Kailash replied. "I will tell you all I know. There's much we didn't discuss while you slept. It would have been too much for you, and I still remember enough of kindness to spare you that until you had the strength."

"Tell me."

"It will be faster and you will understand more fully if we skip the conversation part of this." She raised her hand then paused. "What I held back I'm going to put directly into your mind. It will take you many hours to go through this—and hours more to understand. You won't sleep tonight. Then again, you've slept long enough. We'll talk more in the morning. But remember this, Jay: come morning, the mirror eclipse will be but a day away."

Worry flooded him. *She's said so little of Rucksack and Jade,* he thought. *Or of Jigme and Asha.*

Jay nodded. "I want to understand," he said. "I'm ready now."

"You're awake and time is short," Kailash said. "You no longer have any choice but to be ready."

She touched her hands to his face. From her mind to his, her heart to his, all that had happened over the last month, since he had fled Agamuskara, flowed into him.

At first he screamed and wailed. He clenched his fists, even though his knitting bones ached when he did so. Soon there were no more screams, no more tears. No more wailing.

The night had long since taken over the day when she left. But she was right: he did not sleep.

He thought. He felt.

In the morning, when Kailash stood in the doorway again, Jay looked at her with a surprising strength in his weary eyes. "I understand," he said, glancing at his broken body and shaking his head. "But I don't know what I can possibly do about it from here, like this. Was this supposed to be part of the destiny?"

Kailash shrugged as she came back to the chair by the bed. "I wish I could answer that. These last few weeks while you've healed, I've asked that question of every god I could corner. If anyone knows, they aren't sharing. There are many things I don't know. I'm no god, Jay. I'm a woman, with a bit added on. Maybe this was part of your destiny. If I can draw any conclusion, I can say with some confidence that the choice you made must have been part of my destiny."

"I'm sorry I left and brought all this on you," Jay said. "I should have stayed. I should have forgiven Rucksack and Jade. I felt trapped. I felt manipulated. Cornered. I took the only chance I saw."

She nodded. "And of all the places where you could have jumped from that train, you jumped at the edge of my village, the little haven where I've secreted myself over the eons. I thought I could keep myself safe from the Smiling Fire, you see. Not so much to save myself but to ensure he didn't recapture the power I had taken from him so long ago. It turns out I have to risk that too."

"We know that the destiny is mine," Jay said. "I have to go back. I have to face him."

"Your voice still has bitterness. Most mortals would be so excited to become a god."

"I just want to be me, but there's something far more important than what I want. Life must live," Jay said. "Thrive and strive, that's all that matters."

"That's why the world thought you were such a good choice after all," Kailash said. "It knew you'd get there in the end, and the end is here."

"If I make it long enough to become this god, I don't suppose the dia ubh will heal me the rest of the way?"

Kailash chuckled. "It will do more than that," she said. "Love and power are inverses of one another. The key to destroying the Smiling Fire is to bring both love and power into balance in your own self so that from the depths of your soul to the tips of your fingernails you are both boundless love and unstoppable power."

"So it comes down to me."

Kailash nodded. "First, though, we have to get you out of bed."

Jay tried to shift his legs, but his legs and arms cried out when he moved them. Ignoring the pain, he set his feet on the floor. The moment he rose, his knees buckled and he fell back onto the bed. The agony brought tears to his eyes.

"How can I save the world if I can't even stand?"

Kailash looked away from him, but Jay saw the fear and longing in her eyes. When she looked back, her gaze was hard again.

"That brings us to the worst part. At least, that's what I thought it would be," Kailash said. "Now that this time has finally come, I actually find I'm excited about it. You think of the joy of new adventures, Jay, and I would say that's what I'm feeling. I've been who I am for a long time. I'm ready to be something more. I'm ready to get my balance right."

"I can't even get up," Jay said, "much less go to the heart of Agamuskara to defeat the Smiling Fire."

"And that, dear Jay, is why you're really here."

Kailash squeezed his hand. "You didn't heal enough. So I'm going to finish the job for you."

She reached over and took his other hand. "This will hurt," she said. "But don't worry. Once we're done, you will be completely healed, ready to arrive in Agamuskara just in the nick of time."

"Aren't you coming with me?"

She smiled. "In a sense, yes. What I know, you will know. Who I am will now be part of you. The power I have I now give so that you may be whole again."

"You're sacrificing yourself for me," Jay said. He tried to pull his hands away, but there was no escaping the power of her grip. The aches of his body turned into silent screams.

"Don't think of it as me dying," she said. "Think of it as you helping me be reborn."

Her brown-and-black eyes turned white, and so did all that Jay saw. Rushes of pain and warmth flooded him until all he perceived was only white, calm, and silent.

When he could see the room again, the pain was gone.

So was Kailash.

Jay swung his legs out of the bed, felt the rough-smooth texture of the wood as his feet touched the floor. He stood.

He did not fall.

*Kailash gave her life to save me,* Jay thought. *I have to see this through.*

The new memories from Kailash settled into his blood and his soul. The doubt was gone, as absent as the pain from his healed body.

He had a quick wash. The blue had faded from his

skin, replaced by a soft blue glow. Jay opened the backpack for new clothes. Tan as sun-beaten earth, the trusty cargo pants looked like new. He pulled out the white t-shirt and smiled.

*Seems fitting,* he thought, reading the slogan on the shirt, *though I don't remember where in the world I bought this one.*

The pack seemed to smile as he zipped it closed. He slung it over his shoulders as easily as a pillow. Outside the little cottage where Kailash had lived, Jay stared north at the plains, which stretched as far as his eyes could see. Just at the edge of his sight a mountain, impossible in its size, bigger than all others in the world, stood proud.

Jay thought back to when he met Rucksack. He joined his palms and held his hands in front of his chest. "Namaste," he said.

The mountain vanished into the horizon. Jay could've sworn it winked at him.

"Thank you," he said. "Good-bye, Kailash."

Much closer to him, a tunnel of dust approached.

When at last it stopped, right in front of him, Mim and Pim got out of a taxi.

"Today is the first day of the rest of your life," Mim said, nodding. "Nice shirt."

"Are you ready?" Pim asked.

"I don't have any choice." Jay set his pack in the car and climbed into the back.

"Get me to Agamuskara," he said. "I've got a god to kill."

* * * * *

JADE WOKE ALONE. Her eyes adjusted to the dim reddish light, and slowly she sat up.

"I'm alive," she said. *For now,* she thought, *but I'll take what I can get.*

She swung her legs off the stone block where she lay, noticing as she stood on the floor that a groove had been worn into the surface of the block.

*This is where he slept,* she thought. *On a big stone slab against the wall of a prison. He's been here for so many uncountable years that he wore into the stone.*

Jade walked around the chamber and stared at the walls. The smooth, solid black rock had no cracks or joints, no sections or textures. The entire chamber seemed like it had been hollowed out from one piece of perfect, featureless obsidian.

The walls were warm to her touch. *I'm surrounded by the molten rock of the world,* she thought. *No wonder I'm sweating.*

Above her, in the center of the ceiling, cracks stretched like forks of lightning from an opening that must originally have been rectangular. Now it had been ripped open, breaking and warping the stone. Jade stared up into the darkness of a narrow vertical shaft.

*The world is up there and I'm trapped down here,* she thought. *No way out. Only one way in. It almost feels safe. Then again, you keep the bait safe until it's time to set the trap.*

She stared into the eye of the dark shaft. "Are you up there?" she shouted. "We're going to stop you. No matter what."

Darkness and silence were the only reply. As Jade's words faded, so too did her courage.

"Who am I kidding?" she said, much quieter. "We don't stand a chance."

Despair hovered like a dark shadow over the light of her courage and strength. "I'm scared as hell of dying," she said to the darkness outside and in. "I never knew if I would be or not. But if it takes my death to save the world, I'll die. Whatever it takes to get Jay into that light. Destroying the Smiling Fire is all that matters."

Inside, the despair faded back. While she did not feel brave, she felt she at least knew the destiny before her.

"Destroying the Smiling Fire is all that matters," she said again. "Life must live."

"Why?"

The sound of the rasping voice made her jump back. Jade pressed against a corner, a wall to her right and the worn stone slab to her left. From the opposite corner of the room, a shadow unfolded, stretching taller and moving slowly toward her. Soon she stared once more into the eyes of the Smiling Fire.

"Why must you live?" he asked. "Life is a thief."

"We stole nothing from you," Jade replied, clenching at the wall. *Stay calm,* she thought. *Make him talk. Learn. He won't kill me. Yet.*

"You can't claim rights to something that isn't yours to begin with," Jade said.

"It was always mine," the Smiling Fire replied. "Living things are an accident of coincidences, always on the thin edge of overrun and annihilation. You use continuance and renewal to conceal the decimation of your true nature."

"How is that different from yours?"

"In my time the world was simpler," the Smiling Fire said. "It needed no organisms. The simple physical processes of rock and water, fire and wind were enough. I seek only to remove a scourge and restore the old harmony. Or is that what you would say you yourself intend to do?"

"The world decided merely existing wasn't enough," Jade said. "Life makes the world fascinating, varied. Life fills the world with love, laughter, togetherness, striving."

*He has existed so long in hate,* she thought. *Has he ever tried to understand living things?*

"Am I not alive?" the Smiling Fire said. "Do I not also deserve to live?"

"We defend ourselves against things that wish to kill us," Jade replied.

"If I live, I also seek to protect myself," the Smiling Fire said. "Life kills me. If I am to exist, living things must be killed. Or do you somehow deserve to live more than I do?"

Jade had no reply. Something flickered in the Smiling Fire's eyes. *I've seen that before,* she thought.

"You know nothing. You burn with a fire that isn't yours," the Smiling Fire said. "I seek only to be as I was. You have nothing to offer me but weakness in a world whose every breath makes me less."

Jade closed her eyes. "If you are alive, you should have a chance to live," Jade said. "But not if it means destroying everything else in the world." She stared into the flickering red eyes.

"You cannot stop me. What all stole will be all mine again." The Smiling Fire moved to the center of the room, below the opening in the ceiling.

"When next I return, it will be time."

Then he was gone.

*He's right,* Jade thought. Alone again, she took the photo out of her pocket and looked at the faces of the dead couple, then put it away.

Jade's knees buckled. She slid down the wall until she crouched on the floor. There were no tears to cry anymore. There was no rage to shout with. *I can only hope Jay comes back,* she thought. *He's our only chance.*

Her hand brushed the stone of the worn slab. It seemed warmer than before, though nothing else in the room seemed different. Images flashed through her mind: The Smiling Fire, dim and faint, pounding on the wall. Then, exhausted, he collapsed onto the stone slab. Time passed. The room shook. The figure rose. As he stood, head back and arms outstretched, the Smiling Fire darkened, becoming more distinct and solid with every tremor. The first hint of his fiery grin glimmered, thin and faint, but there. The Smiling Fire stared at the ceiling of his prison, and then he leaped...

Jade's hand stopped touching the slab. The images were gone as quickly as they had appeared.

Jade scrambled to her feet and stared at the impression worn into the obsidian.

*The Smiling Fire has been here for eons,* she thought. *Even after he freed himself, he's kept returning here. His body has worn itself into the stone...* Her eyes widened.

"Has his mind as well?" she whispered.

Jade pressed her hands to the stone and waited for the images to come back.

Nothing happened.

"You've never had anyone to listen," Jade said softly

to the rock. "But you have the most important story to tell. I am here to listen. You are rock of this world. If you know of life, if you know what he intends to do, if you care at all for a world with things that live, grow, and love, then please, please tell me your story."

Jade waited. And waited.

Silence.

She shook her head. *This was foolish,* she thought, ready to take her hands away.

"It would help," said the slow, low voice rumbling in her mind, "if you lie down."

"Of course." Jade climbed back onto the stone and settled her body down into the impression where the Smiling Fire used to lay.

"I'm listening," she said.

The rock's long story wove into her soul like music. It wove into the fibers of her body. She forgot time, hunger, and thirst. Jade lived only the story of the Smiling Fire: how he had come here, all his dark thoughts, the escape, and how different he seemed since the night he freed himself.

When at last the rock finished its story, Jade began to understand, but she did not get up. She stayed only in her deepest thoughts, thought beyond thought, seeing the Smiling Fire as it really was. And as it could be.

She found herself smiling. *I know what that flickering is,* she thought, even though she wasn't yet sure how it could help.

Jade stirred only when a shadowy hand, hot as the fires of the early world yet colder than deepest space, pulled her to her feet.

"It is time," the Smiling Fire said. "The mirror

eclipse comes, and so does he."

"Then let's get going," Jade said, smiling back.


ON THE LAST DAY of the world, Jigme never would have expected the sky to be so blue, bright, and clear. The sun rose toward its summit. Golden light poured warmth on Agamuskara, so different from the burning heat of the fading fires.

In the decimated city, the sun shone on a world of shadows.

From the opposite side of the sky, the full moon rose too. Ghostly silver-white, it hung level with the sun, but they did not overlap yet.

*Soon it will happen,* Jigme thought, staring at the world through the eyes of the Smiling Fire. *One way or another, soon all of us will die.*

"There is still no way," said the voice of his father.

Jigme turned away from the outside world.

*My father,* he thought.

Even now it felt so hard to believe. The man who could not speak. The man Jigme had walked past many times a day for years.

Anger welled in him. So did longing. Then the anger seemed less important.

Then a new feeling arose. It said his longing was not important. Nor was his anger. Nor was anything Jigme felt; it all mattered less than the problem before them. Though his feelings roiled and collided, ebbed and crashed, Jigme tried to focus himself on what was happening and what they could do about it.

Seeing both the sun and moon in the sky, Jigme knew how long they had been arguing and trying to find a way around the impossible. Could the Smiling Fire be stopped in a way that would not also destroy the souls preserved inside? No solutions came. If the Smiling Fire was destroyed, so were they and the children and all the others Jigme's father had sought to protect after being consumed by the Smiling Fire.

But they didn't give up. Amma's concern for the children and for Jigme had brought out a fiery resolve in his mother that he had never seen before. When he or his father felt like their efforts were futile, Amma bolstered them. When Jigme despaired that he should have fully died, Amma pointed out that any life was a chance for them all. No matter how many dead ends they came to, she found another direction.

"We keep getting lost on the how," Amma said now. "Let's assume we know the how. The Smiling Fire can be stopped, and the souls can be restored to living bodies. How does that happen?"

"It's a matter of redirection," Jigme's father said. "The Smiling Fire does not make his own life, he only steals it from others. The only way the Smiling Fire can be destroyed is to empty him of all energy, like turning the flame off a stove. Emptied of all fire of life, he will die. If some of that energy can be redirected, so that instead of fleeing out into the world it comes here, to the souls, then the souls and the energy could form new bodies, and these people could return to the world. There is no guarantee that all will return. The energy is only an opportunity, not a choice already made. Each soul must be strong. Each must want to live."

"If they don't," Jigme said, "Then they will fully die. What happens then?"

"That is a question only they will be able to answer."

As his father spoke, Jigme felt a question spark and burn inside him. "Will we also be able to go back?"

There was a long silence.

"Your mother and I must confer," Jigme's father said at last.

In the longer silence that followed, Jigme looked out into the world again, trying to distract himself from the despair and hope battling in his soul. The Smiling Fire had brought Jade back to the surface. He laid her unconscious body on the obsidian block that covered the entrance to his chamber. Then he tied her to the block by her wrists and ankles.

*But there was a chance,* Jigme thought. *There has to be.*

As the moon and the sun drew nearer to one another, the Smiling Fire set the dia ubh in a small round depression at the head of the stone slab, a few inches away from Jade's hair. In the small crack on the surface of the dia ubh, Jigme saw the barest silver and gold glint, like the birth of a spark.

*Jay has to be close,* he thought. *He has to be coming.*

Jigme looked all around, wondering.

No one came near.

"Son," said his mother.

Jigme looked away from the outside world. The way she said that one word, despair rushed through him. He had feared the answer he already knew to be right.

"You and Father can go back," Jigme said. "But I can't."

"What was his name, Jigme?" Amma asked. "What was the name of the first boy you brought to the

Smiling Fire?"

"I... I can't," Jigme said, feeling the memory of tears. Sadness then filled every part of his soul. Jigme saw the boy in his mind, saw his bright eyes and the hope on his face. Jigme could even still feel the happiness in his grip when the boy held his hand, as they walked through the gleaming, bustling, bright city of Agamuskara, past the empty stand of The Mystery Chickpea, down the alley, past the red door, to the temple...

To the death of the first child.

"Isn't he here with you too?" Jigme said.

"He is not," his father replied, bursting with regret and sadness. "You brought the first boy before I had given myself to the Smiling Fire. I was able to save all those he has consumed since my own decimation. The first boy is lost to us all."

"And because of that," Jigme said, "I do not get another chance."

"You regret," Jigme's father said. "But regret is not enough for redemption."

"But why you? Why Amma?" Jigme asked, anger rushing through him. "Why am I the only one who can't have another chance?"

"Your mother did not act of her own accord," his father replied. "You did."

"But I am sorry."

"That matters," his father said. "But it is not enough." The kindness and gentleness in the old man's voice only further enflamed Jigme's anger.

"Son," his father continued, "you cannot even say his name. Even if you could..."

"It still wouldn't be enough," Jigme replied. "You

were able to live here. You have been powerful enough to save all these other souls. Why not mine too? You said you wanted to do so much for me. Why not this?"

"There are worlds separating what I can do, what I have done, and what I should do," his father replied. "As for me and your mother, we will not return."

"What do you mean?" Jigme said. "You have a chance to live. That's more than what I have. Why won't you take it?"

"To give you a chance," his father said. "To have an alternative, in case there is no other option. I have lived long, Jigme. Longer than you can imagine. My soul's power has waned, but it is still vast. One way or another, my duty in the world is done. There either will be no world to protect from the Smiling Fire or there will be no Smiling Fire to protect the world from. What is left of my life I will give to help these others live again. I give it gladly. I have little hope to offer you, but such that I can is yours, along with the love that should have been yours all your life."

"You've never given me anything before," Jigme said, flooded with spite. "Why start now?"

"My son," Asha said. "I am sorry. And no, that is not enough. I too will pass on, will give all that is left of me. There is nothing left for me in the world, and my life is not as I wish it could have been. I was not the mother for you that I should have been or wished I had been. If I can die and it brings you back, I die gladly. If I can die and bring back these others too, I die gladly. Live with my love, son. I take my regret with me."

"But I just die," Jigme said.

"There may be ways that we cannot see," Amma replied. "We hope that it is so. Even if you must fully die, Jigme, at least you also may choose the manner in which you do so."

"Maybe I should just fade away," Jigme said. "Or let it all happen. Be consumed as the others are. Or watch them escape while I burn. If there's no chance to live again, why bother with anything else? Why not just be done with it all? What did life ever really give me, anyway? All I had was you, Mum. Now I won't even have that."

"Jigme," Asha said. "My son—"

"I don't care," he said. "I just don't care. Let it all burn. What's it good for, anyway? Why bother with life at all when it's just cruel and thoughtless?"

His mother and father had no reply.

Jigme turned his focus back to the world outside. The Smiling Fire was looking at Jade, who was still unconscious. Jigme remembered how smart she was, how beautiful, how vibrant and alive. She had been kind.

*And the Smiling Fire is going to kill her,* Jigme thought. *He has killed so many, and now he's going to kill more. What has she done to deserve this death? Doesn't she deserve to live?*

*If she does, who else does?*

His anger dimmed.

"You have tried to save me and the others," Jigme said. "But it's my own actions that helped bring this about too. If I hadn't helped him... If I hadn't believed his lies... maybe none of this would be happening."

"Maybe," Amma said. "Or maybe this was always the destiny that had to unwind eventually. I know only that, regardless of where we go in life, we must do what we can."

"You are willing to die for me and for the others," Jigme said to his parents. Something in him blazed up, but it was not anger. "Even if I can't come back, it doesn't matter. I will fight for you, for them. I will do all I can to stop the Smiling Fire. Even if it kills me. If by fighting or dying I can stop him, then at least in death I tried to make good for what I did wrong in life."

Before they could reply, Jigme turned back to looking at the outside world.

The moon began to cover the sun. Far at the edge of the Smiling Fire's sight, two people approached.

THE TAXI PULLED AWAY and the blackened city crunched under Jay's feet. He watched the cab disappear. Dust and exhaust trailed up in a large gray plume.

"Before you even start to think it," said a familiar voice, "this isn't your fault."

The plume faded as Rucksack passed through it. In his black clothes, he looked like a walking shadow.

Jay shook his head. "If I had stayed—"

"If you had stayed," Rucksack said, "maybe you would've been killed. Maybe Jade or I would be dead too. Maybe more would have died. I could just as easily say Mum should've stayed, but she didn't and you didn't. All that mattered is what happened, and all that matters is what happens now."

"I shouldn't have abandoned you and Jade. That wasn't right."

"You felt betrayed," Rucksack said. "In some ways, we did betray you."

"You didn't let me have a say," Jay replied. "Maybe I would've chosen to stay, even though I had my passport back."

"I can understand if you're still angry."

They stared at each other and said nothing.

Jay stuck out his hand. After a moment, Rucksack shook it.

"There are more important things," Jay said. "I forgive you, Faddah Rucksack, you evasive gobshite."

"And I you," Rucksack said, returning Jay's grin. "You thick eejit."

They looked at the sky. The rich midday blue was only just deepening and darkening as the moon covered the sun.

"I suppose we'd best be off then," Rucksack said.

"I'd hate to be late," Jay replied. "It could be our own funerals, after all."

They started walking toward the heart of the city.

"Do you think this could've been prevented?" Rucksack asked.

Jay shook his head. "Life has waited a long time for this, Rucksack. All living things versus the Smiling Fire," Jay said. "The world tolerates a lot, but a moment like this was always in the works. The place for it happened to be here. The time for it happened to be now. And it wound up being up to me. All you did was try to keep me on track."

"I wish I could take this burden from you, Jay." Rucksack clenched and unclenched his left hand. "If I were as I once was…"

"You could be all that you were," Jay replied. "You

could be all that you're going to be, Rucksack, and this still wouldn't be your responsibility. Remember what you said to me? The other gods weren't the right gods for this fight. You aren't a god. You're far more, really, but this fight is up to the world, to existence itself. Sometimes things have to come down to regular people who find themselves in impossible circumstances. Then we have to learn that far more is possible than we let ourselves imagine before."

"You would think that it would come down to me, you know?" Rucksack said. "I helped stop this thing before I was even born."

"Not all things work like that," Jay replied. "The Smiling Fire doesn't understand enough of life, enough of us, to have any idea that one is different from another. Maybe he would have recognized Kailash, but I don't think so. The only thing he might see you as is a juicier, spicier meal than a typical human. You and Kailash played a part then, but times have changed. What's needed has changed. So have you."

Jay clapped Rucksack on the shoulder and said, "Long as it is, mate, your story has hardly begun. I don't know the how and why and where of all that's ahead for you, but I got a glimpse. You said that helping me do this would put you back on the path to your destiny. It does. I'm glad it does too. I don't know what's coming, but I know that when you face what you're ultimately here to sort out, the Smiling Fire will seem about as big a deal as a stubbed toe."

"Why, Jay of the road," Rucksack said. "When did you get all wise and profound?"

"Your mother gave me a crash course," Jay replied.

"I intend to honor her sacrifice."

For a moment the men said nothing. Rucksack's eyes dimmed. "I always figured Mum would want to go only when it meant exchanging her mortal life for the good o' another," Rucksack said. "Bittersweet as it is that she's gone, at least I got to see her again."

"Is she dead?" Jay asked.

"Her mortal self is," Rucksack replied. "But I think she'd been ready a long time to let that go. She is the mountain now, Jay. The world mountain. We get through this, I bet we'll be seeing her again."

"That's comforting."

Up ahead stood a dark figure, tall and thin like a flame made of shadow.

"Aye," Rucksack said. "Though I suppose that'll be the last comfort we have for a while."

Jay set down his backpack and checked that the daypack was still fastened to it. With a sigh and a pat, he left his backpack behind.

As they walked on, Jay tried to grin, but fear surged up too. "If I make it out alive, I'm going to be thirsty," he said. "If we both survive this, how about we grab a pint later?"

Rucksack chuckled, but fear shone in his eyes too. "You're on."

"Just in case we don't get another chance," Jay said, "it's been a pleasure. Faddah Rucksack, I'm glad I met you. I'm glad to call you my friend."

"Likewise," Rucksack replied. "There's many the time I've despaired, Jay, but meeting you... earning and losing and regaining your friendship... it gives me a lot to look forward to in the world again."

Silent as they continued, Jay and Rucksack now

could see the red gleam of the Smiling Fire's face. They stopped a few yards away.

The Smiling Fire stepped to one side. Jade was tied to the obsidian block.

"A damsel in distress?" Rucksack said. "I wouldn't have thought that was your style."

Jade strained to look at them. "Who the hell are you calling a damsel?" She saw Jay. "Oh. You came back."

"I came to say I'm sorry."

"Save the world," she replied, "and I'll consider that apology accepted."

The Smiling Fire looked back and forth between them. His eyes flickered.

Jay said, "Rucksack and I are going for a pint later. Will you join us?"

"Sure." Jade laughed. "But you and I have to have a serious discussion after. God or not, you've got some explaining to do, backpack boy."

"It's a date."

"You'll bloody well wait until I tell you what it is."

The Smiling Fire raised an arm. "Enough."

"The dia ubh!" Rucksack said.

The crack in the dia ubh had gotten wider and longer. Silver and gold glinted inside.

"When will it break open?" Jay asked.

"When the eclipse is total," Rucksack answered.

The moon now covered most of the sun.

The Smiling Fire let the dia ubh go.

Instead of falling, it ascended. The dia ubh floated until it was directly above them, just far enough away to remain out of reach, yet so close it seemed they could leap up and grab it. As the dia ubh rose, the sky darkened. The moon continued eating the sun.

"At last," the Smiling Fire said. He reached into the shadows of his chest. The slanted edges of a piece of obsidian, as long as Jay's forearm, tapered to a sharp point that glinted even in the dying light.

The Smiling Fire held the knife high over his head. "Now, you all die," he said. Flames spilled from his grin as it widened. "Beginning with her."

The knife plunged.

JAY DIDN'T KNOW if he was going to scream or speak or find he could not voice a word. He stepped forward, but the air had turned to treacle. His leg must have been moving, but everything about his body was happening way too slowly.

The only thing clear was the absent space next to him where Rucksack had been standing. As the knife began its downward arc to Jade's heart, a blur shimmered in a line all the way to where the Smiling Fire stood. Moonlight—or was it sunlight?—glinted off the black point of the obsidian blade.

*She's going to die,* Jay thought. *She's going to die.*

The blade pierced the last shreds of air between it and Jade's chest.

Then there was no blade.

The Smiling Fire staggered backward, falling and tumbling across the rubble.

Rucksack turned around. He spun the knife in his right hand so the blade pointed out like a fencer's sword.

"Stay out o' this as best you can," he said to Jay.

The ferocity in Rucksack's eyes blazed brighter than

full sun. "All we have to do is hold the bastard off until the dia ubh opens," he said. "You keep yourself alive and out o' his way. Position yourself so the moment that light shines, it shines on you."

"What are you going to do?"

"Whatever it takes." Rucksack glanced down. "All right then, Jade?" he said. Rucksack sliced through the tethers that tied her to the block. He went around to the other side and sliced the ties there too.

Jade sat up and swung off the block, rubbing her wrists.

"Jay," she said. "Whatever you do when the time comes, don't kill him."

"What the hell are you talking about?" Jay replied. "That's been the whole point of my destiny. I have to kill him, Jade."

"There's something you don't know."

"The only thing I know is I don't have a choice anymore," Jay said. "This is how it has to be. It's him or the world. I choose the world. The moment I become the god, I'm going to kill him."

The Smiling Fire stood. "You cannot kill me," he said, moving toward Jay. "But I will have your blood."

"Not yet," Jay replied. He threw a rock. The Smiling Fire halted for a moment then continued forward.

Jade ran toward them. She leaped through the air, and her knees knocked into the Smiling Fire's back.

He stumbled but righted himself and turned. Jade regained her own balance. They circled each other and locked eyes.

Jay ran toward the obsidian block, stopping when he stood beneath the dia ubh.

"Where is it, then?" Jade asked through the sharp

scythe of her smile, her hands balled in fists near her face. "You've spent weeks leveling the city. Flames used to spring up wherever you so much as walked or looked. Surely you can barbecue a former bartender."

The Smiling Fire lunged forward, but Jade was ready. Her right hook caught him in the face. He spun around but stayed standing.

She shook her hand, which reddened under the deep brown of her skin. "I've gotten worse touching a hotplate," she said.

"You will burn."

"Then bring the fire, smiley," Jade replied. "Or do you even have it in you anymore?"

The Smiling Fire took a step back.

She laughed. "You greedy bastard. You overdid it, didn't you? All these fires, all this death and destruction. You spent most of your power," Jade said. "You could've burned us like ants under a magnifying glass on a sunny day, but now you couldn't char a dung patty."

"That... That will not matter soon."

Jade glanced at the sky. Only a sliver of sun remained. The sky was black but for a dim light, a ruddy mix of red and gold that turned the broken city around them into bloody shadows.

The glance was enough.

The Smiling Fire grabbed Jade and thrust her backward.

Jay winced at the flat, wet sound her body made when she hit the obsidian block.

She fell to her knees, slumped over, and was still.

"Jade!" he shouted, taking a step.

"Stay where you are, Jay!" Rucksack leaped so that

he stood between them and the Smiling Fire. Again, Rucksack spun the knife in his hand. He pointed the blade down then angled it back toward his forearm.

"Do you bleed fire or shadow?" he asked, slowly waving the knife in front of him. "Let's find out."

They met in a blur. Jay had never thought Rucksack could move so quickly. *Hero of old,* he thought, *and hero of now.*

The two dodged each other's blows first by millimeters, then by spaces no bigger than a crack in the sidewalk, then by atoms. Neither shadow nor blade could connect. They spun around each other, leaping from side to side, limbs blazing forward, then back or aside as the other blocked or countered. All the while, the last sliver of sun faded.

Just when Jay thought it would never end, the Smiling Fire's arm thrust out. Rucksack bent his knees, ducked, and swept underneath, all the while moving forward, his knife arm held close to his body. He slashed the obsidian blade across the Smiling Fire's torso and side, raking the knife forward with him as he stepped through, as nonchalantly as he would have passed by someone in a crowded pub.

The blade gleamed darker than ever.

Now standing behind the Smiling Fire, Rucksack straightened his body and lunged back toward him.

Before the Smiling Fire could turn, Rucksack raised his arm and shot it forward, plunging the knife into the center of the Smiling Fire's back.

*If the Smiling Fire were human,* Jay thought, *Rucksack would've just skewered his heart.*

The howl was like the growling hunger of a forest fire.

*When I learned my parents were dead,* Jay thought, *this is how I screamed inside.*

Rucksack twisted the blade. The howl rose higher. Rucksack stepped in close, as if he was about to whisper a secret to the Smiling Fire.

"If I could stop you when I was but a babe not even born," Rucksack said, strong and level, "what makes you think you could defeat life now?"

The howling stopped. Silence settled over the city.

The Smiling Fire turned his head. His grin widened as he stared at Rucksack.

Jay looked up.

The moon covered the sun. A black disc hung in the sky.

The mirror eclipse was full.

The air shimmered. To the right, level with the black disc in the sky, a silver-and-gold disc appeared. Both pulsed. Below them, meeting at an angle that reminded him of the obsidian knife, the dia ubh pulsed too.

Just as the silence had washed over his ears, a new sound swept the silence away. But this was no howl, no roar, no scream. The splitting noise was like every tree in every forest in the world breaking, and it knocked Jay to his knees. This was the cacophony of the world splitting in two. The cracking noise kept rising, kept getting louder, harsher. It popped and ruptured until Jay thought his own head would split in two.

Just as the dia ubh split now.

Twin gray halves slipped off the dia ubh, dissolving as they fell and leaving behind a gray-black globe. The noise faded. A spark, then two, flickered from the center of the dia ubh.

"You're too late!" Jay shouted, getting back to his feet. "This ends now!"

The Smiling Fire struck. His left arm whirled back and an elbow connected with Rucksack's head. Rucksack dropped the knife and staggered away. Then he rushed forward. The Smiling Fire swung again.

Rucksack caught the blow in his left hand, but Jay could see how the fingers struggled to hang on, how the arm quivered.

The Smiling Fire's left arm came up.

Rucksack crumpled to the ground and did not rise.

"No!" Jay yelled. He glanced up at the dia ubh. It flickered and pulsed, its gold light getting bigger, smaller, then bigger again.

*It can't be much longer,* Jay thought. *Please tell me it won't be much longer...*

The Smiling Fire's fingers faded from sight as he reached through the shadows of his chest. Slowly, the hand pulled forward again, and the long obsidian blade came free. The hole there closed up like night creeping over the last light in the world.

"It comes," the Smiling Fire said. He walked forward and raised the knife. The black blade glinted. "I return."

"Come on," Jay said. The dia ubh got brighter, but no light shone down. Then he looked at the Smiling Fire. "Fine," Jay said. "Come and get me, then!"

But the Smiling Fire stopped. "I wasn't coming for you," he said. "Not yet."

The Smiling Fire reached down, pulled up Jade, and slammed her onto the obsidian block.

Then he raised the knife.

* * * *

THE BLADE PLUNGED. The discs of the mirror eclipse pulsed faster than the eye could follow.

The golden light of the dia ubh began to pour down.

*I'm destined to be here,* Jay thought. He saw his parents. He saw all his travels. He saw Kailash and her sacrifice.

*I can't let the Smiling Fire destroy the world,* Jay thought. *But how can I become a god yet let him kill Jade?*

He looked from Jade to the dia ubh then back. Fear split him.

Yet in between those choices, Jay saw the path.

The Smiling Fire grinned. Jay met his gaze and grinned back.

For a moment, something seemed to tickle him. Then Jay felt nothing but fear and cold as he leaped forward, moving faster than he ever thought he could move.

Standing on the other side of the block from the Smiling Fire, Jay grabbed Jade and pulled with a surge of strength he had never known. He twisted and let go. Jade rolled over on the ground, away from the block and the knife.

Jay turned back to the Smiling Fire. Golden light glinted off the point of the plunging knife. *So pretty,* Jay couldn't help but think.

*At least it's sharp.*

The blade disappeared into Jay's chest with a bite both cold and hot. He breathed in the last life of the world. Then all his air whooshed out of him. His legs forgot how to keep him standing. Jay no longer knew if he was still grinning or if the pain had contorted his mouth. Jay had no scream, no cry. For a moment, he simply paused.

Until, as even the pain faded, the Smiling Fire let go of the knife. Something in the ancient face twisted, just as Jay's own smile had, but he could no longer trouble himself with what that was. The Smiling Fire stepped around Jay, moving past him as if in a hurry.

Jay's body slid down the obsidian block. *I don't want this to be the last thing I see,* he thought.

With one final ember of strength, he turned his body over so his back was against the stone. He hardly glanced at the knife sticking out of his chest, taking only a moment to chuckle in appreciation of the Smiling Fire's aim.

Jay's punctured heart slowed, slowed, slowed. The blood was hardly spilling out now.

Jay looked away from his broken body. *I don't think I'll have last words,* he thought. *Maybe this will do.*

His smile stretched from ear to ear.

*Top that, you grinning bastard,* Jay thought as the Smiling Fire rushed toward the golden light of the dia ubh. *Smile all you want.*

*You're still too late.*

As golden as every dawn of every day from the first time the sun had risen over the new earth, it all began as the light of the dia ubh surrounded and suffused her. Their blue-and-gold brighter than ever in the brilliant light, Jade's eyes opened wide.

Just as Jay's closed.

* * * * *

INTO THE LIGHT, the woman faded.

From the light, the goddess emerged.


SHE SAW DARKNESS. She saw light. She saw every tendril of destiny, decision, and existence. She saw what was, what is, and what could be.

Above all, beyond all, she saw who she was.

Gold blazed across all things then transformed to white. Then she saw nothing as the light both intensified and compressed, pulling into her like breath and out of her like the force of creation spreading across the universe again.

The light faded. The dim, rubble-strewn world of the city returned. Above Jade, the spent dia ubh faded and vanished. The frantic pulsing of the twin discs of the mirror eclipse slowed then became still. Slowly, the black disc brightened until both discs glowed white.

In front of her, she saw Jay slumped against the block. The blood had stained his white shirt red.

Rucksack got to his feet, staggering but steadying. On the far side of the block, the Smiling Fire lay still.

He had rushed the light, Jade remembered, but the moment he touched it, he had been knocked away.

Jade raised her arm. The Smiling Fire lifted off the ground.

"Are you going to kill him now?" Rucksack asked.

"No."

"He killed Jay," Rucksack said. Anger seared his voice. "Nearly killed you."

"Not nearly," Jade said. "He did kill me."

"And look at you now," Rucksack said. "The Smiling

Fire will continue trying to destroy. Jay was destined for this, you know. He was going to finish this once and for all."

Jade lowered the Smiling Fire onto the obsidian block. She and Rucksack faced each other from opposite sides.

"Instead, Jay chose life," she said. "He chose to save another's above his own."

"So what are you going to do then, now that he changed destiny?"

"The same as Jay did. I'm going to choose life."

"You're going to spare him?"

Jade looked down into the Smiling Fire's face, waiting for the light to return to the dark eyes. "Not exactly," she replied.

"You're a goddess now," Rucksack said. "You have to do things like decide and act, no matter what."

"Being a goddess isn't about life or death," Jade said. "No god controls those things. Life and death are what we serve. Do I have the power to kill the Smiling Fire?" She grinned. "Oh, yes. And oh, yes, part of me wants to. But I see the greater power now. The true power of what I serve, what I am, and what I will always be."

"And what is that?" Rucksack said.

A red-and-black spark came into the dark eyes.

"The world," the Smiling Fire said, his voice weak and quavering, "is so cold."

"Only to those who won't be part of it," Jade replied, seeking her strength, her courage, and finding something new: compassion—and possibility.

*He's never tried to understand us,* she thought. *Have we tried to understand him?*

"You don't have to hate this," Jade said. "What is amazing about life is it adapts. If you are alive, then you can adapt too. The world finds a place for all things. The violent and the peaceful coexist. You could be part of this too. You wandered for so long with nothing living in the world. Then the world changed."

She stared into the red eyes and tried to see the world through them. "It must have been terrifying," Jade said. "But you don't have to stay afraid. Things can be different."

"What would you have me do?"

"Give up your hatred. No longer seek to destroy all life. Infinite power will never be yours again. If you are to continue in this world, you must find a new purpose. I ask you to accept infinite possibility instead."

Jade touched the Smiling Fire's hand, surprised at how cool it felt. "I'll wander the world with you, if you want," she said. "I'll show you that there's a place for you. You don't have to control it all. You can live among us, accept what the world offers, and do as you will in return.

"The joy of the fire of life is not control," she continued. "It's the sheer precious moment of being alive and of sharing that joy with the world. That joy is all around, if you want to find it. I'll help you. You don't have to be as you were. The world doesn't have to be as it was. You were infinitely alone. Think of all you can be, together with a living world. I'm asking you... I'm begging you. Please give life a chance. It's the last chance you have."

His voice rasped faintly. "I would be as nothing."

She shrugged. "We continue because we grow and

change. You are ancient and powerful. Imagine all else you could be. Dream beyond who you were. Think of what you could be if all your power, all that vast power, became something other than a force against life."

"Cold," the Smiling Fire said. "Stolen. Mine."

He flung her hand away.

"You have a chance. But I can't make you take that chance." Jade stared into the red eyes and saw them flicker. She smiled. "Think on what I said. You can still turn away from this path. We can still find a way to coexist."

The Smiling Fire struggled and tried to rise.

Jade waved a hand and he stayed on the block. "I offer you a choice," she said.

"You offer nothing," the Smiling Fire replied. "The world is mine. It will always be mine. I have existed since the first spark. I will wait more. One day I will make ash of you, goddess."

Jade shook her head. "You do not want to learn. You do not want to live. Not in the world as it is. Not in the world as it could be. Only in the world that you lost long ago. Things will not be that way again. Not as long as I live. Not as long as anyone lives."

She leaned in close to his face. "You won't destroy us. No matter how long you've tried, how long you've existed, you're done. And you know it."

"Then... kill me."

Jade stared deep into the red-and-black eyes. "I won't kill you," she said. "But there will be no more prisons, and I certainly can't have you running about as you have been."

She raised her hands. "You're fighting me." Jade

smiled. "But I don't think that's all you're fighting. So this ends now."

Rucksack stared at her. "What are you going to do?"

"Take my hands," Jade said, "and I'll show you." They joined hands, bowed their heads, and closed their eyes.

"Cold!" the Smiling Fire said. "So cold, so cold!"

Soon the words faded and he only screamed.

"Jade?" Rucksack said. But she only clenched his hands tighter.

The screams faded into whimpers and then silence.

They opened their eyes and lowered their hands. The red-and-black gleam of the Smiling Fire's eyes was all but gone.

"I thought you weren't going to kill him?" Rucksack said.

"I'm not." Jade smiled. "Do you remember when your mother said that to stand in the light of the dia ubh was to become the pure form of what was at the core of your being?"

Rucksack nodded. "So, what are you?"

"I am renewal and rebirth," Jade said. "The path that could be taken. I am the goddess of choice and new beginnings." As tenderly as if she were comforting a child, she touched her hand to the Smiling Fire's face.

"Are you still there?" she said. "Can you answer me now, Jigme?"

The voice that replied was no longer the rasp of the Smiling Fire's. It was young, yet sad. "I'm here, Jade."

"Good," she replied. "Here's what we're going to do."

* * * * *

JIGME FINISHED SPEAKING. It still was weird to hear his voice coming from the body of the Smiling Fire. The surprise on Jade and Rucksack's faces said they were still getting used to it too.

"There has to be a way," Rucksack said.

"We have all discussed it and discussed it. We have looked at it from every way," Jigme replied. "There's no alternative. But it's okay. He died because of me. There are many who will remain dead, and that's in part because of me. What happens to me doesn't matter anymore, as long as I can bring back as many people as possible."

"I thought the souls had been preserved and protected inside?" Jade said.

"Only those consumed in his fire," Jigme replied. "Some died from the fires of the city or from smoke or from falling stone. They're not coming back. They've passed on like all others who die."

Jade took a photo out of her pocket and stared at the smiling faces there. She closed her eyes for a moment. "So be it," she said.

Rucksack looked at her. "Are you okay?"

"No matter the bluster you might hear otherwise, gods and goddesses aren't all-powerful," Jade said. "When there is so much that could be done, let's just say it's not easy to accept my limitations."

"Done, only not by you?" Rucksack said.

"Not by anyone but the living and the mortal," Jade replied. "Gods are just a nudge. When gods do too much, then instead of life being full and free, it's just tended, restricted, manipulated. People are not pawns or toys. Often, the best thing a god can do is nothing. Maybe the most important thing to know is when to do nothing and when to act. I am only a power to transform—far as I can tell, anyway. This is all pretty much on-the-job training right now."

"I'm ready when you are," Jigme said.

Jade nodded.

They stood where Jade had been transformed, directly under the twin discs of the mirror eclipse. Jigme could feel it throughout the Smiling Fire's being; they had only a little longer to draw on the power of the eclipse. He stood between Jade and Rucksack, who held hands as they both stared at Jigme.

It began.

From within the silver-and-gold glow of his mother and father, Jigme heard the stirring of the souls, their excitement and their hope. He could both hear and feel the song of his mother and father, joining with Jade and Rucksack's voices, and with his own. They sang to the moon and the sun, to the earth and the sky. They sang to all the gods, to all the living, to all the dead. They sang to themselves and to those they loved.

When the song faded, so did the silver-and-gold glow. "Son," said his mother and father, "it is done. We pass from this world, but we leave our love for you and our hope. We take our regrets and failures with us. May your world be happier without them."

Their voices faded. Then Jigme's father spoke one last time. "Oh." Laughter sparkled in his voice. "So, that's what it is."

Where the glow had been, it was as if all the stars in the sky now surrounded Jigme. The souls whizzed and spun, bright silver and gold.

Each small dot of light was getting bigger. As they grew, the ruddy red dimness faded to a midnight black.

"It's working," Jigme said. "Soon they'll be coming back."

No sooner had he said the words when a red light blazed. Larger than the others, it flew like a spark into the midst of the silver-and-gold souls. The red light flickered, as if flames were unfolding from it. The souls around blurred, trying to flee.

The Smiling Fire screamed. "They are mine!"

Flames roared.


A LIGHT GREW in Jigme, and he was not afraid. "And so," Jigme said, "we at last see the Smiling Fire for what you really are: a little spark that could not live without the fires of others."

He blazed forward, meeting the red light. "But you will not have them," Jigme said. "If this is my end, I gladly die so they can live, so you can hurt the world no more."

Jigme came closer and for the first time he saw the strange mark. A silver-and-gold streak like a splinter or a fragment glowed from the surface of the red bloody gleam of the Smiling Fire. But Jigme had no time to consider it. He moved faster, before the Smiling Fire could consume the souls and try to restore his strength.

They collided.

They merged.

The lights faded. Jigme felt the fire, but it did not burn. He felt the ancient hate, but he did not flee.

He focused only on the strange mark. It still glowed silver-and-gold, so innocent amidst the fire, death, and rage spinning around it.

Jigme understood.

Some bit had survived. The first blood that had put Jigme on this path.

The first child.

The fire raged but Jigme surrounded it. He could feel himself burning away. Parts of his soul disappeared from all existence. But at least it was only his. Jigme surrounded the Smiling Fire and realized that his flames were fading too.

"If we end," Jigme said, "we end together."

Beyond them, the other souls kept moving and growing. They began to escape. The power inside the Smiling Fire and the power of the mirror eclipse funneled through Jade and Rucksack, pulling the souls out of the void and back into the world. Jigme could feel every liberation. He could feel each soul grow, change, flex, and become not just soul but mind and body again.

He himself was almost gone, Jigme realized, but so was the Smiling Fire. The ancient hatred was vanishing, burning up in its own rage and in the smothering strength of Jigme's fading self.

The void was empty. Jigme felt the last bit of his own being waver and flicker.

He curled around the little spark. What would happen to it? "I'm sorry," he said to the silver and gold fragment. "I'm so sorry I brought this upon you, Ammar."

The name of the first boy reverberated around them.

"Ammar," Jigme said again. "It means builder. A good name. A good boy. I hope there's something better for you and better beings than me."

Jigme faded.

The Smiling Fire went out.

The spark grew.

Jigme realized he was watching it grow. And that Jade was speaking.

"The name," she said. "There is a way, Jigme. Say the name again."

"A way for what?" he said, wondering how he could speak. "Ammar," he said. "Ammar."

They all sang the name. As they sang, Jigme saw the red spark flicker again, but not as it had before.

"Such a shame to waste all that power," Jade said. "What if it could be so much more?"

The red spark of the Smiling Fire flared up then scattered into the spark of Ammar. That spark too flared up, growing in size and wrapping around Jigme.

"You are no longer yourself," Jade said. "And the boy is no longer dead. The Smiling Fire is no more, but his power remains. I bring together all of you, the best of all of you. The hope of the boy. The power of the fire. And the understanding, Jigme, of you."

The world flashed silver and gold. Then it turned a brilliant white and Jigme could see no more.

WHEN THE LIGHT FADED, Jigme opened his eyes. The world seemed brighter. Above them, the second disc of the mirror eclipse faded. A sliver of sun began to shine again. People stood everywhere, confused but elated, trying to understand where they were, what had happened, and why they were all naked.

But Jigme had only one thought: *How do I have eyes to open?*

He held up his hands. A hot wind rustled across his skin.

*And when did I turn red?*

"Wasn't anything I could do about the color," Jade said.

He heard her voice through ears. Had to be. He touched his head. Definitely a head. And definitely ears.

"You are now the Smiling Fire," Rucksack said. "At least the body that the spark o' his soul occupied is now yours, only revamped and remodeled."

Rucksack grinned. "You still look like you, only grown up. And red. But a handsome red, I must say. And the eyes are the same, brown and black, only brighter than noon. You can always tell someone's true self by their eyes."

"How am I here?"

"You were willing to die and you were as dead," Jade said. "But when you said the boy's name, the first boy who had lost all, a new way opened for you. For him too. Even for the Smiling Fire."

Jade smiled and the richness of her brown skin gleamed in the growing sun.

Her eyes had changed, Jigme realized. The gold remained but the blue now seemed mixed with green. A silver ring glowed around the blackness of her pupil, reminding him of how the moon had covered the sun.

"But Ammar was dead."

"A small fragment of his soul survived," Jade said.

"And that was enough. When you said his name, you accepted your actions. By being willing to give all to stop the Smiling Fire and save the others, there came a way to save you as well. What power remained of the Smiling Fire is yours. The hope that lived on in the boy, you are now part of. They all come together in you, Jigme."

"Am I a god?" Jigme asked. "Like you?"

Jade shrugged. "The powers are a different degree. You can do more than mortals, live longer than mortals, and you see further. I don't know what that makes you. It doesn't matter, though, if you are god or demi-god or the walking tomato-man or whatever, as long as you are yourself and always true to yourself."

She stared at him. "What do you think you'll do with all that, Jigme?"

"My parents are gone and the city lies in ruins," he replied, staring at the survivors. "And these people may have life, but they have no idea what to do with where they are."

He looked back at Jade and Rucksack. "I will no longer be Jigme," he said. "Jigme did much wrong, caused much death, but he died to save these people. Jigme died so that the Smiling Fire would be fully and forever extinguished. They both are gone."

"So, who are you?" Rucksack asked.

He waved his arm. There was so much more light now.

"See this city? See these people?" he said. "That is who I will be. That is who I am. The Smiling Fire strove to destroy all life. He leveled the city. If I have his power, then as long as I live I will protect life. I will rebuild and preserve Agamuskara.

"I am no longer Jigme," he said. "I am the builder."

A smile grew on his face.

"I am Ammar."


THE CHILDREN RAN all around what had been the city. Their laughter and whoops seemed to hurry along the fading of the mirror eclipse, and the day grew brighter.

With Jade's new eyes, the helixes were part of everything she looked at. The world turned, changed, and stayed the same—whatever all that meant. She gazed at the survivors, reborn, wandering, wondering. Their helixes shone bright and flowed like rivers, each running to its own ways—and none ended in red and black fire. Life lived. Existence continued.

Except for Jay.

Their own elation fading, Jade, Rucksack, and Ammar stood silent around the body.

"I kept thinking he would say something," Jade said. "Like, 'This is better. Never did like the idea of thinking I was a hero.'"

"You can't be dead," Rucksack said to Jay's body. Tears filled his eyes. "I owe you a pint."

They waited for a reply.

Jay lay there unmoving, no rise or fall to his chest, no flutter of his eyelids to suggest that his eyes were about to open.

*He died smiling, though,* Jade thought. *He knew what he'd done. My backpack boy. He gave himself to save me, gave up his life not only so that I could live, but so I could take on the destiny he had surrendered.*

She pulled the obsidian blade from his heart. The

black stone glowed then cracked and turned to powder. Dust ran over Jade's hand, blowing away to be lost among the ashes and rubble.

Blood had trickled down the corner of Jay's mouth. She kneeled beside him and wiped it away. A soft golden light suffused the blood. For a moment, gold flickered in the red then faded and dulled.

Jade touched her finger to Jay's lips then leaned in and softly kissed him.

"All this happened because of Jay," Ammar said. "He made a choice that defied destiny."

"Destiny pulled him along and he didn't always choose well," Rucksack said. "All along we thought he was to kill the Smiling Fire. But if he had, none o' you would have been able to come back. In the end, Jay did better than destiny."

"Do you think he knew that?" Ammar asked.

"We'll never know how much he knew," Rucksack replied. "And how much he decided while dealing with what was in front of him. Not in this life anyway. Here we can only be grateful for what he did."

"We can do more than that," Ammar said, looking at Jade. "He died and we lived, but there are ways he can live on."

"I know you're going to rebuild the city," Jade said. "But he wouldn't have been a man for statues or monuments."

"Those are things for the dead," Ammar said. "He always seemed a man for the living. How about we start with a new pub and hostel? We'll call it 'The Jay.'"

Jade laughed. "The name may need some work. But yes, that sounds like a good way to remember him."

"Will The Management have a problem with that?"

Rucksack asked.

"I don't think so," Jade replied. "I'm sure they'll be in touch, though. Agamuskara is still Agamuskara, and there will always be a Jake or Jade here."

"I'd heard it told he was the world's greatest traveler," Rucksack said. "But all that matters to me is he was my friend. He screwed up but he made good. He gave all. He'll still be a traveler, though." Rucksack grinned. "Someone like Jay, he'd know that death isn't a destination. He'd remember that there are no destinations. There are only more journeys, and it's up to you to decide how your experiences make you who you are."

"What do we do now?" Ammar asked.

"I think I can help with that," Rucksack replied.

The people, adults and children alike, saw the three of them pick up Jay's body. The children fell silent, and along with the adults they gathered close. No one gave any instruction or spoke a single word, but all the people formed two lines, stretching out from the obsidian block, in the direction of the Agamuskara River.

Jade stood in front, her arms stretched high, holding Jay's shoulders and head. Behind her, Ammar's red hands supported Jay's torso. And at the rear, the dust gone from his black clothes, Rucksack held up Jay's legs.

"The man who gave all," Rucksack said.

"The man who gave all another chance," Ammar followed.

"And we will always remember him," Jade finished. "Jay of the road."

They walked between the lines of people. No one

spoke. Some bowed their heads. Some raised joined palms to their chests in namaste.

*In their eyes,* Jade thought, *they all know what happened. They know how Jay died and why. They know what Ammar and I are. What will they do with that knowledge?* She sighed. *In time, maybe I'll find out.*

As they passed each person, with every silent glance the goddess of choice and new beginnings shared her hopes for them, her hopes for the city, her hopes for their futures and for their children's futures.

And as they passed each person, each one said a name, or sometimes multiple names.

"Saakaar."

"Utsavi. Pranav."

"Labuki."

"Debjit. Ecchumati. Tista."

"Giridhar."

"Bavishni."

Jade could feel their sadness. *The Smiling Fire took someone from everyone here,* she thought, *but these survivors have no bodies to grieve over. There's only Jay's body. Through him, they mourn those they lost.*

Each person chanted a name, then kept repeating it. Some sang low and with a hum, or high and with a remembered serenity, or stuttering and with a voice that was almost a wail. Instead of dissonant, the voices and names wove together in a song. A song of the burned city. A song of the dead. A song of the love that lived on.

As Jade, Rucksack, and Ammar carried Jay's body to the end of the lines of people, they came to the river and the song reached a perfect unison. For a moment, the names and notes hung together in the bright air.

They grieved, but out of love they would live fully again, rebuilding homes, regaining work and family, singing new songs that could overpower fire.

Then, name by name, the song faded until all the people were silent and still.

Everyone looked at the goddess. "Let it all be better than it was," Jade said. "Let us all be better than we were."

*Including me.*

The people stood by the shore, amidst the wreckage of boats and a few that, like other random things in the city, had remained untouched by the Smiling Fire.

"That one there," Rucksack said, nodding. "Jay and I... The boat knows him well. That's the only one that's right."

Some people moved the boat down into the water. Jade, Rucksack, and Ammar gently laid Jay's body in the boat.

Another person had brought Jay's backpack and handed it to Jade. She raised Jay's head and laid it on his daypack like a pillow. Ammar set the large backpack in the end of the boat by Jay's feet.

Rucksack laid Jay's folded hands on his chest. For a moment, he stood with Jade and Ammar between the boat and the shore, their heads bowed and hands joined. Jade and Rucksack looked at each other then stepped forward to push the boat into the current.

"Wait."

They stopped and turned around.

Mim and Pim walked through the crowd, down to the boat.

"What are you doing here?" Jade asked.

"In the end," Mim said, "he gave it freely."

Rucksack glared at the two men. "Did you know this would happen?"

Mim and Pim shrugged.

"What happened, happened," Pim said. "But if Jay is going on his final journey, it's only right that he have this."

Pim reached into his pocket and took out a soft, blue light. He handed it to Mim, who opened the small booklet of Jay's passport.

"We said that we would fix it," Mim said. "And we did."

Mim raised the passport so everyone could see. There was only one visa page, and on it was stamped the world.

But not just stamped, Jade saw as she looked more closely. It wasn't a sticker either. There were too many colors and shades. Brown and black, blue and green, gold and silver. The white clouds even seemed like they were moving.

"What is that?" Rucksack asked.

"The last visa he will ever need," Pim said.

"He can go anywhere and everywhere now," Mim said, tucking the passport under Jay's hands.

"What good will that do him?" Ammar asked.

Pim pointed north to the horizon. "Enough that she said it must be done."

Larger than all the other mountains of the world, the mountain stood so high it touched both heaven and earth.

"Besides," Mim said, "all right and good must be done for the dead, if only to remind us of the right and good we should do for the living."

Rucksack snorted. "You know much about that, do you?"

Mim and Pim stared up at a spot above Rucksack's head. The two men smiled.

"More than you may think, Faddah Rucksack," Mim said.

"In time, you'll understand," Pim said. "Maybe even when next we meet."

The men raised their hands in the namaste. "Farewell to you all," Mim and Pim said. "For now."

Then Mim and Pim walked back through the crowd and were gone.

Rucksack stared at the mountain. A small smile came to his face. He nodded to Jade and together they pushed the boat out into the current. As the small boat bobbed on the waves, already it seemed smaller as it went north toward the world mountain in the far distance.

"Where will the boat take him?" Jade asked. "What will happen when he meets with the Ganges and goes toward Kolkata?"

"Oh, that's not where he's going," Rucksack replied. "He'll take the course o' the real Agamuskara River. That flows north into the Himalayas. Jay gave his life so all life may live. In honor o' that sacrifice, Jay will be laid to rest in the Heart o' the World. It's a long journey, but that boat will get him there just fine."

They fell silent. All watched the boat grow smaller and smaller on the massive river. When at last they could see the boat no more, people said a final thanks, a final farewell, and began to wander away. The mountain faded and was gone.

"It's time for me to go with them," Ammar said,

nodding toward the people. "We have much to do, and I owe a man a boat."

"Do you fear them?" Jade asked. "Or how they will react to you?"

"Jigme would have feared them. He had much bitterness growing in his heart," Ammar said. "That bitterness and fear died with Jigme. I do not fear. It is said that even the Lord Brahma, god of all creation, has red skin. I am not Brahma, but I am here to create, to build, to help. I will live through my works and my love. That will see us through."

Ammar left them and walked toward his people.

Jade and Rucksack stood by the river and stared at each other.

"I'll stay a while longer," Rucksack said. "Show Ammar the ropes. Besides, I don't have anywhere else to be."

Jade shook her head. "I don't think so," she replied. "You've done what you needed to do in Agamuskara. I'd say you're wanted elsewhere. A second chance is a new start, after all."

"Second chances," Rucksack said, a trace of sadness, almost bitterness, in his voice.

"Yes." Jade grinned as she stared at a spot just above Rucksack's head.

"What are you looking at?" he asked.

"You mean you don't know?"

"Enlighten me, goddess, if you don't mind."

"Second chances," Jade said. "For me, for Ammar... and for you too."

She stared at the spot again. It was still short and thin, but there was no doubt: a silvery, intertwined tendril of decision and destiny flowed out of Rucksack like a creek that could become a river.

"You said that helping Jay could restore you to the path of your destiny," Jade said. "It did, Rucksack. You're connected to the world again. You are on your path once more."

A shock came over the anywhere face. "Guess I'll always owe him a pint," Rucksack finally said. "I'd hoped... I've tried for so long..."

"He believed in you," Jade said. "And so do I. Whatever you're here to do, Faddah Rucksack, it's going to be magnificent. I know it will be. Because like me, you'll always carry him in your heart. Some part of everything you do will be to remember him, to keep him alive in some small way."

Rucksack smiled but had no words to reply. They stood there for a while, watching the river, thinking of the little boat and of the peaceful smile on Jay's face.

Then, without a word, Jade and Rucksack walked away from each other, heading in opposite directions.

There were still roads to travel. There were still journeys to begin. There would always be another journey on the road—the endless, boundless road.

You could never see all of it or know where you were going, but you could always choose your way.

The road forever, Jade saw, wandering forward and never looking back.

Forever the road.

# IV

BEHIND THE BAR, the comment book lay open to a blank page, reminding Jade of the guestbook she had kept in the pub at the Everest Base Camp. It wasn't the same, though. The Rum Doodle in Kathmandu, Nepal, had no hostel. It was just a bar and restaurant—though a damn good one, if the way they pulled a pint of Galway Pradesh Stout was any indication.

That old guestbook stuck in Jade's mind. She remembered watching Jay scrawl his name in it the day they first met.

*Such distinct handwriting,* she thought. *I'd still know it anywhere.*

After a year of wandering according to destiny and decision throughout India and Southeast Asia, she had followed the silver-and-gold tendrils to Nepal this time, the closest she had ever been to the Himalayas.

*A year to the day,* she thought. *A year since I became a goddess.*

*A year since Jay died saving the world from the Smiling Fire.*

Jade pulled herself out of memory and back to the present. *Why am I here tonight?* she thought, but the tendrils gave her no answer yet. *Maybe I should have gone to Agamuskara instead of Kathmandu. Word is a man named Ammar is doing amazing work cleaning and rebuilding the city, and there's a new pub and hostel that's the talk of India and the globetrotter's grapevine...*

The traveler came back from the toilet, sat next to Jade at the bar, and took a long draw from his own fresh pint of GPS.

*Someone's life is going to change tonight,* Jade thought. *But I don't think it's his. His path seems certain already.*

*So, why am I talking with him?*

Not that the traveler wasn't fun conversation. They swapped stories of the road, the world, of Jay. No matter where she'd gone, travelers and soon-to-be-travelers always loved hearing about Jay, the world's greatest globetrotter. She didn't have the heart to tell any of them that Jay was dead. His exploits, his adventures—*though,* Jade thought, *perhaps I'm adding some Rucksack-worthy embellishments nowadays*—inspired all the more whenever the listener left believing Jay was out there somewhere, living the world, blazing a trail of myth and legend wherever he roamed.

*Or maybe I still have trouble telling myself he's gone,* Jade thought.

The traveler set down his pint. "I come here every chance I get," he said in an accent that reminded her of Scotland. "Most inspiring place in the world."

Jade sat up. She'd come to Rum Doodle in a hurry, no time to learn anything about it other than where it was. There were no notes or instructions like there had been back when she was Jade the bartender instead of Jade the goddess.

Now she listened to the world, and listening brought her to her road. The road followed her heart, and it always took her where she needed to go.

"What's so inspiring about it?" she asked. *I'm still following the path,* she thought, *but I wish it would get around to telling me where in blazes I'm going this time.*

He pointed at the walls. "See all those photos, all those signatures?"

She looked around the bar. Photographs hung here and there on the walls, which were tan and yellow like old parchment. Most of the pictures showed a similar scene: women and men in thick coats, gloves, boots, and goggles, their faces tired but exuberant. Where there weren't photographs, names and numbers were scrawled everywhere she looked.

"Some of this stuff is just the mark of people who happened in for a drink or a meal just so they could say they had written on the wall of the Rum Doodle." The traveler smiled. "But the best stuff? Story goes it started with Tenzing Norgay and Sir Edmund Hillary, when they became the first climbers confirmed to get to the top of Everest and back down again. Since then, after summiting Mt. Everest—and making it back down alive, of course—a climber usually comes to Kathmandu. One of the first places they go is the Rum Doodle, and they sign the wall with their name and summit date."

"Have you gone to the top?" Jade asked.

"Not yet," he replied, pausing to take another swig of his pint. "But I'm working on it. Training hard. In a year or two I'll be ready to give it a go."

"How long does it take to climb Everest?"

"Weeks," he replied. "A lot of it is waiting, making sure your body is adjusting to the different altitudes. It's not a technically hard mountain to climb, but it's high enough and cold enough to be plenty hell on the body and mind. And you could still spend all that time getting to the top, only to be within yards of the summit and have to come down again. Well, that or die trying. Personally, I prefer staying alive."

"Weeks," Jade said. "Quite a feat. What would you say if I told you I knew someone who once went up—and down—Mount Everest in one night?"

The traveler laughed. "I'd say sure, and tomorrow there'll be free beer too."

"Not possible, huh?"

He shook his head. "Not in the slightest."

"But if it were, it'd make a great story, wouldn't it?"

"Oh, it'd be bloody legendary," the traveler said. "But the rest of us will just have to work for it."

They each took a swig of stout. "Let me show you my favorite stretch of wall," he said.

Jade and the traveler carried their pints from the bar to a back corner of the restaurant.

"I'm not a religious man," the traveler said. "But you could say I've made a pilgrimage here."

Jade wondered if her companion was the one who had hung the small blue-and-white Scottish flag over the signatures.

"I like to call it Little Scotland," he said. "It's all the

Scots who've summited Everest. Not a bad list, aye?"

Jade nodded, following the tendrils. Feeling the way destiny and decision were aligning, she touched his shoulder. "Your name will be here someday," she said, looking from the wall to him then back to the wall.

Surrounding Little Scotland were more names, more dates, people from all over the world. Jade read the signatures, one by one, line by line, until she got to a name that made her gasp.

She hardly noticed when her glass shattered on the floor.

Jade ran to the bar. The bartenders had no recollection of the person who had signed that name, and there was no Jake or Jade stationed at the Rum Doodle.

She dashed down the stairs, knocked open the door, and ran outside.

Right into Faddah Rucksack.

"Jade!" he said, staggering back but jumping forward just as fast. "Thank goodness."

"What are you doing here?" she replied.

"I had to find you." Rucksack took a letter from his pocket. "You got one too, right?"

"Sorry. Been on the road a lot. And last time there were letters to you, Rucksack," she said, "a certain pair of jokesters were behind it."

"They're not the reason I'm here, Jade." He stared deep into her eyes. "I'd stake my destiny on it."

"Jay came here after that night at Everest, right?" she asked as she led him into the Rum Doodle, ignoring the unasked questions from the traveler as they walked by.

"No," Rucksack said. "He went straight to Agamuskara. Jay had never been to Kathmandu."

Again she followed the tendrils. *Whose life is getting changed tonight?* she thought.

At the wall in the back corner of the restaurant, she pointed. The date corresponded to all she knew. Beneath it, scrawled in black handwriting she'd recognize anywhere, she read the signature again:

*Jay*

"I know, Jade. I know." Rucksack took a deep breath. "It's why I had to find you," he said. "Jay's boat arrived at the Heart of the World."

"And?"

Rucksack looked at the wall. Then he looked at Jade.

"It was empty."

THANK YOU FOR READING!

Please tell your friends about this story and review it at your favorite bookstore. Reviews are the best way readers discover great new books, and I would truly appreciate it. Even a couple of sentences is a big help. Here's a list of stores:

anthonystclair.com/forevertheroad

## MORE FROM THE RUCKSACK UNIVERSE

The Martini of Destiny
anthonystclair.com/martini

Home Sweet Road
anthonystclair.com/homesweetroad

## SUBSCRIBE TODAY

New story announcements, events, exclusive bonuses and more. Join the free email list:

anthonystclair.com/subscribe

Dozens of friends, colleagues, and relatives helped in some way or another with this Rucksack Universe novel. I am forever grateful for their help, expertise, and patience. If something in this book makes you go "whoa," I wouldn't be surprised if it came from their input. All flaws are mine.

Thank you to...

My friends and family for believing not only that I could write, but that I could quit my old job and pay bills with the scribbling instead; to my publishing A-Team: Chief Reader, Beta Readers (Robin, Jeanette, Choya, Matilda, Bonnie, and Taylor), editor Scott Alexander Jones, and designer Bonnie Donaghy;

To the world for giving not only life, but the capacity to experience, suffer, enjoy and grow;

To all the travelers and locals I've encountered over the years—yes, I was always taking notes;

To the peculiar combination of circumstance, destiny, and decision that enabled me to travel to amazing places such as India, Tibet, Nepal, and Ireland. I am grateful beyond words for all I've learned and seen—and excited for what's next;

To my beloved Jodie, for being the best wife, friend, and partner a man could have, and to Connor for inspiring me not only to live the world to the fullest, but to help you do so too.

# ABOUT THE AUTHOR

Globetrotter, homebrewer and writer Anthony St. Clair has walked with hairy coos in the Scottish Highlands, choked on seafood in Australia, and watched the full moon rise over Mt. Everest in Tibet. Anthony's travels have also taken him around the sights and beers of Thailand, Japan, India, Canada, Ireland, the USA, Cambodia, China and Nepal. He and his wife live in Oregon and gave their son a passport for his first birthday. Learn more and connect:

www.anthonystclair.com

www.ingramcontent.com/pod-product-compliance
Lightning Source LLC
Chambersburg PA
CBHW050953210726
48287CB00004B/1212